LOVING BEN COOPER

LOVING BEN COOPER

CC MONROE

wattpad books — FRAYED PAGES

W FRAYED
wattpad books **PAGES**

Copyright © 2025 CC Monroe. All rights reserved.

Published in Canada by Wattpad WEBTOON Book Group, a division of Wattpad WEBTOON Studios, Inc.

36 Wellington Street E., Toronto, ON M5E 1C7

www.wattpad.com

No portion of this publication may be reproduced or transmitted, in any form or by any means, without the express written permission of the copyright holders.

First Frayed Pages x Wattpad Books edition: March 2025

www.frayedpagesmedia.com

ISBN 978-1-99834-118-4 (Trade Paperback)
ISBN 978-1-99834-159-7 (eBook)

Names, characters, places, and incidents featured in this publication are either the product of the author's imagination or are used fictitiously. Any resemblance to actual persons (living or dead), events, institutions, or locales, without satiric intent, is coincidental.

Wattpad Books, W by Wattpad Books, Wattpad WEBTOON Book Group, and associated logos are trademarks and/or registered trademarks of Wattpad WEBTOON Studios, Inc. and/or its affiliates. Wattpad and associated logos are trademarks and/or registered trademarks of Wattpad Corp.

Frayed Pages and associated logos are trademarks and/or registered trademarks of Frayed Pages, Inc.

Library and Archives Canada Cataloguing in Publication and U.S. Library of Congress Cataloging in Publication information is available upon request.

Printed and bound in Canada

1 3 5 7 9 10 8 6 4 2

Cover design by Lesley Worrell
Cover images © da-kuk via Getty Images, © NatalyFox via Shutterstock
Typesetting by Delaney Anderson
Author Photo by LaShelle Cook

You are seen. You are loved. You are worthy. For every person who said otherwise, it wasn't their right. Keep your shoulders back and push through—life is waiting for you ♡

Author's note

There are some complex themes and difficult subject matter within Sadie and Ben's story. Their relationship touches on sensitive topics and has strong elements of a toxic relationship. They have to face a lot together and don't go about it the right way or get it right each time. It also deals with domestic violence, parental loss, trauma, strong drug use and addiction, as well as mental illness. While theirs is ultimately a love story, if any of the following might be harmful to you, please take care.

Domestic violence of mother and son.
Mental illness and therapy.
Drug use.
Strong jealousy.
Parental loss.
On page abuse and drug use.
Strong language and sexual content.
Mental manipulation.
Toxic relationship.

If you are struggling with mental illness, please know you are not alone. You are loved and you are needed.

Call 1-800-950-6264, chat, text "Friend" to 62640, or email helpline@nami.org

Prologue

Growing up under the pressure of never letting anyone I love break, molded me into a young woman who didn't know herself or what life she wanted. I always assumed I would spend my life chasing the dreams and creating the realities that my parents had built for themselves. There was never a time when I thought my faith would be tested as deeply as it was starting in the spring after I turned nineteen. Everything before that had been predetermined by my life within the walls of my parents' ideals, monochromatic tones that left nothing to chance. But when I walked into that place and looked into those honey-brown eyes, I knew life could offer vibrant colors. Sadly, sometimes colors can bleed and leave stains. My heart was at the mercy of a man I never planned for, one I never knew I would want more with each breath I took. The rock star created a chaos I wasn't prepared for. But I danced in that storm because I wanted to see it clear. That's when it hit me. From the day I met him, this story was never mine. It was always his. It was always about Ben Cooper.

One

SADIE

The warm water rushes out of the showerhead in a steady stream, colliding perfectly against my aching muscles. Twelve hours at the hospital working the night shift has me unbelievably exhausted. It's noon, and I haven't had a chance to get to bed yet. I have one month left of school before I get my licensed practical nurse degree. I'm looking forward to graduating because school and studying will be eliminated, and I can fill that time with sleep and some semblance of a social life. I plan to work at the hospital for a year before going back to nursing school to get my registered nursing degree. My parents call me dedicated, and my best friend, Kate, says I wear the world on my shoulders and need a break. However, I still wonder if I am doing enough. Having a life while fulfilling my aspirations is a balance that I have yet to figure out. Alas, here I am still juggling life on a tightrope.

At some point, everything will fall into place. All the hard work, sleep deprivation, and time spent will pay off. Life is on track. But then, like that, the voice in my head that often places self-doubt, creeps in. *Is it, Sadie?*

There's a tap on the bathroom door, followed by my mama's voice.

"Sadie, I made lunch! And Kate called, she said she's going to stop by soon. She said you didn't answer your phone."

"Thanks, Mama! I'll be out in a few minutes," I holler over the running water.

I'm sure we're the only house left that has a landline. I often tease my parents about it. I remember I turned my phone off at the start of my shift, and realize I must have spaced on turning it back on. When I'm at work, it's all I focus on—no distractions. Do I need to impress anyone? No, but I am a pathological people pleaser, so I do it by habit.

Portland General, the nationally renowned institution where I'm doing my LPN clinicals with Dr. Bailer, has offered me a full-time internship after graduation, and achieving this goal has been on my vision board ever since I started on this path. I've been working hard to get into the nursing program since before I even started school. Completing a successful internship is like trying to find a needle in knee-deep haystacks. The chances of getting in are slim, but I did it. No slipups can happen—not a 0.1 percent decrease in my grades, nothing. I have to make sure I stay focused on being the best at what I do.

I finish washing up, step out onto the fuzzy white bath mat, and towel myself off. Reaching for my plush white robe, I wrap myself up and band the towel around my wet hair. I open the door that leads me straight into my bedroom, where I'm met with my mother's sweet smile. Her long brown hair is pulled up and out of her face, showing off her barely-there wrinkles and the blue eyes that resemble mine. I have my daddy's blond hair, but my pouty lips and the light sprinkle of freckles on my nose and cheeks match my mother's.

"Here are some freshly washed scrubs. How was your shift?"

Though I'm exhausted, it's kind of her to ask, and I don't want to send her away. I muster up enough energy to enjoy some small talk. Grabbing my moisturizer, I take a seat at the end of my bed.

"It was long. I got to help two gunshot victims. That was a first."

"I remember my first time removing a bullet. I thought I was going to pass out. Nearly considered a career change."

My mother's Southern charm coats each of her words, and I can't help the grin that widens across my face. I love the story of how my parents met, and had Mama changed her career, I wouldn't be here.

My dad, Stanley, was an ER doctor in South Carolina while my mama, Raydean, had just graduated with her nursing license. Her first year of nursing was at the same hospital. They met soon after she started, and after a few rotations together, my dad knew he needed to marry her. She couldn't say no to his gentlemanly ways and Southern charisma. My daddy really is a sweet man, with more patience than a saint, and he always trusts the good in people—giving them the benefit of the doubt, if you will. He's the greatest example of a good man I've ever seen, and I hope to marry someone as profoundly kind as him someday.

Shortly after they started dating—three months after, to be exact—they got married, and within a year they had me. We stayed in South Carolina until I was fourteen. That's when Mama was diagnosed with breast cancer. The memory feels as new to me as if I found out yesterday. Even though I'm nineteen now, and she has been in remission for two years, I still remember the fear and the pain we endured during that time.

We left South Carolina to come to Portland, where they have some of the best cancer treatment facilities. Between them and God, Mama was healed and continues to be in remission. My parents are highly religious, and while I wouldn't say I'm as devout as they are, I lead my life with the morals that our faith teaches. It hasn't steered me wrong so far.

"Surprisingly, that wasn't the worst injury I've ever seen."

"You don't say," she says matter-of-factly, putting my scrubs in the closet.

"Yeah. Hey, I can put that away. You should go relax."

She's too good to me. My parents decided she needed to quit working after her diagnosis, and even though she's better now, she still tires easily (a disease like cancer takes a lot out of someone). At first, she hated not working, but now we think she secretly likes being the stay-at-home wife and mother.

For years, she was scared she would leave us and miss out on all the monumental moments in our lives, especially mine. But once she started staying home, the little things, such as cooking for her family and putting my laundry away, make her feel like she's serving a greater purpose—at least, that's what she says. Raydean McCallister is everything that serves a greater purpose. She's the first to lend a hand, the first to open her home to a stranger, and the first to give the clothes off her back. All my life, I've tried to follow each step she has taken—another reason why I simply cannot get distracted and fail.

Sometimes, though, I'm only human, and it can be a bit much when your mother puts away your laundry and cooks your dinner when you're an adult. Sometimes, I almost tell her the naked truth, but I understand the happiness it brings her to take care of us. Zipping my lips and giving gratitude to my mother is best for all of us.

"I'm not tired, and you just worked your little butt off. Get some rest. I told Kate that you were going to take a nap before she comes over. She said she gets off work at five, then she'll be here. Dinner will be ready by then." My mom walks up to me and cradles my face, looking me over with a prideful smile. "We're so proud of you, baby."

She kisses my forehead then leaves the room.

"Love you. Thanks, Mama." I squeeze the words out before the door clicks.

I climb into my warm bed and let slumber not just take me but knock me out and pull me under.

Two

BEN

Our guitarist, Eric, sits on the speakers downstage right, and I'm standing off to the side. We just finished sound check, so now we can enjoy the downtime—something we rarely get between shows.

Tonight, we're playing Portland, our new home. We left California three months ago, right after New Year's, and the atmosphere here is the perfect inspiration for my writing. The greenery, the rain, the normal summers—the fucking women.

I'm the lead singer for the punk band The Roes. We've been a band—with Eric as the lead guitarist, Jason on the bass, JJ on drums, and me as the singer—for nearly four years. We started the group when I was eighteen, playing in dive bars that we shouldn't have been allowed to step foot in. They were shady places that make me question how we didn't get ourselves in more sticky situations. Finally, our song "Run, Baby, Run" became a hit. All that time kissing ass, clawing our way to the top, and opening for bigger headliners, and now we are the headliner on our first arena tour. We aren't at the bottom anymore—we're the penthouse suite.

"Get up and play, shithead." Eric throws the football directly at me, and I nearly miss it. Fumbling it a bit when I grab it, my eyes zone in on my bandmate.

"Fuck you, asshole."

I put all my strength into my throw and release the football back to Eric, hitting him hard in the chest and causing him to lose his balance and fall off the speaker. JJ and Jason join me in laughing. Eric's face looks panic-stricken as he falls and lands on his side with a grunt.

"Dick."

He stands and dusts himself off, bouncing on the balls of his feet. I smirk, giving him the finger, and head toward the booth where they're setting up merchandise.

"Don't fuck with the greatest, man," I holler over my shoulder.

My mood rides high, and I'm on a pedestal no one can knock me off. It's not a matter of if I am ready for the show but if the show is ready for me. Adrenaline pumps through my veins, and my hands are twitching to be behind the mic already. Only a few more hours and I will be on that stage, feeding off the energy of my fans and looking for fresh pussy. Talk about the perks of being a fucking rock star.

I had women before we got noticed, but now I can drown myself in them and never get tired. Sex, music, booze, drugs, and the feel of my face being hit repeatedly—those are my releases. I like to feel pain. After years of trauma, I am scarred and bruised inside. For years, my father abused my mother and me. He thrived off letting me know my mom and I were worthless and didn't deserve happiness.

The older I got, the less he hurt her because I was around to take the beatings and to step up and defend her. The one time I wasn't there—the day I ditched school to hang out with some friends and get drunk—he used her instead. She had to take the beating for me. My father didn't care that I missed school; he never planned on me being a scholar—no, it was more about his reputation. His son skipping school and him having to get the call. I wish they had called my mother instead. Maybe she would still be here if he hadn't known.

When I think about that day, I start to spiral. It is a giant trigger for me. In fact, it is the worst thing for my mental health. All I have left now is missing her. Often before shows, my mind will get in a loop where I wonder if she'd be proud. Would she be in the crowd cheering? Would we have run from him and made it out? All those thoughts bring me back to the same moment. That day. That coward beat my mother to the point of no return, and like the letdown my father always claimed I was, I wasn't there to protect her. Losing my mother at the hands of my father when it should have been me was all it took for me to dispose of my faith in humanity or any higher power. My mother taught me to have faith, but I drove out any morals I had left because of his actions and my failure that night. It should have been me who died, and it wasn't, so now I take each brutal hit with pleasure. I owe my mother that.

Fighting random strangers when I need to release all the unresolved anger isn't heroic. It doesn't bring her back. I'm no vigilante, but goddamn, does it feel fucking good. Pain for pain. You can thank my sperm donor for leaving me with a diagnosis of intermittent explosive disorder. The smallest things can cause me to react with anger. Textbooks might call my actions unwarranted, but I do my best to try to remember that this illness is real. I am not a textbook. I am a person trying to fight back against my own mind. A mind that was formed by the man who was supposed to love me but ultimately fucking destroyed me.

Pulling a joint out of my back pocket, I light it up to help take the edge off this unpleasant jaunt down memory lane. Most of the time, when my mood starts to take a nosedive from high into low, I can barely handle it. I need something that can rein me in.

"Ben, you good?" Our tour manager, Nick, is hanging up our band tees.

"Hey, yeah, perfect," I lie through my teeth. "Looks good."

Doing my best to not show my internal turmoil outwardly, I brush him off, but I know damn well he can see right through me. He's been more than a manager to me, he's been a mentor. A best friend. He knows my past, and he knows what it can do to me.

The drugs, the drinking, the fighting, my mental health issues—all of those make up a concoction that most people don't even want to attempt to address, let alone help me with. Nick stays with me through every rise and every fall. Every. Single. Time. There are not many people out there I can say that about. Actually, there is no one. I have my bandmates, but they all have their own vices and are working through them the best they can. The only one I can truly depend on and be the real Ben with is Nick.

Thankfully, he lets me have a reprieve on this one. "I didn't know we got more shirts. When the hell did we make that one?"

"Came in last week." He moves to the next box.

"We should make a shirt with my face on the front that says, 'If you think his face is fucking perfect, you should see his dick.' That will sell like crazy," I tease. I've lost count of how many times I've tried to drown out the noise in my head. I don't want to think about my past any longer. So I will hide behind my humor and bury that trauma a little bit deeper. Isn't there a saying that what makes someone the most fun to be around is being riddled with trauma?

I, Ben Cooper, live my life with no control and no restraint, barely hanging on to a slippery ledge. I'll never truly find peace again. Only wish for it.

Three

SADIE

"Wakey, wakey, eggs and bakey!"

My eyes fly open as my best friend, Kate, jumps up and down on the bed like a madwoman. Once I realize what's happening, I cover my heavy eyes with my bouncing arms, doing my best to ignore her.

"Go away. I'm exhausted, Kate." My groggy voice sounds like I feel: over it and ready to shut down again. Is there a word that surpasses exhaustion? If so, slam my picture right on it in the dictionary.

"Oh, no you don't. Up, up!"

"First off, I hate that you scared me awake, like I was in the middle of an earthquake. Second, do you ever run out of energy?" I sit up on my elbows and watch her land on both feet on the floor at the foot of my bed.

"You love me. I'm actually a vampire, and instead of blood, I feed off others by stealing their energy."

Reaching for the pillow behind me, I chuck it right at her smug little face. "Ha ha. You're so funny," I say sarcastically.

My best friend is my polar opposite: loud, eccentric, funny, and far from reserved. Kate is also more experienced in the man department. She has a mouth that would make sailors' eyes bulge.

She often says things others find offensive, but I love how she can be all the things I sometimes wish I could be. Kate doesn't take anything too seriously. Sometimes I envy her lack of responsibility and her ability to live life to the fullest without ever thinking about the consequences. If I took on life the way Kate does, hooking up with people I don't know or riding in cars with strangers, I would be repenting daily. Still, I envy it sometimes.

"Get that sexy little ass out of bed and let's get ready." Opening the door to my walk-in closet, she sets herself to work digging through my clothes.

"Kate, I can't. I worked a twelve-hour clinical, and I have a ton of studying to do over the weekend. I need to sleep."

"No, we're going out. We haven't spent any girl time together in weeks, and I need it. Besides, grandma, you need it too."

She steps out of the closet, places her hands on her hips, and shakes her head at me as if I've done something wrong.

"Good thing I brought backup. Do you not own one thing remotely appropriate for your age? Did you buy all your clothes in the early eighteen hundreds? Are there ankles under there somewhere?" She lifts my blanket a bit and pretends to search for my ankles.

Okay, not all my clothes are that bad. I choose not to wear anything revealing. My skirts are all below my knees, and my tops all have sleeves and higher necklines. So sue me if I cover up my body out of respect. Showing off in a way that could be perceived as sexy isn't something I do. I'm not ashamed of my body, and I don't look down on anyone who dresses more freely, but I want to save that part of me. For him. For the man I marry. Even I can understand how that might sound stupid to outsiders. But I was raised this way, and it has stuck.

"There's nothing wrong with my clothes. The whole world doesn't want to see me on display, I'm sure." I throw the blankets off. "Ugh."

Looks like I'm going out tonight. Not because I want to, but if I say no, I'll spend the next hour listening to Kate whine and moan about how we never hang out. I stand up and move to the bathroom to brush my teeth.

"If you ever want to get laid, you have to change what you wear. No man will talk to you if you look like you might just bite him." She pulls out a ton of things from her bag and throws them carelessly onto my bed.

"Not fair. It's not like I'm a prude, Kate! And you know what?" I ask around my toothbrush. "Mike likes me the way I am."

She digs into her seemingly never-ending bag. What the heck is in that thing? She could fit a dead body in there. Her blond hair is already curled, her green eyes are makeup-free, and her curvy body is encased in yoga pants and a loose tank. She looks stunning even when she isn't trying.

"Mike doesn't like anyone but himself."

I roll my eyes. Mike is a stand-up guy from my church, and he and I have been dating for a few months now. We study together multiple times a week, and on a few occasions he has called me his girlfriend. I've never asked him to expand on it; it just feels like something we're supposed to do. Our dates are innocent, with a peck here and there; usually, we go to the movies, the diner, or church. Sure, maybe there's no spark, but we've been friends since I moved here. That's a relationship . . . right?

Spitting out my toothpaste, I rinse then walk back into my room. "Okay, that's not true. And he also respects me."

"I've seen you naked, Sadie Jay, and I must say, if any man looked close enough, past the eighteenth-century attire, he wouldn't be able to keep his fucking hands off you."

"He's a gentleman," I reiterate.

"Whatever. Get dressed and try not to look like you are allergic to the sun. Put on this tank! Oh, and wear this lacy bralette!" Throwing the items at my face, she winks, and I catch the flimsy bra with a shake of my head.

"Kate, please, you know I would never." Holding the barely there material by the strap, I swing it back and forth. This must be a joke.

How does Kate even wear this? Are nipples on display a new trend? This covers nothing.

"It's my night. I get to pick your outfit, so what I say goes! Now get changed and show off your gorgeous girls." Bouncing over to me, she slaps the top of my full, heavy breasts. I squeak, grabbing them.

"You're so annoying," I say, but I do as she asks. I may be tired, and she may be a lot to handle, but she's my best friend. She's *my* handful. And against my mind screaming for me to put my foot down, I give in and get ready.

Four

BEN

"Ten minutes! Ben, no more beer. You need to be somewhat coherent onstage tonight. Thousands of people are here," Nick scolds me as I down the rest of the bottle, my eyes on him while I give him the classic middle finger. We play home shows quite often. In between out-of-state shows, we like to come back and play for the local fans. Most artists in our league don't do this; however, my bandmates and I find it grounds us. When you flip the switch of stardom overnight, you always want to be reminded of the things that got you here.

"Three minutes! You boys ready?"

Setting the glass bottle down on the table, I throw on my red blazer, leaving my chest bare since it's spring. When I start the show, the jacket keeps me warm, but after a few songs, I always lose it. High on adrenaline, and even more high on the crowd, I perform in only leather pants and black shoes. In our sets, I do all kinds of wild shit, and the medication I take for my anxiety makes my body temperature warmer than normal. Combine all of that and I'm a sweaty mess. My lean frame and the V-cut abs disappearing into my pants are always out at my shows. Women love it, and I love women, so it's a win-win.

We stand in the wings for a moment waiting on the go signal. Once cleared by Nick, we bound onstage.

"Portland! How's it going tonight!"

The crowd roars to life, and the spotlight shines down on me, center stage. The buzz has me feeling bold, the slight high helping to keep me relaxed. I have the best of both worlds. The seats up on the balcony are filled to the brim with my fans. There is a haze of smoke, and the smell of booze is thick in the air. Scanning the front row, I'm looking for anything I like but also feeding my ego. I almost move to the next row when I dead fucking stop.

Wait.

My eyes land on the most stunning creature I've ever seen, and my fucking chest kicks. There is no way she's real. Blond hair curled all around a perfect pale face. Her eyes so fucking blue I can see them all the way up here even with the spotlight trained on me. The pouty lips on this goddess are painted a glossy red, and they invite me to taste them. But the body. God, the body. Perfect heavy breasts that I want to suck, bite, and taste all night long.

"Shit," I say into the microphone, suddenly forgetting where I am and what I planned to say next. Her eyes lock on mine, never leaving, even when her friend pulls on her arm and screams excitedly, pointing out the obvious—that I'm fucking stoned off the sight of this woman.

I clear my throat and find my words again. "You guys ready for some good music and a hell of a night?"

The crowd hollers, but I don't break eye contact with the beauty who stole my fucking breath. A cross hangs on her pale neck, lying between her heavy breasts above her low-cut black tank top. The way the lace plays peekaboo makes me want to see what else is hiding underneath.

Her eyes drop, and it's cute the way she's acting like she didn't come here to get my attention. The innocent act never works. Women come here looking for a rock star like me—and I plan to deliver.

I start singing the first song. The words echo back to me from the crowd singing along; it's so loud, I can barely hear the backing track and clicks in my earpieces. Still, nothing else matters except for the distraction in the front. My eyes never leave hers for more than a few seconds. I stay focused, sobering up at the same time as I'm getting drunk on those fuck-me eyes. I'm going to be inside her tonight—the most intoxicating woman I've ever laid my greedy fucking eyes on.

Three songs in and I already have lyrics in my head for the woman with a face but no name. I dance along with each track, teasing her more and more. I lose my jacket and proudly show her the body she will be writhing under tonight, begging for me to stop all while wanting more. Yes, I'm that fucking sure of myself, and I'm more than sure that I want this woman.

"All right, let's slow it down for a second." I take a swig of my water.

"Yeah, let's give Ben another second to talk about himself," Eric jokes, and the crowd erupts in laughter. Looking to the blond angel in the crowd, I see her smile at Eric then me. I shoot her a wink, and she drops her head again. Oh fuck. I can't wait to bite that chin and keep her head up while she watches me make her come.

"I think they like it," I banter back.

"I bet they do, egomaniac. Check out this guy—isn't he such a fucking looker? I don't blame you guys." Girls holler my name, throwing out *I love you, Ben* and stroking my ego just a little more.

"Thank you, thank you." I bow, my abs tightening as I do. Moving side stage, I stand in front of my mystery girl. Her friend screams, but not her, no. She's almost unfazed by our closeness, until I see her throat bobbing as she swallows deeply. Her eyes rake down my body, stopping for a little longer on my leather-covered cock.

"You like that?" I tease.

The crowd screams, and she blushes. She looks down for the hundredth time tonight, but this time, she does something intriguing. She grabs the dainty silver cross around her neck, closes her eyes, and whispers something to herself. When she stares back up at me, she's stone-faced, her wide blue orbs hazy. She looks ... guilty. What the fuck just happened?

"Ben, sing 'Falling from Grace'!" a loud voice screams from the surrounding crowd, and I finally break our trance, knowing without a doubt that this girl needs to be mine tonight—shit, for more than tonight. I want to know what the hell is going on in her mind. No, I need to know.

***

"Nick, I want those girls, the blonds side stage. Go get them."

I wipe my face and chest down with a towel. There is a hunger in me I haven't felt before. Women aren't scarce, and I have no cravings I can't fulfill, but I felt a kinetic pull to the blond goddess. My tongue is begging for a drop of water in a drought. Maybe I drank too much and mixing in the pills and weed made me delirious.

"You got it."

"Hurry before she leaves."

"I call dibs on her friend." Eric slaps my back.

Poor friend of hers; hopefully she can handle him and will recognize when the red flags turn to flashing lights telling her to run. Eric is into some dark shit. I've seen the things he has in his room. I've heard him with women in the bunk above me in the back of our bus and on the other side of hotel walls. I like to keep it wild and adventurous under the sheets, but he is next level.

I light a cigarette and head down the hall to the back room where all our shit is. I take long drags, closing my eyes in an attempt to come down from everything. I need to settle my adrenaline, turn on the charm, and focus on the goddess who is about to be mine. Coming to her wild and wired can go one of two ways: she will enjoy it or she will call me on it. I prefer option number one.

Five

SADIE

"Holy shit, Sadie! He was totally into you!" Kate screeches, her excitement enough for a dozen people. Her excitement is usually contagious—it was one of the things that made the time my mother was sick bearable. But in this moment, I can't agree with her.

"I'm not interested." I try my best to not let her know what kind of things I was thinking when I was looking up at Ben. *Ben.* Such a simple name for a man more mysterious and complex than the Riemann hypothesis.

"Oh please, Sadie. I saw the way you were looking at him. I could practically see your lady bits tingling."

Scolding her with a look, I slap her arm. Yes, I felt a physical pull toward him. The way he owned that stage, the way the words he sang spoke to the musical parts in me, and the way he stared at me. I've never felt something so palpable, like I could reach out and touch the untouchable.

"You're so vile sometimes, Kate. Can we go home now? I'm getting irritable, and I need to sleep."

"Fine."

We make our way out of the crowd into the slightly chilly night air. Ben's there in my mind again, his cocky persona burning a permanent image into my memory. His one arm was covered in tattoos while his other arm and chest were bare. His stomach was lean with amazing abs and that *V* that Kate is always going on about. I get it now.

He made me feel something—desire. The way he looked at me, the way his body bounced on that stage with pure confidence, exuding sex from the veins in his neck all the way to the leather hugging his long legs, had me tempted to haul myself straight into sin.

I envisioned worshipping his full lips, whispering against them while he does things to my body. What things I don't know, since I've never even read a book with sex in it or watched an R-rated film. Right now, my imagination is working overtime. He keeps his hair shorter on the sides and slightly longer on top so it flails about while he's bent over and belting beautifully into the microphone. The way he ran his hand through it to reveal his brown eyes made me feel things I don't want to feel. He is a rock star, and his cockiness tells me to run and never look back. But the way he controlled my inner needs with just his presence tells me the opposite.

I almost feel guilty that I've never felt a fraction of the desire for Mike that I did in that hour watching the rock star.

We're outside the door, immobilized by the crowd in front of us like traffic on the highway, when a tall man with a long beard and slicked-back, dirty-blond hair approaches.

I see his badge, which reads: TOUR MANAGER OF THE ROES.

"Ladies, I'm Nick. Ben wanted me to come find you girls and bring you backstage for a meet and greet. You interested?"

He looks older but still handsome; I believe the statement "aging like fine wine" was made for men like him. If I were to guess, he is nearing forty, but you can only tell by the lines in the corners of his eyes and the one defined wrinkle on his forehead.

Even though he gives off big bad biker vibes with tattoos on almost every inch of skin from his neck down, his age and his soft green eyes tell me something different. Something about Nick makes me surprisingly comfortable.

"Yes! We would love that!" Kate says.

"No!" I reply.

"What? Sade, come on, it's backstage passes to meet the band! Please! I won't ask for another thing tonight! Please. They are my favorite band."

She gives me doe eyes, and I want to fight her on it, but I don't. People pleaser. I'm torn between sleep and the happiness of my best friend.

"Please."

"Fine, but not for too long. I really need the sleep, Kate."

"Yay! I love you, Sadie Jay!" Jumping up and down, she follows Nick. I drag my tired feet behind her.

"You better," I mumble.

We're nearly smoked out when we step into the room, and the polluted air makes me cough a little. I need to physically restrain myself from plugging my nose. I don't want to disrespect anyone, but the smell is pungent, and my stomach rolls.

Staying close to the door, Kate takes charge of the room like she always does, catching the attention of all the guys. I check my phone awkwardly. Seeing a message from Mike, I occupy myself.

Mike: Want to get breakfast tomorrow? I can go over my thesis with you?
Me: Sounds good. Pick me up at 9?

As I wait for his response, I peer up for a quick second to see Kate attached to the guitar player. My phone buzzes again.

Mike: Perfect, see you then

I frown a bit at the bland closing of our conversation. Mike has never called me anything other than Sadie. No pet names or sweet terms of endearment. Just Sadie. What would it be like for him to say, *See you then, baby?* Would it feel as good as I imagine?

I hate to admit that I'm bored, and that's driving my attraction to

Ben, the lead singer. I'm hungry for something, and I don't know what it is. Mike's great, but he isn't exceptional, and the young girl in me who believed in fairy tales wants to feel something life-changing. Like the world is moving rapidly under my feet in the best way possible.

"You know, I can't take my fucking eyes off you. You are intoxicating."

Thoughts of Mike fade away; a few feet away from me is the man who let temptation in, and those feelings are right there on the surface. I need to hush the voices screaming at me to do something I shouldn't—to test boundaries.

"That was the stage lights. Everyone was shining. Really."

"Fuck me, an accent?" His vulgarity might have shocked me, but I'm friends with Kate.

"Yes, I guess. But to me you have one, too, so really, do I have the accent or do you?"

His brows lift, his bottom lip getting caught between his perfectly straight white teeth. My breath hitches, and I nearly choke. He's still shirtless, but now he's wearing a backward flat-bill hat.

"Smart and sassy."

"I'm not sassy," I retort.

"Where are you from . . ." He trails off, searching for my name.

"Sadie. From Carolina."

"North or South?"

"South."

"Sadie from South Carolina, I'm Ben Cooper."

"Do you always say your full name when introducing yourself? It seems a bit like an egotistical James Bond vibe." I debate shaking his hand but decide against it. I will stick with the insult and avoid touching the skin that secretly I want to.

"Do you prefer fucking on buses, or do we go back to your place, gorgeous?"

The crass way he asks me that question catapults me to a different realm, one where my hand wants to slap his face. "Neither. I'm not interested." Stepping back a little, I put some distance between us. He watches as I take two steps away from him.

"You can drop the act. I'm not in the mood to play hard to get. My bunk or your place?"

"Wow, no. I'm not that kind of girl. I'm only here because my friend wanted to meet the band."

When I cross my arms defensively, he blatantly stares at my chest; I forgot for a second that I'm wearing the most revealing top in the world.

"Eyes up here, jerk."

Seriously, is this what the world of men has become? Suddenly, I'm thankful for Mike and his infinite respect, and I regret my lapse in judgment.

"They feel better down there."

"You are such a pig. We're done here." I move fast, pushing past him. Ben—too simple a name for a man with such an obviously big ego.

"Is this the part where I chase you, baby? I guess the hard-to-get thing can be pretty hot—at least you make it that way!" he yells after me.

"Kate, I'm leaving." I exit the room, not looking back.

"What—wait! What happened!"

I don't slow down. I feel so violated, so heated, completely enraged by his audacity. I feel . . . alive. What in the world is going on in my mind? He is an asshole. Not someone charming or worth giving a second thought.

"Hey, wait up! What did he say?" Kate catches up to me as we make our way out of the venue through the now-empty parking lot.

"He hit on me like a real class act. And if you can't tell, I am being sarcastic. It was terrible. I never want to be in the same room with that man again."

"Hmm."

"Hmm what, Kate?"

"You liked it. You liked him. I can tell. You're completely turned on, and the little cross on your neck is burning your skin. Oh my god, Sadie!"

"Kate, no. He's trouble wrapped up in a nice body. It's an illusion, and I can see through it."

"That scares you, doesn't it? Desiring someone and straying from the person you think you have to be. The good girl?"

"Kate, you have no idea what you're talking about." I shake my head. "I don't know him. Our conversation lasted a hot second. I have nothing but pure disgust for a man who thinks he can proposition a woman with sex because he's a rock star. No thanks." My face grows red, my neck itches, and these awful clothes feel tight.

"You're defending yourself pretty hard."

"Because the world's biggest player just hit on me, and I'm exhausted! Kate, can we please go home!"

I'm a mess, an out-of-control, overly stimulated mess. I don't know what to make of my emotions because everything I feel right now is something I've never experienced. Everything happening inside me goes against everything that I am. I'm straddling a line between the woman I am and someone I wonder if I could be. And I don't know which side I'm on. My body is hot, and I feel a pit of wanting in my stomach. There is even a quiver in my lip when I talk. Why would my body feel like that when simultaneously it wants to knee him in the balls?

"Hey, I'm sorry. Take a deep breath."

Kate runs her hands over my shoulders, and I breathe out for what feels like the first time since I got here. I need rest and some time to reset myself. Maybe it's the lack of sleep that has me feeling the way I do. No way can a man I just met have this much power over me. No way should he make me as worked up as he does.

A good night's sleep will fix this. It has to.

Six

BEN

What just happened? I thought for sure she was playing some game with me, but my South Carolina blond left. She waltzed her sassy ass out of here like the damn building caught fire.

"Way to go. Her friend was down to hook up. You owe me," Eric says from the couch with a joint in his hand.

I go to grab it, on edge and fucking irritated. I've never been turned down—I've never been more turned on. Talk about a mindfuck.

Taking a hit, I release the smoke and reply, "World's shittiest wingman goes to me then?"

"She was fucking hot. What the fuck happened with you and the prude?"

"Don't call her a prude."

Even though she turned me down, I feel a pull to defend her. I pass him the blunt.

"Her hot friend Kate said she was standing in the corner cause she's more reserved around people and this shit ain't her scene. Dude, she's probably still a virgin."

"Fuck me."

I could have shot myself in the foot and it would have caused less damage. She's not the type of girl I should have been forward with. I wouldn't usually care how girls feel or if I offended them, but this girl, this woman, made me feel something. Blame it on the lust, but I've never seen a more beautiful woman in my life, and now I'll never have a chance with her because I'm a fucking dick.

"You asked her if she wanted to fuck, didn't you?" Smoke fills the air, and I nod my head as JJ, Nick, and Jason enter the room with some takeout. I probably traumatized Sadie. *Good going, Ben.*

Turning, I punch the wall, almost plowing straight through it. Grabbing my shirt and jacket, I head out to fix my rage with my fist in someone's face. I make it to the door before Nick stops me.

"I'll call Dr. Danivah."

I want to fight Nick on this because I can't see through the fog right now, and the only way I see out is to give in to the urge. To punch a wall or, better yet, have someone hit me.

"Fine. Get me to the bus and get him on the phone. Now."

I'm going to battle against my every instinct, and then tomorrow I'm going to find Sadie.

* * *

"Welcome back, boys."

We sit down on the couch and chairs in the room as Trey and Kingston, our record producers, walk in. After my call with Dr. Davinah, I took my medication and fought a terrible struggle in my mind until sleep took me under. Waking up this morning was equally as taxing. I have a pounding headache, and we had to wake up early to head to Seattle for a recording session. Not only am I mentally and physically drained, but I now have to spend the morning recording and then rush back to Portland for a photo shoot. Today is going to be a long day. And of course, I can't stop thinking about her. I want to taste her.

"Gentlemen, you ready for today? Hope you brought your A game," Kingston sings, far too chipper for me this early in the morning. "Did you miss me?"

"Who wouldn't?" I retort.

"The girl from last night sure doesn't," Eric says. If he could see the death glare I'm giving him under my shades, he'd take that shit back.

"What did you get yourself into now?" Trey asks while he messes with some knobs on the mixing board.

"Nothing. Don't worry about it. How's fatherhood? You two are starting to go gray a bit." I wink, and they both audibly growl. Trey glares at me, and Kingston curls his lip in annoyance. "Sensitive topic? Don't worry, I'm sure Lana and Shayla will stick around for a couple more years."

"At least they have someone," Jason quips, sitting next to me. I can't help but punch his arm.

When are they going to drop last night? I get it, I was rejected, and that's a first, but enough is enough. The more they talk about it, the more worked up I become. Her memory is picking me apart; I'm tied up in knots over how much one woman is occupying my mind. That's never happened before.

"All right, spit it out. Who is the girl?" Kingston asks.

"One who was lucky enough to not fall into his trap," Nick says.

I remove my sunglasses and blink a couple times to adjust to the lighting. Nick stands next to the door, looking me dead in the eye, challenging me to say something back. I debate it, too prideful to let him have the last word, but when he doesn't back down, I shut up. Nick may be a bit overprotective, but it's more than I can say for a lot of people in my life. He doesn't tolerate my bullshit, but often he's the one dragging me out of my own fucking mess. The number of times he has kept me from getting arrested after bar fights deserves some sort of award. Definitely got him a hefty pay raise. Amazing what people will do when a tall, tattooed man tells them to shut their mouths, ice the eye, and take a nice payoff. Well, most of the time, I just egg my opponent on until they throw the first punch, and the rest is simply self-defense.

It isn't only the fights he has to pull me out of, though. Since I'm in the public eye, no dive bar is ever truly hidden enough from the bottom feeders in the tabloids. Nick has helped me repeatedly rebuild my reputation. However, how many times can you rebuild until people stop giving you a helping hand and a forgiving shrug? I guess we will just keep fucking with the system until it bites back.

"Shit, *the* Ben Cooper, playboy extraordinaire, tripped and caught feelings. Whatever happened to the whole 'Only here for a good time, not a long time'?" Spinning in his chair, Trey looks at me, as does everyone else.

"All right, guys, drop it. I think she's hot." They don't need to know what I've got planned. "That doesn't mean I'm in love and shit. I said maybe five things to her. You know what? Can we just fucking record? We have to get back to Portland soon."

Eric and I talked last night before my medication took me out, and he convinced Kate over the phone to give me Sadie's address. I am not done with her, not even close. I don't know what the pull is, but I'm a curious man, and I want to know why one woman is fogging up my brain.

"Let's get to it, boys." Kingston leads us in, and we record one of my best songs yet. A certain blue-eyed muse can be thanked for that.

Seven

SADIE

My parents left town to visit my grandparents early this morning. I wanted to go with them to South Carolina, but they're staying for a week, and I have clinicals, plus I still need to study. There are only a few weeks of school left. I'm feeling a little less light-headed and irritable after much-needed sleep, but I still can't stop thinking about Ben. Is he thinking of me? Why do I care? I wanted to crawl out of my skin last night, but at the same time I was drawn to him. The invisible pull is hard to forget.

Truthfully, I can't tell if I'm mad or if I want to see him again. It's all very confusing. When I talked to Kate earlier, she said she's seeing Eric tomorrow to go boating on the lake. She asked me to come along, but I shot her down. This time, she didn't beg. It's safe to say after she saw how upset I was at the predicament I was put in last night, she won't be pushing me to go. I'm staying home to study, then I will attempt a night of self-care before a long rest ahead of medical madness.

The doorbell rings, letting me know Mike is here. Moving quickly, I throw on my zip-up hoodie and rush to meet him at the door. I'm wearing jeans, some knee-high boots, and a black basic tee. It's raining like crazy today, so I opted for comfy, warm, but still a little more stylish than what I usually wear.

"Mike, hey," I greet him. Leaning in, he gives me a brisk kiss on the cheek.

"Hey, Sadie."

His greeting is warm, but I'm comparing the feelings in my stomach and the thoughts in my head to how Ben made me feel last night. The way Mike makes me feel is so lackluster. Ben enraged me, but he poked and prodded at the emotions inside me that I have always been curious about but pushed deep, deep down.

"You look comfy. Ready to go?"

I did my makeup a little heavier than usual, and I curled my hair, hoping Mike would notice. Truly, what did I expect? For him to drool at the sight of me? Mike didn't even notice; it's as if he is looking right through me.

"Yes, let me grab my bag."

My stomach drops when I catch a glimpse of myself in the mirror in our entryway. I feel foolish for trying to get him to see something else in me. I tuck my hair behind my ear, feeling inadequate. Am I desperate? Is that what is happening? This is new to me, and everything I'm feeling is a shock to my psyche.

Picking up my bag, I fake a smile, and we make our way toward our usual hangout at the downtown café.

* * *

"You want some coffee?" Mike offers as he stands up from the table. We finished our chocolate chip pancakes with orange juice—we order them every Saturday morning, and each time we split them. I like food, but Mike likes fitness, so I've given in, and we share so he doesn't go overboard. I'll sneak snacks when I get home.

"Sure, thanks."

As he leaves, I release a breath I've been holding for what seems like forever.

Ben. That's the first thought that comes to mind. I'm uneasy about the way I'm obsessing over him, the way he makes me think tirelessly about him, dream about him, and desperately try to find attention from someone else so I can forget about him.

Being strong and courageous where Ben is concerned seems unachievable. The point may be moot, though, since I may never see him again. If I'm wise, I will forget he even exists.

"Here's my thesis for my literature class. Read it, make some notes," Mike says as he comes back, sets down the coffee, then takes the papers out from his textbook and slides them over to me.

I read it over, but, to be honest, I retain almost nothing. Mike is going to school for business. His literature class is required, and the contents of this paper show that. He hates reading, hates the idea of anything to do with classic novels.

"What do you think?" Mike asks as I slide the papers back to him.

"It's perfect, I love it. You've made some great points about the book." That's a lie. I look at him briefly over the rim of my coffee before pulling my eyes away. Usually, we can fill breakfast with conversation, but today there is an awkward, prolonged pause.

"You doing all right? You seem a bit off today." He breaks the silence, and I swallow my coffee so fast that it burns going down.

"Oh, I'm good. Nervous about finals, and it's been busy at the hospital. I'm tired."

My conscience screams that I should tell him about last night, but Mike knows that concerts aren't my typical fare, and I don't want to explain that a rock star wanted to sleep with me. That story I will save for a different day.

"Maybe you should get some rest. You look different today." He gestures to my appearance, and I hate to admit my stomach does a slight flip. Is he going to compliment me?

"You like it? I usually don't wear this much makeup, but I wanted to try something different."

He laughs in an incredulous way. My brow furrows.

"What?" I ask.

"Nothing. You should stick to no makeup. You look better without it. You almost look like you're trying too hard."

Wow, a slap to the face would have been less painful. I open my mouth to fire back, then snap it shut, biting my tongue. I don't want to fight with him. Actually, I would like to get as far away from him as possible. What kind of man says that to his girlfriend? Even if he thought it, he could have kept it to himself.

Moments like this are why I never step out of the safety of the cocoon I've built around myself. I hate it, but sometimes I'm too soft for all of this. Being the good girl is like being the world's punching bag. Good girls don't say anything wrong. Good girls don't get too loud. Good girls don't push back. That's me. The only time I did push back was last night with Ben. A stranger. A beautiful stranger. I wish I could have found my voice today with Mike like I did last night in that smoky backstage room.

"Anyway, I need to get home to study," I state. Right now, the room seems to be getting smaller, and the boiling anger in my stomach is climbing up my throat. I not only feel like a joke, I feel hurt that Mike dismissed me. The way that entire interaction went down has me feeling immature, but then again I *am* only nineteen. I've spent my entire life living to please everyone and make everyone proud of me. It's all I know.

"Agreed, you need rest and a shower." He digs that knife deeper, and I bleed a little more.

***

I have stared at the same textbook for the past six hours, only taking breaks to eat and watch the Health Channel. It's nearing 7:00 p.m., and it's dark outside. The day got away from me, but studying kept me distracted enough to not think about Ben or the hurtful comments that Mike made.

I pick through the fridge, pushing past all the condiments and random things but not finding anything appetizing. The thought of pizza has my stomach singing, and even though I could probably choose something better suited to fueling my brain for a long night of studying, I order anyway.

I'm not a small girl; I would classify my body as midsize. I have thin legs and a soft stomach, but my thighs, butt, and breasts are thick. I have an hourglass shape with a little extra weight to it. I work out a couple times a week when I find the time, usually before or after work at the facility provided by the hospital. I'm happy with my body, and being happy with my body is all that matters.

Once I finish ordering dinner, I FaceTime my parents to help fill the time until my food arrives. I haven't spoken to my grandma in a couple of weeks. My eighty-year-old grandmother Maureen, Mo for short, may be the sweetest old lady there ever was in our small town of Chesnee, South Carolina. She leaves her door unlocked, and often the neighbors drop in for a piece of pie or some cookies or whatever roast she's cooking. And, of course, for the best conversation with the kindest woman.

I miss our small town, the way everyone knows everyone, but most of all I miss my eccentric Grandma Mo.

"Sadie Jay, how are you, baby?" Mama answers, struggling to get her glasses on. I see my face in the little box, and I look more than exhausted—like the living dead. Frustrated by Mike's comments, I wiped all the makeup off my face, and now my lips are swollen and covered in lip balm from biting them tirelessly while studying. My hair is in a topknot, and I'm wearing my daddy's old University of South Carolina hoodie and leggings.

"I'm good, just studying. Where's Grandma?"

"She's right here, hold on. Do you think you'll be ready for finals?" Mama asks as she walks through the house.

"Maybe? I don't know, Mama, I'm all over the place today," I admit defeatedly. I wish she was here so I could unload on her and my father. The bond between us isn't typical. They have always been open and honest with me, as I have been with them, and when they're back, I plan to tell Mama about Ben. Maybe she can help me make sense of all this.

"You're smart, Sadie. You've got this."

"Yes, you do, baby girl." My father's voice comes through the phone. My parents never put pressure on me to be this person. But *they* are those people, and I admire them so much that I strive to be exactly like them.

"Thank you, guys. Now where is Grandma? I want to see her!"

"I'm here, angel baby. Oh my—look at you, Sadie Jay, you've grown up so much!"

Her wrinkled yet youthful face comes into focus. I swear her joyful outlook on life has kept her young.

"It's only been six months since I visited last, Mo-Mo."

"But you young kids change so fast. You look like a young woman, like your mama did when she was a young lady."

The twinkle in her eyes warms my heart. Her health hasn't been the best lately, but she never lets that dull her charisma. She's suffered three strokes in the past three years, and it's been extremely hard on us all to be so far away from her. Good thing Mama and Papa go back frequently to visit.

"Thanks, Mo-Mo." The doorbell rings, and I check the time. There's no way that's the pizza already.

"Hey, guys, I have to go. I think my pizza's here? I'll FaceTime you later this week."

"Love you. Be safe and lock up the house, baby girl," Dad reminds me.

"I always do. Love you!" They say goodbye, and I open the door right as the call ends.

"That was fast . . . Ben?" Nearly stumbling as I back up, I'm sure I must be seeing a mirage. Ben Cooper stands on my doorstep all handsome in his skinny ripped jeans that only a rocker could pull off with his leather jacket and wild hair.

"Expecting someone else?"

"I am. I have a hot date with the pizza guy. What are you doing here? How did you get my address?"

"Kate told me. I love pizza, sounds good to me. You going to invite me in?"

"No," I sass.

He's incorrigible. I make a mental note to wring Kate's neck.

"That's not nice. Didn't your mother teach you manners? Aren't people from the South supposed to be more welcoming?"

"To people who deserve it."

"Ouch. I thought you would invite me in and give me sweet tea and cookies. I was wrong about you, Sadie from South Carolina." He winks, his humor both annoying and funny. I keep my face as straight as possible but crack when he stares at me while his smile beams.

"You're insane. What do you want, Ben?" I laugh.

"Invite me in and I'll tell you. Please?"

Pursing my lips, I release a breath and debate the idea for a few seconds. I should slam the door in his face. I almost lost my marbles from our short interaction yesterday. Now I'm debating letting him into my house—inviting the enemy in?

"Fine, but if you hit on me or anything of that sort, you're out."

"Score! Thanks, beautiful." He walks around me, and my stomach flips, filling with flying butterflies. Did he call me beautiful?

I watch, fascinated, as he waltzes into the living room and makes himself right at home. He plops down and stacks his feet on top of one another, using my coffee table as a footstool. Reluctantly, I follow him.

"Health Channel, health books. You into some kinky shit?"

"I said no weird comments!" Grabbing the pillow beside me, I chuck it at him.

"All right!" He laughs, and the throaty sound and his charming smile have my stomach dancing again. "I was teasing, but really, what's with all this?"

"I'm about to graduate with my LPN."

"Wow. Smart, sassy, and beautiful. What else do I not know about you?"

Beautiful. There it is again, that unfamiliar word. No man has called me that. Well, my father has, but that is what dads do.

"None of those, really. I like helping people," I tell him truthfully, sitting crossed-legged alongside him. I can't believe I have a rock star in my living room sitting next to me, less than twenty-four hours after he crudely propositioned me for sex. This new Sadie doesn't even know if she approves of herself.

"There's that Southern charm."

He squeezes my knee, and something happens. The spot between my thighs softly pulses. That turned me on—his touch made my body go all gooey inside. But I ignore it, pushing it down deep, and thank my stars he doesn't notice. I can only imagine what he would say and how much having that knowledge would stroke his already too big ego.

"No, that's God's work. He put us here to help people, and that's my life mission."

"Oh God, that's right. God." He says *God* with such disdain, it throws me off.

"You're not the religious type?"

"No. I don't believe in it," Ben states bluntly.

"If you aren't religious, then who do you thank for your success?"

Somehow, sitting here with Ben feels natural, like it's a regular night between two good friends. It's different, and what's more odd is I feel completely comfortable. Every moment spent with Ben is a new experience I've never felt with Mike.

"My hard work. My dedication. My good looks." He falls back on humor. I see the shield he puts up, and I don't push further. There is something darker there, something he wants hidden. But like I have my secrets, I respect his boundaries.

"You're very full of yourself. I can't believe women fall for that," I say, standing and moving to the kitchen. "Would you like a water or anything, Ben?" I say over my shoulder.

"Beer."

"We don't drink in this house, I'm sorry. I have soda." I peer back at him, and he nods with a sly sideways grin.

"That'll do. Your whole family super religious then?" I fill a glass with some ice and pour the soda into it.

"My parents are, and I try to be as active as possible." I shrug.

Does he think that religion is what drives me to be reserved? To be more guarded? It's not. It helps, but it's not why I am the way I am.

"Hmm."

"Hmm what?" I hand him his drink as we resume our spots on the couch.

"Nothing, just curious. It never made sense to me."

"What? Religion?"

"Yeah, religion. It seems fake—unnecessary."

"I believe in God. I believe in his miracles," I say. Ben grunts, taking a sip of his drink.

"What miracles?" he inquires as I drop my head and start rubbing my neck. It's filled with a thousand kinks from studying all day. "Your neck hurt?"

I nod, ready to answer his question when he grabs me by the elbow and yanks me into his arms, cradling me in his lap. I yelp.

"Ben!" Immediately, his hand goes to my neck, and he begins to knead the knots. Suddenly, I don't know what words are. It feels so good.

"I'll rub it out. Keep talking. Tell me about these miracles." My natural reaction is to run the other way, but the urge to stay is much stronger.

"I—I . . ." Looking into his eyes, I get lost seeing all the emotions gathering in his stormy brown irises.

"Miracles, baby. Tell me about them."

Baby? Am I here in my house, sitting in his lap, inches from his handsome face? This is all overwhelming, but the words come naturally, nearly unstoppable.

"Love. I have seen the power of love in my parents. Or when a new baby is born. When a gunshot victim wakes up from their coma . . . when Mama went into remission." I whisper the last words, searching his eyes as well as every detail of his face.

"Your mother had cancer?" he questions, and I see a new look that has yet to grace Ben's face, a look of sadness, empathy, and pain.

I look down, and he drops his forehead to mine. "Hey, look at me."

Giving him my eyes, I wait for his words, clinging to the silent air around us, waiting for something else to latch onto. "I'm sorry you had to go through that, but I'm glad your mother is in remission."

His words feel more genuine than any I heard while Mama was going through cancer. The same words came from a hundred different people, but the way Ben says them reaches something in me. How is this stranger so deep in my psyche that I am sharing the stories of wounds that I am still trying to heal?

"Thank you."

"Tell me about your parents."

When he changes the subject, I snap back to reality. I go to climb out of his lap, thanking him for the massage, but he stops me.

"Stay in my lap. I like you here." I take a deep breath and smell his cologne and the faint smell of smoke. Surprisingly, it's not repulsive, more unique. I bite my lip and shake my head.

"Really, it's okay. I don't want to crush you with my big butt," I tease, hoping this will set me free. I feel myself growing hot, and my core tightens again.

"You have a beautiful body, Sadie, not an ounce of complaint on my end. Stay here, talk to me. Besides, you have me feeling something . . ." I wiggle a bit, staying in place when I realize he isn't going to let me go.

"What do I make you feel, Ben? I barely know you."

"That's the weird thing. I feel safe with you, like I don't need anything else but your presence. It's like we're old friends catching up on lost time. This is a new feeling for me."

I'm stunned. I thought I was crazy, that I was reading this all wrong. Clearly I'm not because he feels the same way.

"You can get all that from what little time we've spent together?"

"I can. You believe in miracles. Maybe this is something like that," he tells me. I shake my head in response.

"You aren't just trying to get me naked, are you?" I cover my mouth, unable to stop the words once they've come out. Did I really say that?

"No, Sadie, surprisingly, I'm not trying to fuck you and leave you like every other girl I've met."

"How poetic," I tease.

"I'm an artist and songwriter, so I'd think so."

I'm about to respond when the doorbell rings. Before I can move, he stands from the couch with me in his arms. He holds me effortlessly, like I weigh nothing. My insides turn to mush.

"Get some plates, I'll get the pizza," he tells me, squeezing my hip, the small touch electrifying. He lowers me slowly to my feet, and our bodies touch, sliding against one another.

"The cash is on the entry table."

"I'll pay. Consider it an apology for the shit I said yesterday."

"Ben, really, it's forgotten. Don't worry." I go to move to the door, but he steps in front of me.

"Don't try it, woman."

"You can't stop me." I attempt to swerve around him, but he's faster. "Ugh, Ben!"

"Move again and I'll carry you over my shoulder to the door."

"You wouldn't."

"Oh, I would." He turns, challenging me, standing much taller than my short frame.

"Challenge accepted." Before he gets a word in, I duck, moving around him. I've almost reached the cash when I'm pulled up into the air. The room around me is no longer in focus as I'm thrown over his shoulder.

"Ben!" I yell, kicking my legs.

He slaps my ass, and I cease moving and gulp. No one has ever touched me like that. Each time he touches me, whether it be an accidental graze, a massage, or a slap on my ass, I get turned on. A confusing thrill follows each moment. I shouldn't desire someone who doesn't know me. Honestly, I imagine he only sees me as a conquest.

"Settle down or I'll smack it again, Sadie, right in front of . . ." He trails off, opening the door. "The nice man named . . ." He pauses, and I hear the pizza guy chuckle.

"Justin."

"The nice man named Justin." Somehow, he gets his wallet out of his back pocket as I dangle over his shoulder. I should be upset or embarrassed, but honestly, I'm having fun. I always feel like I'm in an imaginary hiding place, and suddenly I realize I haven't been living. Not even a little bit. I'm laughing with a stranger, like Kate does. It's something I envied, and now I'm laughing, playing, teasing, and rolling my eyes at Ben. My stomach is tight, and my core is pulsing with need. Tonight, I am feeling desire in the rawest form.

He rustles around then finally says goodbye to the delivery man.

"That was easy."

He places me on my feet and holds the pizza box tightly. I get my balance back, and the blood leaves my head.

"You're such a pain. You know that? I should toss you out." I grab the soda, and he follows me into the kitchen. Everything in here is white, with light granite counters and silver appliances. The windows open to our backyard, sitting on the edge of a small patch of trees. Rain falls, making a light pelting sound against the windows.

"You liked it, it made you laugh," Ben says. "Tell me more about your parents."

I scoff and grab some plates from the cupboard. "My parents are in South Carolina visiting my Grandma Mo. She's been having some health problems."

That's not what he meant when he asked about my parents, but I'm still feeling him out. I don't want to tell all my secrets before I know him better.

"That's rough. What's wrong with her? If you don't mind me asking."

"Old age. She can't get around as fast as she once did, and she's also had three strokes. Poor woman gets tired easily. The neighbors help her out a lot, but my parents like to go back once every few months and stay with her for a week or two, sometimes more." I hand him a plate of pizza.

"Do your parents work? What are their names?"

"Are you playing twenty questions because you really want the answers? Or are you bored?"

"Neither. I want to get to know you."

"Pickup line—that has to be one."

"Nope, it's the truth. I don't lie, I'm too attractive to need to lie." He winks.

"I don't know if I want to throw you out or learn more about your lack of social skills." I throw a piece of pepperoni at him, and he catches it in his mouth.

"I have great social skills. You're just jealous that I have a better sense of humor than you do." He throws a piece of pepperoni back at me, and I catch it in my mouth as well.

"Oh!" we shout in unison.

Tonight is turning out to be fun and a little less confusing than it was when I first opened the door.

Eight

BEN

The way she laughs, the way she teases, it excites me more than any high or fuck I've had. How can that even happen? Her small glances and little touches feel overwhelmingly natural. I like the way she distracts me from the things that hurt me most. My past. My pain. My struggles. Since she opened the door, I haven't thought about anything but her.

"My mom's name is Raydean, she was a nurse before her cancer, and my father is a cardiologist named Stanley."

"They obviously like helping people too. I see where you get it."

"What about you, Ben?"

I catch her meaning, but I play the fool. "What about me?"

"Who are you? Why music?"

Safe enough. That I can answer.

"I don't know. I've always loved music; it's been an escape for me for years. It's my safe place."

"Your religion—it's your religion." Profound. She is every bit as profound as I hoped she would be. Not only is she the most beautiful woman, but I'm completely stunned by her intelligence, her passion, her everything.

"You could say that."

The pull happens immediately. There's nothing I can do except stand and move toward her. Her body craves mine like mine does hers. We can sit here all night and try not to give in, but the air is thick with tension, and our bodies are calling out to one another.

She tenses under my gaze as I close in on her.

"B-Ben," she stutters.

"What, Sadie?"

I cage her in, my hands sliding around her waist until I interlock them. Her skin is warm against mine; we are like magnets drawn by sensation.

"What are you doing?"

I lean close to her ear, my lips barely touching her. "I'm going to kiss you, Sadie."

"Ben, that's dangerous." She quivers against me.

"What's dangerous isn't the kiss. What's dangerous"—I stop for a second to bite her neck—"is that in less than a day you've made me feel something I've never felt in the twenty-two years of my life."

"Ben," she moans, turning quickly toward me.

She wraps her arms around my neck, and just like that my lips find hers. She tastes like something I have been craving but can't quite place. Something that I can claim and not relinquish to anyone else. I grip her hips and place her on the counter, her face now level with mine.

"Sadie, what are you doing to me? I'm not going to be able to stop," I moan, breaking contact. Her hands find my hair as I suck on her neck. This isn't me, the whole talking thing—or even the getting-to-know-you part. I pick a woman and I fuck her without any intention of seeing her again, but Sadie makes me want to come back tomorrow, and the next day, and the next.

"Oh, Ben. I'm sorry." I kiss her again, and she starts to move her hips in circles, looking for friction. "Sadie? What do you want?"

Licking the edge of her plump lips, I taste her, swallowing her down like a glass of water.

"I don't know," she cries as I swallow her words. I fucking know what she needs. Grabbing her wide hips, I slide her forward, and her core hits my growing cock. She yelps as I move her hips against me.

"What's happening?" She throws her head back, and I look down at the raw and intimate act of her grinding against my jean-clad cock.

"What do you mean, angel?" Her head flies up, and her eyes lock on mine, her jaw lax and her crystal-blue orbs wide.

"What you're doing. It feels ... so good." I stop. Wait a second, is she a complete virgin, as in she has zero experience?

"Sadie, has a man ever touched you, besides me?"

As she speeds up her hips, I feel my pre-come and her juices seeping through our clothes, and I groan, the smell of her arousal noticeable. Shit, it smells sweet.

"No. Ben, this is so bad. I have to stop, we need to ... to ... oh my!"

I match her rhythm, and she tries to drop her head back as she chases her orgasm, but I have other plans. With one hand, I catch her chin and tilt it up so her face is on me. "Look at me while I make you come, angel."

She cries out, and her eyes flood, her orgasm taking over, her face flushed in the most stunning shade of pink. Sadie moans loudly. Wall-shakingly loud, and I almost come right there as if it were my first time.

"Ben, Ben, Ben!" Like a high E minor chord on a piano, she screams my name. I moan with her and watch her come down.

"Oh, beautiful. Feels good, doesn't it?"

I moan as she shivers and spasms all over. I wait a second until we finally stop moving, and I kiss her face all over. Her lips, her cheek, up to her forehead, down to her ear.

"That was the most breathtaking thing I've ever seen," I say.

I kiss down the column of her neck until her hoodie stops me. I would keep going, but the eerie silence brings my focus back to her. Sadie has tears rolling down her cheeks, and the guilt-ridden look she's wearing makes my fucking stomach sink.

"What's wrong?" I cradle her soft cheeks in my hands.

"I shouldn't have done that with you. I don't know what came over me."

My chest tightens a bit. Does she regret it? Me? The harsh sting of that blow hits me.

"Talk to me, what do you mean?"

I cup her face so I can get us closer. I need us closer. My body needs her to feel that I want her.

"This isn't like me, Ben. I don't hook up with people I don't know. I don't hook up at all. I always thought I would save this until marriage, and I'm confused, very, very confused."

She searches my face; her brows are drawn tight with worry. How do I make her see that while she is confused and going against what she believes, so am I? I've never wanted just one person, and now suddenly I do? Maybe that means this is something we should be chasing, a wrench in the works that will reset our direction.

"Me, too, Sadie. You make me want exclusively you. You make me crazy, and I just met you. This isn't me either."

"Then why are we doing this?" she pleads, her face contorted in torment.

"I don't know."

Truthfully, I am petrified. My head is pounding, and it feels like my heart is beating out of my chest. But I want this with her. I want to kiss her, touch her, claim her, and fucking keep her. But what does that mean?

"I want to tell you to fucking run, but I won't. I have to have this. I have to keep tasting you. Touching you. Run. Do it."

Giving her an out is the only option. I can't be the one to turn away. Who am I kidding? I wouldn't be able to if I tried. Her eyes search mine. The storms raging in them are beautiful but tragic, and for a moment, I think she might run. Perhaps she is much stronger than I am and will be able to resist whatever this is between us.

"I want to. I need to, but I can't. I want to fear you, I want to push you away, but I can't. I need *you* to run," she chokes out.

"I won't run. But I am telling you now there isn't a world where I won't fucking ruin you. Ruin you for every other person."

"Ben," she whimpers, this time leaning in and kissing me. I grab her neck and tighten my grip enough to control the kiss. It's messy in the best way. She tastes good. So damn good. I want to bottle up her taste and keep it for myself. I moan against her mouth.

"I want to make you feel like that again. I want to drown in you, Sadie," I say between our heavy breathing and lashing tongues.

"We can't. I can't. Shit. Mike." I freeze, my back going stiff. Who the fuck is Mike?

"Mike?" I pull away, my hand still locked around her gorgeous neck.

"Yes, Mike, he's my boyfriend. I think that's what you would call it. Maybe he's my boyfriend?"

I clench my jaw, my nose flares, and my eyes dilate to full black. Jealousy and rage. Those two feelings start to melt into one, and I want to snap. I tilt my head from side to side and crack my neck.

"You have a boyfriend?"

I'm not mad at her, but there's no way another man is having something that I want. Something I need. I'm jealous that he has it and I don't . . . yet.

"Yes. We don't do things like what you and I did. We never even kissed properly. I don't actually know what we are, but this is wrong. He's going to think so little of me," she whispers, and I shake my head, baffled. Moving my hands to her hips, I give them a squeeze.

"I don't give a fuck about his feelings because I don't care what he thinks about you after you leave him." I tilt my head to the side. Sadie doesn't react. "You are not going back to him, Sadie. You are crazy if you think I will let someone else have you."

"Ben, we aren't thinking straight. Can we pause? Take a beat?"

She tries to move, and my temperature rises. My anxiety is skyrocketing, and I don't have anything on me to help calm me down. I left it back at my place. Stepping away from her, I pace back and forth, trying to self-soothe like my therapist says, but it's not working. I knead at my neck and focus on my feet, trying to center myself. I need to calm down. I'm coming on strong, but I can't help it. Sadie needs to know that this isn't a fling, that she's not a game I'm trying to win. She wants to push me away, and I don't know how to tug her back in. That fucking pull that I have felt since I saw her. That invisible force that ties me to her.

"Please, don't be upset. I shouldn't have let it get this far. I am so sorry, Ben."

Her voice breaks through it all. I abruptly stop pacing and turn my head to look at her. The tears streaming down her face and her shaking hands are all I need to see. We are a mess. Two forces that shouldn't have clashed. I'm on her again, and I cradle her face.

"Taste me. Taste what's yours. Give me you, Sadie. Fuck, give me you."

She cries out and nods, leading with her body. Our mouths collide again, and we all but claw at one another to get closer. I couldn't tear myself away from her taste if I tried. When I step back, she cries out, reaching for me, so I grab the waistband of her leggings. "Lift your hips for me, baby, just a little." Gulping, she does, and I yank them down, thankful she has no panties on.

"Ben?" She calls my name, her eyes widening.

"Open your legs for me, angel."

She hesitates for a moment, the war between the good girl and the one who wants to be pleasured. Her legs open, and my eyes look over her beautiful pussy. She has a light smattering of hair, and I can't help but lean in and nip at her lips.

"Oh God!"

"Not God, baby, Ben. My name is fucking Ben."

Her head lolls, and she leans back slightly. I take her feet and place them on my shoulders.

"Look at me while I eat you, angel. Watch your pleasure. Watch what we can do together," I demand. She nods eagerly, and I move in slowly, making her wait desperately for my expert tongue and mouth to destroy her.

I kiss her clit, and she jolts forward. Fuck. She tastes better than I ever imagined. I lick from her center and up to her clit. Now resting on her elbows, she looks to where I am bent over her. Her eyes gloss over with lust, and she bites her lip. My focus never leaves her. As I kiss the top of her pubic bone then bite it, she moans through a giggle.

"Sadie, tonight you're going to call that so-called, almost, whatever-the-fuck he is of yours and tell him that I fucking claimed you. I tasted your gorgeous pussy, and I made you come against my cock. You're mine now, Sadie." I drop my head on my last word and start to suck, lick, and nip at her. I can't even believe I'm telling her the things I am.

"Ben . . ." She trails off, fighting hard to keep her eyes on me. With each stroke of my tongue, she shudders. Sadie is so fucking responsive. I have her ready and on the edge within minutes, and when she squirts against my tongue, my heart thunders painfully against my chest and a feeling of possession comes over me.

Tonight, I went against everything I thought I wanted. No commitment. Not one woman. And never to chase. I went against everything I stood for, and now—and now, I will not let her go. Mike lost her, and she is all fucking mine.

Nine

SADIE

Everything about tonight has contradicted everything I have planned for my life. We kissed, he made me orgasm, and he made me forget any sense of what I thought life was before him. That terrifies me, yet the way that he made me feel is something I can't explain. It's like life has new colors, and he is the reason I learned about them. Tastes that I never knew existed are now familiar favorites. Everything has changed, and yet I'm still trying to navigate what it all means.

I like Ben. I hate Ben. I'm torn up over how I can feel the way I do about him in such a short amount of time. I'm not declaring love or anything—it's too soon for that—but I'm declaring that he makes me want to explore the unknown. That's the best way to put it because I still don't know him. Who is he, and why am I allowing him to explore me in these ways?

Regardless of where my relationship with Ben goes, I have to end whatever I have with Mike. And what happened tonight—I can't do it again. My virginity is something I have always held close to me because I want love when I give the deepest part of me. Marriage. The knowledge that my innocence won't be taken and then I will be left behind. We crossed too many lines tonight, and I need to reel us back in. Ben kisses each of my thighs, following up with intimate nips and suckles. It's raw. It's real.

"B-Ben," I stutter, and he looks up at me. His face is content.

"Yes?"

He stands at full height now, and he helps me put my leggings back on. Who knew the act of dressing in silence after an unconstrained sexual encounter could be so intimate? I blush with each part of my flesh that he covers. When I'm fully clothed, I hop down from the counter and put some much-needed distance between us. I need to think straight. What is happening is really messy. Shit, what am I doing?

He watches me closely as I move around the kitchen, unsure where to put myself. Can't sit down, don't know if I can keep standing up. Ben doesn't move.

"What do you want from me, Ben? Just sex?"

"I want more than sex, Sadie."

I pause, my back to him, and look up at the crown molding on the kitchen ceiling. Releasing a deep breath, I drop my head and prepare for him to change his mind when I say my next words.

"I can't—won't—do that again. I want to wait until marriage. It might be clichéd and probably doesn't make sense to you, but it does to me, and I won't waver." My words are rushed. I wait for him to say good riddance once I finally stop, but those words never come.

"As long as I can be the only one to have you, I don't give a fuck. You have me by the fucking throat, Sadie. Other women don't stand a chance," he admits, and I melt.

I've never felt so desired in my life. I've never had a man lust for me or desire me like Ben does, and even if lust and desire are the root of this, maybe we can grow outside of them. He makes me want to trust him and see where this goes.

"You can have me, but not those parts," I admit, giving him a second chance to find an out.

"I will respect you. But you're mine now, and I won't share."

"Neither will I, Ben." My tone is firm.

"Deal. If I have you, then that is all I need."

I scoff. Rock stars can't be with women who won't put out. Who is he kidding? "You say that now. But I won't have sex. I'm saving myself."

He moves, turning me to face him. He takes my face in his hands and forces me to look up at him.

"You don't get to tell me what I want. I need to know why you are so fucking stuck in my head, Sadie."

Our eyes search one another. I don't know what to say, because as much as I don't want to be a test subject for him to figure out new feelings, I feel things I don't understand and want to know why as well. I wait a moment, my hands wrapped around his wrist as I look at the ground between us. He drops his forehead to mine and urges me to say something.

"Promise me we won't regret this, Ben," I beg, and he takes my words as a green light.

Dropping his lips to mine again, he peppers me with soft, feathery kisses. The kind that make knees weak and hearts break.

"I can't promise you anything other than whatever is happening between us. I plan to ride it out because it's the realest thing I've felt in years." He searches my face, and I reciprocate; he's looking for approval, and I'm looking for any reason to back out, but I find none.

"Mine. I have my own angel," he murmurs.

He moans against my mouth, sliding his tongue across the swell of my bottom lip. I close my eyes and let the musician take over my mouth, teaching me how to truly connect with someone with just a kiss.

"Mmm. Come boating with us tomorrow." He breaks contact, and my head spins, still feeling the electricity on my skin and the plushness of his mouth on mine.

"I have to talk to Mike. End it with him. What time are you going?" I ask. He kisses the tip of my nose, and I catch myself wondering how a rock star who is so confident in himself has such a gentle touch.

"We'll leave at eleven. I'll pick you up."

I nod, nervous about breaking up with Mike tomorrow. Hopefully I won't make it awkward or, worse, lose a friend.

"Now, how about you let me watch you study while I get my guitar and write some music?"

What does it mean to be with Ben Cooper? That is the question I study instead of my textbooks for the next few hours.

* * *

"Things happened between us, and I feel awful. I didn't want to hurt you or lie. But I don't feel like this is what either of us wants. We're more like really good friends." Vaguely, with as little detail as possible, I explain to Mike that I was with Ben last night intimately. Waiting for him to tell me how hurt he is, I look at him searchingly, but not one ounce of sadness appears, let alone jealousy. In fact, he is looking at me like he is disappointed in what I did with Ben rather than what I did to him.

"What, so you're dating a rock star now after knowing him for less than a day? And ending us because you want to hook up? Seriously? Do you know how dangerous and wrong that is? Sweetie, this isn't like you." Mike scolds me like I'm a child. I stayed up all night tossing and turning as I thought about Ben and whatever journey we are about to take together.

Mike and I are sitting in our favorite café while I break the news. It's styled to replicate the feel of a 1950s diner with checkered black-and-white floors, white walls with framed newspaper clippings, and booths cushioned with a deep red hue that matches the stools at the bar. There is a vintage jukebox next to the restrooms, but it doesn't work. Mike and I learned it wasn't functional after we spent twenty minutes our first time here trying to pick a song before the waitress told us the music is controlled in the back and the jukebox is just for the aesthetic. That's a great memory, and that date with Mike is what solidified this friendship-turned-relationship. Yet now, seeing Mike cast judgment on my choice to be with Ben rather than focusing on he and I breaking up, I see maybe this was just a case of friends who got into a routine and slapped a senseless label on it. That doesn't mean I don't feel bad. I am not a cheater, and regardless of how close Mike and I are, I still don't think it was right. But secretly, I don't regret Ben's touch like I should. Actually, I miss it already and crave more of it.

I set a boundary last night that we wouldn't be intimate again. Am I really going to be able to do that? Do I even want to?

I think about the good and the bad, all of it tearing me up inside, but the good outweighs the bad every time. Last night, after Ben and I talked about having a future together, he wrote beautiful lyrics and played his guitar effortlessly. His voice filled the room, mysterious and longing. All of that is enough for me to trust my heart on this one. It's also enough to make me question if I can—or want to—resist his touch.

"This is sudden, and I'm sorry. But I like him, and I want to explore where it goes. I really am sorry that I did this to you," I admit.

"Explore? What, have sex with him? Sadie, I'm so disappointed in you."

I drop my head, irritated that he's treating me like a child. Each time he opens his judgmental mouth, the guilt from last night slips further and further away. Mike flags down the waitress for the check. We spend a couple of tense minutes waiting to pay. Finally, we make our way outside.

"You don't know him," I say, standing outside the café. Patrons are passing us, and the outside tables are full of people sitting with their dates or their novels.

"I don't need to. Rock stars are notoriously bad guys. *Sinners* is what they're called, Sadie. You should be settling down with a good man, not a sinful, disease-ridden bad boy. To be honest, looking at you and knowing you aren't as pure as I thought, I'm disgusted." Wow, so much for the nice guy.

My mouth falls open, but I refrain from yelling. He's a totally different person from the man I thought I knew. I don't hate him, but I certainly don't like him at the moment.

"And I'm disgusted that you are more concerned about my virtue than us breaking up. I'm not going to sit here and be shamed or have you talk about Ben like that. I wish you the best. I do. Goodbye, Mike."

He scoffs and runs his hands through his hair. I can tell he wants to hit below the belt again, but I won't give him any more of my time. I turn to leave, deciding that he can sit with his own thoughts. If he has to hate me right now, then that is on him. This is the first time in my life that I am going against the grain and leading with my heart rather than my head.

I may be young, but the minute Mike started making assumptions about Ben, I knew exactly what I needed to do.

Maybe I'm playing with fire by dating Ben, but I realized last night that I shouldn't judge him for who he was, only by who he is when we're together. If he can respect me and my wishes, then I can accept him and his lifestyle.

Besides, we're only dating. I don't think we're even a couple. Ben and I could be over before we even start. How dare Mike accuse me and Ben of being bad people? He knows nothing about us—I don't even know enough about us yet.

Hurrying to my car, I climb in. I'm going on an official date with Ben today. I should be thrilled, not feeling guilty. I need to shake off Mike's words and focus on the rest of the day.

It's getting close to ten thirty, so I drive back to my house to get changed. On the way, I call Kate.

"Hello!" she answers.

"What are you wearing on the boat? Ben invited me. My bathing suit from my family trip to Hawaii last year might work." I pull into my driveway, climb out, and run as fast as I can in heels to get inside.

"That bright pink one-piece? Ew, no. I'll be right over. I have some old one-pieces I don't wear. I have a really cute black one that will look phenomenal on your gorgeous boobs."

"Okay," I laugh. "Let's keep it somewhat modest, Kate." I haven't told her that I broke it off with Mike or that Ben and I hooked up yet.

"By the way, I find it weird that you're hanging out with Ben. Got something you want to tell me?"

"I'll explain it when you get here. Bring a couple options. I don't want to be stuck wearing the raciest thing you own."

"That takes away all the fun."

"I'll see you in a minute." I need to make haste; Kate only lives ten minutes from me—more like five with her lead foot.

Ending the call, I make quick work of putting my curly hair into a messy bun. I strip down to nothing and head into the bathroom to put on some sunscreen.

"Sade? You in here?" Kate calls from my bedroom. I throw on my silk robe and bring the lotion out with me.

"Yes, I was putting on my sunscreen. Okay, let's see what you have."

Sitting on the edge of the bed, she dumps out her bag. She's already dressed in a two-piece coral bathing suit. The edges have lace trim around her breasts. Her lean stomach is showing, and the light smattering of freckles on her rib cage is darker than normal, highlighting another one of her many beautiful traits.

"Try this one, it's my black one-piece." She tosses me a bathing suit. Grabbing it, I remove my robe.

My more-than-generous breasts pop out of the suit, and it hugs my butt tight enough that more than half of each cheek is showing. I'll wear shorts over it.

Going to my dresser, I pull out some knee-length denim shorts and slide them on, feeling much more comfortable.

"Sadie, are you dating two guys at once? What has gotten into you? And last I checked, you were repulsed by Ben. What happened last night?" Sitting on the bed next to her, I resume putting on sunscreen.

"I broke it off with Mike this morning. I didn't feel right going on a date with Ben otherwise, especially after we ... kissed."

I want to leave it at that. What happened was private, and I would like to keep it that way—but also, this is new, and this is Kate. My best friend.

"Sadie Jay McCallister! What did you drink? Who are you right now?" She nudges my shoulder, and I laugh with her.

"It's crazy, but he came over last night, and we started talking, then playing around, being totally open with one another, then we kissed."

"And? Oh my god, details, woman!"

"I don't know, Kate, it was wild. We simply clicked. We didn't say much, but what we did say was enough. He made me feel comfortable, like we've been best friends for the longest time. Oh! And then he said these things after we kissed—when I told him about Mike—things that should have me running for the hills but don't."

"Like?" she asks, bouncing a little, her eyes wide in wonderment.

"He said that I'm his now and that I need to leave Mike. It feels surreal, Kate, like we're too young, but I've never felt more alive."

"Wow, you got it bad. Damn, Sadie."

"I'm nervous," I choke out, handing her the bottle of sunscreen and standing up.

"We're young, Sadie, and no one can tell us what to feel because we still haven't learned everything. It's okay to be nervous."

"I know what I want in life, and I'm not impulsive. Besides, this is our first real date. It can't be that serious."

"Last night was the preliminaries, Sade, you are in it now."

"I'm getting that."

I grab a bag, a bottle of water, my towel, and the sunscreen. With my Ray-Bans in my hand, I get downstairs just as the doorbell rings.

Opening the door, I see Ben standing there with a grin on his adorable face.

"Damn, you look beautiful today, baby." Stepping in, he wraps his arm around my waist and pulls me up against him. Leaning in, he pecks me once on the lips then again on my cheek.

"You're sweet. You look handsome too."

I notice his snapback hat and the Ray-Bans that match mine. When he notices mine, he taps the side and smirks at me, speaking without words.

"Well shit, Ben. I didn't think anyone could make Sadie go all gooey in the head. Nice work, but make no mistake, I will break your knees if you fuck with her," Kate threatens.

"Damn, that's sexy, baby. Come here," Eric says, walking up the steps of my porch. Kate squeals and flies past us to jump in Eric's arms.

"Hate to break up the lovefest, but we have to hit it." Ben laughs, and I chuckle. Kate and Eric pull themselves apart and head to the car. I start to follow, but Ben stops me.

Bending down, he whispers in my ear, "I can't wait to have you all day." My heart beats more erratically than it already was after seeing his devilishly handsome face.

"I'm excited too."

Ben smiles, leaning in and kissing my neck. My knees want to buckle at that moment.

"Let's get this fucking show on the road!" he yells, letting go of my waist and placing his hand in mine. I walk on shaky legs toward the car. Today should be interesting.

Ten

BEN

We make it to the lake before noon, and we are on the boat in less than thirty minutes. JJ, Jason, and Nick are waiting with a group of girls when we arrive. The weather is perfect: the sun is mostly out, only disappearing behind clouds for brief moments. The lake looks like a million crystals are dancing along it. Trees line the shoreline. I take a long breath in, enjoying the fresh scent. I love it here.

The women my bandmates brought eye Sadie up and down as if she's in the way of getting to me. She is, and I make sure some part of me is always touching Sadie, ensuring it sends a message: I'm not interested.

Nick owns a decent size cruiser boat that comfortably sits twelve. The best part is the extra bit of space in the front. I plan to lay us under the sun and steal some alone time with Sadie in that very spot today.

"Sadie, this is JJ and Jason." I introduce the guys, pointing to each one as I name them.

"Hello, gorgeous! You're certifiably insane to be hanging out with this guy," JJ says from his place across from her.

"You're telling me. Nice to officially meet you, JJ. Sorry I ran out the other night," she replies shyly, a blush suffusing the apples of her cheeks. Fuck, she's cute.

"It's all right, I would run away from him too," Jason adds, taking a sip of his Corona.

"He should be on his hands and knees thanking you for hanging around," Nick chimes in, and I shut them all up.

"Way to be good wingmen, guys." I sit next to Sadie, putting my arm around her shoulders. She snuggles into me. It's as if the spot was made for her.

"It's our job to keep you humble." Eric laughs, and I wave them off. I didn't come here for them today. I came to be with Sadie.

Leaning into Sadie as the boat glides across the water, I bring my lips to her exposed neck. Leaving a light kiss there, I move my lips to her ear. "I love the way you smell."

Turning to look up at me, she smirks. "It's creepy that you are smelling me." There is something refreshing about the way she isn't afraid to be vulnerable one moment and sassy the next. She isn't here to fuck me or climb some fame ladder. She's here because something that goes against everything inside her is calling out to her. She's curious—as am I. "Maybe I should be running."

"I dare you," I challenge her, placing a kiss in the crook of her neck.

"I can't."

"Good." We stare at one another, my hand lightly caressing her shoulder. "I don't know who I am anymore or where this will go, Sadie, but this is just the beginning. Hold on tight, angel."

I see her physically take in what I'm saying. The boat is far enough out, and that's my cue to end this conversation before it gets too real and she starts to think about it too much. Standing, I pull off her sunglasses and put them next to mine on the seat. Then I pick her up, and she squeals.

"Ben!" I walk us to the edge of the boat. "Don't you dare—"

Whoosh. Into the water she goes. Everyone starts laughing, me included as I jump in right after her. Coming up for air seconds later, she splashes me with a cupped hand of water.

"You're seriously such an ass! I didn't even take my clothes off!" My hat floats next to me. Snatching it, I place it on my head and splash her back.

"You like it when I play? Come here, sexy." I reach for her. She protests, shaking her head, and immediately I want to bite her pouty lip. "Oh come on, don't be like that. You can't stay mad at me, look at me. I'm fucking cute." I wiggle my brows, and I see the slightest lift of her lips as she shakes her head in denial.

"Come on, gimme a kiss and let me make it up to you, sweet thing." I wrap my arms around her waist, placing her round, thick ass in my hungry hands.

We may not be able to indulge in sex, but the way my hands need to feel her skin, that is something neither she nor I resists.

"No!" she yells. I squeeze her ass and bury my face in her slim neck, biting and dragging my scruff along her skin. "Ah! Okay!" She forfeits, wrapping her legs and arms around me.

"You got charmed the hell out of. Call it the Ben Cooper Effect," I tell her, and she snorts.

Sadie looks back up to the boat for a split second, her face dripping, her blue eyes so damn large and innocent looking. I think about her getting off last night and how wet she was when she orgasmed for me. I swear I can still taste her on my lips and tongue.

"You really think so highly of yourself? I took a leap of faith today, Ben. I still don't really understand what is happening. You have to show me that I can trust you to help walk me through this."

We're back to being serious, and I respect that. Usually, I would say we need to take this one day at a time, but what we have is so fragile, it's more like taking it one minute at a time.

"What else do you like? Was there something about Mike that you liked enough to date him?" I can't help but be overcome with jealousy. He had her, and I want to burn the hands of any man who ever put them on her.

"He was nice to me. I could trust him. Can I trust you?" She peers up at me.

I wait a moment before I answer. I don't want to lie. I'm complex, and there isn't always going to be an easy route with me.

"You can, but can I trust that you will be patient with me while I figure this all out?" Sadie and I are both new to this. But we can try. That is a start. Trying.

"One thing about me, Ben, is I always try to give the benefit of the doubt. I want to believe I am making the right choice, but that doesn't mean it's easy. Just because I trust you and you trust me, that isn't grounds for us to mess up over and over again."

"We both have a lot of work to do, then," I admit. I'm new to relationships, and she is new to being with someone like me. How do we take this? Minute by fucking minute.

"Communication. That's what I require. And don't lie to me. Lying to me is the worst thing you could do," she whispers, looking deep into my soul. I want to say I am not a liar, but I have never been in a place with a woman where I have had to lie.

"Okay. I can do that," I promise her. Because I can. Even if that means I will have to unveil parts of me that only I have had to live with. I want her. And I don't care what the cost is.

"Can I kiss you, baby?" I ask after a few moments. I needed a second in order to let that conversation sink in. Now I want to seal our fate with more of her.

"Yes." She lets out a shaky breath. She's as scared as me; it's written all over her face.

"Sadie, I will have you as mine. I've never said yes to wanting someone, not a single person. But I want you. All of you. Exclusively. If you ever let anyone touch you like this . . ." I reach my hand under the water and between her legs, cupping her pussy. Gasping, she peers at the boat, making sure no one is paying attention. I don't take my attention off her. I watch her lips gape a little, enough to lick the seam and taste the tip of her tongue.

"They can't see us," I assure her.

"G-good," she stutters, looking back at me.

"We're two days in, and I plan to make you more and more mine with each day that comes," I declare, going in for her lips, stopping her from countering my remarks with a kiss to end all kisses. My tongue slides against hers, the taste of her flooding my system. I start rubbing her clit through the material of her bathing suit and shorts. Damn me for not letting her take them off before I threw her in.

Looking around, I make sure no one else has joined us. We are in the clear. We are hidden on the back side of the boat, just deep enough that the water clears her shoulders. I rub her clit faster as she begins to push down on me, her tongue messy against mine as the water from her hair falls between our lips.

"Ben. I want to come again, please," she cries against my mouth, her breath hot. Sadie is eager for more, chasing something she has never experienced, and I am glad to oblige.

"You can't make a sound. You fucking moan like you did last night and everyone will see you losing a piece of your innocence, and that's not going to happen. That's my innocence." She nods, dropping her forehead against mine. We lock eyes, and I rub faster. She bites her lip, and I see a storm brewing in her eyes.

"What, baby?"

"Touch me there."

"Where?" I want her to say it.

"You know."

I shake my head, daring her to say what's on the tip of her tongue. "Say it out loud."

"Touch my—" She blushes, halting before she can get the word out.

"Pussy, you want me to touch your pussy, baby? You can say it; it's not a bad thing." She blushes even more and nods. Hesitating, she looks around; her face is flushed with arousal, and her eyes are dilated. I keep watching her, intrigued by the way she's experiencing something so intimate in a setting where anyone could see us.

"Um...you can touch my...um, please touch my..." She's flustered. Her cheeks turn a rosy shade, and her breathing hitches with trepidation.

"It's okay, angel," I reassure her, wanting her to be who she wants with me—a different breed of woman, unhinged and at the mercy of her own pleasure.

"Touch my pussy, please, Ben." I snap and kiss her again, my hand leaving her. She cries out at the loss, and I kiss her harder, the water around us beginning to still. After I get enough of her taste for a few seconds, I pull away.

"Not here, not in a lake surrounded by people. Tonight, when I take you home, I will touch your beautiful body, and I will make it so damn good for you, angel."

Maybe making her test her limits and delay her satisfaction isn't the best idea. Revving her up just to pull my foot off the pedal at full speed before she has time to enjoy the ride may be the worst thing to do to an inexperienced driver. I try to explain it to her.

"I don't respect everyone, but I respect you, and I won't share you or any part of us with anyone. I want to get you home and make sure you are properly worshipped."

"Okay." She nods, her forehead rolling against mine, her body slowly becoming less tense.

"Okay. Now, let's get out of our clothes. We're going to lay out and enjoy my last day here."

I'm leaving for two weeks tomorrow, and it'll be the first time I'll miss being away from home. It will give me something to look forward to for the first time in a long time.

* * *

We're sunbathing on the deck of the boat. I have a beer in my hand, and I pull out the joint behind my ear and light it up. Sadie watches me curiously as I take a drag. The first hit of indica tastes thick and pungent, exactly how I like it.

"You do weed?" she questions, and I all but snort when she asks. Life hasn't tainted her in the ways it has me.

"It's not 'do weed,' it's 'smoke weed.' I smoke weed."

"Sorry." She chuckles softly. "I'm not familiar with that kind of stuff. I sound like such an idiot."

"You aren't an idiot. I like that this lifestyle isn't something you're used to. I don't want to see clean water poisoned."

"Is that all you do?"

"I drink, and I dabble with some harder stuff."

"Harder stuff?" She turns on her side, and her feet connect with mine, tangling together. Sadie may be curvy, but next to my tall, lean frame she looks incredibly delicate. Her hand finds my chest, and her wide blue eyes draw me in like the view of a setting sun.

"Sometimes, when the mood strikes." I pause, not sure if she's ready to know this part of me or if I'm ready to share it. What if it pushes her away? "I do coke."

I watch her for any sign of rejection. Her lips stay in a firm, straight line. Her nose doesn't tighten, but in her eyes, I notice it. Her brows draw in, and I see the familiar look of pity. She doesn't know anything about me, yet she pities me. God, there is nothing I hate more than the idea of someone pitying me. I made my choices, and I do my best to not look back on them.

"I don't know much, but cocaine is dangerous. I see many patients on that stuff, and they always come in from injuries they sustained while on it."

"Nose candy will do that to you. That's why I try not to do it too often." I still haven't told her about the fighting or my intermittent explosive disorder. I don't want to jump the gun and push her away before I even get a fighting chance.

For a split second, I start to see my father and his descending fist coming down on my face—hell, I almost feel it. I hurry and take another long drag from my joint.

"Nose candy?" Sadie asks, bringing me back here.

Her short nails draw infinity symbols on my chest, and I look down at her. "That's what they call cocaine."

Determined not to let her press me for more information in case I tell her all about my dad, my anger disorder, and the side effects of my drinking, I take one last drag, exhale, and then holler up to Nick to come take the rest of it from me. I want to be coherent while I'm with my girl. I had enough to calm me down. Now I want my newest drug—her.

Nick takes it, walks away, and gives the rest of it to my bandmates. Taking the opportunity, I roll Sadie onto her back and dig my face into the crease of her neck. I bite her and growl, running my stubble over the sensitive skin. Squealing, she brings her hands up to my shoulder in an attempt to push me away.

"Ben! Stop, that tickles. Seriously!" I keep going, enjoying the way her laugh sounds like a melody, and in that small laugh, lyrics come to mind.

Bringing my lips an inch or two higher, I whisper singsong in her ear, "She's the girl with eyes the purest blue and a laugh like a melody; she makes me want to get lost and never come back to my lonely reality." Her laughter dies down, and her breath hitches, her hands gripping my shoulders harder with the sudden change of mood.

"Sing it again." The breathy sound of her voice in my ear has me more than willing to oblige.

"She's the girl with eyes the purest blue and a laugh like a melody; she makes me want to get lost and never come back to my lonely reality."

"You're changing something in me, Ben."

"It's only fair. You're changing something in me too."

Sadie turns her head and lays a soft kiss on my cheek. I have a feeling this is the beginning of something neither of us will ever understand. Our connection is something greater. I turn my head and find her lips. Instantly, they fuse with mine. Somewhere deep in my mind, I think this is my mother's divine intervention. Just maybe she forgives me for not saving her that night and is giving me a chance to explore this with Sadie.

***

All day we lie out, play in the water when we get too warm, then laze away. The sun sets, and we're filled with enough vitamin D to sleep like the dead. As the boat nears the dock, Sadie dozes on my shoulder, her curvy form snuggled into my side.

"Sadie, angel. Wake up, we're back." Her long lashes flutter open, and her tired, glassy eyes shine up at me. I kiss the side of her temple, letting my lips linger for a moment as I take in her scent.

Our intimate moment is interrupted when her phone rings. She reaches into her purse and pulls it free. Seeing her mom is FaceTiming her, she answers it quickly. My face isn't in sight, and I try to keep it that way. I don't think she wants to introduce me to the parents quite yet, and I would agree that maybe it's too soon. No, it's definitely too soon.

"Mama, hey!" Sadie's the spitting image of her mother, beautiful and all smiles.

"Where are you? Are you at the lake?" her mother asks as a man enters the room behind her; I assume it's Sadie's father.

"Sure am, Kate and I came with my new friends. Mama, this is Ben." I panic, and before I can move or tell her no, she turns the camera on me, putting me on the spot. Fuck me.

"Well, hi! I don't think you've ever mentioned a Ben before, sweetie.

Nice to meet you, Ben!" Her mom's face lights up, as does her dad's, throwing me off. I can see on the screen that my tattoos are showing, as is the cigarette behind my ear—where my joint was just hours ago. They can't think anything good of this. Not to mention the fact my arm is comfortably draped around Sadie's shoulder.

"Hi, nice to meet you guys." I try to put my best foot forward. What else am I going to do? Stumble over my words and make a complete ass out of myself?

"I'm Raydean, and this is my husband, Stanley. It's nice to meet you, son."

I nod my head. I'm usually great with people, it's the most essential part of my job, but I'm meeting Sadie's parents after less than a day. I'm willing to explore us, but I still have my reservations.

"We wanted a quick chat, but I see y'all are busy, baby. We'll be home later this week!"

"Okay, Mama. I'll call you later. I can't wait to see you guys!"

"We love you, sweetie, and Ben, hopefully we can meet you in person soon, son."

Her father isn't as intimidating as I assumed he would be. Most dads, so I have heard, tend to be aggressive when they meet someone their daughter is seeing. Especially when he is covered in tattoos and has a cigarette tucked behind his ear. In my world, smoking and tattoos are not a sign of anything troubling, but in a world like Sadie's, you can call them a red flag.

"Absolutely."

Thank fuck I'm leaving town tomorrow. I'm not ready to meet the parents. I like Sadie a lot, more than any other girl I've known, but that's exactly why meeting her parents isn't something I'm ready for. If they care at all about their daughter, then when they get to know all of me, they'll make sure she runs far away.

She ends the call, and I release a deep breath. I don't have to look over to know her eyes are on me as the boat rolls into the dock.

"Ben, you don't need to be afraid of my parents. They're great people," she assures me.

Am I that much of an open book? Has my guard completely fallen with her? There is no way I can let someone in so quickly. I have to be cautious. Not just for me but for her too.

"That's the exact reason. You're too good for me, and they'll see it."

"Don't do that." Her head drops, and I am the one watching her now.

"Do what?" I massage her shoulder, kneading the soft, warm skin kissed with the afterglow of sun.

"Don't assume that I don't know what's good for me or decide that they'll make me see you differently than I already see you."

"And how do you see me?" I ask, intrigued to know her perception of the man I am.

"I see hope. I see a man lost but looking. You hide behind the rock star, but underneath that facade, when you think no one is looking, you're real, you're human."

"We're all human, Sadie," I tease, pointing out the obvious in a poor attempt to steer this conversation somewhere else.

"We're all human, yes, but, Ben, you're a different kind. The kind of man who makes you want to be in his world. How many people truly have that gift?" How can she have so much faith in the kind of man she thinks I am?

After my mother passed, I lost all faith in myself—it dissipated with the rest of my heart—and yet Sadie is making the version of me she's concocted sound tangible, like something I desire to have again.

"You should write fucking poetry or music, baby; you make words sound good." I shift the conversation because it's all I can do. Sadie has no idea what she has the power to set free if she digs her hands deep enough into my chest and around my heart. Shit is black as night, and her clean hands would take every fucking drop of it if I let her.

"I do love music. I really haven't had much time to spend playing the piano or going to concerts. Your show was the first one I've seen in years."

"Now you tell me you can sing and play piano. Anything else you want to throw at me, woman? Damn." She giggles, brushing me off.

"Oh, stop. Mama and Papa say I can sing, but I don't know." Everyone starts to pile off the boat, even the women who spent all day giving Sadie the side-eye.

"I guess you'll have to sing for me in the car." I stand, grabbing her hand.

"No, no—no way."

"Come on. If not in the car, then I'll play that gorgeous grand piano I saw at your house and you can sing there," I challenge. I'll make sure I hear her voice tonight.

"Deal."

"Good."

Furrowing my brow, I wait a moment to watch her turn and saunter away, catching up to Kate. The entire time she walks ahead of me, I pay close attention to the way her hips sway; her sultry walk has a way about it. When they get to the end of the short pier, she peeks over her shoulder at me and gives me a flirtatious wink.

"Close your mouth or catch your drool, son," Nick remarks, coming to stand next to me.

"What?" I glance at him, still in a haze.

"Listen, I see your lifestyle and the things roaming around your stage every night." Where is he going with this? "Try not to let any of it take too much of you. Sadie seems like a nice girl, and you don't break hearts, Benny boy, you fucking destroy them. Don't do that to one of the few good ones left."

I would deck any other man if he questioned my character, but Nick's my family. He has a point, though. I destroy hearts, break them in half and scatter the pieces over the girls as they beg on their knees for mercy.

The difference between them and Sadie is Sadie. She wants to look past the persona I show everyone. I'm not a rock star with fame and money. I'm Ben. Someone she sees as good enough to let into her life. Maybe that is why I am drawn to her. She makes me want to be better, to not be so afraid of what is waiting on the other side of the invisible wall I have built to protect myself. Maybe I can still be me, but a version that is worthy of her. A version I can be proud of.

Eleven

SADIE

I didn't miss the way all the other women on the boat looked at me and sneered in my direction the whole day. I did my best to hide it from Ben, hoping he wouldn't think I was delusional. I'm not jealous, simply a little put off by the environment. Ben never took his attention off of me, though, and it made my stomach coil in knots and my skin prickle with heat. I felt truly special for the first time in my nineteen years. My body hummed all day at the memory of him between my legs last night. Ben Cooper is a paradox. He is everything my body craves, and my mind is curious to explore him while also screaming for me to be wary. But I simply can't avoid the pull he has.

I always wondered what intimacy with a man would feel like when it had the passion that Ben gives. Never in any of my dreams did it feel even half as incredible as each touch of Ben's lips on mine. There is a sense of recklessness in Ben, and I chase it. It's been forty-eight hours since I looked him in the eye and told him to take a hike. Now I crave his touch. I want to listen to everything he has to say and look for any information I can to make sense of why I feel this deep desire to be near him.

Minutes in Ben's world feel like hours, hours like days, and days like months. It's intoxicating in the best of ways.

***

"Night, guys, thank you for today!" I climb out of the backseat with Ben in tow as we say goodbye to Kate, Nick, and Eric. Nick and Ben share a quick look that I don't understand, a passing glance of ... concern? I don't know, but for a split second I drown in worry. Turning to Ben as the car pulls away, I go to speak, but before the words even dance on the tip of my tongue, he beats me to it.

"The piano is waiting, and your angel voice better be ready," he teases, and I nod anxiously. I decide it's best that I bury the self-doubt clouding my brain. The more time I spend overthinking, the dizzier I become. I've got a white-knuckled grip on whatever is happening between me and Ben: at any second I could slip to my doom, but at the same time, he could pull me up. Which one it will be? I have no idea.

"I do not have an angelic voice. But I did make a deal, so let's do this." Butterflies rumble in my stomach as we make our way up my steps. I unlock the door and let us in. I've never been one to sing in front of a ton of people. My parents hear it the most, but outside of that, my church choir, the confines of my car, and my shampoo bottles are the only ones that get to hear me sing.

"A Yamaha S Series. Shit, baby, this is beautiful."

In our sitting room, to the right of the front door, our piano sits adjacent to the fireplace in front of the large bay window. The sun is gone, chased away by the moon. Our neighbors' lights are all on, and I see some eating dinner and others watching TV as Ben takes a seat on the bench.

"My mama and papa love playing the piano. In fact, every Sunday, we play it, and I listen to them sing together, humming along most of the time."

"My mom and I used to do that. Of course, our piano wasn't this beautiful, but my mom loved to sing hymns to me. That's how we discovered I could sing." I watch him while he talks about his mother for the first time. I don't miss the apprehension in his voice and the deep sadness in his eyes.

"Do you still sing together?" I ask hesitantly.

"She died," he replies harshly.

I see his grief cruelly etched on his gorgeous face. His mother died. Wow. I can only imagine the feeling. Almost losing my mother destroyed me, and she made it through.

"Oh, I'm sorry, Ben."

I bring my hand up to rest on his shoulder. He peers up at me, pain pinching his face. Behind all that sadness, there is something no one could mistake—anger. I lack the courage to ask him what happened, but I lock that look deep in my mind and keep it there for the day when he may share his story. If we ever make it that far.

"Don't be sorry; it was a long time ago. But enough of this. What's your favorite song?" He shuts down like I knew he would before I can decide who he really is. I let him brush it off because that's who I am—the girl who never pushes for more. I don't want this night to be something that upsets him. Especially after the fantastic day we had together.

"Wow, that's a loaded question. I have so many." I chuckle, leaning on the lid of the piano and staring out the window.

"Here, let me help. Who's your favorite artist? Band? Singer?"

"What if you can't play their songs?" I ask, propping my chin on my hand.

"Oh, Sadie baby. I can play almost everything." He winks, exuding cockiness.

"Full of yourself much?"

"You'll get used to it." With another smirk, he waits for my answer.

"Hmm. Oh! Okay, I got it. I love Lana Del Ray, 'Lust for Life.' Have you heard that song?"

"Yes, I have." He smiles at me like I'm the brightest star in the sky. My stomach flips again. "All right, I'll play and you sing."

Suddenly, my belly begins rumbling with nerves, my heart starts racing, and my throat grows tight. When the first notes start, his joking demeanor disappears, and I see a different side of him. The playfulness fades into a reserved, serious focus. It is a captivating thing to watch.

I relax a bit, and he gets lost in the melody. Finally, two notes before the words start, he looks up at me, his long, calloused fingers playing from memory. I swallow and sing the first few words.

My voice is shaky at first, and my hands are damp with sweat. I've never sung solo in front of anyone, let alone a beautiful, dangerous, talented man like him. Ben makes me nervous, and I'm beyond eager to impress him.

"It's only me, Sadie. Your voice is wonderful—you're incredible," he whispers during a pause in the lyrics, the melody carrying on around us. I nod, still wavering in self-doubt.

His hands are still on the keys, the notes dropping along with my stomach as he speaks. "Sadie, come here."

He holds out his hand, and I take it. Shaking my head, I lower my eyes. I sit astride him in defeat—I really have no idea how to be in a relationship, and that is a very vulnerable feeling. It is hard to let him see that vulnerability, but with Ben I'm stripped naked, bare to him. *Vulnerable* takes on a form, and I am it.

"Hey, look at me." Cupping my face in his hands, he lifts my chin. "Music is a way to be free, to let the world around you fall away. Your voice is beautiful, Sadie. Be who you are with me—don't hide." Ben's brown irises search my baby blues, looking deep into me. It's a sharp sword, being this insecure around someone who is secure in everything they do.

"Okay." I go to stand, but he stops me, scooting us forward to the edge of the bench and placing his hands back into formation. "How are you going to play with me in your lap?" I wonder.

"Baby, I know the keys like the back of my hand, and I want to feel you, feel your voice inside my soul—be the music." My heart thuds loudly in my chest, creating a comfortable beat. That's exactly what it's like with him. Ben has a way of challenging me, making me feel an urge to test the boundaries I've given myself all my life.

He starts us off. I swallow and pick up the next words. The piano vibrates loudly, the melody moving smoothly with the words we sing together. When the chorus kicks in, I find my voice—finally—and pray endlessly that I can keep it.

The smile on his face lets me know he likes what he hears, and the arousal hits my center. It builds alongside the words. We're connected here in the moment, from the music to the physical touch. When he leans in to plant a kiss against my lips, that connection only magnifies as the song crescendos around us. The need on his lips captures my breath for a second.

His tongue seeks access to my mouth, and I grant it, opening and inviting him in. When he plays the next note, I reluctantly pull back to steady my breathing.

He takes the second verse, and my chest rises and falls unsteadily. I watch, intrigued and turned on by the way he gives everything he has, his neck straining and his veins rising in the column of his neck above his Adam's apple. He's different when he sings privately versus the man I saw onstage. There's more intensity, more passion. He feels the music and lets it carry him away. Onstage, he hides behind the funny playboy rock star, the cocky man with no intention of showing his real self.

Within a few seconds, our voices join again, and we find the perfect pitch, my soprano to his tenor. As if we were always made to sing together, we find the groove easily.

"Damn, baby, hit that note!" The keys become louder under his moving fingers, and I hold the last note, smiling infectiously. He laughs, as do I. When the final few keys fade out, the song echoes softly.

Running my hands through his lush mane, I settle my fingers on the back of his neck. I want to get close. I want to know Ben, and with that intense moment we shared, I feel I'm tapping into a side of him that only a few people get to see.

"Let's do that every time I come over," he whispers. I whimper the moment his hands find my hips and start kneading the muscles there.

"I've never seen someone so passionate when they sing." Truly, it was a stunning sight to see a person connect with the music and have his hands blindly find the keys.

"We make great music together, Sadie."

"Do we?" It comes out a question, and we both hesitate. What are we? What is this we're doing?

Staring at him for a few seconds, I watch him snap. It's as if a brewing storm has hit its peak.

"I want you," he growls, grasping my ass firmly and pulling me flush against him, my core directly against his hard length stiffening in his swim trunks. My chest is pressed to his, and our noses are touching with only a whisper of space between our lips.

"How?"

"I want to be the first man to have you. Make you mine."

He leans in and kisses the top of my full breasts peeking out of the scoop in my bathing suit. I throw my head back, and by natural force the lower half of my body grinds down against him. I feel his erection straining in his bottoms, and it electrifies me, shaking me to the core.

"I want to taste your skin," he whispers, licking up the column of my neck. "I want you to break your rules with me—for me."

I swallow hard, and he wraps his large hand around my thin neck, squeezing with a little pressure.

"Look at me, Sadie."

I snap my head back up, bracing my hands on his lower abs. He's wild and untamed, completely unhinged and removed from reality. What I see in front of me is what I imagine intoxication to be like, and I feel drunk on him too.

"Sadie, you have gotten under my skin, and you can't go back," he admits, and I swear the moment is so intense I can hear my heart pounding rapidly. "That's me owning you, angel."

Those words should terrify me, completely turn me off, but they don't. I like the idea of being owned by Ben Cooper.

"Ben." I thrust my hips, the friction of his erection hitting my clit making my entire body tense up then dissolve on a shiver.

"Tell me no and I'll stop, baby. But if you don't, then I'm going to taste you."

He brings me into him even more, and I do nothing to protest when he feasts on my lips. Flicking his tongue against mine, biting my lip and tasting me, he groans, and I whimper. I seem to be doing many things I haven't done before.

He is chaos, and together we are a tinderbox.

Then it happens: he admits something so soft, I am almost sure I imagined it. Separating himself from me, he cups my face. "You're the realest thing I've had since my mother died, and that's the fucking truth."

"Ben," I whisper, locking my hands around his wrists. I tilt my head from side to side ever so slightly and kiss each of his wrists. He looks broken; whatever happened with his mother is still haunting him. In fact, it may be the entire reason for who he is. The rock star, the man with no plan except a ticket on the fast track to disaster. He has demons, and the voice inside me tells me he may not be ready to unveil them. I take on everyone's hurt, but if I take on his, I won't be able to let go. Self-sabotage? Or the realest connection I have ever found?

"You know what? Let's relax tonight. Maybe watch a movie and eat really fucking shitty food." Ben stops us from spiraling, as if he could sense it in us both.

"I would like that."

"Good, let me run home and change."

His attempt at relaxing me is the waving white flag I need. I don't push him further on his mother, and he doesn't dig more into how I'm feeling. I can ride our new relationship out and let time and my feelings work themselves out. Right?

"Up, up!" He slaps my ass, and I jump up.

"Ouch, that hurt."

"Dirty baby likes it a little rough?" Growling, he scoops me up and presses me flush against him, one arm around my waist and his other hand on my rib under my breast. My curvy frame is small and dainty against his tall, lean figure. Dipping his head in the crease of my neck, he growls and tickles me with his scruff, a small act that he does frequently. It's slowly becoming one of my favorite things.

Twelve

BEN

My apartment's ten minutes away, allowing me to run home, shower, and change. Entering my apartment, I notice the space feels so empty. The silence is a bit of a shock to my system after the loud music in my car. I've been attached to Sadie like a magnet, and now I feel her absence. There is no Southern drawl or loud laughter. Has it always been this quiet? Maybe life has always been dull without her. When I leave for my next shows, daydreaming about her and calling or texting her is all I will have. She is taking up such a large portion of me, I feel it all around. The walls are closing in on me, and there isn't any way I can stop them. Hell, I don't want to.

When I return to her place within the hour, the silence explodes and bursts of Sadie ricochet around me.

Entering the house, I see she has changed into another pair of skintight yoga pants and a loose tee. My hands are yearning to touch. Her large breasts are playing peekaboo, and I don't think she knows it. I see the light tan of her tight nipples straining through the white top she's blessing my eyes with.

This sweet-talking, innocent angel has made a hostile takeover. She's released a new kind of narcotic in my brain, and it's both thrilling and damn near terrifying. I've never wanted something past one night, never dreamed of staying celibate in hopes of getting a taste of something off-limits.

Her voice—God, that voice—echoes in my head, louder than the damn piano did. She's a melody, her angelic soprano voice therapy for my tortured soul. If she let us, I would have stayed seated at the piano and played every song I possibly could, all so I could hear her voice over and over again. Then she reached out to me for answers, called for me to make sense of our connection. Hell if I know. I'm as unsure as she is about what's happening between us. Whatever is happening contradicts everything we believe and who we are as individuals. Sadie wants the white picket fence, and I want an empty highway where I can't be slowed down.

I'm the rock star who never settles for anything other than a quick fix, while she's wrapped in her innocent purity, hiding from men like me. We're the very things we never planned for. And that makes me want her even more—makes this all the more tantalizing. Sadie leads us to the kitchen as I stay locked in my own mind, which is often the most dangerous place for me to be.

"I can scoop us some ice cream with about fifty million different toppings. Dessert before dinner is always a good idea." Sadie interrupts my wayward thoughts. My eyes scan her beautiful body as she reaches up to grab some bowls from the top cabinet. As her heels plant firmly on the floor, her round ass bounces delectably, and my cock grows hard again.

Fuck.

"Ben?"

I zoned out again.

"Shit, that sounds great, angel."

"Perfect. I have some vanilla ice cream."

"My favorite," I add.

"Mine too." She blushes, another small thing about her that makes my heart feel like it's being squeezed lifeless. "I have chocolate sauce, whipped cream, and a ton of sprinkles." Her giggle sounds delicate in the big space. I smile proudly as I watch her busy herself. Finally noticing my silent stare, she shakes her head and rushes to assess her body.

"What, is something on me?" She lifts her arms, and I rap my knuckles on the granite countertop.

"Nope, nothing wrong. Actually, there may be one thing." I round the counter, and she stays stock-still, her eyes following me as I close in on her.

"What?"

"You see..." I stop in front of her, placing one hand on her hip and collecting the whipped cream. "I've always wanted to have a whipped cream fight. But no one was ever willing to go up against me."

Swallowing, she tilts her head up. "Ben..." She trails off, but before she can leave my hold, I attack. Lifting the can, I shake it and spray her right in the face. Squealing, she gawks at me through her cream-covered face.

"You freaking jerk!"

I step back and hold the can up in the air, feigning innocence.

"I have no idea what you're talking about. This thing just went off," I tease, and she reacts like a bolt of lightning. She grabs the can and catches the side of my face as I turn to run. Laughing, she points at me mockingly. I keep my face turned, wiping some whipped cream off my cheek and bringing it to my mouth, savoring the taste with a sly grin.

"You think you got me?" Slowly turning my head, I squint and shake my head. Widening her blue eyes, she takes two small steps backward.

"Three-second head start, and if I catch you, you'll regret it," I rumble. "One..."

Finally setting herself in motion, she drops the can on the counter and runs toward the living room.

"Two!" I raise my voice, listening closely so I can hear her pass through the living room. She yelps on a soft giggle, and that's my cue. I cheat and take the doorway from her kitchen to the entryway.

I see her already on the landing between the first and second set of stairs. Fuck, she's fast. Peering back to see where I am, she lets out a scream and keeps running.

"Baby! Don't you dare lock yourself in a room. I'll fucking break the door down if you do!" I yell, taking two steps at a time.

"Then don't chase me!"

"Too late for that, tease!" I make it to the top of the stairs right as she shuts herself in what I'm assuming is her bedroom. I hurry to get to the door before she locks it, and just in time, I grab the knob and turn it as she laughs hysterically.

"Ben! Ahh!" I push the door open, and she backs up. Now I have the upper hand, and I slowly corner her. At this point, whipped cream has made its way onto our clothes, but there is still a little bit left on her button nose.

"You can't win against me."

"Real confident there. You chased me, but looks like I'm in the running to win."

Lifting my brows, I challenge her on that. "Okay, fine." I close the gap and swoop her up swiftly, dropping us onto her bed. She doesn't fight; instead, she throws her head back and laughs without regard. I let Sadie enjoy herself while I lie back and admire her. Her laugh, her smile, everything about her is beautiful to watch.

"Wait, wait, you win 'cause you're cute," she chokes out between laughs.

"Every time you laugh, it reminds me of a melody." I relax, and our laughter dulls naturally. We settle into something I'm not familiar with: a safe place. Somewhere comfortable.

On a tired breath, she whispers, "You going to write me a song, Ben Cooper?"

I let my hand trail lazily over her shins the way the breeze passes against you, almost like a whisper. "If it will make you fall in love with me, then I would write never-ending sonnets. Different poems that tell the story of who you are and what you've done to me."

"I don't need the song. Keep talking like that and you'll waltz right into my heart." Her accent is thick, only increasing how precious she is to me. I want to roar valiantly that she is all mine and I will keep her captive.

For a few more moments, we look at one another, each feeling the other out. Though I wish I could explain how we feel, I can't—but it feels real. It's indescribable, like seeing love in the darkness or hearing it in silence.

I have to put a stop to this moment. If I don't, I will dissolve into nothing.

"We're a mess. Guess I could shower in the guest bathroom." I start to sit up, assessing the now-destroyed shirt that I changed into barely an hour ago. Checking the bedside clock, I see it's nearing 11:00 p.m.

Sadie doesn't respond, and I risk looking back at her lying on the bed. I see the haze in her eyes, and she looks me up and down as she wages a war inside: Does she go left or right?

"What?" I ask softly. Behind Sadie's look of wonderment, I sense lust. I can smell it, see it, feel it radiating off her.

We stare at each other silently. My fingers keep caressing up and down the length of her leg. I bet if she didn't have on leggings, I would feel a thousand goose bumps of desire.

"What, Sadie?" I ask again.

"If I weren't a girl with particular morals, I would beg you to wash me clean."

I nearly choke out my last breath when she bats her long lashes as her husky voice whispers such a temptation. I hurriedly stand up and start pacing around her room.

"Sadie, fuck. Don't do that. I'm not a man with much control. Putting that out there makes me more than ready to take what's mine," I growl, my cock growing in my jeans. Shit, I don't want to get hard because if I keep this up, I'll get a severe case of blue balls.

"What's yours?" Like a lioness, she slowly rolls onto her stomach then positions herself on all fours. The way she slithers toward me is sin. Pure sin. Her dancing eyes entice me. I halt at the end of her bed and watch her. My eyes are glazed over.

"You're mine, Sadie—I won't let you out of my calloused, scarred hands. You could beat me black and blue and I would still keep a death grip on you."

Her breath catches, releasing with a shudder. "You're a rock star, Ben. You'll forget about me just like you forget the cities you've played in as they fade in the rearview mirror of the tour bus."

Now on her knees at the edge of the bed, she leaves only a few inches between us. My thighs touch the bed, and she brings those tiny, soft, feminine hands to my shirt. They sneak under the fabric to touch my sizzling skin.

Those giant blue eyes of hers are staring up at me under long, thick lashes, teasing me in tandem with the touch of her hand. My heart rate is jacked up to a hundred, my head is spinning a mile a minute, and I can't grab onto anything surrounding me. Well, there's one thing that can steady me, a talisman in a clusterfuck of "what is happening to me" moments—Sadie.

"I couldn't shake you or drink you or drug you out of my system. I want you there, Sadie, fucking stuck."

"Make sure you don't break my heart." Those words in that Southern accent melt me to nothing, and I'm a damn servant at her feet. Sadie has no idea the power she has over me or what it means for her to be able to make my black heart feel something.

"Sadie, you have no idea what a mistake you're making," I admit. I'm telling the truth. I won't be able to handle her hurting me—in any way—rationally.

"I do. I know the risk, but I'm ready for the fallout. What will it be? That will be up to you, Ben." She pushes me back with a wink and rises from the bed. Rounding me, she looks over her shoulder as she saunters toward the bathroom, looking like anything but the saint she claims to be. There may be a little sinner in her waiting for the devil in me to entice her to bite the apple, to show her a different side of this world that's waiting to ravish her and twist her innocence in a vise.

"What will it be, Ben? Will you mess it up? Do you have any idea what dangerous waters you are putting us both in?" She pauses. "Guest bathroom is down the hall, towels are in there. See you soon." With one last smirk, she disappears behind the door. The second it closes, I can take a deep breath. Every time I'm in her presence, she steals all the air from my lungs. I can only compare it to what I imagine drowning would be like.

As I walk to the bathroom down the hall, the insecure voices start thundering loudly in my head.

You're no good for her.

You can't settle.

You can't be tied down by one woman.

You're a monster. An anger-ridden disease, hooked on drugs. You'll fucking destroy her.

Run.

The only man I have ever been speaks so loudly. But the man I want to be for her, the man I promised I would be for my mother and have failed time and time again to be, comes out of nowhere.

You could be good for her.

You can settle down.

She's more than enough. She's perfect. You could never get tired of her.

Maybe the monster can be captured by the saint. Maybe she can change you.

Stay.

Which voice do I pick? Which part of me do I go with? My brain telling me to run or my heart telling me to stay and find a light to shine into the cracks of my darkened soul?

The only certainty is that if I stick with my heart, Sadie has to know about my intermittent explosive disorder and the way cocaine affects my rage fighting—the terrible parts of me I can hide for only a short time.

How do I even fucking begin?

Thirteen

SADIE

I wake to warmth wrapped around me, a tight squeeze holding me close to a bare chest. Smiling, I remember where I am and who I'm with. Last night was incredible. We played music together, we laughed, we touched. God, did we touch. All night, my hands roamed his body, avoiding the stiffness between his legs because I knew it could get me in trouble. But his skin, it was soft, his body strong, and some areas were covered in intricate tattoos.

When I finally had enough, he whispered lyrics against my skin from head to toe—praising my thicker curves and the way they make him feel. He compared me to art crafted by the delicate hands of gods. He hushed the doubts that creep in with even more words of poetry. He's changing me, and I cling to it. I finally feel alive after what feels like a lifetime without a pulse—it's hard to pull away anymore.

"Mmm, is it really time for me to go?" Ben wakes with a groggy voice that moves through my body. A sultry, exotic rumble.

"Yes, it is, unfortunately. I need to study. Reality calls." Graduation is coming up soon, and even though I'm sure I have everything memorized for my finals, I still want to be prepared for anything I may have missed.

"It does." Ben kisses the top of my shoulder, his tongue moving against my flesh. We don't speak for a little bit, knowing that goodbye is closing in on us.

"What now, Ben?"

"What do you mean?"

I look down and examine each of his fingers in my hands. "What do we do now?" He sighs, and my eyes flutter closed. I have an overwhelming urge to cry. I'm afraid I won't be able to handle him leaving.

"I'll be gone for two weeks, then I have two days off, then I'm gone again for months. Touring is crazy busy right now. We're hitting the East Coast."

Ben runs me through his tour schedule, and it leaves little room for us. An average day consists of waking up, grabbing breakfast and a quick workout, then heading to sound check for several grueling hours. Once that is done, they spend time doing press before getting ready and playing until late, then they party. Wash. Rinse. Repeat. I feel a sting bite my nose, tears begin to puddle in my eyes, and without catching myself, I sniffle. I regret it when he hears me.

"Baby, are you crying?" He turns me, and I roll over willingly, nodding my head in response as I wipe away the sneaky tears that gave me away. In a flash, his brown eyes are staring down at me as he leans over me with his hands on each side of my head. His arms extend, and I hold onto them, wanting to feel his skin in my hands. "Hey, don't cry."

The connection we've built in these few short days has brought him close to my heart, and the thought of his absence cuts like a knife.

"It's—I didn't know that I could build a bond like this or feel this way with someone so perfect."

"I'm not perfect, baby, and I feel the same way, but I promise these last few perfect fucking days are just the beginning." Our lips touch, and our tongues stroke along one another. Ben is closing in on me, pulling me into his quicksand.

With one hand, he reaches between us and grabs my thigh. Pulling it up and out, he settles between my spread legs.

"Mm-hmm," I moan into his hot mouth ravishing me.

My hands claw at his lower stomach, and he starts to grind against me, his hips rolling like a smooth wave.

The room is now warm, the exchange of body heat dampening our skin. I feel Ben inching through my bloodstream like water moves through tight spaces.

"Ben, we should stop ... I can't ... oh."

He lightly bites down on my ear, and I lose my words. I see little white spots dancing in my vision as I fight to keep my eyes on the ceiling. I can't keep doing this to him—have him take care of me while I leave him high and dry. It isn't right, but goodness does it feel amazing.

"Ben, I have to stop. I don't want to keep doing this to you, and it's wrong. This is wrong." Finally, for the first time in days, my moral compass points me in the right direction.

"Fuck." He lets out a hot breath against my neck, stilling his hips in the process. I feel a tinge of guilt eat at me, and my embarrassment spikes. Stopping because I want to stay pure until marriage isn't common nowadays, especially in a rock star's world. Ben is surrounded every night by beautiful women who would give up anything for him in a heartbeat. I'm inadequate. I want to wait because it's worth it to me to be with one man for the rest of my life.

"Fuck, you're right. Shit, sorry, Sade." Pushing up and back, he stands from the bed, turning his back to me with his hands clasped behind his head. I watch uneasily as he takes a few breaths. I shouldn't expect him to understand me or change who he is.

I don't want Ben to leave me and go to anyone else. We are starting to get to know one another, and it's been all-consuming and passionate. I don't want that to end because I can't give him sex. I search my brain for the right words, thinking about what I could give him that would make it worth him staying for a little while longer.

"Don't think less of me. I know it's uncommon—staying a virgin until marriage—but it's what I want."

"Sade, angel, I don't think less of you. I just need a second." He's facing me now; his erection's gone, and his bare chest rises with heavy breaths. I appreciate his sincerity, but it's probably an attempt at making me feel less like a timid prude.

"I . . ." I pause, rethinking what I want to say. I want to be 100 percent me. The truth can be good or bad, who's to know, but I need to try to find a reason for us to not walk away from this.

"I can't give you what those other women can give you, but I can offer you something better." Swallowing, I embrace him with a look. Here it goes. "I can give you my heart." A hush passes between us; the only movement is his chest exhaling and his expression softening.

"You should be careful giving me your heart, Sadie." Grabbing my hands in a fist, he brings my palms to his bare chest. I nearly stop breathing as he looks at me in the most vulnerable state I've ever been in. I offered my heart to a stranger, offered my love for the first time in my life. I'm both thrilled that I found him and scared that my heart is in the hands of the world's biggest heartbreaker.

"Why?"

"Because I don't know how I will ever let you take it back—I've told you that. When I walk out that door today, you're mine, and that means you don't get to push me out when shit gets rough."

"It's already rough, don't you think?" Honestly, we're a recipe for disaster. He and I are both openly admitting our wounds to one another.

"It is, baby." We fall into silence.

I'll let this play out, trust in myself, and beg for God to keep us going.

Fourteen

BEN

Sadie and I have talked every single day during this first week. The band has gone all down the East Coast, starting in New York and traveling to Florida. That's where we are tonight. All this talking isn't enough to keep me completely sane, but I have poured all my extra time into her instead of spiraling. There were some close calls, but I focused all my energy on Sadie and therapy.

Sadie keeps me centered. It's nice having something else to get me high. Week one is almost over, which brings me one week closer to getting back home to her. How is it possible to miss her so much? After my mother was murdered, I didn't think I would ever be able to let someone in again. My sperm donor made it easy for me to not trust a single fucking soul.

My father's abuse started when I was six. That was the first time I saw him hit my mother.

* * *

The smell of our house and the creak of the wooden floorboards are familiar as I pad toward the kitchen to beg for a taste of the pie my mom is baking. That's when I hear it. Her soft, sad whimpers. I can hear the sound of skin on skin violently coming together. With fear in each step, I walk into the kitchen to find my dad slapping my mother then spitting in her face as she lies on the floor in front of him, his body towering over her.

Her favorite blue dress with flowers on it, the one she wears every Monday, is covered in blood from her nose. At first, I don't move, afraid of what I'm witnessing. Despite my young age, I understand that my father is hurting my mother. When he lifts his fist, still unaware of my presence, I watch her close her eyes, grab the cross on her neck, and whisper, "Please, God." Before my father brings his fist down, I scream, rounding his body faster than light.

Jumping in front of my mother, I wrap my arms around her and catch his fist right between my shoulders. I wail, the pain unlike anything I have ever felt. But I take it willingly because she is my mother, my goddamn mother. My screams mix in with hers as she hurries to grab me and shield me from his descending fist. When he catches the side of her head, she cries louder.

Here we are, mother and son, dangerously defending and protecting one another.

***

My entire nervous system is on overload because of the memory. After the first time, my father began to hit me more and more and her less and less, causing me to act out and find outlets like drugs and drinking at a young age—as young as fourteen. If I had to take the hits for my mother, I would do it. Shit, I'd do it all over again, except this time, I would fight back and get us out of there. No matter what, I would save us.

But I didn't. Now I see my mother's dark hair and the brown eyes that look like mine in my dreams. I hear her sing soft melodies to me, the vibrato in her low, sultry voice carrying through the house on days when Dad wasn't home.

I remember running my hands through her hair to help her sleep as she cried in pain with fresh bruises. I remember the apologies she whispered and the forgiveness she begged from me for not being able to save us. My father would have killed us both before he ever let us leave, and many times he nearly did. No one saved us. Instead, we drowned, and he took my mother away from me. There I was as a young teenager, angry that I, unfortunately, survived.

Fuck. I need to get out of here. I can't think about this any longer. I'm on the verge of ripping my hair out and tearing at my skin.

"Nick. Let's go grab some food. I need something to eat." Sliding out from my bunk, I search out Nick in the front of the bus.

"Let's go. The other boys already left to go to the bar. You didn't want to go?" He sounds surprised. He's not the only one. I'm surprised at myself. Sure, I still drink and smoke some weed when my palms begin to shake a little too much. But as wrong as this is, Sadie's the drug in my life right now.

"Have a little faith in me. I'm exhausted, and Sadie worked a shift at the hospital, so I want to be back in time to FaceTime her."

Shaking his head, Nick stands, and we head out of the bus to catch an Uber.

Nick and I have known each other since I was nineteen. He was a roadie for another band when we played a festival in Portland our first year as The Roes. I was the inexperienced mess of a human I admittedly still am. After my mom died and the old man was hauled off to prison, I became a ward of the state. Out of all the families I was tossed around to, not one wanted me. When I was eighteen, I left the state's care and slept on people's couches—friends and friends of friends—just living for the drugs, alcohol, and women. I was an adolescent punk with an attitude and an ego bigger than myself. I was all over the place at shows, high, drunk, and forgetting lyrics left and right. One time we got booed offstage. I told the crowd to fuck off, dropped my mic, and stormed off.

There Nick was, stopping me and shaking the shit out of me, giving me a real wake-up call. One thing led to another, and we've been thick as thieves ever since.

I'm not totally clean, but I've cleaned up a lot since then. Back then, LSD, cocaine, even fentanyl was an everyday occurrence. It took me two years to clean up as much as I have now. I'm not really one to admit that I still have a lot of work to do—but I do. People can praise my growth, but it's up to me to figure it out. I've never tried to forgive myself for what happened to my mother. When I met the band, we were all lost boys looking for a home but never finding one. We were alone in the wild, and soon enough it became just us four. Nobody wanted the fucked-up teenage rebels, not one single soul. Often, I find myself wondering what my life would be like if one person helped me before I got so lost. Nick could have been the one to help me, but by the time I met him, all the damage had been done.

It is what it is, and I have to cope the only way I know how, and that's with music, fighting, and unfortunately the chemicals. Nick is the person who's helped me rein it in. I owe this man a lot; he helped save my life.

We made it big when I turned twenty-two. That's when we signed with Lightning Rock Records, and our first album went platinum within six weeks of its release. Time moved at record speed, and then the money came, the headlining tour hit, and I'm still only twenty-two. In less than a year, my life has turned on its axis. I didn't think I would ever experience something that cosmic again. Until I met her.

"The shows have been going good." Nick's voice slices through the silent car.

"Actually, today was one of our best. I like playing daytime festivals. Much fucking nicer."

"It was hot as fuck, though," he responds.

"I'm used to the heat."

"True." I can tell he wants to ask about Sadie. He's not making eye contact, and the gnawing on the inside of his cheek is a dead giveaway.

Shaking my head, I tap out a quick drumbeat on my thighs and go in for the kill. "We're great—she's great. You know you can ask me, Nick." I have no reservations about Sadie. I've accepted how I feel: I'm falling for her. At least, that's what I assume this is. I've never experienced something that almost feels like a birthright. Sadie belongs on my lips, grazing against the tips of my hungry fingers and cradling my damaged heart in her delicate hands.

He stiffens. "I don't want to pry into your business."

"You're my best friend, man. You aren't in my business. Besides, I would tell you to fuck off if you were." We both laugh.

"True, you would. But still—Ben and one woman. What is it about her?" he asks, seeming a bit peeved.

"What was that?"

"Hmm?"

"You did that shit where you secretly don't agree with me but you wear it on your face. What, you don't like Sadie?"

"I don't know her," he answers and shrugs.

"Exactly, and I do, so don't go making judgments about her. She's different, man." My anger begins spiking, that familiar tingle running up my spine and the hair on my neck standing, like a dog when he feels something circling whatever he is protecting.

"It's not that, Ben. I'm not worried about you. It's her. Sadie seems different—she's in this for you. I saw the way she was with you on the boat."

His words help ease out my next breath, because I was one wrong word coming out of his mouth from snapping. I didn't tell him about the flashback I had on the bus, so he has no idea that I am on a hair trigger. Relaxing my clenched fist and closing my eyes for a second, I even out my breathing and wait for my heart rate to decline. I despise my IED—hate that I have it at all. Hate learning after the state therapist diagnosed me with it at seventeen that it came from the long line of abusers on my dad's side. My grandpa died when I was nine, but I watched him beat his wife and hit my dad, his own son. Then the cycle bled on.

"Nick, I would fight hell for her before I ever let her go. Yes, I have some fucked-up shit to work through, but I'm feeling this. Let me have this and don't give me shit." I'm growing heated between thinking about my mother and defending myself in the name of wanting Sadie.

"All right, I'm sorry, you're right. Take a breath." Sensing I'm worked up, Nick attempts to soothe me, but it's useless. I need to get back to the bus, light a joint, and wait like a puppy dog for Sadie to answer her phone and throw me a fucking bone.

"Get takeout and take me back."

Knowing better than to fight me, he tells the driver to go somewhere fast, and within thirty minutes, I'm back on the bus with a blunt between my lips and my phone in my hand, waiting for it to ring. Some days are better than others, but today wasn't one of them. Digging up old memories and hearing Nick tell me he's worried about me being with Sadie worked against me. There are days I hyperfocus on bitterness toward the people who push me past my limits, but at the same time, I remember that the world can't stop turning to cater to me. The eggshells around me are bound to be broken down and smashed, and I have to accept that.

Seconds later, my phone goes off, and like a beacon of light, Sadie's picture fills the screen. I leave the bus so I can have privacy.

"Angel, look at you." Her blond hair is tied up in a messy bun, and her blue eyes are piercing. She looks tired but still hauntingly beautiful. The angel of temptation and desire. The perfect combination of sexy and cute.

"Hey, how are you!" Her enthusiasm isn't lost on me. It feels good knowing that she's excited to see me, even if it's late and on a small phone screen. That shit sobers me up.

"Could be better. I can't stop thinking about you," I tell her truthfully. With a frown, she nods. "I miss you. Are you outside?"

I look around me at the empty venue parking lot and the night sky. "I am. I wanted privacy, and you know that musky bus has everything but privacy," I tell her, and she chuckles. "You alone?" I ask, lowering my voice. I need a fix. What would she do if I told her that my addictive personality has latched on to her? That I need to feel a connection with her after the day I had? There were too many flashbacks. They consumed me and turned me inside out. Nick questioning me on what my presence in her life could do to her—once again, a hair trigger. Now I have her, and it's a need. Not just a want but a need. One so deep that I would take a life for a second of her time spent whimpering my name.

"Kind of. Mama and Papa are downstairs, why?" She misses the way I'm focused on her. I wish I could crawl into the screen and taste a little bit of my innocent Sadie.

"What are you wearing?" I ask. She gulps with a blush and shakes her head.

"Ben, my parents are downstairs."

"Then be a good girl and lock your door. Go to your bathroom and stand in front of your mirror. I want to have some of you. Just a fucking little, baby," I groan.

"Then play your guitar or something, Benny," she sasses, and I laugh with a sly grin—that's my fucking girl.

"I want to play with my innocent Sadie. Can I have that? I'm dying for some peeks of skin." I'm not ashamed to beg at this point. I want some of her. I crave it. Going from having women on the regular to not having one at all is one thing. But to have Sadie and not be able to get inside her is a true testament to self-control.

"Fine, but only a little."

"I'll take what I can get from you, angel."

I watch as the ceiling comes into focus as she moves around her room. Seconds later, her face is in frame again and the bathroom is surrounding her. "I can't believe I'm doing this."

"I promise I'll reward you so fucking good, baby." She gulps and nods, biting her lip and whimpering. There she is. The virtue she has held onto so tightly is slipping away. All for me. We are both sacrificing parts of ourselves.

"What—what do you want to see, Ben?" The way she says my name, as if it is a blessing and a curse.

"A bit of skin. Flip the camera and show me what you're wearing." I lean against the bus; my cock is already hard, and I haven't even seen anything yet.

"Okay." When she flips it, I almost choke on my next words.

"Is that my shirt?"

"Yes, you left it here after our whipped cream fight. I washed it, and now I can't take it off." Her creamy, luscious thighs play peekaboo, inches away from showing me that sweet spot between her legs. I moan, looking around to see if I'm still alone in the shadows behind the bus. When I see the coast is clear, I get to work.

Reaching into my jeans, I grip my hard shaft and free it from its confines. Yup, I'm pleasuring myself outside this bus.

"Turn around," I demand with a growl. She does, holding the phone over her shoulder and peering back at the mirror. Sadie watches the screen while I watch her.

"Lift up that shirt and let me see that ass, baby." My cock's warm and stiff, my veins throbbing as I stroke myself slowly, building up at record speed.

"But, um, I'm not really wearing anything sexy ... I don't own those kinds of panties." *Fuck me*, I groan, squeezing myself tighter.

"You sound so sexy saying *panties*. You're fucking fine, baby. Show your man what kind of panties you got on, don't be shy," I entice her, ready to see whatever she has on because she could make anything diabolically sexual.

"Please don't laugh." If I were there, I'd kiss those pouty lips, take them between my teeth and bite down, and make her take those words back.

"You don't need to be shy or embarrassed around me, baby. I'm going to show you what it's like to really be worshipped. Those books you read about worship will pale in comparison when I make you mine completely." Her breath hitches, and her eyes widen in the mirror.

With her other hand, she reaches around her back painfully slowly, lifting the fabric to expose the ripest and most lusciously round ass that I have yet to bite. What the hell does she mean those aren't sexy? The material curves around the top of her buttocks, exposing the bottom part to my hungry gaze.

"Fuck, I want that ass. I want you so bad, angel." I don't hold back as I use my pre-come as lube and start to stroke my nine inches fast and violently. "Turn around, let me see the front of those panties. Let me get a glimpse of your pretty body—show me some stomach too."

"Like this?"

As she turns, I see the white material lying against her perfect lips. A real vision of my beautiful virgin. The grooves in her stomach, showing off her fuller figure, bring me to the brink. What the fuck has happened to me?

"Ben, are you . . ."

"Fuck yes, baby, I'm touching my cock. Want to see me come?" I stroke faster, watching her curious face debating what to do.

"Y-yes," she stammers, and I tilt the camera, still going strong on my rock-hard shaft. I watch the spot between her legs as I chase the orgasm, but what sets me off is when I look for a split second at her sexy face and see her lip caught between her teeth.

"I'm coming, fuck, angel, I'm coming for you. Let me see it, please," I beg, my balls drawing up. It feels like a volcano ready to set off, and fuck it does the moment she pulls her panties down and she shows me the light smattering of hair on her tight pussy.

Just like that, I see stars shining in my eyes as I come. Hot spurts shoot from my cock.

"Sadie, oh baby, fuck, Sadie!" I don't care if I get caught.

"Ben..." she whimpers, and fuck me I feel that sound. She's aroused and needs her fix.

"Go lie down on the bed. I want you to come, too, angel." Flipping the camera back to my face, I let the last spasm leave me before cleaning myself up.

"You don't have to do that, it's okay." She makes a terrible attempt at hiding her lust.

I have this desire to make her come, to feel closer to her and make her vulnerable enough to want me as badly. I love being secure with her, love the intimate way we talk and touch, the depth of our conversations.

Oh, my angel is going to feel me as if I were there, and if she lets me, I will make her touch herself for hours, spiraling into a comatose state of pleasure.

Fifteen

SADIE

Work and studying have drained me, and it shows. My eyes nearly drift shut during Mike's sermon in church. I went with my parents today because my father is also giving a talk. I feel horrible because I've been neglecting Kate, my parents, and even Ben since I'm cramming in as much study time as I can while working at the hospital and finishing up classes.

To add more salt to the open wound that is my life, Ben's been a little off lately, mostly silent on our nightly calls, and his texts seem forced. I don't know why, especially after the phone sex we had the other day. I showed Ben parts of me that no one has ever seen, and I saw parts of him that I've never seen. For me, it built up my bond with him even more. It gave me a sense of closeness, a feeling inside me where I want to be only his. It's special. I hope he feels the same way. Did I rush into this? Did I fall for a game? Was I a pawn? I self-sabotage and spiral. Yet I cling tightly to my phone and watch it like a lifeline as I wait for his name to appear on the screen. I am holding onto an unseen force, and I have no idea what will hold me in return.

My mom nudges me and wakes me up a few times at church, and when it ends, I drag my butt home and fall face-first into bed. When I wake up three hours later, I immediately start to feel guilty for all the things I seem to be lacking in. Has anyone told me I'm lacking? No, but I feel it in my core. If I am not everywhere at once, then I am nowhere at all.

I have plans to meet up with Mike for dinner. I want to remain friends regardless of what happened before Ben. I've decided to forgive him and move on from the nasty things he said to me. Holding grudges only holds you captive.

Halfway there, I realize I forgot my phone, meaning I will most likely miss a few texts from Ben before our nightly call. This doesn't work in my favor, as I have been questioning exactly who I am to him for most of this second week apart. He has a show tonight in Atlanta, so I will get back just as he finishes.

"How are things with your new 'rock star' boyfriend?" Mike asks as we're packing up to leave. It's nearing nine o'clock, which is three hours behind Ben in his current city. I missed him before the show, and I add that to the list of things I am failing miserably at. I need to rush home if I'm going to be there to answer his call before he either goes to bed or spends the rest of the night with the guys.

"Things are great—a little rough since he's on tour, but I like him a lot."

Mike looks at me for a moment, giving me a questionable nod.

"What?"

"Nothing." He waves me off. "It's nothing. Be careful with that life, Sadie. Guys like him only want one thing and can't be trusted."

Part of me wants to be upset with Mike, but we already did this, and the rhetoric is tired. Everyone thinks they know what I want—or what I should want—but no one cares to ask me. What do I want? When will it be okay for me to explore these parts of me that I didn't know I had? The curious side? The sensual side? The girl who wants more than what she had? Yet how do I do that without losing the parts of me that I love? The kind one, the one who would take a dagger for others—she is still there.

"Thank you, Mike. I appreciate it. But I trust myself. I don't want to fight or go backward. I told you how I felt last time," I warn him.

"Hey." He reaches out and places his hand on my shoulder reassuringly. I peer up with a soft smile. "I am always here to talk. I respect you and your choice to do what you need to do. But we're friends; let's not lose that. And I will get better at sealing my lips."

I return the innocent touch, placing my hand on his wrist and giving it a reassuring squeeze.

"I agree. Thank you for meeting up with me and talking tonight." Tonight the main topics of conversation were school, church, and our families. Innocent and a lot less heavy than my other conversations lately.

"Anytime. Now get home safe and text me when you get there."

"Will do. Night!" With a bounce in my step, I hurry to my car to get to Ben, the person who's overtaken all my thoughts all night. Is he ever going to leave there? I quietly rush through the front door and up the stairs to my bedroom, doing my best to not wake up my parents. I drop all my things at the foot of my bed and look around for where I last put my phone.

I don't see it at first, but then I hear it between my pillows. I quite literally jump onto the bed, dig it out, and answer it.

Just in time.

In a heap of messy hair and heavy breathing, I answer the phone. "Hello!"

"Well, hello, you okay?" Ben asks, and his face steals my already frantic breathing from my chest. He is so stunning. The kind of handsome that magazines showcase, the kind starring in movies and written in the pages of books.

"Sorry. I just got back from dinner with Mike, and I forgot my phone, and I was scared I would miss your—" I'm rambling, but he stops me before I can finish.

"Wait. You were out with Mike? You missed our call because you were too busy with your boring ex? Does my time not mean anything to you?"

"Ben, that's not true. I care about your time, and you don't need to take digs at Mike. What's wrong?" His questions are throwing me off, as is the deep scowl on his face. I want to immediately get defensive, but clearly there is something else going on here. I notice the neon lights of the bar behind him and hear men and women walking by.

"You would rather spend your time with someone else and not me."

"That's not true, Ben. You are blowing this up for no reason. I am sorry, but we have time to talk now." I push for him to calm down a bit so we can start over. I would like to talk to him about why he is acting this way, but right now I need to get him back to square one.

"Forget it, Sadie. Go hang out with whoever else." His words sting. This is a side of him I haven't seen before; my stomach drops, and my heartbeat slows down.

"Ben! No! It's not like that, please, I don't want to end our call." The tears build in my eyes, a reaction I wasn't expecting. The last thing I want to do is hurt Ben, but the look on his face and his response tells me I in fact hurt him deeply.

"I don't want to talk."

"Ben—"

He ends the call, and I'm left stunned.

What just happened? Why is he acting this way? Why do I feel guilty when I didn't do anything? Clearly, I respect our time together.

I rack my brain for a few more seconds before I try to call him back. He had no right to react so harshly with me. After I wrap my head around that, the guilt wears off and my good sense kicks in. That was uncalled for.

Ben doesn't answer; instead, he denies my calls repeatedly. I stand up and pace my room, deciding to send him a text. One that I write, erase, and rewrite a hundred times.

You're such a jerk, you didn't have a right to say that.

No.

Ben, call me. That wasn't cool. You're overreacting.

Ugh.

Ben, listen. That was uncalled for, but I still want to make this right. I don't want to fight with you. Call me back.

Finally, something that seems reasonable. I hit Send and watch it go through. After it says it's delivered and read, I wait for a response. But after a minute or two, nothing comes—nothing at all. I release a defeated breath, and my heart aches even more. I've never fought with someone like this, let alone a man that I am falling for. I pace more and feel that familiar rise of anxiety. I do the only thing that comes to mind and that's call Kate. She'll make this right. She has to help me see this clearly, because I sure as heck don't know what to do. Falling for him? Not knowing where I stand? Fighting with him? This is all new to me, and I don't know how to navigate it. That terrifies me. This all absolutely terrifies me.

***

"Sounds like he doesn't trust you." Kate came over shortly after I called in a panic, dressed in her PJs and ready to stay.

"He has no reason to not trust me," I point out. "For it to escalate that quickly, that isn't normal, right?" Taking a sip of my water, I squeeze the pillow closer to me, the one Ben laid his head on when he slept here our last night together.

"No, I don't think that's normal. You accidentally forgot your phone and missed his calls; he took that as purposeful. Have you talked about him having trust issues?" she questions.

"No, in fact, I told him I need to be able to trust him. This all feels really rash, and I don't know what to do," I admit.

"I'm sorry. I wish I had a cure-all. But you need to talk to him."

"I tried. He won't answer."

"Want to text Nick? I got his number."

"Really?"

"Yeah, here." She rattles off the number. Standing there in Ben's shirt and my sleep shorts, I text him. I feel Kate's eyes on me as I bite my nails, waiting for an answer.

> **Me**: Hey, Nick, it's Sadie. I'm sorry it's late. Kate gave me your number because Ben and I had a fight and I wanted to make sure he's okay. He won't answer me.

Is there such thing as rambling in text messages? If so, I am sure as heck doing that.

> **Nick**: Hey, sweetie, Ben's here with me. He passed out. He was upset at the bar and drank a little too much.
>
> **Me**: Oh, okay. I'm sorry. This is all my fault. I feel terrible that he's upset. Can you tell him I'm sorry and I want to talk about this? To call me when he gets up?
>
> **Nick**: Yes, I can do that. And don't worry, this isn't your fault. Okay?

I'm stunned that he's not telling me to take a leap. He must think I did something awful to cause Ben to go out and drink himself into oblivion.

> **Me**: You're kind. Thanks, Nick, have a good night.
>
> **Nick**: Sadie, he has a lot of things about him that make him hard to understand.

But be patient with him. I see how close he is to you, and he's right on the brink of telling you everything. Please give him that time. You may be his last hope.

The last text doesn't need a response. What would I even say? I am falling in love with someone I know only from small glimpses of his complexity and beauty. The lines are blurred, and I feel a building pressure. In this moment, I wish I could run to Atlanta and be with him, talk about everything. But school and life are in the way, and honestly, I'm not that girl. Nevertheless, I can't walk away from this twisted, codependent need we have for each other. I'm his last hope? What exactly am I supposed to be saving?

Who is Ben Cooper, and how deep into this did I get?

"What did he say?" Kate interrupts my thoughts.

"He's wasted. He went out and got drunk over this stupid fight," I groan.

"Is that why you look like you've seen a ghost?"

"No." I roll my eyes and sit back down. "Nick said something to me, and now I want to puke."

"Like what?"

"Here." I shake my head and hand her the phone. I don't want to explain it. I'm not really sure what to do with this information—that was a lot of vague stuff to dump on me.

"Damn, what the hell is he hiding? Oh my god, maybe he owns a sex compound, and he plans to turn you into a nymphomaniac," she teases, and I laugh a little.

"Ha ha, so funny. No, Kate, I'm serious. I don't know what to do."

"Sleep on it and say a little prayer." She winks, and I push her shoulder.

"Whatever, you're no help."

Closing my eyes, I say a silent prayer in the hopes that we'll work this all out tomorrow.

***

Waking up with a stress headache the size of a boulder, I roll over and see Kate is still asleep. It can't be later than seven o'clock. My internal clock wakes me up at all kinds of odd hours. I have hospital clinicals to thank for that. Rolling out of bed, I slip out of the room silently, not wanting to wake her—she's a beast if you wake her up too early.

Heading downstairs into the kitchen, I see Mama and Papa already having their morning coffee and the muffins that my mother made.

"Morning, sweet girl. How you feeling today?" my dad asks, and like always, I hide nothing from my parents.

"Not good. Ben and I had our first fight."

"Fight? What on earth about, sweetie?" Mama chimes in with concern.

"Maybe it wasn't really a fight, more of a misunderstanding. I don't know, it was stupid." I take my coffee cup and slump down at the table. I'm sure I look like a million bucks.

"Couples have disagreements, baby. But you have to make a choice: Was it something big enough to break up over or something you can talk out and resolve?" That sounds so much easier said than done. I could work through this with him if he would call me, but that's not the point. The issue is more why he was so upset.

"I've never been in this position before. Did you and Mama ever fight?" I look between the two of them and watch them share a glance then laugh.

"Did we? Oh, honey, we still have fights. Sure, they have become less heated and more mature, but we've had years of practice." Papa grabs my hand and rubs the back of it with his thumb. "Besides, you and Ben are young. You have a lot of differences. You'll learn how to compromise with one another. Promise. But don't give up all of who you are to fit what he wants. It's give and take." I'm only nineteen—I'm still figuring out who I am, so how will I know what's a worthy sacrifice? For the first time, I can fully admit that what I'm feeling is love.

"True. But I hate that he's on the road, and I can't see him to work our problems out." Then something hits me. I was wrong. Maybe I *can* be that girl. My life right now is all about trying new things, especially in my relationship with Ben.

"I bet. Speaking of Ben, once you two work this out, we want to meet the young man." I nod, my brain is already planning my next move.

"He gets back Friday. We can have dinner or something?" I say quickly, taking out my phone and searching for the earliest flight. I am going to see him. Why not? He has two shows scheduled in Atlanta, one last night and one tonight. We agreed in the lake to give and take, and I don't want to sit idly by.

"Sounds perfect! You bring the dessert." Mama winks, and that's that.

"Will do. Hey, I'm going to stay at Kate's for my next couple days off. We're going to have some girl time."

I have never lied to my parents, but they would most likely tell me to sit back and wait it out. Not this time. I'm going to him; I need to see him.

"Sure thing, baby, you have fun."

I hurry up the stairs and shut the door, and Kate stretches off her sleep. "Any more disasters?" she teases. I'm sure I look deranged.

"No, but I need you to cover for me. I am going to see him, Kate. And I have less than an hour to pack my bags and get to the airport. You down?"

"Holy fuck, okay, Sadie! Damn." She's proud of me but still shocked. As am I.

"What do I pack for Atlanta in the spring?"

Sixteen

BEN

I never called Sadie back last night, and this morning I woke up hungover with a throbbing headache. And by morning, I mean nearly two in the afternoon.

"Boys, sound check in forty minutes, get up!" Nick passes our bunks, banging on the wood above each one. I drag my hands up and down my face and turn over to see my phone next to me. After blinding myself with the harsh light and nearly throwing my phone, I turn it down and squint through my blurry, hungover eyes.

Seeing all the missed calls and rereading the one message from Sadie, I take a deep breath.

I fucked up last night.

The boys start moving around outside my closed bed curtain as I call Sadie and wait for her to answer. Before I start anything today, I need to make it right with Sadie, if I didn't already lose her for good with my fucking jealousy.

She doesn't answer. Fuck.

"Ben, you got thirty minutes. The boys and I are headed to sound check. Hurry up!" Nick hollers, but I don't respond. I call again, and she doesn't answer. Shit. I clench my phone and climb out of the bunk. I may need Nick to get Sadie to talk to me. My feet hit the bus floor, and I call again, but before I can bring the phone to my ear, I hear her.

"Hey." Sadie's angelic voice comes from the front of the bus. I turn, and like a dream, she stands there. Close enough to fucking touch. Her hair is in some side braid draping down her shoulder, and she is wearing a pair of jeans and a white V-neck T-shirt. She looks so fucking good. Is she real?

"Sadie?" She nods. Fuck, she's real. I am on her in seconds. "Baby, I am so sorry." I wrap my arms around her and pick her up, squeezing her tight, as if she might evaporate.

"I caught the first flight I could—nearly missed it, actually. We can't fight on the phone. I don't want to do that with you, Ben."

"I'm sorry. I fucked up last night. I shouldn't have reacted that way." Coming out of the gate with an apology seems only right.

"It's okay," she mumbles into my chest. Her voice is soft, as if she is cowering, and that is all my fault. Sadie feeling like she has to take more shit from someone without speaking up makes me nauseated.

"No, it's not."

"Ben, why don't you trust me? You know what trust means to me," she asks as she untangles herself from my suffocating grip.

"I do, it's—"

"No, you don't," she says, cutting me off. Good. I deserve her calling me on my shit. "If you did, you wouldn't have acted that way. You hurt me last night," she admits. She looks down at her hands, which are picking at each other.

"You're right. I didn't trust you, and I have no reason not to." I lift her chin. "But you're here—fuck, you're here." What made her come to me when I don't deserve to breathe the same air as her?

"Because I said that I would be open to this, that I would talk things out. But I need to know that you will too."

"Baby, I broke our trust. Joke's on me. Clearly, I'm the one who can't be trusted." I smile.

"I do trust you, though. You have been from New York all the way to Florida and now here in Atlanta, and I haven't once worried that you have done anything to break my trust. I deserve the same thing. I deserve honesty. You can have moments where you doubt me, but talk to me about it, Ben. You have to tell me."

I don't deserve her forgiveness. I haven't had to plead my case or beg her to forgive me; instead, she just showed up here. How do I make this right? I should be kissing her feet.

"I'm working on that one minute at a time," I whisper.

"One minute at a time. Next time, I won't fly out when I am in the middle of school to make it right." She smiles. My girl.

"I can't believe you did this. How long do I have with you?" I run my hands up and down the smooth skin of her arms.

"Until tomorrow. I have to get back to studying, and my shifts start back up at the hospital."

"Good. That will give us some time to talk about this. After sound check?"

She nods.

"Thank you for this, Sadie. Thank you for not running."

"Don't give me a reason to."

Softly, I slide my thumb up and down the slender column of her neck. I want to mark her. Leave love bites everywhere I can.

"It doesn't make it all better, but can I taste your lips? It's been too fucking long since the last time," I ask. She nods. Her breathing becomes labored. Aroused. Craving me and our closeness. There is an intimacy that goes beyond physical touch. The way we shelter our relationship from the outside world to make it our own draws us so much closer. That is the most intoxicating thing about us.

"We have an instant connection. You make me feel alive. When you touch me, I'm actually breathing for the first time," she whispers.

"Me, too, baby."

"You came in and flipped my world upside down in a matter of days."

"Look who's talking, angel." With that, I seal our lips and brand myself with her taste. I want her scent all over me.

I could have easily lost her over something so damn small, but instead she's telling me she doesn't want to leave me. I revel in the fact that she wants me as much as I want her.

***

"Good night, Atlanta!" I holler into the mic, grabbing my water bottle and putting the mic back in the stand. Sadie is at the side of the stage, and after that amazing show, all I want to do is get to her.

"That was electric, Ben!" she tells me as I run up to her, wrap one arm around her waist, and spin her. I kiss her neck, and she giggles. Fuck, I missed that sound.

"Ahh! You are so sweaty!" she hollers, and this time I run my mouth up her jaw, over her cheek, and back to her ear.

"Am I? You want to be this sweaty, baby?" I groan into her ear, my cock getting hard.

"Ben, there are lots of people around." She lets out an aroused moan.

"There are . . . so how about we go back to the bus?" I lean back enough to look at her.

She bites her lip and nods.

"Nick, clear the bus for the next hour. The boys can stay here and party," I holler to Nick. Sadie keeps her head low. So shy. I will work on that.

"One hour. That's it, then we have to hit the road; we need to be in Nashville tomorrow. We can't be waiting on you two." I brush him off and get us back to the bus in record time. The second the door shuts, the silence around us makes our breathing more pronounced.

"What now?" Sadie asks, placing her hand on her stomach. We stand in the small living area, and yet it feels like the feet between us are miles.

"Now you're going to let me say sorry. You are going to let me kiss you up and down, all over your body." I drop my blazer on the couch and slowly move closer to her. I admire the way her throat moves as she anxiously swallows, the way her nipples pucker under that white tee. She backs up, and with each step I take, she repeats that action.

"You want me to say sorry like that, Sadie?" She nods eagerly when I ask.

"Yes, please, Ben," she moans, and now I am on her.

"Such a good fucking girl," I groan into her neck, one hand gripping her waist and the other taking her hand and pinning it above her head in the hallway.

"Oh," she cries.

"Let it out, no one is here." I kiss the nape of her neck, then bite it.

"God!" she cries, and that's my cue. I pick her up by her ass, and she wraps her arms around my shoulders. We have a room at the back of the bus, and I make a beeline for it.

I lay her down and hover above her the second we get to the queen bed. The room is modern, with a white headboard, black silk sheets, and a white comforter, but the icing on the cake is the mirror above the bed. I laughed when I first saw it. Such a cliché, but now it will be used in anything but cliché ways. It will be another way I can show Sadie what pleasure and sexual freedom look like. I start with her jeans, our eyes never leaving one another. The button first, then the long trail of zipper that I swear feels never ending.

"So beautiful. You know that? Look up at the mirror, pretty baby." I want Sadie to see what I'm doing. Finally, she looks up, and as she does, I pull her pants down. She lifts her hips slightly to help me move the tight fabric over her curves. I slide them all the way off. She is left in nothing but a pair of nude panties.

"Look at you. See it?" She shakes her head. "Look again, baby." This time, my hands trail down her thighs, over the peaks of her knees and down to her ankles. I grab them and lift them effortlessly; she is under my control now, and she is letting me lead. My favorite fucking thing.

I place her feet shoulder-width apart, flat against the bed. "You are the embodiment of sex appeal, Sadie. And now it's all mine," I tell her. She gulps, and I move her panties to the side, exposing her center to me. "Fuck, there you are. My girl is so wet for me," I praise her.

"Touch me, please."

"Gladly." Without another word, I drag my knuckle up and down her center from her entrance to her clit, and she shudders. I insert my middle finger, and she cries out my name.

I place my wide-open palm on her lower stomach to keep her from moving away from my touch. The pleasure will drive her to the brink, and I want her to be enthralled in it. I tilt my finger up slightly, hitting that spot deep inside her warm cunt, and I massage it with pressure.

"I'm sorry I fucked up. How could I do that to my girl? So fucking special." I praise her through my apology.

Her moan hollows to a cry. Her eyes start to close. "I know you are, baby." She accepts my apology, and the way she calls me *baby* is music to my ears.

"Don't you dare close your eyes. Keep watching, Sadie. Watch how beautiful you look when you come."

"Ben, I am so close." She tries to scoot away, but my hand on her stomach is keeping her locked in place.

"Holy fuck. What would you do if your parents knew you snuck away to let me finger-fuck your gorgeous body? To claim you. You know that this is mine now? All of it?" I add my thumb on her clit, and her back bows slightly.

"Yes," she cries.

"Prove it. Come on my finger and prove that I own this body." On command, she orgasms, fast and hard, screaming my name and grabbing the sheets in pure euphoria. Her core pulses around my finger, her juices now sliding down my hand. I am going to drink her in.

I lap lazily at her center as she comes down from her orgasm, taking all she will give me. So responsive and so giving.

"Angel. Angel," I repeat over and over.

"Ben, I might come again," she rushes out, her stomach tightening and her chest rising and falling with deep breaths.

"Ride that out, you can come again. I'm still craving you. Feed me more, pretty baby." Her second cry is softer, a lazy, almost overwhelmed sound.

"Oh, Ben." Her juices coat my mouth, and I swallow it all down, thirsty for all of her.

* * *

"I'm glad I came here," Sadie whispers in the dark room. We stay locked in the back room, going at one another as the bus leaves the venue. There is more pleasure in pleasing her than in getting off. I want to wait for that, travel her body first before we even get to mine. Respecting her wish to only go as far as she is comfortable with isn't an inconvenience to me.

Every once in a while, we pass a car, and the lights shine against the wall next to us and dance by quickly.

"Me too. Thank you for listening to me. I haven't really learned how to talk and be heard before," I admit.

"What do you mean?"

"Sometimes when I am hurting and I talk about things, it's like people want to jump in or fix it. But I don't want that. I want to be heard. I want them to listen. When they try to fix it, I feel like a burden." The darkness may be why I am so willing to share more with her. There is still a barrier keeping me safe, but I let Sadie in a little bit more.

"You aren't a burden to me, I hope you know that. And sometimes people want to fix problems because they don't want to see the hurt drown you anymore. Fixing it sometimes means an act of love," Sadie says, running her hand slowly up and down my abs and chest.

"I guess that is something I don't know how to differentiate," I admit. Sadie stays silent for a minute before she says one simple word.

"Trust."

I nod, looking up at the ceiling; even in the dark, I can slightly make out the shape of us. "Trust," I repeat.

Sadie isn't wrong. Trust is everything, and if we have it, then we always know where we stand. I have to remember that.

"Sadie?" It's been several minutes since we said anything.

"Mm-hmm."

I can tell she is almost asleep. She won't remember what I am about to say, and that is okay because I need this for me. I avoided it all my life until I found her.

"I love you."

"Mm-hmm," she repeats, confirming that she is in fact slipping into sleep.

"Good night, angel." Kissing her forehead, I let slumber take us both.

* * *

We finished our last show in Michigan yesterday, and today we start the long drive home. The two days with Sadie were needed. I knew when I dropped her off at the airport in Tennessee that I would be seeing her in a matter of days, but the goodbye was shitty nonetheless. I wish I could keep her with me every day.

Nick, Jason, and I spend the day on the bus drinking and playing cards. Eric spends the day fighting with Kate because she found out about his random hookup a few nights ago, while JJ sleeps most of the day. Nick, Jason, and I finally call it quits as we get ready to pull into some town for dinner. I head to my bunk to grab my phone and my jacket as the guys head out.

"I'll meet you inside!" I yell as they climb off the bus. Grabbing my phone, I see a missed call and a voice mail waiting. I don't notice the number, and I instantly regret listening to the message.

The call came from a California state prison: "Son, it's me. I get that you don't want to talk to me, but please come see me. Forgive me, son. I love you. I don't know what else to say. All I have is begging. Please."

This is the third attempt the old bastard has made at reaching me in the past few years, and like every other time, I despise him. Tunnel vision fills my eyes, and I blink away the blur taking over.

Forgive me, son. I love you.

I can still hear his voice.

The hell you fucking do, bastard! You hurt me over and over again. You beat Mom to death and fucking took the one person I loved in life. You're a guilty old son of a bitch looking for forgiveness in all the wrong places!

In the confines of the small bunk, I slip into a manic rage. Blackness takes over, and I become the Ben in the shadows that no one is ever prepared for—not even me. I punch the wall then grab at my hair, pulling at the strands in agony. Reaching for my backpack at the foot of my bunk, I dig deep and find my special vial—the vial filled with my medication, the nonprescription kind. Cocaine. I should take my other medication and lie down, but tonight my prescription won't be enough.

Dumping some on the back of my hand, I sniff the bump faster than it has time to settle on my skin. It stings my nose, and my eyes instantly water—but it's the good kind of burn. The burn that promises a release, a darker side of vengeance.

I put the vial back on my bunk and grab my jacket. I head in the opposite direction of the restaurant and search out the nearest bar.

Tonight, I will take on my mother's pain and beg her to forgive me.

It is Thursday night and tomorrow I will be with Sadie, but right now all I can think about is that call, and I'm only seeing red. Sadie's face is slipping from my mind as my mania sets in. We've stopped for dinner on the outskirts of Idaho, and there is one seedy local bar crawling with lowlifes—exactly what I'm looking for. I sit at the bar, my eyes watering and my nose itching as I down another shot. My skin is coated in a light sheen of sweat, and I swear I can feel the hair on my head growing, or even the littlest of pieces falling out of place.

All my senses are heightened while I look around for someone—the unlucky bastard I want to fight—to numb me from the outside in.

"Come on, baby. Wearing a dress like that means you're looking for a quick fuck." A deep voice down the bar from me is talking to the waitress. She's young, and I bet she's only in this dump to make enough money to leave this shithole town.

The man has a beer gut busting out of his greasy, stained shirt, and his trucker hat hangs sloppily on his gray hair.

"Sir, please pay your tab and leave," the young woman tells him, and I watch as he basically fucks her with his greedy eyes.

Bingo.

"Don't be such a cunt. Come on, give big papa a ride. I'll make it feel real good." He grabs her ass, and she turns, slapping him hard enough to leave her handprint on his cheek. Her body moves again, stepping into his space to knee him in the balls, but there is no need. I will gladly do the honors.

"Hey!" I stand, running my hand over the back of my head, cracking my neck from side to side.

"What?" He stands up like he's about to intimidate me with his size and age. I don't care if he's forty years old and over two hundred pounds of hamburger meat. He's not only a piece of shit, he has the perfect-sized fist for bruising my face.

"Why don't you back off the girl and go home and play with your small dick, fucker?" I challenge, getting closer.

"Excuse me, son? You might want to rethink who you're talking to."

"The town asshole? I'm good." I smirk, flicking my left nostril and sniffing. "You're a piece of shit I will gladly fucking set straight."

"Is that right?" he yells, taking a few steps closer, his alcohol breath pungent and his shirt stained with God knows what. Getting in my face, he points to the exit. "Why don't you set me straight, then?"

He pokes my chest, and I look around the bar, making sure all the attention is on me. That's how I like it. Even the waitress has her eyes glued on us, and the other people in the bar have their jaws on the floor. I nod.

"Gladly." With that, I see it all happen before it even starts, and I do nothing at all to stop it. I welcome it—fucking count on it.

Pulling his fist back, he flings his arm forward with all his might, catching me right in the eye. That was a good one, and I'm sure it'll leave one hell of a black eye. But I always say, if you want to throw a punch, you better make it a damn good one.

I tackle the man to the floor and give him the special treatment. The father treatment. With each punch and each failed attempt at retaliation, the real man disappears and my father's face comes into focus, taking each hit like he deserves.

"Fuck you, you piece of shit!" I hit him for the third time, seeing him begin to weaken. People scream, then a loud commotion comes from the door at the front of the bar.

"Ben!" Turning at the sound of Nick and Eric's voices calling to me, I catch a fist to my jaw and topple over onto the floor.

Fuck.

The stocky man stands to kick me, but before he can, Eric stops him, and Nick grabs my arm, pulling me up off the floor.

"You son of a bitch! You better hope I don't fucking run into you again!" the man spits as Nick rushes us out the door. I never lose the shit-eating grin on my face.

That one was for you, old man.

* * *

"What the fuck were you thinking!" Nick yells at me a short time later. The second we got back to the bus, Nick woke up our driver and demanded he get back on the road. He's been working on damage control, ensuring no charges are pressed. To be fair, I did make sure the asshole hit me first. Sprawled out on the bus couch with an ice pack on my eye, I don't answer. I'm still messed up from the high of pummeling the jackass who didn't know how to treat a woman. My eye is throbbing, and my head feels like it is being repeatedly hit by a sledgehammer, but I don't regret what I did even if the room does start to spin if I keep my eyes open for too long.

"Don't fucking ignore me, Ben!" Nick shouts.

Releasing a deep breath, I count in my head, doing everything I can to keep from snapping on him. It's one thing when it's a stranger, but it's another thing when it's someone I care about.

"Ben!" he yells for the third time.

"What! What the fuck do you want me to say!" I throw the ice pack against the wall adjacent to me, and it dents instantly.

"You can't do this. You know that it's going to lead to you self-destructing. You are doing really good, Ben. Stay with me."

"But the dick deserved it!"

"Ben, I can't keep pulling you out. One day, I won't be able to pay someone off. You will get arrested. You can't be getting hopped up on drugs and going out to fight someone. You could kill someone—or yourself—one day, Ben! This shit isn't a game! How many people who love you, how many therapists, need to tell you that for it to stick!"

"You don't think I get it?" This time I stand and punch the wall, nearly breaking my hand as the pain gallops up my arm. "Fuck!"

"Goddamn it, Ben! Sit down! Now!" My blood singes my veins, spreading to each limb like a wildfire. Shit. I breathe in and out while the pain in my hand duels with my internal pain. The room begins to turn to a smoky gray haze. Words form deep in my chest and begin to rise to a boil, ready to spill over the top.

"Don't fucking tell me what to do!" I go to hit him, but he dodges my fist and moves behind me fast enough to catch me off guard. Hearing the boys coming from the bunks as Nick wraps his arms around me, I try to fight, almost breaking free from his bear hug until he grips me tighter.

"Ben! Relax!" he yells in my ear, dragging me to the couch and pulling my body on top of his. I yell out, still attempting to break free.

"Let me go, Nick!" My bandmates are watching me as I lose myself to the rage.

"Get the shot, Eric. It's in my shaving kit."

"Don't fucking knock me out, Nick!" I fight against him even harder.

Whenever I'm too far gone, Nick takes the sedative my doctor gave me and injects me with it. The worst part is, it knocks me out for hours and leaves me lethargic for nearly a day afterward.

The room spins, and I blink rapidly, thinking of anything in the world that could calm me down. First, I see my mother, but that only reminds me that she's gone. Music—I try to think of my music, but it still does nothing.

"Get me Sadie. Fuck, please get me Sadie!" I growl out, tears coming from my eyes not from sadness but anger. I'm too wound up, with no way of controlling what's already lost. I have to find my center again.

"No, I won't let her see you like this. I won't let the one good thing in your life leave," he says, and Eric appears with my medicine.

"She won't. I can calm down if I hear her. Call her, let me hear her." I'm desperate. Maybe she can help me; she has centered me before. Never when I was this far gone, but I am willing to do anything.

"Maybe we could try it, man, maybe it will help," JJ chimes in. I nod my head, thankful I have someone on my side.

"Please." I stop moving because I have nowhere to go and only one way to get what I want. Already, the thought of talking to her has me able to think straight.

"Call her." Nick holds me still, and Eric takes my phone off the table. With each ring, my heart rate drops closer to its normal rate.

"Hey, baby! Sorry, I'm barely leaving the hospital! I didn't want to miss your call."

"Sadie." Her name is a plea.

"Ben, is everything all right? What happened?" She sounds worried.

"Nothing. I just had a rough night. I don't want to talk about it. Please, say anything, just—just tell me about your day. Anything." There is a long pause. Sadie will push for more. She will. And I might regret this call after all. Except she doesn't. As if it's just another fucking call, she changes her tone and does exactly what I begged her to do.

Nick's face relaxes, and he loosens his grip on me slightly so I can grab my phone. Eric hands it to me, and I cling to it.

"I had a busy day with studying, and then I had to help Mama and Papa clean out the garage. Then I had clinicals. That's about it. What about you?" I nudge myself out from Nick's grip and move away from them, heading toward the sleeping quarters.

I climb into my bunk and close the curtain. In the background, Nick's calling Dr. Davinah, stealing quick glimpses at me to make sure I am still lying here and not doing anything I shouldn't be, like taking another bump. I will talk to my therapist next, but I need Sadie this very second. I'm shaking uncontrollably, and I can still feel myself lost in the blurry mist that happens when coming down after an episode.

"Today was shit, but I'm here. That's all I care about. Where are you going now? Home?"

"Yes, I put a pot roast on before work. It's my turn for dinner, so a Crock-Pot meal it is. Did you eat dinner? What town are y'all in, anyway?" Her Southern drawl hums soothingly in my ear. I'm coming back. *Keep bringing me home, angel.*

"We just left some town in Idaho, and no, I haven't eaten yet."

"It's almost eight here, so I'm starved!" She giggles.

"I bet you are. Hey, Sadie . . ." I trail off as she hums into the phone. The sweet noise is enough to set me free, to let me take my first full breath in hours, and it feels like the rarest type of air. "Thank you."

"Whatever you're thanking me for, Ben Cooper, anytime. I'm here when you're ready."

"Did you think about me all day?" I inwardly beg her to say yes.

"Always. In fact, you are becoming quite the distraction." She laughs.

"How?" I push for more. Nick waits a few feet away, watching me. He says something to Dr. Davinah, but I block him out.

"I think at one point today, I was jotting your name down in my notes at the hospital when really I should have been writing this sweet lady's chief complaints for my mentor." She giggles again. That sound is the drug that I need.

"No one died on your watch because of me, did they?" I swallow thickly.

"No, but it was a close call," she teases.

"Good, baby, that's good." As I hoped, Sadie has helped put me in the clear. With her, I am out of the woods.

"How was the last show? I get to see you tomorrow!" She is so fucking thrilled about being with me. I feel that familiar swell of comfort in my chest.

Tomorrow, I'm going to have to tell her about my eye, about my current mental state, and—fuck me—about my father. Knowing that Sadie has the power to pull me through a rage means that out of anyone in the world, I feel safest sharing that part of me with her. No one has ever been able to pull me through that without my medication or a swift kick to the fucking head.

The night doesn't fade away effortlessly, but she eases me enough to talk to Dr. Davinah. But when I talk to him, I lose myself again. My peace is gone, and my demons are left breathing down my neck.

Seventeen

SADIE

Ben is due home any second, and I've been sitting at Kate's table biting my nails (a nasty habit). We all agreed to meet here before going our separate ways—meaning he's coming to meet my family.

"Nervous Nelly over there, you excited to see your rock star?" Kate interrupts my nail biting.

"Are *you* excited to see *your* rock star?" I retort.

Eric and Kate have had a terrible week. Even though they aren't exclusive, Kate thought that the two of them sleeping together meant they were only sleeping with one another. He, however, understood it differently.

"I don't know if I'm nauseated because the thought of seeing him excites me or if it's because I'm repulsed and still pissed that he screwed some groupie. She probably had fake boobs that could fit the entire circumference of my head." I frown, feeling for her. I don't know what I would do if Ben was still seeing other women, especially if he were sleeping with them.

"I'm sorry. Did y'all work it out?"

"Yes and no. I explained I'd forgive him this one time."

"And?"

"He agreed, and then he went on and on about how much he likes me and how he only thought of me. I get that we aren't exclusive or anything, but why have sex with someone else if it 'meant nothing' or he was 'only thinking of me'?" I understand fully what she means as she peppers air quotes through her speech.

"Are you going to be able to trust him when he goes back out on the road?"

"Maybe. I don't know. Who even knows what we'll be after this weekend."

Kate's showing her hand for the first time. She is vulnerable over a man in a way I've never seen, and my heart aches for her.

"I'm here if you need me. We're both busy, but I am never too busy to talk."

"I love you for that. And hey, you still have to tell me all the details of what happened when you got that wild urge to fly to your man. Was it hot?" She wiggles her brows at me, and I blush, remembering the way we made up. The mirror. God, his touch. It was electric. I'm glad I flew to him, and I am even more glad we are making progress on the trust aspect of our relationship. My mouth opens to tell her a very PG version of what happened, but there is a knock at the door.

"Kate, baby! Open up, I'm home!" Eric yells from the other side of the door.

My body reacts because he is here. Ben's back. My stomach runs wild with butterflies. I stand from the kitchen chair and make sure my new skinny jeans are fitting me snugly and my cute floral chiffon V-neck top is showing my cleavage yet leaving some mystery. The perfect combination of sexy and cute. My low-heeled booties compliment my smaller frame and give me some height, making my legs look longer and leaner. Kate was shocked I bought this whole ensemble, but for Ben I want to look sexy while keeping my own sense of style.

I fixed up my hair, curling it in loose waves, a mix of wild and messy on purpose. Completing the look is my makeup—winged liner with some blush and a layer of nude gloss on my already pouty lips.

The door opens, and Eric immediately wraps Kate up in his arms.

They share a kiss and whisper, Kate and my conversation forgotten. Biting my lip, I see Ben skate around them in his gray beanie, matching gray T-shirt, black leather jacket, and skinny jeans. But what has me gasping and rushing to him worriedly is his black eye.

"Oh my gosh! Ben! What happened!" I crowd him, still only reaching his shoulders even with my heels. I peer up at him and lightly touch his swollen yellow-and-purple eye. His hands grip my hips, and he clings to me extra tight, as if he's checking that I'm in front of him, cementing him to the ground.

"Your hair is different. You look stunning." He looks me over, completely ignoring my question.

"Ben . . . Your eye, what happened?" I whisper softly, changing my approach.

"Let me take you to my place, and I'll explain. Nick's waiting for us in the car."

* * *

Ben and I settle into the backseat for the ride. I half expected him to take the front seat to avoid me pushing for answers. He isn't putting physical distance between us, but his body language is screaming for me to let him have a moment. He looks out the window with our interlocked hands bouncing on his bobbing knee.

"You look so fucking amazing," he whispers, slowly turning to face me and leaning in for a kiss. I taste the mint he must have popped in his mouth after a recent cigarette, and I'm surprised that it's a taste I enjoy. I think I would enjoy anything that is Ben Cooper. His highs, his lows, his flaws, and all the devastatingly beautiful things that make him chaos. We linger, his full lips on mine, sharing soft, gentle kisses. Our lips barely touch, yet it's still more intimate than most kisses. I scoot closer, dying to get nearer to him, and he grabs me without pause. My hands claim his chest as Nick turns up the radio a little to grant us more privacy.

I want to be close to him. Pull him in and heal his wounds. I want to take all of him and never let go. Wrap him in a bubble of my love and shelter him from the outside world. The distance made me yearn for him; it gutted me to not be within reach of something I never want to lose.

"Your eye looks painful. I hate that you're hurt. Promise me you're okay," I whisper, my head moving against his gently.

He nods. "I am now. You make everything feel right again."

"You, too, Ben. I missed you so much." With barely any words, he pulls me in close, my legs dropping over his, my head on his shoulder and his lips against my forehead, peppering it with kisses. The short drive to his apartment is painfully slow, most likely because I need answers. By the time we pull up, I am ready to beg for those answers.

"Stay out of trouble, you two, and Sadie, I'll see you soon, sweetie," Nick says as he sends us off.

"You, too, see ya!" We climb out, and I help Ben with his luggage. We climb up the stairs silently, and I follow him inside his third-floor apartment. I've never been here before, and Ben's touch is all over the place—it's the first thing I notice. There is a piano next to the flat-screen TV mounted on the wall. Opposite that, there is a guitar on a stand. An intricate epoxy-covered coffee table with white and black rivers woven into cedar sits in the middle of the room, and it pairs well with his black sectional. Their debut record, *Longest Hour*, hangs in a glass case above his couch with a picture of him and the band outside the record studio.

I admire his smile in the picture, reaching from ear to ear like a little kid's. I love seeing him happy over what he has accomplished. It makes me unbelievably proud to call him mine.

"Come sit down, baby." I didn't even notice him sit.

"Okay, what happened?" I ask now that we're alone.

"All right, Sadie. Some of the things I'm going to tell you are not going to be easy to say, and they may not be easy to hear." He's terrified.

His hands shake in mine, and I do my best to surge some strength into him, tightening my grip.

"It's okay, Ben. It's me, remember?"

Dropping his head, he gnaws at his lip. "I have intermittent explosive disorder. I was diagnosed when I was in the foster system at seventeen, after my dad was taken to prison for killing my mother."

"Ben." The anguish in my voice can't be avoided. I feel his words deep in my chest. An onslaught of emotions hits me like a crashing wave. It's as if a bomb was dropped on my protective bubble.

"The drugs are a way of coping. The weed calms me down, and so do my meds—sometimes—but the cocaine gives me adrenaline." He pauses, and I stay silent. The space around us is for him. I don't need to fill it with words.

"My father used to beat us. Bad ... really fucking bad. It was almost every day, starting when I was six. God knows how long he beat my mother before that."

"He beat your mother to death?"

"Yes." With that, I watch his eyes dilate as if he's seeing it all again in his head. "It was my fault. It should have been me."

"You? How is it your fault, Ben? Please don't say that." I all but jump on him, his words frightening me, snatching my heart in a deadly grip.

"Because he was mad at me. I ditched school to get drunk with my friends, and he knew about it. And instead of going home, I stayed out so he wouldn't beat on me. If I had been there that night to take my beating, my mother would still be alive." His eyes squeeze shut, and he pinches the bridge of his nose. He's attempting to chase away the demons in his mind, but it isn't working, and he is growing more agitated.

"Ben, what he did was not your fault. Your father is at fault. Not you. He would have killed both of you."

"Then it should have been me too! Damn it! My mom was a fucking saint. She put her faith in me, and then life ripped her away savagely!"

He stands up from the couch in a rush, kicking the coffee table, causing it to scuff the floor.

I jump a little, taken aback by his outburst. Quickly, that passes, and the urge to comfort him takes precedence. His reaction is intimidating, but it's also a cry for help. It makes sense now why he looks at life as a series of letdowns where you can only hold on to the moment you are in.

"No, Ben. Your mom wouldn't have wanted that . . ."

I'm up and on him, comforting him. I was raised to take on the pain of the world. To wear the wounds of the ones I love and stitch them back together. I did it for my father every day that my mother was sick and for my mother when she was worried about how he and I would go on if she didn't make it. Being in the medical field has put me in places where I have watched people's last breaths. I have been in the room with families as they are told their loved one has passed, and they've fallen apart in front of me. But right now, in this moment, it is different. This isn't a stranger I just met; this is someone who owns pieces of me, who has sown the seeds of their being into my heart. But I do my best to apply some of my training. I want to understand him and give him the space to grieve. Has he ever even had that? I don't know.

"Sometimes I fight because I owe it to her. No punch can bring her back or compare to the ones she took that night, but I damn well deserve to understand the pain." His voice is eerily quiet, and I keep my focus on him, surprised by what he has admitted. "I take a sniff of cocaine and then I rage fight. I find someone who deserves it, and I fight. When I hit them, I see my father, and I feel I've vindicated my mother. Avenged her death. It's the least I can do for being a coward when she needed someone to protect her."

"No, stop. Ben, you can't do that. That's not the way you remember your mother. You can't bring violence on someone to make up for the violence done to her. You could get hurt, and then her legacy will be for nothing."

He shakes his head. "Her legacy? Her abuse is not her legacy, Sadie."

"No, but *you* are. You're her legacy, Ben. I didn't know her, but there's love in your eyes and in your actions. You are the best thing she gave this world, and if you keep fighting, that legacy might fade away." I say it calmly; however, inside I am haunted by the image of Ben lying there bloody and lifeless.

"You don't have to fix this," Ben says. "This is who I am. I've been alone for years now, and I've come to terms with how I live my life."

"I'm not trying to fix this," I explain, shaking my head adamantly. "I'm trying to understand what happened to you. To be there for you. Because I don't think anyone really ever has." I pause, looking out the window then back to him. "Ben, you mean something to me. I . . . I love you, Ben Cooper, and you hurting yourself like this scares me. You being abused all those years and losing your mother breaks my soul. I hate that someone hurt you. My parents told me to never hate people, but I hate that man for what he's done to my best friend."

His lip quivers, and I witness him cry for the first time. "You love me?" he questions, and I nod, reaching up to grace his lips with a whisper of my fingertips.

"I do love you. You're the first man I've ever loved."

"Sadie . . . I love you too." In that instant, we collide, his lips on mine. Like Romeo and Juliet, we share our first *I love you*s after such a short time knowing one another. I'm his first great love, as he is mine.

He's opened his soul to me and let me into the darkest parts of him, the places only he and I know. He brings me down on his lap, and I straddle him, pulling at his hair and putting all of me into this kiss.

Ben's hands skate over my back and up into my hair, where he mimics my movements. The warmth of his tongue against mine overwhelms me. I lose my breath in him. I'm hurting inside for the small child who was abused, for the teenager who lost his mother, and for the man who is suffering.

"You feel like home," he whispers as our lips part, our foreheads still touching.

"Is this the first time you have felt like you know what a safe home is?" I want to make sure that he tells me the truth. If we are to continue building, I have to make sure he feels safe with me.

"You can make it even better."

"How?"

He tightens his grip on my face and traps me in his longing gaze. "Marry me." It isn't a question, and I'm not sure if it's a joke.

"What?" If it is, then the joke isn't funny.

"Marry me, be my forever. Be my fucking home, Sadie." He smiles, and it's coming from a place of vulnerability. He's afraid and wants something to make him feel whole. I can give him that, but this is without a shadow of a doubt coming from an emotion that will wear off, and he'll regret ever saying it.

"You're emotional—we both are. You don't mean it."

"Whatever you want to think, but I've never been more sure of anyone or anything in my entire life."

I shake my head and chuckle hysterically.

"We're late to meet my parents, and we aren't in a place mentally where we can think about this," I start. "Besides, it's only been a couple weeks. The entire world would think we're insane."

"I don't give a fuck what the world thinks. I give a fuck about what my girl thinks."

I lean in and kiss his lips gently before pulling back and whispering, "I love you, and today we shared something personal. Let's just adjust to this and comfort each other." If the feelings weren't so raw and palpable, I would think this were a dream.

"Fine. Think what you want. I've never met anyone who can make me feel whole the way you do, Sadie. I may be young and new to this whole love thing, but I'm not new to knowing what I want, and I want you." I nod again and let his words settle like ink into my skin. I want him forever, too, and there is no doubt that I would marry this man in a heartbeat, but we would be crazy to do it this soon. This young. Wouldn't we?

"I love you. Ask me again tomorrow when you've had a night to sleep on it." I wink, attempting to lighten the mood, knowing come tomorrow he will forget about this little slip-of-the-tongue marriage proposal.

"Will do, angel."

The thought that he may not ask again seems logical, but I also feel a slight sting of disappointment. I know I want Ben forever, but I haven't thought about how long forever is for him. Is it a fortnight or an eternity?

It's the emotions. Today was a big one. His homecoming, his tragic life story—all of it was a lot to take in. I can't think logically right now. Shutting off my brain and taking my own advice, I drop the subject and get us up and moving.

Time for him to meet my parents. We will address this when we can breathe in fresh air.

Eighteen

BEN

Sharing my past with Sadie was liberating. I no longer feel like these secrets are mine to keep. Now that she knows, they aren't weighing me down as heavily as they were before. Not only does she know but she made it feel better—she made me feel like my still having a fucking heartbeat instead of my mother is for a purpose. One my mother planned.

You're her legacy, Ben.

How profound, how perfect those words are. They may not take away the rage or the guilt, but they help it feel a little less cancerous. While we drive to the grocery store to buy a pie, she sings every song on the radio without a care, absentmindedly checking her phone and watching people as they pass.

Sadie thinks I asked her to marry me because I'm an emotional wreck, but she has no idea that I want her to be mine for good. It's only been two weeks, but time cannot define who we are or the love that we have built.

I never wanted love—I thought it was for complete morons—but Sadie makes the idea of love and marriage sound like a gold nugget in a world full of stones. She's the treasure I've searched for, the home I've been dying to find, and with her, in the weeks of having her, I've found all that and more—I've learned that there is still a place inside me that can love and accept love.

"Mama is going to kick my ass when she sees I brought a store-bought pie." Sadie turns down the radio as we pull into the parking lot of the local grocer.

"Oh really?" Climbing out, I rush to her side, open her door, and take her hand to help her out. I take that same hand and bring it to my lips, giving the back a long, open-mouth kiss, biting the skin before releasing it.

"Ouch! And you can count on it. She taught me how to bake and always says that the store stuff is all preservatives."

"Agreed, but time got away from us," I say.

"That's okay, more time with you is better. We won't get much of it because of the touring schedule. Where do you head next?" She rubs her thumb along the back of my hand, tracing the thick veins.

"We head back to the Midwest."

"Touring is odd to me. One minute you are in New York, then Florida, and then they send you back to New York. Why not do all the shows in one place at the same time instead of ping-ponging?"

I chuckle. "Depends on ticket sales. Some places have higher tickets sales during weekends or certain times of year, and some other things. I never really asked." I shrug as we enter the grocery store and grab a shopping cart. When you first step inside, there is a floral department, and the smell of roses and lilies fills the air. Sadie's nose flares, and I sneak a peek at her taking it in.

"Do you like touring?"

"I did. I still do, but there is something that makes traveling a lot less enjoyable these days," I hint, looking down at her as those fucking dimples break through.

"Careful, what would the world do if *the* Ben Cooper said mushy stuff to some nobody," she teases.

"You aren't nobody, Sadie." She was joking, but I believe behind every joke there is an ugly truth. Sadie is more than somebody. She is fucking everything.

"To you, maybe, but to the world, I am just another girl." She shrugs.

"You—"

"Ben Cooper? Oh my god, we are huge fans. Can we get a picture? Oh! And your autograph!" We are interrupted by two fans. They look to be my age, and they rush up to us. Sadie backs away, jolted by the sudden intrusion. I am used to this—it happens a lot—but she isn't.

"Sure thing." I hurry and sign a grocery receipt and the back of one of their T-shirts before snapping a picture. I say goodbye and instantly look to Sadie. She has the slightest deer-in-headlights look on her gorgeous face.

"Sorry, baby. You okay?" I ask her, pulling her back into my side.

She nods. "Does that happen a lot?"

"Yes, it does. Usually at the shows we have security, so you haven't seen too much of that." I pause and look around. A few people look in our direction; one guy even whispers to the clerk, and they both look at me. I'm usually not this hyperaware of fans, because I've grown used to it. I continue, "I should have brought Nick; he could have grabbed things for us. Sorry, that was a lot."

"No, no. It's fine. Really, it's kind of interesting to see."

I look her over and make sure she is all right. Once her body isn't as tense, I take her hand and continue to push the cart with the other.

"What about tabloids, angel? You know that you are going to be in them, right?"

Tabloids and paparazzi—now, that shit is the part of my job I fucking loathe. Scum. The things people say and the lengths they will go to to find a story (or make one up) are enough to send me over the edge if I think about it too much.

"I haven't thought about any type of publicity. I've tried to keep us in this bubble. I guess reality was bound to slap me in the face," she says, but she doesn't look at me, instead eyeing the items around us with great focus. Clearly, she is avoiding my gaze. I'll let her.

"I will do my best to keep us in this bubble. I don't want people getting into it anyway. But ignore the tabloids at all cost. More than half the shit they put in them is a lie."

"So avoid past tabloid stories about you too? What would be in them?" There is a hint of worry in her voice. She's asking about my history with women without directly asking.

"They have some pictures of me that I don't want you to see."

"Ben, can I ask you something?" She stops abruptly and turns to look up at me.

"Always."

"Am I safe? Health-wise?" Oh, there it is. She *is* a health care professional; I should have told her sooner.

"Yes. I got checked right after we met. Clean."

"Will I always be safe?" she pushes. Wait . . .

"Sadie, I am only with you. You don't think I would cheat, do you?"

"All men and women are capable of it, whether they set out to do it or not. You are a rock star, and I know what that means. I have also been with you, felt the way you touch me. You're clearly . . ." She stops and looks down at her feet.

"Clearly what?" I take her chin in my hands and force her to look at me.

"You have experience. You are really good at it. Great at it. I mean, I—" She stumbles over her words, gnawing at the side of her cheek.

"Baby . . ." I pause, pulling her flush against me, her breasts pressing against my body, just below my pecs. I don't care who's watching. Let the world see me get close to her. I love her. She is mine. "The way I touch you is for you. I don't remember anything before you, and all I think about is all the ways we are going to keep touching and learning each other. I love you. I don't say that shit lightly. I don't say it at all. Those words"—I lean in close and kiss her lips—"these hands"—I move to her cheek and kiss there—"and this cock"—I tighten my grip as I whisper the last part in her ear, taking her lobe between my teeth—"are locked up in a fucking vise by you, Sadie McCallister. No one is ever going to please me like you do."

Her breath rushes across my cheek in a soft, nearly inaudible moan. "Ben."

"Exactly, so ignore the tabloids, baby." I separate us, leaving her breathless. I do this on purpose. I want her to feel my words and know that I am not one to cheat on perfection. I haven't even had her fully and yet there hasn't been one moment where I have wanted to fuck someone else. I don't even glance at the women who come to my shows. This is it for me.

"I'm going to go grab some candy. Meet me at the register?" I look back at her; she stands, barely functioning.

Even though I walk away with my composure seemingly intact, I am anything but calm. That exchange left me desperate for her. I want to take her back to my place, slide her panties to the side, and have her slide her greedy cunt against my hard length. Shit. I'm meeting the parents; I need to get my head far away from that thought.

I grab a few things for later and something for Sadie she can't say no to. Meeting her at the register, I check us out while she takes a call from her mother. I hear her telling her we're on our way and that we lost track of time. I get all my items in the bag and walk us to the car as she ends the call. As we drive, we talk more about her clinicals and upcoming finals. Her eyes light up when she tells me about her internship with Dr. Bailer, a highly esteemed doctor.

* * *

"If they get to know me and decide they don't like me, I still get to keep you, right?" Walking in the front door, I smell something, and my mouth salivates instantly. I haven't had a home-cooked meal in God knows how long.

"My parents don't hate anyone, but yes, if they don't like you, you can keep me. I make my own decisions." She winks at me, earning a smug smile back. So sassy. Taking my hand, she leads me into the kitchen.

"Mama, Papa, we're here," she announces us as we step into view. Stanley stops setting the table and faces us with a warm smile, and Raydean wipes her wet hands on the towel hanging from her apron.

"Ben, how lovely to meet you in person!" Sadie's mom greets me first, giving me a gentle hug.

"Yes, Sadie has told us a lot about you. Come on in and have a seat. Ray is almost done with the food." Her father shakes my hand, and he isn't hostile, but he isn't as warm as his wife is. I can sense him feeling me out. Let us not forget about my fucking black eye. Shit. I didn't think up a lie to tell them.

They're the embodiment of Southern charm, and at first, it's off-putting. It's not the type of setting I'm accustomed to.

"It's nice to meet you guys. Thanks for having me over for dinner." I follow her dad to the table while she stays back with her mom, prepping the last few things before they bring them to the table. Sadie stands barefoot, helping her mother out with a smile on her beautiful face. Looking at her brings me clarity. I want this. I want a home with her happy and smiling. But the question is, can I give her that?

I'm not cured, not even close. And no way in hell can that happen overnight, but still, I want to try for her. Sadie settles in next to me, and surprisingly my nerves slowly fade away the more we all talk.

I see instantly where Sadie's kindness and acceptance for others comes from. With every question they ask, I sense genuine interest from both her parents. For a moment, I feel jealous over the fact that I never had this life.

My home was always peaceful when it was my mother and me alone, but it became a nightmare every time my father stepped back inside. I do my best for the rest of dinner to not wear my thoughts on my face and enjoy the small talk, paying close attention to the way they all finish one another's sentences and the way her parents constantly beam at their pride and joy—Sadie.

"Sadie tells us you got her to sing in front of you. That's impressive;

she doesn't even take solos in the church choir. Her mother and I are the only ones who really hear her sing."

"She has an incredible voice, like an angel." Blushing, she drops her head modestly. I lean in and kiss her cheek, whispering, "Beautiful" against the shell of her ear.

"You're beautiful," she whispers back, giving me a soft kiss on the lips. I linger in the moment until we notice the silence around us. Looking back at her parents, I see they're both staring at us. Raydean wears a smile like Sadie's, but Stanley looks wary. He is welcoming, but there are flashing red lights going off when he watches me with his daughter.

Sadie said I get to keep her, and her father may be the reason she needs to make that decision. He is the one I will have to win over.

"Sorry."

"No, no, it's fine. I'm not used to seeing Sadie in love." Stanley looks to Raydean.

"It *is* new. Anyway, how about dessert? Then, Ben, I'm dying to hear you and Sadie Jay sing together." Her mother starts to collect the plates while I stand to help Sadie with the dishes.

"Not so bad, are they?" Sadie nudges my arm. We're alone for the first time at the kitchen sink.

"No, not at all. I really like your parents. They're more accepting than average. Your dad may need some more of my charm, though."

Handing me a wet plate to dry, she nods. "He's very nice, but I think he worries about my heart," she admits.

"I appreciate that. He and I both care about the best interests of your heart." She blinks slowly, her cheeks rising with a soft smile.

"I think I spent so much time focusing on taking care of him and his heart when Mama was sick that he feels he owes it to me to protect mine." She hands me another dish, and I dry it.

"Did that ever become too much for you?" I ask. We had many conversations while I was away these last couple weeks, but we never talked about what made her so inclined to be the reserved people pleaser.

"It taught me lots." She shrugs. "Remember, it taught me true love." She pauses, peering over her shoulder, making sure no one is there. "But it also put so much pressure on me that I felt like I could never let anyone down, especially my father. If he lost my mother, then I couldn't ever be another reason that he had his heart broken. It was a heavy burden. But I don't regret it."

"Not at all?" She is doing it now, hiding what that pressure did to her so she doesn't talk badly about her family. I want her to know she can let all her walls down and tell me everything like I did with her.

"Maybe a little. Being the only child and the sole reason for my father to stay stable and my mother to keep fighting. That's laying the world on my fragile shoulders and asking me to carry it without faltering, isn't it?" Her head turns, and our eyes meet.

"It is. And you aren't a bad person for feeling this way," I reassure her.

"Aren't I?"

"No, you aren't. I'm sorry that you had to go through that for so long."

"Don't be sorry. I'm fine now, but it feels like a huge part of my youth was taken, and I feel so guilty thinking this way. I almost lost my mom, and my dad almost did too."

"Hey." I reach into the soapy water and find her hand. I grip it in mine and rub soothing circles over the back of her hand. "Being a teenager and having your life molded into something you didn't get to pick yourself isn't fair, and you are anything but selfish for thinking that."

She gives me a soft smile.

"Thank you. I haven't told you this, but being with you is the first thing that I have done just for me. Being with you is showing me exactly what I want." What a compliment—both a blessing and a weight I will carry on my shoulders.

"Maybe now you can be a little selfish, angel. Don't be afraid to test out the things that you want. You don't need to please everyone and take on the entire world as your mission. Do something for you for once." I lean in and kiss her shoulder. In turn, she kisses my bicep when I stand back up to my full height. I hope she keeps doing things for herself from here on out. The world has so much to offer her, and I want to watch it from the front fucking row.

We wash the rest of the dishes in silence. I see it, the difference between us, but we are both going day by day and becoming more raw with one another. When I opened myself up to her earlier today, she had words to comfort me. Now I stand here returning the favor. I want her to know she doesn't always need to be the fixer, the one to heal everyone's sorrows while hers don't have space to exist. We are navigating this newness together. Sadie and I are falling further and further into the unknown, and I wouldn't want this with anyone else.

* * *

The action movie we decided on rolls by quickly, but my eyes stay glued on Sadie as she wraps around me like a vine, her closed eyes and slightly agape lips giving her features a delicate flawlessness. I could stare at her in this state for fucking hours, running my hands through her silky blond hair.

"Just like her mama, I tell ya." Peering up, I look to the other side of the sectional where Ray is fast asleep against Stan's side, his hands also playing with her hair.

"She's a great woman, and so is Sadie—it only makes sense." Sadie shifts with the vibrations from my voice, snuggling in deeper. Her warm, plush curves mold against me.

"When her mother got cancer, I was terrified I wouldn't be able to even look at Sadie, let alone be around her. It was like looking at a reflection of Ray, and the thought that I would lose my wife crushed me. I didn't know how I could look at Sadie and not break down every time."

The way he talks about loss is so familiar. It kills you from the inside out without any way to stop it or slow it down, and all you can do is hope to survive it. Not a day since my mother was murdered have I been without her memory.

"I don't know if you are a religious man, but we are, and I swear God helped me see it differently." I stiffen a bit, and Sadie readjusts. I am not a religious man, I don't even think there is a higher power, but her family clearly believes there is. Isn't there a saying about avoiding religion and politics in conversation? I would very much like that. "If I lost Ray, Sadie Jay would be a reminder of all the things that made Ray beautiful. She wouldn't be a reminder of what I lost but a reminder of all the great things that I shared with her mother."

"She's perfect, sir." This is the truth, and I'm grateful he doesn't press for more. I'm trying to win him over, not add another red flag to his list. I'm surprised he feels comfortable enough to share something this private, but I don't complain.

"You love my daughter?" Faster than I can blink, he changes the subject. With a quick shift in gears, he nails me to a wall with a simple question. I love Sadie, but I debate what to say to him. I feel possessive over my feelings for Sadie. I'm not ready to share what we have with anyone but her. However, if I want to marry Sadie, I might as well tell him exactly how I feel.

"I do. She silences them." I keep my eyes focused on the angel against me—the only belief I've ever had in any type of heaven, higher power, or supreme being lies wrapped around me tightly.

"Silences who?"

"The demons inside me."

"We all have demons, son. But it's all about the choices we make and how we handle those demons. It's also about not using the ones we love to fix all our broken parts." His words have the slightest snark to them. I debate saying something, but that would be strike three. Sadie has shared how she was programmed to always fix her family. If I wanted to, I could remark that this is rich coming from him, as he is one of the people who raised Sadie to carry the world on her shoulders.

"She helps them. No one can cure them. But she makes me want to find a way. It's only taken me a matter of weeks to know she is all I want in life." Bringing my eyes back to Stan, I let them linger with purpose. This is it, the moment where he will either accept Sadie and me for what we have or have my ass kicked to the curb.

"Son?" He picks up on what I'm saying and meets my strong gaze. "Are you trying to ask me something?"

"I want to marry Sadie. I've never wanted anything more than my next breath, but she is it. Can I marry your daughter, Stan?"

His face grows impassive, giving no sign of what he's thinking. My hand in Sadie's hair stills, and I stare down at her, no longer able to keep my eyes on him because I need her strength. She said that no matter what they say, she would choose me. In this moment, I cling to that promise. Swallowing past the very large lump in my dry throat, I press on.

"I can love her, sir. I can make her happy. I can give her what no one else can. I can give her my soul. No one will ever love her this deeply."

Planting a kiss on her forehead, I keep my lips there, my eyes closed. My heart is full of things that I never believed I could feel, especially the gripping vise of her soul intertwined in mine. I would be dumb to walk away from Sadie just because I used to be the playboy who believed in love only being for everyone else. Fuck me, I tripped right into the arms of the most beautiful melody, someone who happens to be everything I once found foolish. Who knew it was all real? That she could be real?

A girl, her soft peace, and her pure heart. Three things I want more than the very air I breathe.

Stanley stays eerily silent; I start to think he might be gone when I look up. Eventually, I tear my eyes from Sadie to see him sitting, staring at me. Perplexed?

"I can't say yes to that, Ben. I am a man of honor, and I do respect you for asking, but I don't think my daughter could survive what you would do to her." My heart drops.

My knuckles tighten into fists, and my jaw clenches tightly. He doesn't know me, and yet, as angry as it makes me, he is right. Sadie may not be able to survive me in the darkest hours that I haunt. We sit there for a moment, not saying a word, both of us unsure of what the next move will be. Stanley breaks the tense standoff.

"You're welcome to stay in the guest bedroom. You be a gentleman now, Ben." With that, he leaves.

He said no without any reservations. Her father denied me. But I can't stop. I will not let anyone tell me and Sadie what we can and can't do. If I have to burn down buildings and wage war on the people around us in order to seal her to me for the rest of our lives, I will do it. She said she would keep me, that I would be her choice, and tomorrow I will beg at her feet to run away with me like some sort of star-crossed love affair. I always did live for the dramatics. No. I will have to prove how far I am willing to go.

After a time, I slide away from Sadie, grab the item I bought at the store earlier, and bring it back to her. I look at the object and lean in to whisper against her ear, "I will keep you forever. Against all. I will keep you. You and me."

Nineteen

SADIE

The smell of bacon wakes me, the scent making my empty stomach growl. I open my eyes, and I'm met with Ben's big brown eyes, fuller lips, and brown hair. His face is covered in the lightest smattering of five o'clock shadow, and it's by far the best sight I've ever woken up to.

"Good morning, angel."

"Morning, handsome. I can't believe I crashed and slept all night." Bringing my hands to my eyes, I yawn and wipe away the rest of my slumber. That's when I feel something sticky scratch the skin of my eyelid.

"Ow, what the heck?" Pulling my hand away, I see a peach candy ring on my finger. "What is this? Did you put this here?" I chuckle, going to remove it when he stops me.

"Ben, what..." Grabbing my chin with his strong fingers, he brings his lips to mine and takes me with a deep need. He controls our kiss so effortlessly. Our tongues touch, and I become powerless under his soft yet rough touch.

Putting less than an inch between our lips, he pulls back slightly and opens his eyes. They search mine as mine search his. "Marry me, Sadie."

"Ben..." I trail off, and my eyes move to look around my bedroom. My chin is still in his firm grasp. Holding it tighter, he gains my attention once more. He really must have lost his mind.

"I love you, Sadie, and I know more than anything that you were meant to be mine. You were put in my life for a fucking reason." I can't believe he's talking about this again, not because it's bothersome—it's not—but because it's shocking. In the beginning, I didn't believe this version of him was possible. Now he is sitting here professing his love for me.

"Ben, it's been two weeks. You don't go from who you were to this..." I gesture at him with my eyes.

"I can. You made me want this, Sadie. You got inside of me and stirred me all up, and I want this with you." He kisses my cheek, then my nose, then my forehead. Such a simple act, yet it feels like he's handed me his beating heart in my hand.

"You want to marry me, don't you, angel?" he questions.

Shocked still, I think for a second. Do I want to marry Ben? I guess it's not a matter of want but more a question of being ready or not. I'm nineteen, he's twenty-two; we're young, and this is completely reckless. But my insides are all twisted up and excited. What would it be like to act on love and not stop to rationalize the millions of reasons why this could go wrong? What would it be like to give in and do something for me?

Does that make us young, naive, and careless or profoundly in love and more mature than we have ever been?

"You don't want to?" he questions, his face drawn down with rejection.

"No, Ben. I mean yes, I want to. Don't look so upset. I just need to think about this. What will people think? What will my parents do? What will we do?" He moves, sitting down and nestling me in his lap.

"The only question I give a fuck about is what we will do. We'll be happy," he states simply, as if he's picking out what to eat for lunch. He's serious; this is a definite decision that he's already made.

"Ben, you tour all the time, and I have my internship for the next year and then nursing school coming up. How would we even make a marriage work?"

"We will. I don't have the answers, but I have a feeling. Damn it, Sadie. I feel it all inside me. Let's spend forever getting to know each other." His poetry is convincing, and my head spins. My eyes keep looking into his as I think of any reason that this may be too rash, but I only find more reasons to fall off the edge with him.

"My parents. I don't know what they will do."

Ben cups my face. "You told me yesterday that no matter what, you would keep me. You said that, didn't you?" Our eyes search one another, and I stutter.

"Y-yes, but Ben. This is marriage. You would have to pick me over anyone," I remind him. His life as a bachelor would be over. There would only be me. I can do that, but can he?

"I don't want to touch another fucking body ever again. I want to spend every night lost between your thighs, touching you, kissing you, tasting you. I don't want anyone but you." My body visibly quivers. "Yes, baby, I want to fucking ruin you for anyone else. I want to program that body to respond to only me. I want your heart to pump blood for only me."

My breath catches, releasing on an unsteady exhale. "You have to bend and break for me, too, Ben. I want you to only exist because I am written all over your heart," I admit. It's the most reckless thing I have ever said.

"We can do that. Now answer me. You said you would let me keep you if they didn't want us together, right?" I nod ever so slightly, fiddling with his shirt. "Then marry me, Sadie. Don't make me beg. Because I am really fucking convincing." He winks. I giggle and lightly slap his chest. "Marry me, Sadie," he asks again, all humor now lost.

I search his eyes one more time, waiting for something to stop me, for some divine intervention to step in, but nothing happens. I only see him. I see peace. I see everything I have longed for: being in love, wild, untamed, and free. I don't know what the outcome will be, but one thing I am sure of: he holds the key.

"I will marry you, Ben." His eyes flutter, and he chuckles as he releases the breath he was holding.

"You will?" He brings his hands up into my hair.

"Yes. I will." He controls my head and brings me in for a kiss that I have branded as ours, one I am convinced we invented. My eyes water, and my brows draw in tight. I have never felt more seen, more needed, more desired. I have never felt more whole than I do right now.

"Marry me today. I want to do it now." He finally releases me, and my eyes all but pop out of my head.

"What is the rush? Ben, we just agreed to do this."

"I want it now. There is a rush, a rush to seal you to me. I want this to start right now." I stand, untangling myself from him. Ben tries to stop me, but I don't let him. I have to take a minute to get my head screwed back on.

"Ben, this is crazy. You're crazy." I laugh. But the comment isn't funny. Saying yes was crazy, but this would make us batshit crazy.

"I am. I warned you how I am. When I had you on my lips, I said I wouldn't ever let you go. What makes you think I would tame that crazy down now? There is more at risk here." The way he says that last part, I sense his fear. He is scared I won't do this.

"Ben, I won't change my mind." I rush to him and straddle him again. This time, I am the one to cup his tense jaw.

"I would if I were you," he warns me.

"You said you want me and only me. Why would you warn me?"

"Because I love you enough to tell you that you should run. Your father is right. You aren't prepared for what it is that I could do to you if this goes wrong."

My chest tightens. He asked my father? Wait.

"Ben, you asked him?"

Ben nods slowly, his eyes soft and sad.

"I did. He said he won't give me his blessing. And I don't blame him. But I won't take no for an answer. I will have you even if that means I leave here today with you handcuffed to me until we get to the fucking courthouse. I continue to breathe every day now because of you. I am fucking crazy, Sadie, but I won't let you go." My head starts to spin. Ben is telling me to my face that this is wrong and we should listen to the flashing warning signs while simultaneously saying to hell with it—let's run the tracks and see if we can beat the train heading straight toward us. It's a contradiction, but it makes sense. How does it always make sense with him?

No one can tell us that we can't chase this. I feel protective of him. This will be the first time I've ever gone against my father. My body tenses. I will let my father down, but I would choose Ben every time, over anyone, over everything, and in every world. Reckless and wild as it is, it's true. Ben is worth losing everything I have for everything unknown. I've never been more excited and terrified for what's around the corner.

"I choose you. But it may cost me, Ben. You can't let us break." His face lights up like a child's.

"Angel, I won't let you down. There is no purpose for me if you aren't the center of it."

* * *

My palms are sweating, my fingers visibly shaking with nervous tremors. Ben and I have decided that we will get married. The small peach candy ring stays on my finger until breakfast. We have committed to us in a way that only fools do. But I am his fool, and he's mine.

My parents don't know Ben, and they will most likely tell me I don't, either, but this is something I'm not going to change my mind on. Ben and I could have a million lifetimes together or only fleeting moments where we are lost in a trance of soft touches and whispers of life's victories and sorrows—either one would feel right. This. Us. Right now, in the moment, this feels like the most right thing I have ever done in my life.

After breakfast, Ben explains he's got rehearsal today and quietly slips out of the house. I convinced him it would be best for me to break the news alone. It's Saturday, and I don't have a shift, so I can study while he's gone and do my best to wrap my head around how we're going to do this whole wedding thing. But first, I need to talk to my parents.

***

My parents are finishing cleaning up the kitchen. I enter the room, Ben's goodbye kiss still fresh on my lips. The seconds since he left somehow feel shorter. A millisecond? Is there a time that speeds by faster? If so, the universe and I invented it together. I am terrified to tell them. I tried to catch my breath between the front door and the kitchen, but it was no use. I arrived here in the briefest time, and now I can't turn back.

Maybe we could run? Maybe I can pack a bag, run out the door, and tell him to floor it through the fields. We will live like star-crossed lovers running from the warning signs tailing us.

No. I couldn't do that to my parents. They would be devastated. I will take disappointment over devastation any day. With one last release of breath, I sign my death certificate. *Please be okay with this*, I think behind my tightly closed eyes.

"Honey? You all right?" My mother speaks first, and I open my eyes, swallowing past the lump in my throat. My mouth drops open, and I go to speak, but there's nothing but rattled breathing.

"That son of bitch," my father says in a low, incredulous tone. My eyes and my mother's fly to him.

"Stan?" My mother's eyes are drawn with worry; mine are shocked. My father rarely uses any strong language or even seems agitated, so his tense body and foul language is a first.

"I told him I wouldn't give my blessing, and that arrogant boy didn't listen." My dad pushes himself from the island and starts pacing. My heart drops out of my chest, landing in a pit in my stomach.

"What? Wait, what are we even talking about right now?" My mother shakes her head, looking back and forth between my father and me.

"Ben asked me to marry him, Mama," I whisper, one hand playing with my wedding finger, where there are still little scratches from the sugar on the peach ring. I don't know why, but it brings me some comfort.

"Oh, honey, well." She pauses, watching my father pace back and forth between us. His hands are making his hair a wild mess atop his head. My mother's voice is a mix of worry and a hint of understanding. She has to get it. My parents got married after knowing each other for three months. They were us. Weren't they?

Ben and I are young, and that plays into our need to be so consumed by one another, but it's what my heart is craving. Ben's name has been stitched into my heart since the night he showed up here and solidified that all my life I have never known something so cosmic and wild. That I have been missing him the entire time. We are entwined now. There is no way someone can break that connection. No one but me or Ben.

"Ray, don't tell me you are even going to entertain the idea of her and Ben. They don't know each other. And she has so much ahead of her. How is marrying some rock star going to work? It will ruin everything."

"It won't, please," I say, but they speak over me.

"But we agreed that whatever Sadie wanted to do in life, we would let her. We should at least hear what she has to say."

"Yes, please," I agree.

"No way, Ray. She can't. I won't let her throw it all away for some boy who's manipulated her into thinking she's in love."

"Dad, I am in—"

"How do you know they aren't in love? Who decides that?" They keep talking as if I am not standing a few feet away.

"We do! Her parents! We are supposed to stop her from making stupid mistakes, Ray!"

"Ben is not a mistake!" I find my voice, tired of being talked *about* and not *to*. Tired of not being heard. I have never yelled at my parents, but God, did I need to. They both look at me, stunned silent by my sudden outburst. "I love him, Papa. Trust me, I understand you think I'm making a mistake. I can't explain to you how much I have questioned my own sanity in the past twenty-four hours. Heck, in the past weeks since I first met him. But I love him, and I want this." I drop my shoulders and release the longest breath, one that has been hidden in chambers behind my lungs for years.

"Sadie, you are only nineteen. You have so much ahead of you. Don't you see that?" My dad's sad eyes search mine, and my heart breaks. I can see how much this is hurting him.

"I do. And that doesn't have to change. Marrying him isn't me signing away my life and my wants." I cross my arms over my body. I'm chilled to the bone now, shaking and consumed with a need to protect myself, to hold myself together as I brace for impact.

"But it does. Sadie, you'll have to compromise. You have to take on his wants and dreams, and he has to take on yours. Is he willing to make sacrifices? Is he willing to mold himself into the version of him that you want?" Dropping my arms, I tighten my hands at my sides. I love Ben for who he is: damaged, flawed, broken, kind, talented, smart, and all the things I ran from my entire life.

"I don't want him to change. He is flawed, yes, but we all are, and I choose him this way. He picked me, too, and we will work out all the trials that I'm sure will come."

"Some things are bigger than trials, Sadie. I think right now you are seeing this relationship in a bubble, but that will pop, and then you will be left with nothing but trouble." I shake my head. The only man in my life I have loved before Ben is now the one I want to protect my love from. My heart is broken in two.

"I am doing this. I finally want to do something for me and only me, and I'm sorry if it hurts you, but it would hurt me more to not be with him." I choke back the tears.

My mother doesn't hide hers; I hear her sobs and see her wiping tears away.

"All right. Then you are on your own. I can't support this. If you are going to marry him, you are on your own." The last tiny string that was holding the two halves of my heart together severs. My eyes begin to water, my lip trembling as I look at my mother, and she shudders.

"Stan." She touches his shoulder, but my father stands his ground.

"She is right. This is what she wants, and if so, then she can do it all on her own." I look to my mother once more, but she shakes her head.

"Honey, how about we take a minute?"

"No, Mama, it's fine." I stop her. Papa is right; Ben and I knew the risk going in. I don't hold back the tears. Rain starts to hit the window. Isn't that comical? The weather looks like the tragic scene in every movie you've ever seen. It pelts loudly, picking up with each passing minute that I stand here in silence.

"I love you both, and yes, this isn't like me. I know you're upset, but I love him, and I want this with him. For me. For us." I hesitate for a moment longer.

"Baby, we love you. We just want you to think this through." Mama speaks so softly.

"I did. I want him," I whisper, seeing his brown eyes in my head. I feel his kisses all over my skin. Hear him whispering those sweet words of love and praise. The way he adores me. It is my talisman, and I cling tightly to it.

"Then leave. If you are old enough to get married and make your own choices, you can leave," my father bites out, but there is no missing the way his lip slowly trembles behind his tough facade.

"Stan. Don't, please." Wanting to spare my mother another blow of heartache, I put on the brave face I always have, shake my head, and walk up to her.

"I love you, Mama." I wrap my arms tightly around her, sending everything I have in me into her. When I walk out that door, it will create a line in the sand, the first divide of our family.

Moments pass, and I finally let go and wipe away her tears. "I'll be okay," I tell her.

I look over at my father, but he keeps his head low and tilted slightly in the opposite direction, avoiding eye contact. Another shot to the soul. I back up slowly and leave the kitchen. I grab my purse, my keys, and the small bag I packed before Ben left. I open the door, and the sound is deafening, as is my mother's crying and her soft whispers asking my father to go after me and make this right. Taking one last breath, I step out, shut the door behind me, and make my way down the patio stairs. The rain starts to hammer down on me, and I'm drenched in seconds. I look up at the sky, and my tears mingle with the rain. The perfect daughter has created the biggest disaster in her family. The woman who learned to never let anyone down has single-handedly broken the two most important hearts she's ever known.

And now, I will run to him. I will fall into his arms and pray that he doesn't prove them right and me wrong. Dad is right: marriage calls for sacrifices, and I've taken the first step. I sacrificed my parents' approval and support to leap into my relationship with Ben headfirst.

Twenty

BEN

Leaving Sadie's house after we packed her a small bag is both terrifying and relieving. I've spent my entire life believing and preaching that love is a con, that the world lied to us, and now I am eating my own words. But each moment I spend with Sadie makes me realize that I don't want anything or anyone like I do her. She's my lifeline, the pulse in my chest, the blood rushing through my veins. If I don't have her, I will be as good as dead. I'm tortured in the best way by her. Sadie makes me believe that I have good left in me. That I can breathe and let my walls crumble when she is around. In the quiet nights since I have known her, when the world is asleep, my brain has searched and searched for reasons that I should end this. Reasons to run. To ruin it. To sabotage the one good thing I have let myself have—not just good, but life-altering. Sadie is a miracle that I can touch. She's sonnets and poems and the lyrics that I wish I could write, but I fall short every time because no words created since the beginning of time can describe Sadie. She is what life is meant to be lived for. I would be a fool to let that slip through my fingers.

I told Sadie I'd asked her father for her hand because I didn't want to lie to her. I want to honor Sadie. As I drive home, I replay all the wrongs I have done in my life, and the list is longer than the things I got right. All those demons I have—the ones that linger in my shadow and come out in my lowest moments—are things I will have to fix. I can desire to be the man she wants, but desire is just a wish without action.

I will have to fight to be worthy of keeping her. I have to do everything that I have been trained and programmed not to do. Love. Open parts of me I shielded from the world. All for her. If not, I could ruin her, and to ruin her would be to murder both our souls. Two graves and one gun, and I would be the one who pulled the trigger.

Sitting in my living room, I wait for Nick to walk in. I called him and said it was an emergency then hung up. That will get him here.

"You better be fucking bleeding out to hang up and then ignore my calls," he announces, swinging open the door.

"You're here. Good. I need a favor." I stand, and he looks at me incredulously, hands on his hips. He looks like a disappointed parent.

"You're not bleeding out, so I guess I need to beat your ass. You gave me a fucking heart attack, Ben."

I smile at him. "Hold on, because I might actually give you one in a second."

He tilts his head and shakes it at me. "Ben, what the fuck did you do?"

I grab my laptop and hand it to him. "I need you to find someone who is ordained and somewhere that can marry Sadie and me."

"What!" Nick's eyes are practically bulging out of his head.

"Yes, oh, and we want to do it in the next two hours or so. Thanks, man." I hand him the computer, but he stays stock-still, shock etched on his face.

"Are you fucking on something? Is this a joke? Does Sadie even know about this?"

I head to my bedroom down the hall and look for the suit I wore to a friend's wedding a few months back.

"She does. And we are doing it today!" I yell from inside my closet. He finally sets into motion, and I hear each boot-clad step he takes down the wooden hallway into my bedroom.

"This isn't right. Holy fuck. I leave you alone for less than a day, and now you want to get married. You need to stop and think about this." He sets the computer down and puts his hand on my chest, stopping me from laying the suit on the bed.

"Nick. I am not going to listen to anyone. You, her dad, anyone who wants to object isn't going to stop us. So you can help me as not only my employee but my best fucking friend, or she and I will do it without any of you." My jaw clenches.

"Fucking hell," he groans after a minute.

"Good. Now find me someone who is ordained. We can do the legal license as well."

"Are you kidding? You know that takes days, right?" he tells me, opening the laptop again.

"Fine, we will have a ceremony, and when the license comes, we'll sign it then."

"I am aging every fucking day at a rapid rate because of you, man," he grumbles.

"Good. Aging looks nice on you, buddy. Don't complain." I pat his shoulder and go to grab more things. Nick does as I ask, and once we get everything I need, I pace like a madman. I haven't heard from Sadie in almost an hour, and she told me she would call when it was good. How long is it going to be until it's good, and what does *good* even mean?

Shit. It isn't good. Good would mean I'd heard from her by now. I go to grab my phone off the counter when there is a knock on my door. I rush across my apartment and open the door.

Standing there, rain-soaked, is Sadie with tears in her eyes. Her body is trembling, and not an ounce of her is dry.

"Baby, what the hell. Come here." I reach for her and pull her into me and the apartment.

"I couldn't b-bring myself to come in yet, so I st-stayed out in the rain for a minute," she stutters, her chattering teeth loud. Nick rushes to my thermostat and turns up the heat.

"Fuck, you're going to get sick. Come on." I pick her up and carry us to my bathroom. I turn on the shower, shut and lock the door, and leave the bathroom fan off. The steam billows up around us as I strip her down to nothing. I've seen parts of her, so many, but never all of her completely naked. Once she is bare to me, I strip down as well. She wraps her arms around herself tighter, still chilled to the bone.

"Take a shower with me?" I ask for her permission. My hands cup her face, and the pads of my calloused thumbs run along the cheeks of the woman I love. Her nod is so subtle I almost don't catch it. I step in first before reaching out and taking her freezing, delicate hand in mine. I help her in, bringing her flush against my skin.

Never have two bodies felt more perfect together. We mold to one another in an unlearned and unrehearsed dance. We are so close that no amount of water or even air could pass between us. That's when I feel it. The hard thrumming against my chest. Sadie is sobbing. Her breathing is bereft, and it's everything I need to know. She picked me. The greater part of me feels guilty about this, but that selfish man—he closes his eyes tightly and thanks whatever power is out there that she chose me.

"Breathe, angel. Breathe," I whisper against her temple, peppering it with soft open-mouthed kisses.

"You should have seen his face. He was so hurt. I did that. I caused him that hurt," she cries, tightening herself around me. Inhaling, I get ready to say something I might regret.

"Sadie, we can wait. You don't have to do this. You know that. I can wait for us." Her head leaves my chest, and she looks up at me, her face tear-stained and red from the cold outside and the heat of the shower. Her bright blue orbs pierce through me, and it hurts to see that pain. I caused it. All of this. All because I wanted to make her mine and not give her the chance to run.

"No, Ben, no. I choose us. I choose you. You can't leave us," she says frantically, clawing at my back and trying to bring me closer.

Fuck. I'm really doing a great job of making her feel better. Bang-up job, buddy.

"I won't. I'm sorry. I just wanted to let you know I will respect what you want, and I don't want you to lose them so we can get married," I tell her. She shakes her head.

"This is the first time I've let my parents down. The most important people. I never wanted to be that person, but this is the first time I am doing something I want. For me. I guess I don't know how to come to terms with it. But I love you, Ben. I want us."

She repeats those words over and over. *I want. I want. I want.* She wants me. Leaning in, I kiss her, taking that soft, angelic face in my hands, and I taste the want. Our tongues dance, and this kiss, this is ours. We invented it, and we've perfected it to be something that only we will ever have, know, or crave.

"Make it stop. Make it all go quiet," she cries against my lips, and I know exactly what she wants. What she needs. I slowly walk her back to the bench in the shower, and when her legs hit the marble, I guide her down. I tower over her. How beautiful she looks when she is broken, and how twisted of me to love it. I will fix that pain. I will calm her worries as she settles my chaos. I take her chin between my thumb and pointer finger, lifting her head slowly. Her eyes peruse my body, taking in every inch of defined muscle, each piece of ink, even some of the scars I've won in my fights.

"I will always heal what I broke. You know that, right?" I tell her, and she nods ever so slightly.

"You have to," she whispers, swallowing deeply. Her eyes look over all the parts of me that she can see from the position I have her locked in.

"What are you thinking, angel?"

A tear slowly sneaks out of the corner of her eye and mingles with the water droplets from the shower. She sniffles.

"How beautiful you are. And how much I love you."

"You shouldn't tell me those things. I won't let you forget it. I will use it."

"Then do it. Use me."

"I don't want to use you right now, baby. I want to heal you." I run my thumb over her plump lips. These lips are all mine. Every inch of her is branded by me, and I can't wait to explore her pleasure. Explore the creature crafted just for me.

"Give me your hand," I tell her. Without hesitating, she does what I ask. Her long, slender fingers land in my palm, and I bring them to my lips then place her hand on my heart. I bend, my lips within inches of hers, the water that soaks my hair now dripping onto her face and chest.

"You have a grip on my heart. You have no idea how much it hurts me and soothes me all at once. It's us two now." Her breath catches, and she starts crying again, but this time it is in desperation.

"Please, please, please," she begs me, and I oblige.

"Keep your eyes on me." I drop to one knee and lay my hand against her ankle. I look back up: her lip is caught between her teeth, and her eyes have glazed over, the tears fading and lust replacing them. I slyly smirk up at her; my angel is fucking ravishing.

Goose bumps arise as I move my hand inch by inch over her shin and up the side of her calf and thigh.

"Spread your legs for me, angel." She does as I ask, her trembling knees parting. "Such a good girl. You're beautiful, you know that?" She doesn't respond, and I tut at her before dropping my head and nipping her thigh.

"Ow! Oh God. Yes."

"You know how many men would kill for the chance to touch you?"

She shakes her head back and forth slowly.

"The entire world, and I thank God they will never get the chance. I don't have enough time on my hands to end them all. I'd much rather spend that time between here." I bend, my head slightly tilted as I peer up at her. My lips kiss the top of her slit, and she thrusts forward.

"Ben!" The way she moans my name. My name. Her lips. I move back down to her inner thigh, and that's when the idea hits me. I start to lick, bite, and then suck. The entire time I do this, Sadie circles her hips, searching for relief.

Each time I move even slightly, I admire my work. I mark her in the most vulgar way. *B. E. N.* My name left on her inner thigh in hickeys.

"Look how beautiful that looks." I sit back. She is breathing heavily and staring at me, confused.

"W-what?" She looks down and sees what I did, and she, too, admires it, her nipples calling to me. They are peaked and a rosy shade against her skin. I lean in and take one between my teeth.

"Oh!" she cries, her head falling back against the shower wall. I flick at the puckered tip and heal it after each bite. Her hands skate to my hair and grip it tightly.

"Pull hard and hold tight, angel. I want to make this feel really good," I whisper against the skin between her breasts, above her heart.

"Please," she whines. Taking the pad of my thumb, I rub it in soft circles over her slit, and she shivers again.

"Beautiful. So fucking beautiful," I tell her. This time she agrees with a nod of her head. "You know how I taught you to play with your clit and use your fingers inside?"

"Mm-hmm."

"You are such a good girl. Responsive. And God, do you take instructions so well."

"B-Ben," she stammers.

"Good." I circle her clit with my thumb a few times, and her moaning fills the bathroom along with the steam from the hot water. A new wave of arousal spreads between her legs; if I circle it one more time, she will come apart in my hands, and I am not ready for that.

Moving down a little, I insert the tip of my middle finger. She's so fucking tight.

"Shit," I growl. Sadie adjusts a bit as I go the slightest bit deeper. "Is that okay?"

"Yes, it just feels different. But it's good different." I can't wait to show her the real difference.

"Good. Now, eyes on me. You look at me while I do this," I tell her.

"I would do anything for you." I use my free hand and cup the side of her cheek and the top of her neck, her ear sliding between my long fingers. "Such a good girl. Breathe in, real deep." She takes a deep breath, and when her chest rises to the hilt, I slide my finger all the way inside, curving up and finding that spot deep inside.

"Oh God! God! Ben!" She screams my name, and I swallow it with a messy kiss. I add pressure on her clit with my thumb, working both my thumb and finger to bring her close to the edge. She's warm, tight, and I want to be inside her then. I want to slide my finger from her and claim her. Slide my cock into her snug pussy and take her innocence.

"Ben, I think I am going to—"

"Ben, we have to get going! The officiant gave me a time." My entire body turns hotter than the water coming from the showerhead. Did Nick interrupt us? Fuck. I put my finger to her lips and mouth for her to be quiet. She does as she's told, and I keep finger-fucking her, making sure she gets to feel pleasure after everything today. My plan is to erase everything from her mind, everything but me.

Her brows are drawn in a pleasurable, tortured pain that shadows the contours of her face.

"We will be right out! Give us a minute," I holler over the water, working Sadie harder, and in seconds she detonates. I hurry to cup her mouth and stifle her sighs.

"Just like that, shh, ride it out for me." I coach her through the orgasm. Her core tightens and releases over and over again on my finger, and that death grip will end me. Sadie has me by the heart, throat, and fucking cock. I am at her mercy and will bend to her will.

"I love you, Ben." I will never get tired of her declaring her love for me. It is something I could listen to day in and day out.

"I love you," I tell her back, kissing her through her post-orgasm bliss. "Let me go get us some clothes before we go out there, all right?" She nods.

"I need to call Kate," she adds.

"I will have Nick give her a call. You wait here for me." I help her out of the shower and wrap her in a towel. I kiss the skin of her shoulders, then reluctantly I leave her. With a towel around my waist, I take our clothes from the bathroom and step into the living room.

"She all right?" Nick asks, and I give him a nod.

"She is. Hey, can you call Kate? She wants her to come here to talk."

"Sure can. But we only have an hour before we have to be at the courthouse. The rain is supposed to stop for three o'clock. Try to hurry." I raise my hand in understanding.

Every time we bring up Kate, Nick's energy shifts. After the first few times it happened, I realized what it was. He likes her. But she is with Eric, and I don't see that changing anytime soon. I want to ask him about it, but he will deny it. Nick doesn't talk about anything unless he feels it is necessary.

Nick is a man of few words and doesn't lean too heavily on anyone. Given his upbringing, it makes sense. I envy the type of man he is even though he had a troubled past. Nick is controlled. Grounded. Centered. All the things I hope I can achieve. That's what my music is for. The therapy. The medication. My on-again, off-again relationship with AA meetings. It all has to get me somewhere. Right?

With Sadie, I'm confident I can. I only hope my brain and heart will catch up with one another so I can be a man of my words. I start the washer and head back to my room, hearing him on the phone with Kate as I go. Nick's got it handled.

I throw on some gray sweatpants and a black V-neck shirt. I grab another pair of sweats and one of my band tees and make my way back to the bathroom. Opening the door, I see Sadie seated on the lip of the bathtub beside the shower. Her hands are in her lap, and she nervously picks at them; she is teary-eyed again, and I debate asking her what I can do, but maybe the best thing I can do right now is let her feel and tell me when she is ready to talk about it.

"Nick called Kate; from what I could hear she is on her way. Let's get you in some warm clothes. We don't have much time before the ceremony," I tell her. Her soft blue eyes travel to me, and she gives me a half smile.

"Thank you." Sadie is shutting down again. I felt her opening to me in the shower, but in the moment I left her alone, she's built up a wall. I have done many things in life that made me feel this low, but letting her down can't be one of them. To see how much this is hurting her only makes me want to call this all off. Does she really want this, or is she clinging to me because she is feeling pushed out? Is it because she feels I'm all she has now? Her parents will come around. And if they don't, I will make them. Sadie broke one of her most sacred values—letting her parents down. Who knew falling in love could be such a letdown? But she did that for me, and I will make sure that she doesn't regret it. Part of that? Getting her parents to come around.

I won't let Sadie lose everything because of me. My mom lost everything because of me. I can't let that happen to another woman I love.

"Can I dress you?" I ask her, taking her hand and helping her stand.

"Yes." Her voice is raspy and low. Setting the clothes on the counter, I take the sweatpants first. Dropping to my haunches, I let her lead. She lifts one leg, and I slide the material over her foot, repeating the action with the second foot. She holds herself up on my shoulders. I admire the smooth skin of her legs with each inch that I cover. When the pants are around her waist, I tighten them.

"Good thing my ass is big enough to keep these up." She laughs, and I shake my head with a smile.

"I have no complaints." I love Sadie's large breasts, round stomach, and full, curved ass, winding roads that all lead to perfect destinations.

"Of course you wouldn't." There is a little more lightness in her voice this time. *Keep her comfortable. Take care of her. That's what she needs*, I tell myself.

"Sadie!" Kate's voice comes bellowing through the apartment.

"That was fast. I forgot that she only lives a couple minutes away." Sadie chuckles.

"You think she is going to wring my neck?" I ask, standing and helping Sadie put my shirt on.

"I wouldn't rule it out." She shrugs.

"Great. Well, here we go." I am more worried about Kate's response then I was her parents. Why? Because Kate is demanding and unafraid to prove her point and go for the jugular. Sadie's parents don't seem like the kind to do that. I need to see if Sadie is more afraid of disappointment or anger.

"She's going to think we're crazy," Sadie whispers. I place my palm against her cheek and bend to place my forehead against hers.

"Then let's give the world hell," I tell her.

Her eyes close, and she smiles. "You're a professional."

I shrug. "Yep. Come on." I kiss her once on the lips before taking her hand and going to the living room. Here we go.

Twenty-one

SADIE

"Woah, wait, Sadie, you want to get married?" Kate asks. Her eyes widen so far, I'm afraid they may get stuck that way.

"Yes. We do." I lift my head and stay firm. Kate is going to either be supportive or lay into me far worse than my parents did. I disappointed my parents. Kate? Kate doesn't get disappointed, she gets mad, and she makes sure everyone in a twenty-mile radius hears what she thinks.

"I take you to one concert and you end up marrying the guy? That's the last time I get you out of the house," she says, scoffing. Nick, Ben, and I all look at one another, and after a few seconds we all start laughing. Kate stops pacing a hole in the floor and looks at us.

"What is so funny!" I lift my hand and try to stop my laughter. Part of me is laughing because it was truly funny, but I also feel delirious. Today has been a whirlwind of emotions, from waking up to a proposal to watching my parents lose all faith in me to being intimate and vulnerable with Ben. I'm overstimulated, tired, and sad, but overall, I'm in love. My heart is devastated over my parents, but I can't help but feel proud. Being with Ben and deciding to prove my parents—and anyone else—wrong is something I did for me. I picked love over all other things. Over logic, over my parents, over the life I thought I should have. I chose the good, the bad, and the ugly, and I chose to do that with Ben.

"Nothing. It's funny because you have a point."

"Well, I am glad you find this funny, but why can't you just date? This isn't the eighteen hundreds, guys. You know dating is a thing, right?"

"Why can't we get married? Why is that such a fucking issue for everyone except the two people it will affect if it goes to shit?" Ben speaks up; he is growing agitated now.

"Because—well, because!" That's all Kate can say, looking defeated. What is one reason we shouldn't? Everyone is telling us that we are too young, that marriage is a compromise and so much more, but no one will tell us what it is that we are going to compromise on.

"Kate. I love you. I love my parents. I hope you guys know that I appreciate you looking out for me. But this is the first time I am doing something that I want to do. Something that makes me happy. He makes me really, really happy, Kate."

I'm standing in front of her, with her hands in mine. Both of us have tears in our eyes. Our years of friendship have been filled with so much love and a sisterhood that I grew up wishing I could have.

Every person in my life means so much to me, to the point that my heart could burst, and that is undoubtedly my biggest weakness. An empathetic heart is often the one that gets used, abused, and broken the most. Caring for others and putting their needs first doesn't always get you rewarded; in fact, most times, it leaves you bleeding and alone.

"Damn you, Sadie." She takes one of her hands from mine and wipes away a fallen tear. Kate has never been a crier.

"I need someone in my corner, and you are my best friend. Please, trust me." Her eyes look to Ben and Nick behind me then back to me.

"Fine, but I swear to the gods above, Ben, if you hurt her, I will castrate you myself and put it in a blender." She sniffles through her warning.

"You have my word. Scout's honor," Ben says behind me, and I smile.

"I guess we get you married. Yup. I guess that's what we're doing." She is mostly talking to herself, processing everything. A slight sting hits me, realizing I won't have my parents there.

This isn't what I thought would happen. Having my parents beside me at my wedding has always been included in my dreams of the future. There was going to be a soft breeze blowing around my husband and me in the wooded chapel built in the Portland forest. But plans change, and for the first time the details I've calculated about the outcome of my life are unraveling before me, showing me life will never be what I plan it. But that doesn't mean the new plan isn't going to be as beautiful. As painful as it may be to not have my mother and father with me, I have him. Ben Cooper. He will be right there with me.

* * *

"Thank you for letting me borrow this dress," I say to Kate as she curls the last strand of my hair. The dress is a maxi style, the straps are thin, and the top hugs my breasts like glue with braided trim woven around my breasts to give the dress more shape.

"You keep it. It looks better on you. My boobs are too small for it." I reach up and place my hand on hers where it sits on my shoulder. She is looking at me in the mirror. We came back to her place to get ready, agreeing to meet Ben and Nick on the steps of the courthouse at three. We have a few minutes left to head out the door, but I need time alone with her.

"Thank you. I needed you, and you didn't walk away." I start to tear up again. No. *No.* I don't want to cry again.

"They will come around. I promise," she comforts me. Kate squeezes my shoulders, kisses the top of my head, then finishes the last touches on my hair. We sit in comfortable silence.

God, I hope she is right.

When we climb out of the car, I see Ben first. He's in a black suit, with a white button-up shirt, a black tie, and shiny dress shoes. He looks handsome standing on the steps of the courthouse, and my heart picks up speed. In a few minutes, he will be all mine, and that thought wrecks me in all the right ways. Nick stands behind him, and when I smile at him, he returns it with a wink.

"Here's to us and nights out at concerts," Kate whispers in my ear teasingly, and we giggle. Happiness surrounds us, and even though there is a big hole missing, everyone here is doing their best to fill it with love and acceptance. She walks me up the steps, and we hug before she lets Ben take over. He softly takes me and pulls me flush against him. There is nothing traditional about today, all the way down to how he holds me close to him, leaving no room between us.

"I got you now, trust me, angel," he whispers, and I visibly relax, falling into the arms of my best friend.

The officiant begins, and in the late afternoon sun on a Saturday, we get married with only a few witnesses, two simple gold bands, and our young, untainted love, declaring that it is officially us against the world.

We decided that we wouldn't exchange vows at the ceremony; instead, we want to do that on our own time. Intimacy and privacy will be our number-one priority. Our connection will be made in those sacred moments.

"Sadie Cooper. Wow. The woman who changed the man," Nick teases once the ceremony is over, enfolding me in his arms. Ben is on a call with his bandmates, filling them in, and Kate left to get dinner with her family for her mother's birthday. It was hard to let her go, but I'm thankful to know that she is in my corner.

"No, he's changing me." I smile, returning his embrace. I've grown comfortable with Nick; at first, I was a little intimidated by his rough exterior, but over the past two weeks, we have grown closer, and I adore how he takes care of Ben.

"If he ever gives you shit, I'll kick his ass."

"You love him too much to do that." I wink.

"Don't tell him, but I may love you more." He returns my smile.

"Thank you for being good to him. I think he looks at you like a father figure, even though he doesn't say it," I admit as I watch Ben smile down the steps as he tells the guys what we did—given his infectious grin, I assume it's all congratulations and a bit of hazing. He looks so handsome, utterly carefree, and it melts me. I love him.

"I love him like a son, and sometimes he tests me like a son, so I'd think so."

"Yup." We both laugh, and Ben makes his way in our direction.

"Can I have time with my wife now?"

"Sorry." Nick shrugs.

"No, you're not." Ben laughs, pulling me into him, and I close my eyes against his warmth. The rain has stopped, but the clouds still hover over us. I take in a deep inhale of his scent, and it smells like . . . home.

"True. Now come on. It's almost four, and we have to drive into Seattle."

"Seattle, why?" I lean back slightly and look up at him.

"Because I got us a suite in a luxury hotel. You think I'm taking you back to my apartment on our wedding night? Hell no." He shakes his head. "I'm taking you for a small honeymoon before I leave tomorrow." Caught up in all that's happened today, I forgot he leaves on tour again tomorrow. If I didn't have finals coming up, I would go with him; that way, we wouldn't have to leave each other right after we got married. But such is life, and we knew what this meant. Married or not, we have lives to live that require we work extra hard. As much as I want to go with Ben, I still want my career.

"You didn't have to do that. You could have taken us home," I whisper, playing with his tie. A blush breaks out over my skin, heating my body. I know what comes tonight, and now that the wedding is over, reality is sinking in. Tonight, I will finally give myself to him—all of me.

"All right, there is a car in the underground garage, and it's ready to go. Be back here by two o'clock tomorrow; the bus leaves at two thirty." Nick interrupts to hand us the car keys.

"I'll see you then. Thanks, man." We share quick hugs with Nick, then he is gone.

"I want to make sure tonight is perfect for you." Standing on my tiptoes, I feel my body flame with arousal, anxious to become his completely.

"Take me away, then." I blush more. The truth is, I'm petrified knowing I'm going to have sex. Ben growls, taking my lips in a feverish kiss, our tongues at war and our hands clawing to get closer.

Our lips drag apart, my body still flush against his bent frame.

"Fuck." Ben separates us and takes a deep breath, trying to calm down. I am practically panting. After the shower we shared, I want to get to that hotel and share more with him. I want to feel all of the man I love and offer myself up to him like a beautiful sacrifice.

"Let's go," he growls, taking my hand. He is as starved for us as I am.

"Please." With that, we are off to Seattle.

* * *

I'm a complete wreck. We left right after our heated kiss, and my stomach's been in knots the entire drive. Ben sings almost every song on the radio to me, and we share laughs and intimate touches. We really don't speak much about what's going to happen in the hotel room, but my mind is sure having a fit over it.

We pull up to the hotel, and I admire the beautiful glass high-rise. The sky is dark and the clouds are heavy with rain, and I can smell the ocean from here. I stay a few steps behind Ben, my hand in his as I take in the elegant lobby. The floors are a beautiful white marble, and the ceiling has multiple intricately designed chandeliers hanging down.

The bellhop loads up the cart with our two small bags; we could have carried them ourselves, but that's not the kind of place this is. I thank the bellhop while Ben checks us in. In what seems like mere seconds, we are in the elevator. The ride is quiet, but our discreet touches feel loud. His hand rests on my hip with my back touching his front. He plants kisses on my shoulders sporadically and massages the skin of my hip. I can't help but shiver.

As each floor takes us closer and closer to our room, my stomach gets tighter with nerves and my heart races at an uncontrollable rate. The door slides open, and Ben grabs our bags and tips the bellhop.

"I got it from here, thank you." I gulp when his hand takes mine. "Don't be scared. Breathe, angel." Sensing my uneasiness at the threshold of the closed door, he tries to calm me. Swinging the door open, he sets the bags down inside, freeing up his hands so he can scoop me up. I yelp and giggle, my feet dangling and my arms around his neck. "Now come on."

Once in the hotel room, he places me back on my feet, and I scan the crisp white and silver accents adorning the room. The bed is a silver four-poster with a bright white duvet paired nicely with gray and white pillows that accentuate the bed. Walking over to the window, I look at the scenery. The ocean water is dark. The floor-to-ceiling windows in the presidential suite have the clearest view of Seattle.

All the details, from the fireplace to the mirrored nightstands topped with stunning silver lamps, are riddled with a sense of romance.

"What do you think, angel?" Ben whispers behind me, his hands on my shoulders rubbing little circles.

"Ben, this is beautiful. You didn't have to spend this much on me," I admit, looking to the left of me, where the tiny kitchen and dining area are located.

"I only get one night with my wife before I go back on tour. I want tonight and tomorrow morning to be the best we've ever had." I blush, turning around and banding my arms around his neck, my body extending on the tips of my toes to meet his bent frame for a kiss.

Dancing his tongue against the seam of my lips, he asks for

entrance, and I grant it without hesitation. My stomach is coiling in knots, my fear building at the same time as my arousal—yearning with pure lust for my husband.

We really did it; we got married and declared our love to one another. A young love, deep and running into a passionate storm.

"Mmm, what do you want to do? We can go to dinner, or we can order room service and watch a movie?" He breaks our connection, and I cry at the loss. As he peers down at me with his hungry eyes, my skin prickles. His hands roam my body aimlessly.

My mind is hyperaware of what I want. I've waited for this since I knew what wanting a touch was. I don't want to wait anymore, but I feel reserved. I've never done this before; how do I even start? Biting my lip, I drop my eyes to the buttons of his dress shirt. We've been intimate before, but this is—different.

"Maybe we could . . ." I trail off, unbuttoning the first button slowly, my eyes traveling up as I undo each one. I keep going until I am under his tie. I look right at him then.

His throat bobs, and he eyes me hungrily. I mimic that look, wanting him badly, his touch so close I can almost taste it.

"Maybe we could make love now." I blush, pushing through my wall of insecurities. He smirks at me, and I'm not sure if he's laughing at my blatant lack of experience or if he likes that idea. Either way, I'm growing more nervous with each passing second.

"Sorry, I probably sound stupid. I'm really scared . . ." I trail off, starting to button his shirt back up. I'm sure spending tonight with a virgin isn't going to be fun for him with all his experience.

"Baby, don't be scared. I want to make love to you, but I only want to if you're ready. I don't want to rush you."

"Ben, we got married after two weeks of knowing each other. I think it's safe to say you aren't rushing me," I joke, stepping back, completely out of my element.

"Hey, why are you scared? What's going on in there?" He kneels in front of the bed as I sit. I'm not even sure what's going on in here. I'm all over the place. I'm elated and in love, terrified and insecure, ready to give myself but unsure how to. I'm not ready to be ready, but oh, am I ready.

"I want you, but I don't know how. I'm scared . . ."

"You're scared of me?" he questions, and I cradle his face gently.

"No, no, not that. Ben, you've had tons of women, more than I care to think about, and I don't want to be compared or feel subpar to the best you've had." Once I say how I'm feeling out loud, I feel less heavy. I'm still a young woman trying to find the right way to womanhood.

"Sadie, I don't want anyone but you. I married you so I could claim that forever. Before you was nothing compared to what it's going to be like with you." My eyes pivot back and forth quickly over his face.

"You'll be patient with my inexperience?" I gulp nervously.

"Sadie, I don't like this. I fucking hate when you're insecure. You're more than exceptional: you're the perfect aphrodisiac. You aren't inexperienced. You are innocent, and that's mine now," he tells me, his face still wedged between my hands, his brown eyes lusting over me. I feel that look deep in my soul.

"Okay." I nod. It's truly amazing how just a few words from him can reset me and build me up. Tonight, he is choosing me; today he chose me forever. Ben is a man who does what he wants and doesn't care who he leaves hurt in his wake, so if he really didn't want me, all of me, he would never have asked me to marry him.

"Do you trust me?"

"Of course, more than anyone."

"Good." He stands over me, removing his tie and the rest of his shirt. His lean abs bare themselves to me, and I gush on the inside, loving his tall, lean rock star body.

"Undo my belt, baby." With trembling hands, I take hold of the buckle. I watch him watch me as I undo his belt clumsily. "Don't be shy; don't be afraid. It's you and me, Sadie," he whispers, his thumb grazing my cheek.

Nodding, I undo his belt, the button, then the zipper. His boxer briefs show slightly, and I gulp. He is starting to grow under my hungry gaze.

"Ben, wait. Um, can I go freshen up real quick?" My voice is a hushed tremble on a rushed breath.

"You still with me?" Pulling me from the bed, he brings me flush against him.

"Yes, I am."

"We are on your time. You call the shots, Sadie. You are in charge." He hands over the power to me, and I ease up a bit.

"Thank you." I kiss his chest and walk away slowly, looking up at him before I slide the frosted glass door shut. He smiles and nods, and that damn smile grips my heart. Finally, alone in the bathroom, I release a deep breath and grab the lip of the sink. I may actually puke. What do I do now? My first thought goes to what to wear. I have no lingerie. I don't have anything sexy other than a basic pair of undergarments. Is that really a thing? Wearing lingerie on your wedding night? Oh lord, I am too in my head.

"Crap, crap, crap." Leaning toward the mirror, I straighten my arms and grip the sink tighter. Looking at my reflection, I scold myself. "Don't be afraid. Be who Ben makes you want to be. Confident, Sadie. Be confident." I talk myself off the ledge a little bit.

I can't seem to properly wrap my head around anything for a multitude of reasons. I'm afraid of myself and my lack of ability to please Ben. Pile that on my insecurities and you get a full-fledged panic attack. But I have nowhere to run, and I can't turn back now, nor do I want to, so I need to buck up and get on with it. This is the moment where I become a new version of myself—a better one. With one more deep breath, I blink tight and release the sink from my now red hands. I strip down to nothing. I take off the dress, my panties, my strapless bra. Everything. My flesh is his for the taking. No barriers. He has seen it before, but somehow this feels like the most vulnerable way he could ever see me.

I'm sure this means more to me than it does to Ben, because he has had his first time. I'm in love, and it's different when it's your first time. I peer out and see him looking out the windows. "Ben?"

"Hmm, what's up, angel?" He turns his attention back to me, seeing only my head. He sits up on the edge of the bed. Sensing my hesitation, he guides me—thank God, because I have no idea what I'm doing here. "Come here." He signals me with his words and a small flick of his fingers.

Nodding, I step out, my hands in knots covering my most intimate parts. I haven't brought my eyes up from the floor when I hear him groan.

"Fuck." Worried, I look up, still using one arm to cover my chest and the other to safeguard my bottom half. He's grinning.

"What?" I ask frantically. He stands quickly, reaching me with only four strides; I purposely count them as a way to distract myself. I back into the wall next to the bathroom, keeping myself covered. Did I do this all wrong? Sure, Ben has seen me naked, but was he hoping for me to be wearing something sexy?

"Are you kidding me?"

I'm such an idiot. "I'm sorry, I didn't have time to buy anything." I wanted to make this special, but I don't know what that would entail.

"Are you kidding me, Sadie? You look like an angel. Like mine. You bring me to my knees with your body, but it's different now."

"How? Is there something wrong?" My throat feels like it's going to come out of my mouth, and my stomach is in coils of nerves. I am a curvy woman, not made like the models that he is used to, and for the first time I feel wary and insecure.

"No. It's because now, I've made it mine. Forever." With that, his grin fades, and I realize what I saw on his face was joy, not laughter. He grabs my wrist, rips my hands from my body, and drops to his knees. I stand, vulnerable.

"Look at these legs." His hands trail from my ankles up to the apex of my thighs. "Look at this beautiful pussy, made for only me." His lips come down on me, kissing me right over my patch of hair.

I jolt back harder against the wall, the action so intimate I can't help it. Each time he does this, I nearly pass out. It feels so good. Every time, it feels brand new. Will it always be like this?

"These hips, they were made to fit my hands." He grips my hips then squeezes my ass. "This stomach, curvy and feminine, this belly button." He licks the skin, and I watch, completely removed from reality. I want to be made a woman, a wife who gives pleasure to her soul mate—her husband.

"That feels good," I moan, my hands digging in his hair as his tongue lashes against my skin.

"Your breasts fit perfectly in my hands. Look at that, Sadie." He cups my breast in one hand as the other massages my hip. That's when I feel that confidence I've been craving like a drug.

"Kiss me." I lick my dry lips.

"Where?"

"Everywhere."

"Forever, angel." With no more words, he finishes undressing, removing any barrier between us. Stripped to nothing, he lays me down on the sea of blankets.

"My everything laid under me, surrounded in white. My virgin. My wife," he whispers, his hand running up and down his shaft. He's larger than average. He's at least nine inches and thick. I know this is going to hurt me.

"Relax, it's you and me, Sadie. I promise to take care of you."

"I trust you."

"Open your pretty little legs," he tells me, and I obey.

"Like this?" I seek guidance, planting my feet shoulder-width apart and spreading my knees.

"Yes, just like that." He looks me over, spending time on each part of my body. Dropping to his knees, he grabs my hips and drags me to the edge of the bed, my legs still bent as he pulls me lazily to him.

"So beautiful," he murmurs. I lift my head as far as I can and watch him descend on me.

"Oh! Oh my god!" I cry, the velvet feel of his tongue spreading my lips and circling my clit, catapulting me off the bed.

"Say my name, baby," he moans into my core, his thick finger slowly entering me. I writhe, the sensation slightly uncomfortable yet incredible.

"Ben, Ben!" He increases his speed on my clit, licking and sucking hard, alternating the action enough to keep me chasing the tingle that builds in my stomach. The room feels dark; only a small tunnel of light filters through my vision. Adding a second finger and more pressure on my clit, he reaches his tattooed arm up to grab my breast.

"Ben, it feels different," I admit, unafraid. Earlier I had the tingle, but this time, it's more intense, and my center feels more sensitive than before.

"That's good. Chase it, baby, chase that feeling and come on my tongue." Gripping his hair, I move my hips in tandem with his tongue, and I let myself feel everything. He pinches my nipple, the pain adding to the pleasure on my clit, and I scream.

"Ben! Right there!" I scream out, my stomach tightening and my core shaking. Peering down, I see my orgasm coating his nose and mouth. Is that normal? I ride out the orgasm, my toes curling and my fingers going numb in the sheet. That feeling was unbelievable; I swear I floated from my body. "Oh . . ." I slow my hips, and his fingers draw lazy circles around my pulsing entrance. Lifting his face a bit, he wipes his mouth against my thigh.

"So good. Such a good little wife." I shake my head, still dazed.

He climbs up my body, kissing my skin as he goes. Stopping on my breast, he licks around my hard nipple. I feel his cock against my clit, and my whole body lights a new flame.

Lying beside me, he runs his large, strong hands down my stomach, squeezing and releasing the extra flesh. His fingers reach my pelvic bone, and he rubs more circles around my swollen clit.

"You're beautiful, Sadie. I'm never going to be able to quit you," he admits, our lips barely touching. Reaching my hands up in his hair, I make direct eye contact with him. We fall silent for a moment as he circles my clit before moving down to my entrance.

"We can't quit now, it's legal, baby," I tease.

"It is. You are mine. Come again like a good wife would for her husband." My eyes roll back the second he starts to relentlessly rub my clit.

* * *

I run my hand over his cock as I come down from another high, breathing heavily as my fingers touch the warm skin of the smooth, pronounced head. This is the first time I have touched him this way. I picture what it will feel like when he's inside me, and I quiver from head to toe. I get the hype now; I understand why people can't resist this temptation. I've only had a glimpse, a small taste, and I'm starving for the entire meal.

"I want you. Let me have you?" Climbing between my legs, he settles himself on his calves, his hands running up and down my thighs.

"Is it going to hurt?" I mumble in fear.

"Yes, it will, but I promise I'll go slow. I'll take care of you, angel." I trust him. I don't know what kind of lover my husband will be yet, but in a few seconds I will. In a few short moments, I will be a woman—his woman.

"Relax. Deep breaths." He kneads my sides first then trails his hands up the center of my stomach and over my breasts, squeezing and pinching as he goes. The sensation has me even more wet. I hope that and the two explosive orgasms I've had will help with the pain.

I nod, staring up into his brown eyes. "Okay." He nods with me. He maneuvers himself between my legs, his cock sliding up and down my sensitive clit, increasing my desire tenfold. Hovering above me on his extended arms, he never breaks eye contact with me.

"You need to talk to me, Sadie. Tell me if it's too much so I can take care of you, okay?" I place my hands on his face, submitting to him completely and putting all the trust I have in his hands.

"I promise." My nerves grow wild, feelings raging inside me—fear, excitement, and love. I feel every emotion lying under my husband.

Reaching between us, he breaks our eye contact for a moment, his head tilting down but staying in my hands. I follow his gaze and watch him grab his cock. He takes it and runs it up and down my slit. Wetting his tip, he coats himself in my arousal, and I whimper. It feels unbelievably good.

With one more look between us, he lines himself up at my entrance. Focusing in on me, he drops his mouth open and slides his wide head inside me, pushing me open, and I can't help but cry out. Oh my god, that's painful.

"Ow, Ben!" I try to slide out from underneath him to stop the burning pain that starts from my core and disperses through my entire bottom half.

"Angel, you need to relax. I haven't even taken your virginity. I need you to breathe and relax your body." He peppers my face with kisses. Taking one of my hands, he extends it above my head and digs it into the bed with his weight.

"Please keep going." Without words, he enters me more.

"Fuck, Sadie!" He curses my name, and I feel fuller; he has to be all the way in. I feel wet tears roll down the sides of my face and disappear into my hair. I hate that I'm crying, but the pinching pain and the sting is nearly unbearable.

"I'm there. This is going to hurt, baby. Can you breathe with me?" Nodding, I brace myself, doing my best to relax. With one more hard thrust, I feel my insides burn, filled past the point of return.

"Ahh!" I scream out, crying a little more.

"Shh, that was so good, angel, you're there. Such a good girl." I wish I could feel anything but the pain right now. Staying still, he doesn't move inside me, giving me a moment to adjust. I look up into his longing eyes and see his guilt. He drops his head and gently laps up my tears with his tongue.

"I'm sorry. I know it doesn't feel good, but it will. Relax, angel, and let me help you."

"I can't, it hurts too much to relax." I've surpassed feeling like a complete idiot. This is mortifying because I don't know what I'm doing. It's more embarrassing that I can't even let my husband make love to me without crying like this. I tuck my head in shame. Undoubtedly, the connection feels amazing, and I want to enjoy each moment, but the pain is so prominent that I can't focus.

"Want me to stop?" He kisses my lips, lingering for a moment. There is a long debate in my mind. No. That's not what I want. My body does, because she is struggling to take the man that he is. But my heart—she knows better. She is louder.

"No, I want this, I do. But I need you to make it feel better."

"It will. God, look at you." Ben looks me over, and I smile sweetly at him. There is adoration and appreciation for me in his gaze. I wish I could take a picture of this moment and never forget that exact look. "You belong in my fucking soul." He lets out a moan, and those words ignite my insides, making me painfully but deliciously press upward against his cock. I focus on our connection—we're consumed with one another.

"I fell for your heart first, then for your words. It was all-consuming and reckless. I fell in love backward, and now I'm falling headfirst into your depths," I confess.

"I was never made to get it right, but somehow I did." He starts to increase the pace of his thrusts. On the borderline of pain and pleasure, I writhe under him, his cock inside me filling me. "Sadie, you're mine. Every damn inch," he whispers, his eyes on me the entire time. Using his hand, he explores my curves, spending time on my breasts and hips, then, lifting my thigh, he finds the perfect pace. The feeling of pain begins to slowly dissipate. Pleasure is taking over. A sheen of sweat covers our bodies, and the room feels hot. It's a strange, almost abstract feeling being so completely connected to someone. Not only are we physically connected, we're emotionally in tune to the point where I only see, feel, hear, and want Ben, as he wants me.

This is what love is. It's the invincible feeling that you always chase. The desire that even the littlest things they do can bring. The way you feel you are no longer an individual but a part of someone else. Ben and I are extensions of each other; where he ends is where I begin, and that alone is inconceivable. I'll never be able to find enough words to do this feeling justice.

"I love you," I repeat. All the things I feel, I want him to feel too.

"I love you, too, Mrs. Cooper." He winks and drives his hips home, thrusting into me with blunt force.

"Ahh! Baby!" I scream out, my back leaving the bed and my eyes closing.

"You like that? My pretty baby likes it rough?" I blush.

"Ben..."

"Don't blush. This is real, so damn real." He groans, sliding in and out slowly this time, altering his thrust. My legs are going numb with the intense sensation, and I try to stay focused, but it's impossible with his skillful hips and dirty words.

"Make me come. I want to feel it for the first time with you inside me."

"Come on my cock, let it go." Leaning up, he grabs my hips and starts to slam into me without missing a beat.

"Look at your damn body, Sadie. Fuck, you're a goddess." I reach up and grab my breasts. "Dirty little angel. Like that, squeeze your tits like I like it, baby."

"Oh my god!"

"No, baby, it's Ben." He laughs, taking one hand from my hip to graze the back of his middle knuckle against my clit, and with that, I orgasm without warning. The build was so fast, I didn't have enough time to prepare myself. "I'm ruined because of you—fucking addicted."

I feel my orgasm from my head to the tips of my curled toes.

"Shit!" Before I've even come down, he pulls out, and I cry out.

"What, baby?" I ask. My breathing is labored, and my eyes are fuzzy. I try to get him back.

"I didn't wear a condom. I need to come, baby, can I come on your stomach?" he asks, stroking himself.

Biting my lip, I shake my head. "No, come in me. I'm not ovulating, it's okay."

I am not on birth control, but being in the medical field and always wanting to be prepared for my menstrual cycle, I'm a counter.

"Fuck, are you sure, angel?" he questions, but before I can even answer, he enters me again.

"I'm positive."

"Fuck, lay back, let me see that body, Sadie." I fall back down as his hand grips my stomach, and his thrusts become choppy. Within seconds, he groans, throwing his head back and letting my name slip past his lips.

I bite my lip, watching him orgasm. Seeing it is insanely raw. I don't know how to explain it. My stomach warms as his hot spurts of come shoot into me, leaving me in a coil of butterflies.

Today I became Mrs. Ben Cooper, and for the first time, I felt the touch of true love.

Everything that happened today, even the heartbreak, will be worth it, because now is perfect.

Twenty-two

BEN

Sadie lies beside me, asleep, and the image of her under me as I took away her innocence and made her mine for good plays on a constant reel in my head. She drifted off after she let me take her a second time. Her poor body is going to be sore tomorrow, and fuck if that doesn't excite me. What a bastard I am.

My wife. I'm never going to get tired of those words.

I wish I didn't have to leave; more than anything, I want to drag her on tour with me. I worry what being away from her will do to my mental health. The drugs are still there, the need to do them is still there, but only when she isn't around. My rage disorder takes over sometimes when I least expect it, and what will I do then? More therapy. More AA meetings. It may even be time for a medication change. There are so many things that I still need to work on.

"You're thinking of something. What is it?" Sadie whispers in her post-slumber voice. I didn't even see her stir.

"You were supposed to get more sleep before dinner."

"I couldn't stay asleep knowing you were right here for me to take advantage of." Her hand roams over my flat abs, stopping right above my cock. As she trails her fingers across my stomach, my cock stirs, and I get hard again. Damn it.

"You're not ready for more yet. You're going to be way too sore." I groan as she grips me tightly. "Shit."

"I can use my mouth or my hands. Maybe even my breasts." My brain is going foggy, and she isn't helping. She's still so innocent, yet curious, and it has me by the damn throat.

"You're a bad little thing. You love my cock in you?" Her stroking slows down. Looking down, she blushes and curls her lip.

"That's . . . when you do that, it's . . ." Sadie struggles.

"Sexy? You can say you like dirty talk."

"But it doesn't seem normal," she confesses, circling her thumb around my tip, causing my entire body to shiver.

"You expressing yourself, your desires, is normal. I will teach you how to feel more confident with your wants."

She whimpers, climbing me then straddling my hips. My cock is wedged against her swollen core. "Can I confess something to you without you looking at me differently?"

"Of course. You can always trust me, angel." Reaching up, I graze the tips of her tight nipples. Her curvy thighs tighten around my hips with the simple touch, and her entire body is recharged.

"It turns me on, this . . ." She begins to fuck my cock against her clit, sliding my shaft between her lips.

"So fucking sexy, fuck, baby, take what you want from me," I say through a moan, watching her face contort with pleasure.

"I want to do this every day." I knew that somewhere inside my good girl Sadie there was a bad girl waiting to get out. The rock star's wife was hiding in the shadows, waiting for a sinner like me to rock her world and flip her upside down.

"We can do this every fucking day, and I will never complain," I groan, dropping my head back and swallowing more moans.

"Vows, tell me them," she says, still lazily gliding against my shaft. Her eyes widen, and that plump lip is caught between her teeth.

"I promise to love you through the hard times, the bad times, the fucking great times. Fuck," I hiss when she reaches down and circles the tip of my cock with her thumb each time she slides down. "I will worship you like you deserve and never let you live a day without knowing your worth. I'll live this life for you, with you, and beside you, Sadie. Now you, tell me your promise." I grab her hips again and watch her intently.

"I promise to never let you go. I will be your family, and I will give you a safe place to come home to every night. I'll be your best friend, your muse, your everything." I trace my thumb over the soft skin of her inner stomach, between her hip and pubic bone. "I will show you real love every minute, every hour, every day." Intimately, in the confines of this room with no one else around, we share our vows. Just like everything we have done, it's unorthodox, but it's exactly who we are.

***

The hotel bar is convenient, so we pick there to eat. Sadie gets a sweet tea, and I order myself a beer. Her crystal-blue eyes roam all over the dining area, taking in the lights, the people, and the scenery outside the window, but my focus is on her, enjoying the best view in the entire world.

Apparently, Kate added some clothes to Sadie's small bag. The tight-fitting red dress she's wearing hugs her hips perfectly, showing a generous amount of cleavage and the roundness of her ass. She wears red lipstick to match and has teased her hair. I'm not complaining about what she's wearing. This isn't how she usually dresses, but I like the innocent Sadie too; it's the only way I've known her.

I watched the way she checked herself out in the mirror before we left the room. She was glowing, and her confidence was evident. She not only feels sexy, but I see the new woman in her, and, like a bastard, I want to bang my chest knowing I'm the one who made her a woman.

Reaching over the table, I grab her hand and kiss the back, bringing her focus back to me. "You look beautiful."

"You look handsome." I went with casual black skinny jeans, a cream shirt, and a leather jacket. Compared to her, I look like a normal guy out of his league. "I'm ready to eat. I'm starved," she adds, running her nails over the back of my hand.

"Me, too, we worked up quite an appetite because someone couldn't behave and keep her hands to herself." I wiggle my brows, and she laughs.

"Whatever, you're as bad as me. Anyway, can you believe we're married?"

"Yes and no. It's a bit surreal." I take a swig of my beer. "You doing okay? You want to talk about your parents? You haven't told me much, Sadie." Her face drops; long gone is the newlywed glow. We're supposed to be stuck in marital bliss, but I won't leave for this tour without making sure she is okay.

"There isn't much to say. They were worried. My father more than anyone. He is scared, and I don't blame him. I am too." She rubs her lips together, takes a sip of her drink, and continues. I don't interrupt. "I've never done something that my parents disapproved of. I lived for their approval. My father just doesn't want me to get hurt."

She looks at the table next to us. The couple there are laughing loud enough to gain her attention. Her father knows what a risk I am; what if Sadie thinks that too? I silence the doubt instantly. She still believes the good is greater than the risk.

"He told me to leave, so after you leave tomorrow, I'm going to stay with Kate. She went to my place tonight to pack a couple bags," she adds. My brows draw in.

"You aren't staying with Kate, angel, you're staying at our home." I take her hand and bring it to my lips.

"I don't want to barge in and take up your space." She laughs. I chuckle back.

"Sadie. We got married. Did you think nothing was going to change? That we would live in different places?"

She shrugs. "I don't know. I have no idea what comes next." There is so much worry and hurt to unpack here, and right now Sadie is looking for a beacon in the night.

"What comes next is we take it day by day. You continue school. I go on these next tour dates and then come home. Until then, you will barge in and take up all our fucking space. Because it's ours. I will provide for you, Sadie. And I am sorry." I pause, running my thumb against the back of her hand. "Sorry that your parents didn't want this. Sorry you had to marry me without them. And sorry that this is a bumpy start. But I promise you that your parents will come around. I won't let you live life without them. Okay?" Sadie is now teary-eyed, and she nods rapidly.

"Mm-hmm," she hums behind closed lips and trembling jaw. She doesn't want to cry in public, and I don't want that either. But she needs to have some hope so we can start this marriage off right. "I still can't believe it happened so fast." She laughs, wiping away the tears and taking another sip of her tea in an attempt to keep them away.

"We make our own rules."

"True." Sadie and I have done everything from day one backward. Even the guys in the band told me we were insane, but the only person I care about is Sadie. I don't care if everyone thinks we are making a mistake; I only care if Sadie thinks we are.

"Ben?" She hesitates, keeping her eyes on my hand in hers.

"Hmm, baby?"

"What was your mom like?" Her question comes out of left field.

"Um . . ." I pause, thinking of how the hell I want to answer this. I don't ever talk about my mother with anyone but my therapist, and even he gets only a highlight reel. I have never opened up fully about the life I had before she died.

"You don't have to talk about it if it's too hard. We can talk about something else." She tries to brush it off, but I decide it's only right. She bared her wounds, and I will bear mine.

"No, it's all right. There is so much about her, I don't know where to start. She was incredible."

Sadie smiles.

"She loved music. It was a huge part of her life. She was always singing—in the kitchen, driving, while doing laundry, in the shower."

"I bet. You have an incredible voice, it had to come from somewhere."

"Thanks, baby. She would have loved you." I think of all the things I've accomplished with music, and hands down, my marriage to Sadie outshines them all. My mother would be beaming if she could see me now.

"I would have loved her too."

"Her favorite thing to do other than singing was baking. She could cook and bake anything from scratch, swear it."

"Oh really? Good thing you married yourself a Southern girl. Mama taught me how to cook."

"Did she?" I smirk, leaning in to kiss her gently.

"I could be a world-renowned chef at this point"—she pulls away—"and maybe if you're real good, I will have a home-cooked meal on the table every night that you are home from touring." I appreciate that she let me give her those little bits of information without pushing me. Slowly, I will be able to tell her more and more.

"I'll be a real good boy, baby. I swear." I kiss her again, and she lingers a little bit longer.

"Thank you for telling me a little about her. When you're ready, I would love to know more." She kisses me again, not pushing me past that.

Her cherry lip gloss stains my mouth, and I taste it on my tongue as I lick my lips. Damn, she's good. Pulling back with a shake of her head, she watches me hum her praise.

"I need to use the restroom. I'll be back." I watch those hips sway, because she has a body that is worth admiring. And I have the right as her husband to look.

Our food comes to the table while she's gone, and I wait to dig in, not wanting to start without her. As I take a swig of my beer, I see her over the rim of the glass, but she's not alone. At the bar, a man who looks like a frat boy fresh out of a catalog has his hand on her waist and her attention on him.

That same waist where my hands were an hour ago, owning her. The smile she wears as he flirts with her is mine. A stranger is grabbing my wife in a bar and doesn't bother to keep his hands off her body, and she's fucking smiling like she enjoys the attention?

I start to feel the mania set in, that heat up my spine trickling through all my nerve endings. I clench my fist and stand, attempting to rein myself in before I reach her, and by hell, I almost do until his lips touch her cheek.

"Hey!" I'm on him in a few strides, pushing his chest and coming between him and Sadie. "Want to keep your fucking hands off my wife?" I push his chest again, this time causing him to lean up against the bar. The other restaurant guests start staring.

"Ben! Hey, stop!" Sadie grabs my arm, and I use all my weight to stand tall, not backing down.

"Your wife? Sadie, what's this guy talking about?" He tries to brush me off and looks at Sadie over my shoulder.

I get in his face. "Don't fucking look at her, you look at me. I'm her husband, and as far as I'm concerned, your hands don't need to be touching her."

"Ben!" Sadie grabs my arm and tugs again.

"No, he was touching you, and you let him." I turn to her and glare.

"I know him. He's a family friend, he's Mike's brother!"

Mike. Fucking Mike, the perfect ex whom I have yet to see. If he looks like his brother, then I hate the dick more. This guy is at least six foot four and two hundred pounds of football muscle. Add in his frat boy haircut and khakis and he's the perfect poster child for every parent's wet dream.

"I don't care," I snap.

"Well, I do!" Sadie comes and stands between us, and for a split second, I watch his eyes wander over her backside, and I snap.

"You don't know when to stop, do you?" Moving around Sadie, I grab his shirt. All the rage seeps in, and I throw him down on the bar.

"Ben! Stop it!" Sadie is pulling at me along with the fucker's buddies. Before I can set the asshole straight with my fist, my arms are yanked, and I lose my grip on him.

"Dean, I'm so sorry," Sadie apologizes, and when I turn to give her an incredulous look, I'm met with her retreating figure. I see security coming in my direction, so I pull back. Looking over at the guy she called Dean, I shrug his buddies off me.

"You and your brother make sure you find yourselves anywhere but near her, got it?" He nods, doing the right thing by shutting his preppy little mouth. "Good."

Security comes up and asks me to leave the bar or I will be asked to leave the hotel. I do so willingly, still angry but more concerned about getting to Sadie. Because tonight, she saw it. Saw a glimpse of the anger that lives in me. The beast that lurks in the shadows came out of hiding and nearly scared her out of her skin. The way her eyes looked before she walked away? That look may stick with me forever.

I fucked up, but more importantly, I can't control it. Fuck me, I wish I could, but I can't. I go to therapy and take my medication, but there is something that still won't work. What it is? I don't know. It eats me alive. Catching an elevator before it closes, I hurry up to the room. Bursting in the door, I yell for Sadie.

"Baby, where are you?" I step further in and see Sadie sitting by the window, looking out over Seattle's skyline.

"Can I have a minute, please?" Her voice is distant.

"Hey, listen. All I need is my medicine and I'll calm down, okay?"

"Sure, go ahead. I think I need a minute to myself too." She looks over her shoulder; her eyes are red, and mascara lines make their way down her defined cheekbones.

I all but growl as my fists tighten at my sides and my jaw clenches so tightly I could break through wood.

"We aren't done here." Grabbing my bag, I go into the bathroom. I rummage through my bag and look for my medication, but when I sift through everything, I realize I left it at home. Great, fucking great. I take a few deep breaths as my body twitches, the sweat still rushing out of my pores. That's my fucking body trying to calm down, all because I worry that if Sadie sees me in a full-fledged rage, a damn annulment may be in my near future. Thank God I still have the pre-rolled joint. Pulling it out, I get my lighter from my bag.

You don't forget your lighter, but you forget your meds? Nice, Ben. Real nice. I take a long drag the second it's lit.

"Ben?" Her soft voice sounds from the other side of the closed door.

"Yeah?" I take another drag, the smoke filling my lungs.

"Can I come in?"

"Give me a minute." That came out more agitated than I intended, but I'm angry and manic, and she's confused and hurt. I don't want to add anything else. Day one of marriage, and I'm undoubtedly fucking it up.

"Don't push me out like you did last time. We talked about this, Ben." There's a touch of irritation in her voice.

"I'm trying to calm down, and you're the one who told me to give you space."

"Please calm down with me. Help me understand." Her voice lowers again, and I hear the damage my fucked-up problems have the power to cause. I take another drag, a long one, and hold the smoke in for an extra few seconds before I release it. Wetting the tips of my thumb and pointer finger, I put out the cherry and pinch the edge.

With a deep breath, I open the door, and she's standing there, still teary and afraid. "Talk to me. What was that?"

I walk past her, keeping my hands to myself, fearing I'll grab her and fuck the anger out of my system.

"Ben?" Following me, she comes to stand in front of me at the edge of the bed. I sit, shaking my head, hanging it low with regret. The weed is doing its job, but it still needs to fully settle in my system.

"Yes. I was angry seeing another man's hands on you, okay?" I snap.

"But is that normal for you to become that upset? You could have talked to me, told me how you felt."

I shake my head repeatedly. "It's not that simple, Sadie. I can't control myself sometimes. I can go from zero to sixty and act completely manic." Her hands go to my shoulders, and she rubs through the thick knots of tension. I'm not sure why she is even talking to me. She wanted space just minutes ago, and now she's closing the distance between us.

"You can't react like that over me. You have to understand that you can control your anger when it comes to me. I don't cheat."

Scoffing, I stand, separating myself from her touch. "I can't control it, Sadie. Really? If I could control my anger, then I wouldn't have a fucking problem! For you to think it's as simple as deep breaths just shows you have no idea how bad this can get."

"You're right. I'm sorry. But we talked about trust. Surely you know that you have no reason to not trust me."

"Yes, I can trust *you*. It's other people."

"I can't control that, Ben. But what you and I can both control is our commitment. We just got married. That means something, doesn't it?"

"But his hands, Sadie, his fucking hands touched you!"

"Then let them. Did mine touch his? Did I look like I wanted it in that way?" she replies. I move back to the bed and sit down.

"No, but what if he took it too far? I have to keep you safe, and I don't want men touching you. You're my wife."

"I am your wife, baby," she says, softening and straddling me. "I love you for wanting to protect me. And yes, if it went too far and I needed you, I would tell you." She kisses my forehead a few times.

"Goddamn it." I grip her hips and bury my face in her chest, right above her heart.

"Ben?"

"Angel," I say against her skin. Her comforting me instead of pushing me away feels welcome but wrong. I don't deserve that.

"You're in therapy, but you don't talk about it much. What is your therapist's name?"

"Dr. Davinah," I tell her, finally looking up at her. She moves a piece of my hair that covers my eye.

"What would Dr. Davinah tell you to do in moments like this?"

"There are a lot of things. Take my medication, but that shit knocks me on my ass, so I avoid it. He tells me to talk about it..." I hate fucking talking about these things with people.

"How often do you see him?" Sadie keeps rubbing my shoulders. It feels good, and now the high is starting to kick in. Her softness, the high, her touch, it is all merging together to bring me back down to earth.

"Once a week."

"Please tell me if it's too much to talk about. But maybe you can see him more than once a week. Is that something you would be willing to do?" I think about this. Is it? I already hate the weekly sessions and the occasional emergency meetings. Therapy hasn't clicked for me like everyone says it's supposed to.

"Maybe I am broken, angel. Therapy isn't working. Everything he says feels easier said than done." I search her face. It's still so soft. How is she so damn calm? I wish I could channel that.

"I can come. Maybe having someone there with you to support you would help? Has Nick or one of the guys ever gone?"

I shake my head rapidly. "No, I would rather saw my arm off than let them see me in therapy."

"You don't have to shut off your feelings with me," she whispers.

"But I want to. Look what happened." I grip her hips and knead them in my hands.

"And I am still here."

"For what reason I will never know," I admit, showing all my cards.

"Because I love you. You deserve someone to work through it without judgment."

Fuck me. How did the universe decide that a saint like her should pick me?

"Can you just be my therapist? Look how much you fucking calm me down." I point out what we both clearly see. She is a necessity to me now.

"No, I'm your wife. But I want to be your partner, and I want to help you. Let someone be your support, Ben. Land with your feet on the ground. Stop trying to take flight when it gets hard. Land. I am here."

"I'm not ready to share that part yet, but I think one day I will be." I have to try something on my own. Sadie can tell me to land, but I have to set boundaries too. If I land, I will crush her.

"That's okay."

"Can I hover? Is that okay for now?" I ask.

"Yes, you can hover, but don't let me be the enemy. I'm not. Trust?"

"Trust." We both wave the white flag.

"What can I do to make you happy, angel?" I want to make this right, to flip this night back around. I leave tomorrow, and the last thing I want to do is leave with us fighting.

Twenty-three

SADIE

One week married, and it has been a lot. I do not regret marrying Ben, and I'm still crazy in love with him, but I have a lot of work to do in order to understand him better, and he needs to make more strides in trusting me.

I am still navigating how to live my life without talking to my father. My mom called, and we talked a little. She admitted that she regrets not being at the ceremony that day. I didn't know what to say. There was a time I thought she wouldn't make it to my wedding because of her cancer. And even though she has recovered, my best day still had moments of the worst day. She wasn't there after all. I promised her I would come see her when my dad is ready, but I need time. He hurt me. And truth be told, I'm not ready to see that pained, disappointed look again.

Thankfully, I've been busy moving into his apartment with Kate's help, all while getting ready for my graduation in a few weeks. That has helped keep my mind occupied. Ben has been so distracted with shows, interviews, and more that we barely have enough time to say good morning and good night to each other.

I miss him, even though I was aware of how lonely this life is. He is a rock star and is only growing his brand. We may be apart more than we are together, and it's a sad reality that we will both have to adjust to.

Friday night, I take a break from studying to make dinner, and it feels surprisingly normal. I've never lived with anyone but my parents, so there are some small moments of unease, but for the most part, I like being in a new home that I'll share with him.

Kate is due over any minute to have a girls' night in. I haven't spoken to Ben all day. He had a daytime show and then he has a huge meet and greet with fans tonight. God, I want him home already.

My thoughts carry me away before the sound of Kate arriving distracts me minutes later. She makes me forget, for now.

* * *

Being away from Ben over the last two weeks has been a lot harder than we both thought it would be. The knowledge that he tours for six months out of the year is starting to weigh on me. Our phone conversations and FaceTime calls are the only interactions we get, and it makes me long for him.

Tonight, I agree to have a study session with Mike at the café, and the entire time I am distracted, thinking about Ben and checking my phone frequently to see if he has been able to step away to call or text me. But that doesn't happen until two in the morning. I wake up to my phone ringing, and even though I am exhausted, I'm more than excited to talk to him. I would forfeit all my sleep for moments with him.

* * *

Running around the apartment like a chicken loose from its pen, I get ready for today. My graduation is in a few hours, and Ben is due home any minute after three weeks away. My morning at the spa went longer than Kate and I planned, so I'm behind schedule. And today my mother let me know that she and my father will be there. Seeing them for the first time in weeks at my graduation isn't ideal. But it's a step. Dad wants to be there. He has to know Ben will be there too. Baby steps. Ben said baby steps.

My hair and makeup are done. I'm wearing a red lip with winged eyeliner and highlighter on my cheeks. I chose a simple black slip dress with lace lining the V-neck—completely unlike me. It has spaghetti straps, and it makes my fresh spray tan pop.

As I put on my nude pumps, I hear the front door open, and Ben's voice carries through the apartment.

"Angel, I'm home!" My belly coils in butterflies, and I leap from the vanity chair in our walk-in closet.

"Ben!" I run down the hall and jump into his arms, wrapping myself around him. Before he can give me a proper hello, I move my hands to his face and take a kiss from him selfishly.

I bite at his lip. Adrenaline, excitement, arousal—all those things thrum inside me. I moan against him, using my legs to climb higher and closer. He tastes like cigarettes and mint, a taste I've come to love.

"Mm-hmm, baby, baby." He pulls us apart, and I whimper when our lips separate.

"Welcome home, handsome."

"What a homecoming that is." I wipe my lipstick from his mouth. "You look—fuck, I missed you." He gives me his lips again, and we push and pull, giving and taking equally with each second that goes by. I want him. I don't want to wait. I can't wait.

"I have thirty minutes left before I need to leave." I pull away, and my blue eyes meet his deep brown ones. It feels almost surreal that he is here.

"That's good, but what will we do with the remaining twenty-nine minutes?" He winks, and we both laugh as he carries us back to the bedroom. I missed him and his jokes.

"We can do it twenty-nine more times."

"Challenge accepted." Ben makes the most of those thirty minutes, giving me enough orgasms to keep me sated for the rest of the day.

***

My graduation is perfect. Ben, Nick, and Kate are seated in the front, and a couple rows back are my parents. I do my best to focus on the speakers, and when they congratulate us, I risk a look at my parents. My father is clapping, and his face holds so many mixed emotions that it instantly sends me into a fit of tears. He's not on board with my marriage, but I'm still his daughter, and he's proud of me for achieving my goals. Love is complicated at the best of times, and two things can be true at once—my dad knows how hard I worked even if he doesn't believe in his heart that I should have married Ben so soon after meeting him.

I hold my LPN certificate in my hands, proof of the time and effort that I put into getting one step closer to nursing school. This certificate guarantees me my dream internship with Dr. Bailer at Portland General at the end of the summer.

Better yet, before that, I will be touring with Ben, meaning no more weeks apart and lonely phone calls. This summer, I will be all his.

I find Ben, Kate, and Nick in the crowd.

"Come here, angel." Ben holds out his arms, and I throw myself into him and kiss him. He lifts me and spins me around.

"Get a room." Kate breaks us up, and I give her a side hug.

Ben's hand never leaves my lower back, a small gesture, like many others, that I missed while he was away.

"So, your parents planned a dinner tonight. Don't yell at me, they just told me," Kate tells us, putting her hands up defensively. Great. This day was nearly perfect.

"Hey, baby steps," Ben whispers in my ear.

"This feels like a leap. It's been three weeks." My dad tossed me out, told me he didn't want me getting married, and we haven't talked since. This is a leap.

"Whatever happens, I'm here. We have each other."

"What if he says something that triggers you?" I say quietly enough for only him to hear as we approach the car.

"I will remove us before something like that happens. Nick can help me if need be. Tonight is for you. Stop worrying about anyone or anything else but you." He kisses me quickly on my lips and opens my door, signaling me to get in. I groan and throw my head back. Why am I worried this dinner is going to be anything but a good time?

Pulling up to the Southern-inspired restaurant, I can't help the huge grin that spreads across my face.

"I love it here. I hope you like all my favorites that I'm going to make you try. Might overload you so much on food that you puke." I climb out and take his hand. He looks edible in his basic black jeans and band tee, his full mane of hair combed back and styled on his head. I lost my cap and gown, throwing on the leather jacket Kate convinced me to buy. This is a new style I'm trying. It's an adjustment, but I have been feeling more and more comfortable in the new outfits Kate and I picked out.

"So I should have worn stretchy pants?"

I chuckle, kissing the back of his hand. "You should have."

Shaking his head and smiling, he opens the door and lets me go first. "You're so fucking adorable." Pulling me in for a kiss, he grips my ass in front of the hostess before she ushers us back. Normally, I would scold him for it, but I'm riding a high.

"Congratulations!"

Everyone at the table cheers, and I note that more people are here than I thought would be, including Mike. Great. My parents and Mike. So much for the giddy feeling I had seconds ago. Reality is slapping me in the face, isn't it?

Mike and I are still friends, but after the way Ben reacted over Dean, my stomach ties in nervous knots. Taking a deep breath, I risk a peek at Ben and see his eyes zeroing in on Mike as he leaves his chair to greet us.

"Sadie, great job, we're so proud of you!" Mike hugs me, and I hesitate at first but then return it with my free arm. My other hand stays in a purposeful grip with Ben's.

Pulling back, Mike turns to Ben, and I swallow thickly. "You must be the infamous Ben. I'm Mike, nice to meet you."

My husband's eyes grow wide, and his lips get tight.

Oh no, please, not again.

Twenty-four

BEN

I'm not a man who gets intimidated or insecure, but this Mike guy sure makes me a little fucking uneasy. He's like his fucking brother, tall, preppy, built like a football player, and of course his eyes keep glancing at Sadie's body.

My body. My wife.

I look at his hand and take a moment to assess everything around me. I could explode and tell this guy to shake his own dick, or I could whip out mine and show him what a real man Sadie belongs to, but I take the fucking high road, because this is her day, and I am trying to convince her parents that they aren't right about me. With acid in my gut, I shake his hand and nod.

"Nice to meet you."

"Sadie's told me lots about you. Nice to put a face to the name."

"Oh really? Funny, can't say she has said much about you, but hey, any friend of Sadie's"—I emphasize *friend*—"is a friend of mine." Yup, there's my dick. Guess I couldn't help myself.

"You know, I'm starved. Let's sit and eat." Sadie breaks up our pissing contest and guides us to our seats. If I had my way, I'd put an entire table between us.

"Hey." Everyone settles in and starts conversing as Sadie whispers to me, one hand on my thigh and the other on my arm.

"Yes?"

"You didn't need to have a peeing contest, but I will say thank you. You being here means a lot to me. My dad won't even look at me, and I need you right now." That's exactly why I didn't do anything.

"I'm sorry. You tell me when it gets to be too much, and we can go."

"Thank you." She kisses my lips, and I let her order for me. Usually, I'm the life of the party, but now I sit back and watch everyone in the room. Their eyes stay glued to Sadie, and she beams. They hang on every word that comes out of her mouth. Her charm, her grace, her smile, her love—she's captivating. I'm the lucky bastard who gets to claim that.

My mood is laid-back until I look at Stan, who is staring at me. His jaw is tight, and I almost feel the daggers he is mentally throwing at me. I get it. He told me no. I didn't listen. And his daughter chose me. I don't blame him one bit. I nod at him, and he shakes his head before looking back down at his plate. I do appreciate that he hasn't caused a scene. That wouldn't be fair to his daughter, and I would like to think that even if he doesn't agree with us, he loves her enough to not make this even harder on her.

"Yay! Okay, try this, baby, I promise you will love it." Bringing a forkful of food to my mouth, she pulls me back into the moment. She feeds it to me, and it's pretty fucking good. Everyone watches me and waits for my reaction.

"Damn, all right, you win. That's pretty tasty," I finally say, and the table erupts in laughter—everyone but Mike and Stan. Mike not laughing makes me feel better: he sees how much Sadie loves me, and that bothers him. It would eat me up inside, too, but I'm not the poor bastard. Stan, on the other hand, isn't a victory for me. I want him to see how happy we make each other and let it be enough for him to see this is it for Sadie. That nothing can come between us. Not even him.

"Told you! Mama and I make the best kind, but I can make that for you another time." The table goes back to eating, and I lean toward Sadie.

"I'm proud of you; you did such an amazing job."

I rub the back of her exposed neck. She lost the jacket when we sat down, and her freshly tanned skin is exposed.

"Thank you. I'm excited to see if I get into the nursing program. I really hope my internship helps."

"You will, with or without it. You're that amazing."

"She's pretty special. I think she'll get in, hands down," Mike interrupts. So he was listening in on our conversation—dick. "I've always told her that." I hate him. He's purposefully trying to get under my skin, and it's working. I wasn't expecting someone like Sadie—I never wanted to be a boyfriend, let alone a husband, yet here I am, and along with that sudden love comes my insane jealousy.

Maybe I'm deflecting because I think Sadie can do way better than me, but I don't give a fuck about that right now, because this man is looking for a one-way ticket to a back-alley brawl if he doesn't mind his place.

"I'm sure you did, man." I give him as much attitude as I can, and the others at the table take notice. Fuck.

"Sorry, didn't mean anything by it," he replies. "Just think she doesn't give herself enough credit." I watch in slow fucking motion as he moves his hand up from under the table, grabs hers, and gives it a squeeze. I feel Sadie tense next to me, her body turning to stone.

"Hey, you know, it's getting late, and I still need to pack. Baby, why don't we head home?" Sadie interrupts before I can react, standing and grabbing her jacket off the back of the chair. I look up at her, and her brows draw in, begging me with a look to please let this one go.

"Sure." I go against everything in me and walk away—for Sadie. I stand and grab my wallet. Pulling out a couple hundred-dollar bills, I place them on the table.

"Thank you, everyone, for coming, and thank you, Mom and Dad, this was perfect." Sadie bends to kiss her mother goodbye. She turns to her dad, and they share a look before he stands, tells her something, then hugs her. Good. I take the chance to say something I need to get off my chest. Bending down, I lower my voice so only Mike can hear me. "She's mine now. Make sure you understand that."

"Is that a threat?" He looks affronted, and I take pleasure in it.

"Only if you don't listen."

With that, I turn and give Raydean a kiss on the cheek. I would attempt to shake Stan's hand, but he already left the table to go to the restroom. I am sure it was to avoid me. I don't blame him. "Night, guys, thank you for having us."

"Anytime, Ben, and hey, he will come around too. Just keep focusing on you two," Ray says, and Sadie can't help but tear up. That is my cue to get us out of here. Today is a day for her wins, not a day I want her to think back on with heartbreak.

***

We don't talk on the way home. Her head is most likely riddled with questions over the situation with her father, and my mind is imagining punching Mike over and over. He knew what he was doing, and he can act as innocent as he wants, but I saw with my own two eyes what he wants, and that's my wife—but he will never get the chance to satisfy that hunger.

When we enter the apartment, I go straight into the kitchen and grab myself a beer. Sadie still doesn't say anything. She removes her shoes and heads for the bedroom, and I stay put in the kitchen, staring at the wall in a trance.

My phone pulls me from my thoughts, and I tug it out of my pocket. Nick's name flashes on the screen, and I answer it quickly.

"What's up?"

"Hey, you good? Dinner was rough. Mike and Stan weren't ideal."

"No, but at least her father showed up, and I saw him say something before hugging her. I'm trying to calm down and give her space. Let her be the one to talk about it."

"That's probably best. You need anything from me?"

"No... well, maybe a life jacket and a miracle drug?"

"I can get you a life jacket, but I am fresh out of miracles. But hey, I also called because *Portland Monthly* wants to do an interview with you. It's one of Portland's hip mainstream magazines." Swallowing another sip of my beer, I hear Sadie in the hall getting something from the closet.

"Sure, sounds good to me. When is that?"

"Tomorrow morning. They can either stop by your place or you can meet them at their corporate office downtown."

"Send me the address, and I'll be there in the morning. I gotta go now."

"Sure thing. Night, man."

"Later." Ending the call, I go in search of Sadie. Walking into our bedroom, I see her sitting in the middle of our bed. She has her bible open in her lap. I haven't seen her read that in front of me before. Her fingers move over the cross around her neck as she concentrates, and I take a moment to watch her.

"You okay?"

She peers up, and for a second, I think she's going to shrug me off, but when she shakes her head and shuts her book, I'm thankful that she's willing to talk. "No. My dad said that he's proud of me but he still needs time. His hug felt so good, Ben, and I realized how much I miss him." She wipes at her tears.

"I know you miss him."

"These three weeks have felt like months. I don't know how to get used to not seeing them and talking to them every day."

"Do you want me to talk to them?"

"No, I want to give him time. And I want to focus on us." I move to the side of the bed and reach out for her. I set my beer on the nightstand, and she crawls to me. Sitting up and planting her feet on each side of me, she pulls me in, and I run my hands through her hair, massaging and tugging gently. She hums a delighted moan.

"That feel good?" I ask. She nods.

"Tonight, you didn't react the way I thought you would with Mike." She rests her cheek against me, puts her chin on my thigh, and looks up at me.

"I'm trying."

"It's working, Ben. Thank you." I grab my beer and take another sip.

What she does next catches me off guard. Her hands find my belt, and her seductive eyes bore into mine. "You have no idea how much I've missed you. I'm really, really wet, and I want it."

"Fuck, Sadie."

"Please fuck me, Ben. I need it." Every time we are intimate, Sadie becomes more vocal with her needs, wants, and desires—and fuck me I love it.

I sip my beer but keep my eyes on her. She opens my button and zipper, slipping her hand into my jeans. When her small hand grips my growing cock, I growl.

"You're such a good fucking girl, baby." I want her to own me tonight. To take it all out on me—everything holding her back.

Lifting my shirt with her free hand, she latches her mouth onto the defined *V* of my abdomen. She wets the skin with her tongue and blows on it softly. My spine tingles. Her hand moves up and down my shaft as much as it can with my jeans in the way.

I hiss when she circles the tip, spreading my pre-come around the head. "Tight pussy, fuck-me eyes, and that sinful mouth. You aren't such a goody-goody anymore, baby. I tainted my little angel, didn't I?"

"Maybe. Maybe I can get a little more bad. You still have so much to teach me; I still haven't had you in my mouth." She blushes and giggles sinfully.

"That simply won't do." Setting my beer on the nightstand, I grip her chin in my large, calloused hand. She stands, and I help her jump and wrap her legs around me. Our lips lock, all tongue and teeth. I lay her down on the bed. She's still in that sexy little slip dress she wore today, except she lost her bra when she got home, and her tight nipples brush against my thin shirt.

Laying us down, I break our kiss and flip her over on her stomach. She yelps as her silk dress rides up, and I get a glimpse of her new panties. It makes my dick twitch to see her in something more risqué, but I still miss her old style of underwear, the ones with more material. Sadie is changing day by day, becoming this version of herself that was hiding somewhere. She is growing into her own independence.

"Did you get some new panties for me?" I lift her dress and expose her entire ass with the tiniest black thong wedged between her smooth skin.

She nods, looking over her shoulder. I can smell her arousal from where I stand.

"What does a man have to do to fuck this ass?" I slap her cheek and watch her ass vibrate.

"Ah! I don't know, anything. Just let me have you." I could bang on my chest, I feel so high right now.

"You had me a few hours ago." I wrap one finger around the fabric covering her pussy and move it aside. "You're still swollen; your cunt is greedy. Did your husband make your pussy hurt, angel?"

"*Ben.*"

She doesn't simply moan my name, she begs desperately for me to fuck her.

"Maybe I'll slow it down a little, take care of you, make sure you don't get too sore. Especially since I plan to fuck this cunt every day for the next three months."

She thrusts back against my finger circling her entrance, and the tip slides in. The tight hole squeezes me.

"I want to be bad, though. I want to be really, really bad," Sadie cries, fucking the tip of my finger. I finally give her what she wants and thrust my finger inside her snug heat.

"Why?" I ask, ready to hear more.

"Because you're my husband, and I can be your servant. I can worship you like a king in our home, and I want you to take everything from me. Use me, Ben."

"I don't want to."

I stop my hands, and she cries at the loss of my finger. I want gentle tonight. That's right, me the fucking playboy wants the plain missionary shit. Her dirty side turns me on, but I don't want her to be this woman just because she thinks it's what I like. I started out wanting to be her cocky, demanding lover, but suddenly, I'm insecure. Never in a million years did I think that would happen to me.

"Is it me?" she inquires, flipping over and sitting up, her hair a wild mess and her makeup smudged slightly. "I thought maybe we could be a little more wild tonight, like you like it."

"I like anything with you. I love the dirty talk, I do, but I need *you* tonight. I need that connection," I admit.

"Everything with you is a connection, Ben."

Tonight, I want to show her my soft side, my worthy side, not a dirty-talking bad boy with a rap sheet of one-night stands.

"Let's make something new tonight; that can also be our thing." I lift her off the bed, and she follows. Understanding what I need, she smiles, running her hands through my hair.

"Okay."

Grabbing the hem of her dress, I lift it up and off her body in one fluid motion.

We don't speak. Instead, our hands do the talking. Sadie slides her hands against my warm skin, and they climb up my sides, taking my shirt with them. Dropping to my haunches, I keep my eyes on hers as she looks down at me. I kiss from her knee up one thigh, then back down and up again on the other leg, ending with an open-mouth kiss right under her belly button.

A shiver runs through her, and there is an inferno burning in my bloodstream. Removing her panties slowly, I slide them down her thighs with purposeful ease.

She looks beautiful, curvy, petite, and womanly. The extra weight on her molds to my hands perfectly, like her soul was made for me, her body crafted by design for me. Her smell fills my lungs, and I take a drag like the last one on a burned-out cigarette.

I kiss my way back up to my full height, paying attention to all the places I can: her legs, her pubic bone, her stomach, and each hip bone. We haven't been together long, but I know her body like the back of my hand. I spent hours on our wedding night memorizing every detail of it.

Switching positions, she drops to her knees and finishes removing my jeans and boxer briefs. Once I'm completely naked, she stays there, leaning against the back of her calves. Tracing her thumb across her lips, she smirks at me; this time, it reaches her eyes. Her sweet dimples indent deeper than normal, and without words she leans in, kissing the tip of my hard cock.

A low growl thunders in my chest. Sadie's touch nearly knocks me on my ass. My hands seize some of her hair as her hands travel up my thighs, waking every nerve ending along the way until she holds on to my hips and takes an inch of me into her sweet mouth.

With every force on this damn planet, I restrain from breaching her completely and ramming my cock down her throat. Sadie is exploring, and I'm enjoying the expedition thoroughly. Her eyes, which are still focused on me, begin to water when she takes in another inch.

She gags as I try another inch but stays strong, rolling her tongue on the underside of my shaft. Using one hand, she circles my wide girth and jerks what she can't fit into her warm mouth. Our eyes stay locked as she switches from bobbing to holding me halfway in and rubbing her tongue around my length.

I've had head, tons of it, but never has it been this raw and incredible. Once again, there's something sexy about a girl with no experience, especially when she's my wife.

"I'm gonna fucking come, baby."

My balls grow tight, and she slows down, letting me slide in and out at a gentle, leisurely pace. This is different; this is intimacy. I match her rhythm, and in a second I shiver and orgasm, releasing hot stream after hot stream down her willing throat. I groan, and she moans, the sensation vibrating against my shaft. I come down from my orgasm, still massaging her head where her hair is in my hands.

My cock is still rock hard and ready for more, but first I want to return the favor.

"On the bed, angel." Standing, she wipes her lips on the back of her hand, and watching that, I react swiftly. I grab her arm and spin her around, pushing her face-first into the bed.

"Ah! Baby!" She giggles, and the sound echoes in the room.

"Ass up." The lover in me is still there, and I plan to look her deep in the eyes while I fuck her gently, but right now is the warm-up, and I'm going to make it count.

Climbing onto her knees, she peers back at me, shaking her ass like a tease and biting that already swollen lip.

"Don't throw that thing around begging for it because you might get it," I growl, and she laughs knowingly.

"I'm counting on it, ba—oh!" Before her sassy Southern drawl can tease me back, I open my mouth and suck her enticing center in from the back side, her lips spread wide, her clit playing against my tongue and her sweet arousal traveling down my throat as I fuck her wildly with my mouth.

"Ben!" Thrusting my pointed tongue in and out of her tight hole, I flick her clit with my finger a few times, and I prepare for my reward. Sadie is the only woman I've been with who can release her juices in abundance, and believe me, the reality is better than the fantasy.

My girl isn't only responsive, she's thankful, showing me as she comes against my tongue, and I drink her in like a fine fucking wine. The warm juices taste sweet.

"Wow," she huffs out, going limp on her stomach, her legs giving out.

"Oh no, we aren't done. You need to be on top. I need to see you. Watch you. Take you all in. I need you to show me how much you love me," I whisper against her skin as I kiss the curve of her silky ass, leaving gentle love bites.

I move us so I'm on my back and she's straddling my cock, her entrance kissing the tip.

"Slowly, you need to go slow," I remind her. She lets my hands on her hips guide her down my shaft. I slide into her heat, and we both lose our fucking breath. My eyes nearly roll back in my head, it feels that good.

I groan. "Damn, angel." Being inside Sadie is like being on the most intense drug. It's euphoric.

"All for you . . ." she moans, lifting off me again. I'm mesmerized by her lust-filled eyes focused on me, watching me take pleasure. I don't let my eyes wander from hers as my muse and I connect. Our lovemaking is writing the perfect song in my head; I find the words with each thrust and jolt of her body. Her breathing makes the perfect sound, a melody to accompany my song.

"Do you know what control you have over me?" I groan, pinching her nipple between my fingers.

"No, why don't you tell me—oh." Sitting up, I lose my hands in her hair and fuse her lips to mine.

My arms cross over her back and bear down on her shoulders. This action helps her thrust up and down, hard, in very defined movements.

"You're the deadliest weapon. You have so much power over me."

"More," she moans, our faces inches apart and our thrusts like rolling waves.

"You're my religion."

"Oh my god, Ben." Throwing her head back, she comes without warning, my words bringing her to a burn.

"Sadie, look at me. Look at me now." I hold her shoulder blades as she reaches back, grabs my legs, and rides out the rest of her orgasm. Her eyes lock in on me. I steal a glance down at our connection, where her lips drag along my cock, then back to her face, torn between which is turning me on more.

"Fuck, I'm gonna come." I'm chasing my orgasm as hers settles and pulses around me.

"You have to pull out, I'm ovulating." We had to do this earlier, and it truly tested me, but I sure as hell don't want to get her pregnant. Growling, I flip us. Towering over her, I pull out right as I explode, unleashing ropes of hot come all over her stomach.

"Fuck, fuck, fuck." She watches, mesmerized, as I focus on my orgasm.

Moments later, we are slowly coming down. No longer in a fit of labored breathing, I trace lyrics along her back. I move Sadie to lie across my chest so we can stay skin to skin.

"Ben?"

"Hmm?" Staring up at the ceiling fan, I wait for her to continue.

"Do you want to have kids?" My breath catches like someone sucker punched me in the gut. Kids. I've never thought about having kids. I never thought I would get married, either, but here we are. What do I say?

"I haven't given it much thought." I give her half-truths. "Why?" There isn't a chance she is pregnant; she wouldn't have asked me to pull out, and she definitely wouldn't tell me she was ovulating if she was already pregnant. Would she? No. No. She wouldn't do that.

"We don't use protection. Ever. And the counting method only works perfectly when you aren't sexually active. We take a risk every time we have sex." She has a point.

"I am not going to have anything between us. No condoms." I come right out with it. Skin on skin with Sadie, being bare in her, is a form of intimacy I never want to give up.

"Pull and pray isn't as effective, though."

"Why not the pill?"

"I've never tried it, but I worry it may make me sick. We can try it?"

"I don't want you to be sick." I pull her in closer, moving her to a position where she can prop her chin on her hands against my chest. "What is best for you, baby?"

"I know, and I love you for that. Why don't we try it and if it doesn't work, we can talk alternatives?"

My body is on fire. We aren't talking directly about kids, but if you look deeper, aren't we? The result of failed birth control is a chance of pregnancy.

"Sadie, we have a lot of things going on in our lives, and I want to be selfish with you. I want you to myself. And there are parts of me that I still want to work on." The air seems to have been sucked out of the room. My body temperature is rising with each passing second. "Baby . . ." I need to calm the fuck down. "I love exploring your body, and while it is mine—all fucking mine—I won't tell you what to do with it. You tell me. If we need condoms . . ." I groan, the idea annoying me. "Then I will buy a giant fucking box."

She giggles. "Okay, caveman. I can tell that you love that idea. But I like it—you—inside me . . . bare . . . It's something I enjoy too." She blushes softly. I love that she craves us as much as I do. "I will talk to my doctor about the pill. I'll make an appointment tomorrow. They have same-day."

"You sure?" I lift her chin. The fear of becoming a parent is slowly subsiding, but I still want to lock this topic away and not talk about it for a long while. I don't know if I will ever be ready or if being a father is in the cards for me.

I need more time to work on me and us before we can open that Pandora's box.

"I'm sure. Kids one day, just not today." She smirks, kissing my chest, and my stomach flips again.

"Maybe one day." She cuddles in closer, and silence claims us. Outwardly, we are quiet, but inside, my brain is running wild. Baby talk wasn't on my bingo card for tonight.

Welcome home ...

Twenty-five

SADIE

The tour starts off amazing, and we spend the first month getting to know one another better, making love any chance we get and laughing every day. No one can make me laugh the way Ben does. I still have six weeks before I have to get back and start my internship, but that time seems like it's going to pass faster than I want. Ben performs every other night, getting better and better and never slowing down. Even though they're playing the same set, it still seems new and exciting to me every time I watch it.

Ben has agreed to do therapy twice a week, but without me. He says it's a part of him he isn't ready to share. I'll admit, that hurts. How are the most difficult and complex times in his life something he doesn't want to let me in on? I want to be his friend, not just his wife and lover.

Nick and I are becoming extremely close, bonding over our shared love of cheese fries and terrible action movies. And he is my saving grace on Ben's low days. I'm not a big fan of the parties the band goes to after each show, so Nick tends to come sit with me on the bus while Ben has fun, and we watch the best of the worst action movies. Some nights, we stay in hotels—the nights when we have time between shows and don't need to be on the road as soon as the show ends.

The band has been very welcoming and is trying to be a little less crude around me. They have been cutting back on the perverted jokes, they've stopped talking about girls they hooked up with in the past, and they aren't bringing random women back to the bus.

The band didn't need to change because of me, and I feel guilty because they have. I may be more reserved, but I don't expect everyone to live the way I live. Hell, I married Ben, and he drinks, parties, has the foulest mouth, and also uses drugs—and I still love him more and more each day.

I will never force anyone to be just a version of me and my lifestyle.

***

"That fucker called again!" Ben yells from the back of the bus. He comes barreling through the bunks to where Nick and I are playing cards.

"What happened?" I ask, standing along with Nick.

"Sperm donor called again; I asked you to make that stop. Get me a new fucking number, Nick!" Ben throws open the door and storms out.

"Shit," Nick mutters, running his hands through his hair. He moves, attempting to go after Ben, but I shake my head.

"Let me. Work on getting the new number. I don't want him calling Ben anymore."

Nick nods, and I rush out the door of the bus. The sun is glaring: it's a hot day in Pennsylvania. I shield my eyes with my hands and watch Ben storming toward the two large metal doors that shield our bus and the trailers that haul the band's equipment.

"Ben! Wait! No!" I hurry now, running as fast as I can. I catch him right as his hand touches the handle, security following behind him. I push past them and place my hand on Ben's shoulder.

"Hey! No, please, there are fans out there lined up for tonight, and God knows how many photographers. Please, Ben." I am grasping, hoping it is enough.

It is. He stops.

Thank God.

"Ben, no!" I watch him lift his arm up and back, his fist in a tight ball, ready to hit the metal door. I am fast enough to jump in front of him, but my arm hits the metal, and I wince. "Ow!" I cry out, but I don't focus on it for more than a second.

"Sadie, stop, you just fucking hurt yourself!" Ben hollers, and I shake my head. I don't care.

"So? You almost did too. Let's go back inside. We'll talk, and you can call Dr. Davinah." I place my hands on his abs and rub soothing circles on them, eventually lifting the material to place my skin against his. He closes his eyes tightly, and I look at both guards. I nod and mouth for them to give us a minute. They walk away from us, and finally it's me and my husband alone.

"Look at me, Ben. Come on, look at me." I need him to look into my eyes. I need to see him.

Slowly, he does as I ask.

"Are you okay?"

He shakes his head. "No. Why does he keep calling me? Why!" I jolt slightly as his voice rises.

"I don't know. I told Nick to work on changing the number. Let's go in, and we will focus on you, Ben. Nothing else." I cup his cheek.

"Is your arm okay?" His voice is low.

"Yes, I'm fine. I will be even better when we are inside. Okay?"

"Okay." He leads, and I follow. Releasing the breath I was holding, I thank God he didn't go out there.

I wish I could fix these times. That I could bottle up the pain, the rage, and the trauma and throw it into oblivion. There are days I even wish that it could be me who carries his burdens. Nothing prepares you to watch the man you love fight himself any chance he gets, all to make it through each day, desperately trying to survive.

***

Ben calms down before the show, but after is a different story. We are traveling to Massachusetts, and Ben has been up with Nick and the boys the entire time, the life of the party—but this time he is overdoing it. Usually, he can find a balance, but tonight he isn't his normal self. I remove myself and head to the back room.

A little while later, I'm sitting in bed, reading my book, when he comes stumbling into the room, laughing.

"Baby! Babe! What are you . . . you doing?" he slurs as he plops down on the bed next to me. I smell the heavy stench of alcohol coming from his breath.

"Ben, you're drunk. Why don't you get some rest? Tomorrow is a busy day."

"Pfft, I am not drunk." He laughs and attempts to look me dead in the eyes but fails miserably, going cross-eyed.

"Okay, yeah you are. It's time you go to bed and sleep this off." I close my book and go to stand, but I'm stopped before I can even get up. Grabbing my arm, he pulls me to him and slams his mouth sloppily against mine. I pull away instantly; the taste of his alcohol is overwhelming. I hate the bitter taste of beer.

"You're drunk. I'm not doing that when you can't even look at me straight," I tell him. Standing, I move to the foot of the bed to remove his shoes.

"God, you're such a prude. You could just say you don't want to fuck." He laughs, and I cease moving. Did he honestly say that to me?

"Excuse me?" This isn't the first time he has gotten high and drank too much, but it's the first time he has said something mean to me. Since when did he resort to name-calling and demeaning comments?

"Come on, you want to sit here with your nose in your book and avoid sex." I remove my hands from him and back away as if he stung me. He didn't need to say that. Regardless of whether he's drunk or not, it was still mean, and I refuse to be on the receiving end of his insults.

"I'm sleeping in the bunks. Get some rest." He blows me off and flips onto his front to fall asleep. This Ben is someone I don't know, and seeing it tonight has turned me off mentally, physically, and emotionally. I honestly hope this will all turn out be a dream and I'll wake up with him back to his normal self.

What am I supposed to say now? How do I bounce back? Sure, he's drunk, but that came from somewhere. Is that really what he thinks? Am I a prude? Is sex with me mediocre and lackluster? I'm starting to spiral now. I close the curtain of the bunk and curl into a ball on my side. My hand rests over my heart; it aches in there, like it was ripped from my chest. I cry enough that it physically knocks me out.

* * *

I wake up to the sound of Ben in the bus bathroom losing all the contents of his stomach from the night before. I debate going in to help him, but the memory of last night comes back. It's still too fresh, and I don't know what to say. I climb out of the bunk and go to the front of the bus to grab a water and start some coffee.

I hear him brush his teeth then drag his feet through the bus. Everyone else is asleep, and our bus is already at the new venue. We must have arrived sometime early this morning. Checking the clock, I see it's nearing eight. Ben doesn't say a word to me and vice versa. He plops down at the breakfast table in the small kitchen area.

I place the water and some ibuprofen in front of him, but he doesn't even look up at me. His head stays in his hands. His hair's a mess, and you can smell the hangover. He takes the pills as I pour myself some coffee, and finally he peers up at me. I can feel his eyes searching me, waiting for me to speak first. But I have nothing to say.

"I didn't mean what I said." He breaks through the silence.

"I'm sure. I'm going to shower." With that, I head toward the back of the bus, ignoring him calling after me. Nights like last night make me wish this were one of the times we stopped at a hotel so I could get another room or go somewhere with more space. Create some distance between us. Stepping into the small bathroom with the world's tiniest shower, I climb in and try to enjoy the slow-running water. It's not much, but it's a moment away from the crazy cluster that this tour has become.

Maybe we've spent too much time together, and we aren't used to it. We've only been together for a couple months; this could be one of the pitfalls of falling in love and getting married faster than the time it takes to break a habit.

I'm bending down to grab my loofah out of my shower caddy when the door opens. Hurriedly I cover myself, embarrassed, assuming one of the boys has walked in on me naked as the day I was born.

"It's me." I look over my shoulder as Ben comes into the small space, shutting the door and closing us in.

"Ben, I'm almost done, give me a minute." I hurry and lather up my body, wanting to keep distance between us. The building tension feels like it will spill over any minute and lead to an even bigger fight.

I'm starting to rinse when his chest touches my back. I turn, and he's standing there naked. I don't know what to do or how to react when he's this close to me with his sad, sorry eyes—I almost want to give in.

"I fucked up and got way too shit-faced last night. You didn't deserve me calling you a prude."

"I guess I'm a prude compared to the women you slept with before me. Sorry I'm not up to par." I turn again and drop my head, regretting what I just said. I don't want to let him affect me, but I am only human. Not only was what he said hurtful but that word struck a nerve in me. It has me swarming with insecurities. I've tried to be the rock star's wife, tried to be the sexually progressive woman he needs, but I'm still trying to keep my identity.

Who I was before Ben is still important to me. I still want to hide my body from everyone else while wanting to show it off to Ben. I want to be more experienced in the bedroom, but I'm not used to acting like an experienced woman. It feels like he may one day need something that I can't give, and that breaks me.

The things he said last night shone a light on our issues. For the first time, Ben didn't make me feel worshipped; he made me feel inadequate.

"I didn't mean it like that. I was drunk, and I said stupid shit. Please don't be upset with me." He grabs my hips, and I back into what little space I have, cutting off physical contact.

"You can't say something cruel then say you didn't mean it. It doesn't make it okay."

"You're right. Please, what can I do to make this better?"

"You can figure that out, Ben, but for now let me have some space." I climb out and grab my towel. Covering myself in my silk robe, I leave him in the shower to think about how much he hurt me.

Once I'm dressed and the guys have left for sound check, I call Kate and vent to her. I need some girl time. As we talk, we sum up my life.

My husband and I are fighting. He won't let me in on what's going on with his therapy. And my father still thinks I made a mistake. Maybe . . . maybe he's right.

Twenty-six

BEN

Sound check finished early, but I stay behind alone. After my fight with Sadie, which was my fucking fault, I need a minute. I don't know what possessed me—other than the drugs and alcohol—to say what I did to her. She's not a prude. Our sex life is fucking phenomenal, and I don't want anyone else. Simply put, I'm a fucking prick.

Sitting center stage, I strum a few chords on my guitar, my cheek resting against the body. My hands move across the strings effortlessly, and Sadie's song finds its way out. I sing it over and over again, wanting it to be perfect for tonight when I sing it to her for the first time.

If this shit doesn't make her forgive me, I don't know what will, because in the time we have been together, I have said sorry for my poor behavior on multiple occasions, and those apologies are becoming meaningless. I need something grand to get her to listen to me.

My fingers change from Sadie's song to my mother's. The acoustic sound of "Amazing Grace" echoes in the venue, carrying out over the empty chairs. She would sing me to sleep with this song when I was little, and it was the first song I ever learned to play on the piano.

The chords sound peaceful, and I feel isolated in my own safe space, as if the entire room has gone dark. Keeping my chin resting on the guitar, I swear I can see my mother sitting front row center wearing her favorite blue dress, smiling up at me with her big brown eyes glistening with pride.

What I wouldn't give for her to be here right now to help set me straight. An image of Sadie standing next to my mother consumes my mind, and it shatters me. I keep playing, the melody slowing as I let a few tears travel down my cheeks and onto the body of my guitar.

Sadie is the only good thing left in my life, and if I don't make this right, I will lose her. That loss would be as hard as, if not harder than, when I lost my mother. Sadie means that fucking much to me.

"Ben, baby?" Looking up into the audience, it's as if I'm dreaming. There Sadie stands, peering up at me with her face drawn down in remorse. I don't answer; instead, I place my chin back down and keep my eyes on her, finishing the last of the song.

She watches me as I watch her. I'm no longer crying, but she is, taking on my pain for me. "Hey," I croak out, my voice thick.

"Your mom?" she questions, moving up the stairs at the side of the stage. "You don't have to do this to yourself anymore, Ben." Taking the guitar from me, she places it on the bench of the piano. I wish it were as simple as she makes it sound.

"It's never that easy, Sadie. I'm not that easy." She looks beautiful in one of our band tees and a pair of skinny jeans. Her hair is hidden under a baseball cap, and she's not wearing makeup.

"We can find another way to help you cope. We can see another doctor if you want. Please understand what this is doing to us, and more importantly, what it's doing to you." I keep my hands in my lap and my eyes down, poking and prodding at my jeans.

"You're right." The thought of seeing another therapist and opening fresh wounds is enough to make my stomach turn. It brings me back to those two years I was in foster care. I sat in rooms with state therapist after state therapist, and all they did was nod their heads and hand me pills.

"Ben, I can only do so much. We are only a couple months into our relationship, and this is starting to happen more and more. I can tell you're upset. I have no doubt that you don't do this to hurt me, but it is hurting me, and what's worse is you're hurting yourself."

"You're right," I repeat. I can't defend myself anymore. All I can do is learn to control my temper and not say stupid shit when I'm fucked up—if that's even possible. "I'm sorry, and I'll get better, I promise." Finally, I touch her, my hands moving up her legs, ending under the curve of her ass.

"Ben, something has to give. I'm starting to drown here, and I want to make this work. Please start letting me in instead of pushing me out." I nod, thankful that she's here offering herself up on a platter for me. Her willingness to be my keeper and my own personal form of therapy is astounding after what I said to her last night.

Sadie is not weak, and she's not submissive. The way she behaves with me shows strength in multitudes; she is a fighter.

"You're way too good to me." Leaning forward, I kiss her stomach, resting my forehead there. Her hands massage my shoulders up my neck then into my hair.

"It's because I love you."

"And I love you, angel." Once again, she lets this one slide. I don't know how I got so lucky, but I can't keep doing this to her. To us. To me.

***

"Boston, you fucking killed it tonight!" The crowd roars to life, and the house lights come on over the sold-out show. "Tonight has been amazing! You're one of the best crowds we've seen. But before we go tonight, I wanna slow things down and play you an exclusive song that I wrote for our new album." I take a seat, and Nick brings me my guitar. I adjust the mic stand. The crowd yells out an array of whistles, screams, and declarations of love.

"I love you guys." I laugh. "So, as many of you know, I recently got married to my beautiful wife, Sadie. She's right over there, take a look at her." I point to side stage, where she stands next to Nick, and the crowd hollers. She shakes her head at me as a blush creeps across her cheeks.

"That little thing knocked me on my ass, and I haven't been the same since. So I wrote this song for you, baby. I hope you like it." The lights dim for a second. I play the first notes, and the blue light that matches her eyes comes on and shines down on me and the guitar as I start to sing.

You were unexpected
Like a freight train into my heart.
Unpredicted, coming into my world
Breaking it all apart.
I never had much faith in believing,
But you came in. Changed my every meaning.

I peer at her, at those blue eyes filled with tears, those high cheeks rounding with her smile. She holds a hand over her heart, and I feel the same heartbeat that I feel against my chest every night when she lies across my bare chest.

You're my heartbeat, my everything and more.
You took my love and
made me beg on my knees at your door.
I never wanted you, but then I found you, and that changed it all.
You're my religion, my hope, and baby, please catch me as I fall.
Maybe it's those baby blues,
or that sweet Southern style.
Or, baby, it's that sassy little way about you,
that perfect, delicate smile.
I know I've got my demons and I'm broken inside,
but here in this moment, I'm better by your side.
You're my heartbeat, my everything and more.
You took my love and made me beg on my knees at your door.
I never wanted you, but then I found you, and that changed it all.
You're my religion, my hope, and baby, please catch me as I fall.

I keep repeating the chorus, and each time I do, the fight slips away. The song ends, and the crowd goes wild. The boys and I take a bow, and I grab my blazer, throwing it on over my sweaty bare back.

"Night, Boston! Thank you!" The lights dim, and I head offstage. I put my hands on Sadie, and the sparks ignite. Her hands roam my chest as our lips lock, and we taste each other. I moan and pull away, looking back to find Nick.

Sadie loses my lips but finds my neck, sucking and leaving kisses against my throat.

"Nick!" He comes walking over after I yell his name. Without removing my hands from her ass, I give him a knowing look.

"What's up?"

Sadie pulls away and hides her face in embarrassment, but I have zero shame.

"Get us a hotel, now," I demand, and he nods, pulling out his phone and walking away from us again.

"You make me crazy. That was beautiful," Sadie whispers the second he disappears. Her body is alive, her nipples grazing my chest, her hands touching me all over, her cheeks flushed.

"I thought you'd like that."

"I loved it. I don't understand how it's possible to love someone as deeply as I love you."

"I don't know either, angel, but it's real, and I will fight for this to work."

"You're worth it." Thank hell, she believes that still.

Twenty-seven

SADIE

"You think he'll like this?"

"A cherry oak Fender T-Bucket 300CE guitar? Yeah, Sade, I think he will." Nick and I are in a local guitar shop in South Carolina. Ben has a photo shoot with the band, so we took the chance to sneak away and grab him a gift for his birthday tomorrow. The summer has flown by, and I have only a few days left on tour before I go home to gear up for my internship.

"I was thinking of engraving it with our wedding date. Then I was going to get the strap embroidered with his mama's name." Nick's eyes stay on the guitar. He nods without saying anything.

"What?" I nudge his shoulder.

"Nothing."

"Come on, tell me. Is it a bad idea? You think he'll get upset?"

"No, no. It's—I'm shocked he's told you so much about his mom. He doesn't usually talk about Grace."

"He told me not many people know." I start walking, looking at all my options, just in case. This has to be his best gift ever.

"I barely even know anything. He told me about his dad and the beatings, about him killing her, but other than that he's been tight-lipped about it," Nick tells me.

"It's therapy he doesn't want to talk to me about." I smile at the other customers as I pass.

"He won't. Whenever he does, that's when he seems to drown himself in booze. He has a very dark side, Sadie."

"Are you trying to warn me or inform me?" I'm not sure where this is going. He, out of anyone, knows that Ben and I are having more lows than highs lately. Haven't I seen him at his worst? It can't possibly get any worse than it is now.

"Both. Listen, you're the greatest thing to happen to Ben since I've known him, but he has a side of him that you haven't really tapped into, and I hope you understand that. Be patient with him, and hopefully when he's ready he will let you in and the help he is getting will work."

"You think he'll get there?" I appreciate his honesty, but Ben and I are very fragile right now. This isn't helping.

"Maybe. With you, I think he'll do whatever he can to make this work."

"You're good to him. So good."

"He's like a son to me, and even though I don't agree with half the things he does, I love him, and the choice he made to marry you is the one thing I support more than anything." I welcome the compliment from this six-foot, burly man. I adore him, and knowing Ben has him after the shitty life he had before makes me hopeful for Ben's future. Maybe both of us can help him stop running from his past and face his future.

I want to give Ben a home, a family, a safe place where he never has to feel unloved, hurt, or alone, but he needs to be willing to lay down his cards and hold up his end of the bargain.

"Thank you." Giving him a hug, I relax enough to focus on the task at hand—Ben's birthday.

"All right, let's get him this guitar and go. I'm excited to see his face." I change the subject. Today I'm not going to think about everything that's wrong in our marriage but rather the things that are right.

***

Today is Ben's birthday, and the boys throw him a tailgate party before the concert. The guitar is hidden in Nick's bunk, and I plan to give it to him when we are alone later tonight.

I feel sick toward the end of the party, so I sneak away to get some rest during the show. I should have known that wouldn't be the best idea, with the alcohol and drugs the boys always consume during my absence.

When I wake up, he is someone different.

Sneaking back into the venue through the back entrance, I head toward the meet and greet, wanting to be here for some of the night and not totally leave him hanging on such a special day.

"Hey, Nick."

"Oh fuck, hey, Sadie. I didn't know you were coming." He blocks Ben from my view, and I step back a little.

"Well, I'm feeling better, and I wanted to come see him. What's going on?" I attempt to move around Nick, but he stops me, grabbing my shoulders and holding me in place.

"Listen, it's just his meet and greet. Why don't you go rest and make sure you're one hundred percent better?" I glare up at him; he's doing a terrible job of hiding whatever it is he doesn't want me to see. I step aside again, clearing him before he can stop me.

I stop dead in my tracks as I watch Ben sniff cocaine off the bar top in the back area. One of his fans laughs, and I nearly lose my dinner.

My knees buckle, but before I fall, Nick catches me under my arms. Knowing Ben does drugs is one thing, but seeing it out there in the open, so raw, is another.

Ben hasn't noticed me, and I'm glad because I feel like I'm losing myself.

This is what I imagine a heart attack feels like: there is a strong grip on my heart, like it is actually being broken in two. Gaining my equilibrium, I snap back into the moment and go into fight or flight. I push Nick off and make a run for the bus.

The night air hits my skin the second I clear the door, and the breeze slightly cools my heated skin. I have no time to think about anything; my flight reflex is fully engaged, and all I can think about is calling a cab and getting a red-eye back to Portland.

Climbing on the bus, I pack whatever's in sight, dumping it all into my suitcase with no method. Picking up my phone, I dial Kate, realizing anew that I can't call my parents. Maybe I was right all along and I'm not meant to be a rock star's wife. This isn't the life I wanted, but I signed up for it. How naive of me to think I could help him.

"Hey, Sadie Jay!"

"Kate, I need you. Please find me a flight home to Portland," I cry into the phone, moving around the bus on autopilot, feeling completely out of my body.

"Oh my god, Sadie, what's wrong?"

"Nothing, Kate! Just please get me a flight and send me the flight information. I'm in South Carolina—fly me out of Charleston International."

"Okay, okay. I'm doing that now. Call me when you get to the airport, but, Sadie?" She pauses.

"What?"

"Tell me you're okay?"

"I'm fine. Please help me."

"Okay, I'm on it." Ending the call, I find the number for a taxi and wait for them to show up. When the taxi pulls up a few minutes later, I see Nick running toward me.

"Sadie! Damn it, don't run!" I throw my bags in the taxi and slam the trunk.

"I don't have a choice, Nick."

"We can help him together. We can do it, I promise, but you can't give up on him."

Opening the door of the cab and climbing inside, I turn on him.

"Don't make excuses for him. He has choices, and he makes the ones that hurt him the most. The ones that hurt me."

"Sade, I'm telling you it's not that simple."

"Stop defending him! I can't stay here, Nick. We rushed this, all of this."

Trying to stop me, he grabs the taxi door before I can close it. "This is going to set him off. He's going to go off the rails."

"I can't feel guilty about that. He's already fallen off. He promised me repeatedly that he would try to work on this. He hasn't." My words render him speechless. Nodding his head in defeat, he lets the door go, and I tell the cab driver to leave.

It isn't until I'm at the airport that my phone starts blowing up with calls and messages from Ben, that I realize everything that is happening. Ben is an addict. He can't simply change for me; he needs more than that. My leaving isn't to prove to him that I am serious; it is for me. I need to do it because I don't know where my place is in Ben's life. He may do therapy and take medication, but there is a place deep inside him that is shut, and he is refusing to unlock his hurt in order to heal.

It's blindingly obvious how young we are, even in how I'm choosing to handle this. Running—it's all I can think to do. I've never been in love before, let alone with a man who can be my best friend and a stranger all at once.

I do everything in my power to restrain myself from looking at the messages he's sending me. Now what do I do? Does going home mean it's over for Ben and me? I can't tell my parents; it would kill my father to know I let my life get this dark.

What about Ben? He comes home this Friday, and that's only two days away. We share an apartment—we're going to have to face each other sooner rather than later. What has my life become? A few months ago, I was in bliss, and now I'm spiraling down a rabbit hole of hows, whys, and what-ifs.

There is no right answer, no magic solution to fix my problems—I believe I'm a lost cause. My heart is broken. I am breaking in this marriage.

Twenty-eight

BEN

"What the fuck do you mean she left? Why?" I yell and sprint back to the bus. I don't know why I'm running. Nick told me she left, so it's not like she'll be there. The second I saw Nick, I knew something was wrong, and before he even finished telling me Sadie had left, I was on my feet.

"She saw you do coke, Ben. She left."

"Fuck!" Damn it, I shouldn't have done that shit, and I knew it the second after I did it. I promised Sadie I would stop the hard drugs, and not only did I lie but she saw it with her two eyes.

"You let her fucking leave me! Where the fuck is my phone?" I never bring it with me to shows, and I can't find it anywhere on the bus. I look like a madman throwing things around and leaving everything in disarray.

"Calm down and let me find it."

"Don't tell me to calm down! I need to go home! I want to leave now. Get me a flight." He hands me my phone, and I call her. Straight to voice mail.

Fuck. I keep trying, and it sends me to voice mail each time. Each time I send her a message, it says *Delivered* but never *Read*.

"You can't. Tomorrow, you have interviews with three different magazines."

"I don't care!"

"Ben! Calm down or I will make you calm down. If you go home or call her when you're fucking high, you're going to make it worse. Give her tomorrow to cool off. You can go home to her once you both have a second to think."

"She can't expect me to change overnight!" My anger is growing more impenetrable by the minute. I'm becoming bitter because she left me instead of fighting for me.

"No, but Ben, doing cocaine isn't exactly a winning scenario. You knew what kind of girl Sadie was when you married her."

"And she knew who I was!" I grab the glass next to me and slam it on the table; the impact causes it to shatter and cut open my hand.

"Damn it, Ben! Calm down!" Nick yells, moving around the bus to find me something for my hand. Only problem is, I don't want it. I want to bleed, want to hurt, want to punish myself for hurting Sadie.

"Here." He wraps my hand, and I drop down on the couch, the night catching up to me. "You two have some shit you need to work out, Ben, but she has sacrificed a lot to be with you, and you need to learn that this isn't all about you." He defends Sadie's honor, and as much as I grow jealous over it, Nick's right. Sadie has put up with my rage, my drug use, and my jealousy. She went against everything she knew in order to be with me. Even gave up her family. Her parents mean the world to her, and I have selfishly sat back and watched as she has given up so much of herself to love me.

All she asked me to do was to stop the hard drug use and open up to her about therapy so I can be healthy and free from all the bad shit that weighs me down.

But the truth of the matter is, I'm an addict, and we can't shed our skin overnight.

"After the interviews, I want to fly home earlier. Move me to the next available flight. Charge my card."

"Fine." That's all he needs to say, because the fight is dead. I fucked up, and the only way I'm going to get better is if I work on this with Sadie and commit to the help I've been getting.

"I'll do anything for her. I love her, Nick."

"Good. Start acting like it, then. Now come on, we need to patch up your hand."

The next twenty-four hours need to fly the hell by. If I lose her like this, I won't bounce back. I won't even stand a chance at surviving.

Twenty-nine

SADIE

It's nearing six in the morning when my flight lands, and Kate is waiting to pick me up. I told her everything on the phone from start to finish as I waited to board my flight, knowing I couldn't go the entire trip without someone hearing what I have to say. Even then, I was losing my mind the whole flight. The flight attendant came around with tissues more than I'd like to admit, and if my sobs had gotten any louder, they might have stopped the damn flight.

Ben has called repeatedly and sent me an ungodly number of messages. I resisted reading any of them with the strength of a saint. But what if he sucks me back in? That's what keeps happening. We've fallen into a cycle, and at this point, I don't know if either of us knows how to break it. How did we get here? How did it get this bad so fast?

"Oh, Sadie," Kate says empathetically the second I clear the sliding doors. She leaves her car running and comes to hug me. I fall into her arms and sob, exhausted and emotionally run dry.

"I hate this," I cry into her shoulder, not caring if I'm all tears, snot, and drool in public. I feel like I'm living in a parallel universe and I can't find my way back home.

"I'm here, babe. Let's get you home. Your parents are waiting."

"You told them?" I didn't want to tell them until I was ready to admit that they were right and I need their help. They have never been disappointed in me. My father warned me, and I didn't listen. Plus, regardless of how hurt I am, I don't want them to judge Ben. They don't know the whole story, and they don't know the man deep inside. The one I keep fighting for.

Kate's face is scrunched up, and I return her look quizzically. She grabs my luggage and packs up her car. We both slide in at the same time.

"I didn't know what to do, Sadie. I was worried, and I think you need them right now. They want to be there. Let them. Let us all be there. Please?" she begs. I look over at her, tempted to tell her she is wrong, but she isn't. I do want my parents. I need them. God, do I need them.

"Am I in the twilight zone?" I ask, sliding on my seat belt.

"That or a really bad horror movie. Either way, we got this." She tries her best to comfort me, but it's a lost cause. Off to face my parents . . . here we go.

***

"How long have you two been struggling with this?" my mother asks from the opposite side of the kitchen table. My father hasn't said a word. Instead, he sits there with his arms crossed over his chest and his tight jaw tilted to the ground. My palms are sweating. I want to throw up, and I worry he may flip the table.

"I knew about his disorder and the drugs, but when we first met, there was this string of really good days—weeks, even. It got bad a month into me going on tour with him," I admit. Kate is sitting next to me holding my hand in a firm, comforting grip, and I draw as much strength from her as I can.

"Why didn't you call us?" My father's tight voice slices through his silent standoff, and my body shivers. I have never seen my dad so cold.

"I didn't want you to worry. And . . ." I pause, finally looking up at him. His eyes are glazed over. That look. That look right there is what I wanted to avoid. Why did I look up? "Because I love him, Papa. I love him, and I didn't want you to tell me you were right and try to convince me to leave. I hate this, but I can't let him go." I break down again, dropping my head in my hands and falling against Kate's shoulder. I'm so ashamed of how weak I am. Ben has molded me to bend and break at his will, but he always comes back and heals me.

"I wouldn't throw that in your face, Sadie. You're our daughter, and regardless of whether we agree with your choices or not, we don't want you to suffer. God, sweetie. Come here." He stands and rounds the table, opening his arms and letting the tears leak from his eyes. I stand on shaky legs and fall into him, crying from deep in my chest.

"He's a good man, the greatest, he just needs someone. I promise. Help me figure this out? Be there for me and for him. Please. That's a lot to ask, but for me?" I beg him to give in. To let go of any preconceived ideas of Ben he may have, even if some of them hold weight.

"Shh, we are here. We love you, and we will help you through this. I am sorry we went this long pushing you out." My mother's warmth surrounds me. She closes the circle, and I'm engulfed in my parents' love, something I didn't think I would still crave like a child into my adulthood.

"I don't know what to do. I really don't," I cry. Their soft voices try their best to soothe me, but it's futile. These past few months have challenged me. Caged me. Changed me. Freed me. Then lured me back into the cage. There must be a con they can sell a fool to get over this faster.

For the next hour, they focus on calming me down. They tell me I need a breather and to put some space between us right now. My father says I shouldn't react or come up with a plan when I am this emotional, and my mother and Kate agree. They are right. Kate takes me to her place. Like I should have known she would, she goes to the extreme in attempting to keep my mind off Ben by convincing me to go out the following night. As if it's possible to not think about him.

***

I continue to ignore Ben's messages and calls, moping around Kate's house and hardly getting anything ready to start my internship—at least I have that to look forward to. I miss Ben. I miss his dirty jokes, his thundering laugh, his touch, his voice, our conversations. But no matter how much I miss him, I can't forget that my love isn't enough to save him. The hard drugs and him shutting me out when he needs to let me in—these things are a threat to us, and my fragile heart doesn't have what it takes to compete with that. I can't watch him destroy himself anymore.

"Kate, I don't know if I'm in the mood to go out. I don't think it's a good idea." Rising out of the chair, I drag myself to the bed and climb in, lying on my side and staring at the opposite wall, ready to zone out.

"But it is, and you need it. Girls' night, don't you want that? You can forget everything."

I scoff. "I can't forget about my husband, Kate." I blink rapidly as my eyes begin to water.

"I didn't mean it like that, but you need to get out. Besides, he's gonna show up everywhere until he finds you when he gets into town, so maybe being out will buy you some time." She has a point.

"You're right. I'll put something on and come out."

"Okay, good. Do you want me to do your hair and makeup? We can talk about everything."

I debate for a moment. I could use a thousand and one vent sessions. "Sure. I'd like that."

"Perfect, go shower first."

Before I stand to do as she said, I read Ben's last messages over and over again.

I'm sorry.
Please forgive me.

You're my wife, you can't give up on us. We made a vow, Sadie. Please—I'm sorry.

"How about you don't do things you have to be sorry about?" I say under my breath. Turning off my ringer, I drop my phone in the heap of blankets and go shower.

* * *

"I'm jealous of your hair, Sadie Jay. I swear, is there anything wrong with you?" I keep my eyes focused on the floor while Kate curls my thick hair into waves.

"My marriage."

"I knew you weren't done talking about it. Let it out; stop getting in your head and blocking me out." I peer up and look at her through the mirror. Kate's eyes don't meet mine, and it's purposeful.

"Kate, we're so young. We fell in love too fast, and we got married even faster." I bite my lip, playing with the gold band on my finger. "You know when I'm sad because I miss him? Well, I want to call him and tell him how bad I'm hurting and what I'm going through, but then I remember he's the reason I'm here. He's the reason I'm drowning."

"Oh, Sade."

The tears have escaped against my will, and I do nothing to catch them. I want them to fall; I want to waste my tears on him, waste my pity, because no one else can heal this.

"Why am I not good enough for him? Why did we get married so young? Did we make a mistake, Kate?" I ask, wiping away my hot tears.

"No, Sade, you didn't. Most people search the world and spend years building a love like yours, and you two found it right away. You're enough. It's Ben who needs to work on himself." Standing beside me, she wraps her arms around my shoulders, and my face drops against her. I shake uncontrollably, feeling reduced to nothing.

"Shh, Sade, it's okay."

A loud sob rips through my chest, echoing in the silent room. "I miss him so much." My back aches with the weight of the world, and anxiety collects in my chest. What do I do? Seeing Ben doing those drugs was a dagger straight to my heart. I can't unsee that, not even if I tried. "I can't believe we're here, that within such a short time we fell so deeply in love and now we're heading for what? A divorce? Am I making a mistake? God, Kate, I have so many questions." Rubbing my back, she hushes me some more, finally loosening her grip a little.

"I can't answer that for you, babe. This is a choice you two have to make." I wish she weren't right.

I finally dry the well of tears enough to continue getting ready. "Now that I look like roadkill, can we focus on getting me ready so I can get out of this house?"

"Of course. I have the perfect outfit."

***

Beach waves in my hair, red lips, and a smoky eye later, I'm dressed in a skintight strapless dress with a thick choker and a leather jacket. My heels add a few inches, and although I'm dying on the inside, surprisingly, my body looks alive and well tonight. I'm shocked Kate could hide the dark circles under my tired eyes.

"You look so damn good, babe!" Stepping away from the closet, Kate looks me over, zipping up the side of her strapless romper. She looks stunning. Her long, lean legs and slender torso make the outfit. Kate could make a trash bag look couture.

"You look great, Kate." I return the compliment, still feeling a little out of my comfort zone with this whole look. Ever since I got married, I've slowly started wearing more revealing clothes and doing my makeup a little differently. I stopped being the doctor's daughter and became the rock star's wife.

"Don't. Don't think of him. We're doing so good, we're almost out the door. Come on." Grabbing my clutch, she hands it to me then ushers me out the door and down the steps of her porch.

Catching an Uber, we head downtown. I'm not sure who's playing here tonight, but getting out after twenty-four hours of wallowing does make me feel a little bit better. The air is crisp, and it glides against us when we climb out of the cab. I straighten my dress, my legs erupting in goose bumps. I don't miss the men passing and gawking at Kate and me.

"Keep walking, boys, eyes on someone else," Kate hollers. They smirk and whistle. "Pigs."

"I agree." We weave around the crowds. Entering the venue, I'm instantly hit with the smell of smoke, and it reminds me of Ben. The only thing missing is his spicy cologne.

"Kate, where do you want to go?" I ask as I turn, but she isn't behind me; she's stopped at the door to talk to someone. I shrug and head to the bar, not really concerned enough to put in any effort.

"Can I get a Coke, please?" I order as I find a stool. The scratched-up wooden bar top holds my attention while I wait for my drink.

"Sadie?" My back stiffens, and my eyes widen. That voice—the only voice that can paralyze me. It's both inviting and daunting. I pivot, and my eyes meet Ben's honey ones. His head is covered with a snapback, his eyes are heavy and dark, and the scruff on his face forms a five o'clock shadow. The way his black jeans and leather jacket fit is lethal, and my knees quickly feel like buckling.

"Ben, what are you doing here?" I ask, exasperated. How did he know where to find me?

"I invited him. I think you two need to talk," Kate says. Feeling betrayed, I stand abruptly, throwing down a ten-dollar bill on the bar top.

"Wow, thanks a lot, Kate. I thought I could trust you." Looking back and forth between her and Ben, I shake my head. "Forget it. Have a good night." I push past them.

"Sadie!" Both Ben and Kate call after me, but I make a hasty retreat. I feel cornered and vulnerable, which doesn't help. Seeing him slammed my heart back into the ground. I thought tonight I was going to be able to forget him, even for a short reprieve, but instead I was faced with him head-on.

"Sadie, baby, wait! Come on."

Stepping onto the sidewalk, I start walking, not bothering to slow down while I try to hail a cab. I'm not ready to make nice with him, not ready to face all the things that have ultimately put us in this very spot.

"No, Ben! Stay away from me." I try to walk faster, but the uneven sidewalk doesn't give me much of a head start in my black pumps. Within seconds, he's on me, grabbing my arm and turning me to face him.

"You can't avoid me anymore, Sadie. You have to talk to me." I look up at his sad expression and see a mirror of my own broken reflection. That's the most twisted thing about this—we're both deeply broken, and the only cure is each other.

"Yes, I can, because there is nothing to say."

"To hell there isn't, Sadie! You're my wife; you can't throw in the towel when shit gets tough," Ben yells, throwing his hands in the air. The breeze hits us, and his smell wafts over to me, assaulting my senses. That smell and the sight of him have my eyes welling with defiant tears. How the hell do I still have tears left to cry? I've missed him, and my wires are getting jumbled. I don't know if I want to scream, cry, fight, or make up. This is exactly why it's dangerous for us to be in the same vicinity.

"You don't want to commit fully to healing. You are using everything but the things that can help you and keep you safe, Ben. On top of that, you won't let me in. You push me away when you know it will only make things worse. I can't sit around and watch you kill yourself for the high. I can't—I won't!" A group of girls walk by, and they chuckle, mumbling about my sudden outburst. If it weren't for how overwhelmed I am, I would say something.

"You think it's that easy, Sadie? It's not. I can't be cured overnight!"

"I've tried getting you to talk about therapy to see if we need to try something different. I've tried to be another outlet for you to lose yourself in instead of drugs and violence. I've begged for you to let me in."

"Damn it, Sadie. I can't be cured so easily. This shit is real. You don't love me enough to stay and work through this?"

"How can we work through this when I don't even know what the hell is going on beneath the surface! Don't try to make this my fault. I have sacrificed a lot to make you happy and to help you, so don't you do that to me!" I poke his chest, shaking my head back and forth.

"What the fuck have you sacrificed for me, Sadie? Huh, what?" he yells, throwing his arms out to the side with a shrug.

"I gave up my life before you to create a new one with you. My life was set before you came along and changed everything!"

"So what? I'm the prick who ruined you? Is that what you're saying? Because I was fine before you, too, Sadie, but I made a choice when we got married that I would fight for this and I would learn to be a different man for you."

"But you aren't! You are using my love as a crutch to excuse your choices! You're still the same! Don't make it sound like I forced you into this marriage, Ben. You wanted this, too, all so you could get me in bed."

"I didn't fucking marry you so I could get some. I can get any woman I want. I married you because I love you!" I cling to those words; they're all I've been craving to hear. It's still not enough, though, for me to forget everything.

"Stay away from me, Ben. Go live the life you wanted before I came to screw it all up. I get that you don't understand me and why I want to help so badly, just like I don't understand your need to self-medicate with drugs and women and fighting. We rushed this, our marriage was a m—"

"No, don't you dare say it was a mistake. You can't take it back once it's said."

I drop my eyes, and the grooves in the sidewalk hold my gaze as the tears fall. "Ben, we both have so much we want in this life, but all the things that hang over us are bound to end everything we want."

"The things I want in this life are you. All of you—every part of you."

I shake my head, and my chest shakes with my sobs. "Ben..."

"Give me tonight, please." He steps toward me, grabbing my elbows.

"I can't..." I don't lean into him, but I don't push away either.

"Why?" he asks, moving the hair away from my face and wrapping his hand around the column of my neck in a possessive way. That is a power move. It's ownership. And he knows it's something I crave. My desperation for him is growing stronger by the second, completely shattering my resolve.

"I can't answer that because I don't even know why," I admit.

Before we question each other further, he pulls my smaller frame to his taller one, and in a flash our lips fuse together. I taste mint and tobacco, an acquired taste but one that, since the day I first had it, has become something I constantly crave.

Gripping his leather jacket in my hands, I feel a rush of butterflies low in my stomach. My legs get weak, and my mouth opens, kissing him back with as much force as he is giving.

His hands leave my neck and reach around to grab the underside of my ass. He leans in to get a complete handful, and I moan into his mouth. Nipping, sucking, biting, and licking, our tongues fall into the dance we've both learned so well.

I barely notice that we're moving until my back is against the side of the brick building next to us.

Ben moans, his erection growing against my stomach. We both know we're in public, and I hear the passing strangers and the honking horns, but all I feel is Ben against me.

Bringing one hand up beside me, he lays his palm flat against the brick while his other hand keeps gripping my backside. I finally pull away, knowing if we continue, we will be arrested for public indecency.

"Ben..." I put a few inches between us by pushing on his chest.

"I've missed you, Sadie. Please let me take us home," he begs, kissing my cheek, then my neck, then down the swell of my breast. I moan and shake.

"I've missed you, too, Ben." I add fuel to this fire, forgetting everything other than lust for my husband. I want him, no matter the consequences. "Okay," I whisper against his ear as he sucks on the skin of my neck. Pulling away, he smirks down at me. Giving me one quick kiss, he hails us a cab.

In the cab, we sit so close it's hard to tell where he starts and I end. I let him whisper in my ear all the ways he is sorry, how beautiful I am, and how much he wants to save us.

Before we even make it in the apartment door, he's on me from behind, his hand coming to my front and going up my dress to cup my pussy. His mouth is latched to my neck.

"Ben, baby, wait. Let me lock the door," I tell him, shutting the door with shaking hands.

"I want you," he groans in my ear. His hand travels up my thigh and under my dress. I went with full coverage tonight, not really prepared to spend time with him. "Tell me something." Finally, I get the door locked, and I'm able to turn to him. I let him remove my jacket, and I help remove his.

"What?" I ask breathlessly, all hormones and need at this point. He puts me against the wall, lifting my legs up and around his waist. I grab his neck and kiss him, nibbling at his full lips.

"Did you wear this because you wanted to find another man? Tell me you don't want someone else, Sadie." My confident playboy is anything but.

"No, I don't want anyone else, ever. I'm never going to want anyone other than you," I whisper, feeling bad that he thought that I would ever do that. But I've been on the opposite end as well, wondering if he would ever cheat on me. The women he once preferred are the kind that still crawl around his stage each night.

"What . . . what about . . . about you?" I stutter, scared. I don't know what it will do to me if he ever gives in to temptation.

"Never. I haven't been with another woman since the day I met you, Sadie. And I never will," he confesses. At first, I don't believe him. I don't know who I trust anymore.

"Promise?"

"Sadie, don't question my desire for you. I only want you."

"What if I'm never going to be enough, Ben?" I ask, and he moves, carrying me toward our bedroom at the end of the hall. The walls are full of framed pictures of us. My heels fall, and I cross my arms around the back of his head, gripping the lush fullness of his hair.

"You're more than enough, Sadie. More than anything, you are enough," he whispers, his breath moving across my face.

"Show me. Please, Ben, because you're losing me," I admit in a low cry, my voice cracking.

"I'll never let that happen," he professes. But until I see him actually changing, tonight isn't going to fix anything. Passion cannot mask the dark side of things. He has to put in the effort and get better or he will lose me for good; that is one thing I will not waver on.

I sit on the edge of our bed and anticipate his next move. I'm letting him take the lead tonight. Ben grabs the hem of my strapless dress and lifts it from my body, leaving me in my black panties and matching strapless bra.

"You look like you but so different, and it's only been a fucking day." He removes the shirt that adorns his body, showing off his abs, his V growing more pronounced. "You're my muse, the most beautiful creature I've ever seen. Those lips tell me beautiful tales and truths—they tell me they love me." I stand no chance when he whispers to me, blessing me with his poetry—the perk of being married to a singer.

"Ben . . ." I don't even have words to reciprocate.

He doesn't say anything. Instead, his hands start to work on me. Starting at my thighs, he trails his fingers up the length of me, all the way up my stomach, laying me back on the bed. When I'm flat, he leans in and kisses my stomach right under my belly button.

This is real intimacy. Those random kisses are deadly to my psyche.

"Relax, baby."

I stay focused as the kisses continue to go lower and his hands find my ankles. Lifting them up, he places them on the bed. Now between my legs, he casts his eyes over my desperate body, kissing me one last time atop the fabric covering my pubic bone as I grow needier.

"Oh, Ben..." I cry, ripped in two with pleasure and despair. Moving across my pubic bone, his hand slides into one side of my panties at my hip while his mouth latches onto the fabric on the other side. In a slow, steady move, he drags them down my thighs, over my knees, and down my shins, where he lifts my feet enough for them to drop from his mouth and fall on the floor.

The lover my husband is. I've never before known what desire could be, but now I believe he invented it. I'm entranced as he kisses his way back up my legs, finally ending with his tongue against my center. I cry out, gripping the sheets, and my toes curl. He doesn't just lick me, he feeds on me, eating me with a purpose. This is Ben spoiling me out of both need and guilt, and I don't stop him.

My legs fall further open as he alternates between biting, licking, and sucking. As I'm chasing the edge of glory, he stops, kissing my thigh and bringing his face to mine.

"You're beautiful. You taste so sweet," he tells me, letting me taste my own arousal on his lips. We are a mixture of moans and heavy breathing. His fingers trail lazily down my body before two enter my dripping core. I bite my lip, breaking our connection and dropping my head back. The cry that leaves me is animalistic. The high-pitched sound earns me a moan of appreciation from Ben that vibrates against me.

He works his fingers up and down, round and round, deeper and faster. Ben has always known how to get me off in record time. That's why he drives me to the edge then pulls away before I can jump headfirst.

"I can't lose this. I can't lose you, baby. Don't leave me." His voice is hoarse, and I nod my head, giving in for the moment. The haze of love messes with our judgment, and right now we are deep in that fog.

"Ben, make love to me, please." I'm physically aching inside for him, for his touch.

"Anything, angel." Sitting up, he looks over me while he slowly unfastens his pants. I wiggle under that gaze, my blood pumping heavily through my veins as I eagerly anticipate his next touch.

His large cock springs free, hard and ready, pre-come already wetting the tip. I lick my lips and reach out for him. He comes to me with no words—we're always connected in a silent understanding. Spreading my legs, he opens me enough to make room for him while he lines his cock up with my entrance. His arms around my head and his hands lost in my hair, he gives me a gentle kiss. With one thrust, he's all the way inside, deep and thick—I feel it all. My home. My husband. The antidote to my broken heart.

"Oh!"

"God, Sadie, you're killing me." My feet move against his calves as he starts thrusting in and out of me, fast yet steady. The closer we get, the more I want to cry. This seems like we're saying goodbye. Each touch feels like the last touch, and I savor it.

We kiss, our lips only breaking apart when we need to breathe out the pleasure. Reaching my hands down, I grip his ass, pulling him in deeper with each thrust. He's everywhere right now; my senses are overtaken by him. I smell him, see him, feel him, taste him—he's in every pore.

"What do you want, Sadie?" he questions, keeping his thrusts strong and giving me his eyes, a connection deeper than the physical. I shake my head as the tears start to fall.

"I want you. I want you to stop hurting yourself because it's killing me, Ben." I run my hands over his face, holding his cheeks in my hands. We're in the shadows right now; I don't know what's lurking around the corner, and all I want is to feel safe again. I want to step into the light.

"Isn't this enough for you?" he questions, thrusting into me with a hard drive of his hips. I choke on a cry, but I don't go silent.

"If it's not all of you, it's not enough," I admit, speaking from deep inside me because if he doesn't get it now, when we're soul to soul, he never will.

He doesn't respond. Instead, he speaks with his body, making love to me. I let it go for now, knowing that though I may never get through to him, right now I can pretend—even if it's for a moment of temporary bliss.

* * *

The storm of our lovemaking has slowed down for a short time. I lie on my stomach pretending I'm asleep so I can hold off the inevitable goodbye for as long as I can. The longer I lie here, the more I realize he will not change unless he really wants to, and there doesn't seem to be an end in sight for him.

My eyes stay closed while he worships me. He lies across my lower back, kissing up and down my spine, running his hands over my curves.

"You're beautiful. You're my drug. My everything," he whispers. I wish I could believe that. The soft sound of "Skinny Love" by Birdy plays on repeat over the speakers in our room. It's not loud enough to overshadow his sweet words, but it definitely makes them more painful to hear. It's the soundtrack to our devastation. "I could kiss your skin every second of every day and never get tired of it. I never knew I could fall in love, baby." I feel the tears threatening to fall—although I don't think they've ever really stopped. "Let me fix us, angel. Give me a chance to make this right." With his whisper, I feel him stand at the side of the bed. His cock stands tall against my ass as he moves. "Wake up, Sadie, I want you again," he whispers in my ear, moving me onto my side and pulling me to the edge of the bed, my knees lifting out in front of me.

I open my eyes just as he thrusts into me. I'm on my side, so I can't move too much, making it hard to squirm away from his invasion. "Ben, baby."

"I need you again." I have to fight the urge to ask him if it's me he's craving or if I'm something he's using instead of the drugs he can't use when he's around me. Leaning over me, he grabs hold of my full breast, the large globe spilling out of his hand.

"I love your breasts, baby. I love your entire body. Fuck, you're like a masterpiece," he moans, kneading my breast, his other hand gripping my hip for leverage as he pounds into me. "Make me come, Sadie, take everything from me," he groans, skating his hand between the valley of my legs. When he lands on my pussy, he rubs my clit in fast circles, speeding up my orgasm.

"Then give me everything, Ben." I look at him with my lips parted, one hand gripping the sheet as the other one moves along with his over my clit, adding pressure.

"Shit, beautiful, just like that. Give it to me, you're squeezing me so tight. Squirt on me, angel." I clench down on his cock, his words driving me over the edge. I come fast, seeing stars and hearing symphonies.

"Oh my!" I scream, bearing down on him.

"Fuck, yes! Take it all, baby." He releases. His head falls back, and his lip is caught between his teeth. His eyes are dilated when he finds mine again, his thrusts slow and lazy, giving me every last drop.

"I love you."

"I love you, too, Ben."

Thirty

BEN

Sitting in a chair on the balcony, I take a long drag of the devil's stick. The smoke fills my lungs, burning deep until I release it again. The sun should be rising in a few hours, but I can't close my eyes. I don't want to sleep. I don't want to do anything other than wait for Sadie to wake up so I can make love to her again.

I'm an addict; my compulsive urge to latch onto something is inevitable. I'm itching for a drag of weed to calm me down; my fists are pain-free from the lack of fights recently. Three cigarettes and five orgasms later, I'm still craving something.

Sadie.

My phone interrupts the silence, and I reach into my pocket to pull it out. Seeing Eric's name, I pick up.

"What's up, man?"

"Hey, I have Lars here. He's selling me some new shit, you want a hit or no? You can pay me back later."

I bite my lip and take a drag of my cigarette, looking over my shoulder to check if Sadie is still asleep. The lights are still off, so I answer, keeping my voice low.

"Get me a bag." The exact thing we are fighting over is snaking its way back in.

"All right, brother. See you tomorrow at the show. You bringing Sadie?"

"I think so, if she wants to come."

"Kate will be there, so she'll most likely come. See you then, dude."

"All right, man, bye."

If Sadie had any idea that I bought drugs on the balcony of our apartment, she would snap, and my ass would be done for. I hate lying to her, I really do, but I can't stop. I'm an addict, and like I told her, that doesn't mean I don't want to try, but it's not as easy as snapping your fingers. Is it doable? Yes. Have I stopped taking other drugs cold turkey? Yes. But fuck, it was like someone was yanking each tooth out one by one. Getting high and fighting fucking feels right. It's momentary, but it never seems unnecessary. How do I tell her that? How can that make sense? It makes sense in my mind, but then again, I walked a different path, and while I can't pretend to know hers, I do understand that we both need to give here. Even if that means we have to share the good, the bad, and the really fucking ugly.

When the drugs hit my system, they fog up all the bad memories, and when I am hit with a hard fist, the blow eases the pain and guilt I feel. It's a slippery slope, but it lessens all the bad a little, sometimes enough to make my memories seem like someone else's story. I have to escape those memories, because most days, they are enough to fucking strangle me.

Sure, I've gotten myself into some not-so-good situations when I'm high, but maybe if I can stop doing that, she'll be okay with me getting high on the bus or in the privacy of our home. There has to come a point where I no longer lean on cocaine or fighting, but in order to do that, I have to face wounds so deep that healing them would be as bad as pulling the trigger of the gun resting against my temple.

I take my last drag for the night and finally get my ass to bed. Tomorrow, I have a shit-ton of ass-kissing to do and a hometown show.

＊＊

I wake to the smell of bacon and the sound of rain from our open window. I'm used to California summers, so these rainy Portland summer days throw me off. I only moved here in January, and with being on the road six months out of the year, I haven't really adjusted to the change.

Climbing out of bed, I open my top drawer and slip on some sweats before heading in search of Sadie. I stretch and yawn all the way down the hall, my body sore and my eyes heavy. It's only nine, meaning I got maybe four hours of sleep.

Coming into the kitchen, I watch Sadie read her bible while she lets the bacon fry, flipping it sporadically. I've noticed that whenever we get bad, she leans heavily on her religion.

Her hair is in a wild bun on her head, little hairs falling out and touching her rosy cheeks. She's wearing my shirt, the sleeves too long for her and covering almost all of her hands. I see the bottom of her sweet little ass, and I want to bite it.

"Morning, angel." I let her know I'm behind her.

"Ben, you scared me." She turns toward me with her hand above her heart. My eyes travel up the length of her thick, creamy legs and end on her baby blues. "Breakfast is almost ready."

"Thank you." Like that, we dance around the elephant in the room. I will wait for her to bring up what we are going to do next, but there is one thing I'm sure of. She isn't leaving me. I will drown silently in my misery before I let her leave.

I check my phone as we eat, scratching down some lyrics in my notes. Sadie makes little noises as she reads, and I smile, loving the small things that make her who she is.

"What are your plans today?" I place my hand on her thigh and squeeze gently, placing my phone down.

"I'm going to do some laundry and clean up, that's all for now. What about you?"

"I'll help you around the house, then I have to go to sound check at four. Doors open at six tonight, you gonna come?" I bait her, leaning in and kissing her cheek.

"Sure. I'll come." She smiles then marks her place in the book. Shutting it, she stands and collects our plates.

"I'm gonna shower. I'll be back in a few minutes." She leaves, and I watch her swaying hips disappear down the hall. I take that shit as an invite.

* * *

"Run, baby, run. Pack your bags, and I'll take you far away. Don't look back, you're gonna drown here if you stay," I sing into the mic, testing out my earpiece.

Eric is to my left on his guitar, messing with tuning, Jason has his bass, and JJ is on his drums. When everything sounds right, we start playing the first couple verses of each song. Sadie has to run some errands before she gets here, meaning I could take a few puffs from the new shit Eric bought. I only smoked enough to take the edge off how I've felt since my last high.

"Nick, turn up my earpiece, it's too quiet on track three. The guitar sounds too loud."

I adjust my earpiece, then the familiar sound of Kate comes bursting through the venue. Looking out in the empty room, I see her and Sadie walking in. Sadie's hair is a perfect wavy mess, and she's wearing skinny black ripped jeans with her boots, looking like a badass rocker wife.

All morning we cleaned, fucked a little, cleaned some more, then fucked again. I don't think I have anything left in me to give until I see her walking in looking like that. She's wearing my band's logo on the oversized black tee that she has tied in a knot at the left bottom side, showing me a little bit of her hip and stomach.

She isn't excited to be here; I can see it in her eyes. We both know we're nowhere near better, and if she knew about the blunt I smoked thirty minutes ago, we would be worse off. Lie. Lie. Lie. Even though I see this cycle happening, I can't help but do it. It's selfish, but I have to do it because I have to keep her.

"That's good. Let's go on back to the dressing room and get you guys ready." Nick gathers us up, and I look down at Sadie. "Come to the back, babe." She nods, and I head back.

She comes walking in a few seconds later. All the guys greet her, and I change out of my sweaty sound check clothes. Slipping on my leather pants, I leave my shirt off and take my earpiece out of my ear, letting it hang loose around my neck.

"Hey, baby, did you get everything done?" She nods and returns my quick peck.

"My parents want to come to the show tonight. You think we can have them side stage?" My eyebrows lift. Shit, did she tell them?

"They want to come here to the show?" I ask, knowing exactly what she means.

"Yes, they want to be supportive. They know we are going through some things, and I asked that they be here for us. Is that something you are okay with?"

Is it? Do they know how bad it is? I would ask, but if it isn't the answer I want, it may set me off, and I can't do that before a show.

"I think it's more about if this is going to make it worse for us. And for you?" Her parents could use this against me, and I wouldn't blame them. Worse, they could use it to pull Sadie in, and that isn't fair to either of us.

"What do you mean?"

I shrug. "We aren't good right now, and I don't want something else added on to make it worse." I look around and nod at some stage crew.

"My parents are kind, Ben. They realize that we all made choices here and the past can't be undone. But they wouldn't use it to hurt us. I promise." Sadie isn't put off by my worry. That was a risk, telling her that I fear they may use this huge fucking wedge between us as a way to save their daughter from me.

"Okay, I want what you want. You take the lead, angel." She gives me the most gentle and hopeful smile I have seen since I came back. "Have them come to the back door, and I'll tell the crew to bring them in." We will have to talk about exactly what she has told them. For now, I go along with it and take them coming as a good sign. I watch her closely as she takes a seat and stares at her phone.

"Dude, that one chick I fucked last time is a major clinger. She showed up outside," JJ says next to me, and we all laugh.

"Don't know why, your dick can't be that good. But hey, never say no to round two," I say, punching his arm and looking back at Sadie. She smiles and shakes her head.

"Can we get some music in here?" I holler toward Nick. A few seconds later, some AC/DC comes on over the loudspeakers.

"Oh fuck yeah." The boys and I join in a circle and start singing and hyping each other up. We do this until it's showtime.

Putting on my red blazer, I head down the hall toward the stage. Sadie's hand is in mine as she follows a few steps behind me. I drink the rest of my beer, taking the edge off my preshow jitters.

"Kiss, baby." Turning to her, I give her a kiss, my tongue moving against hers. I don't like simple with her; I like full-on taste. I need it on my tongue while I perform.

"Good luck." She smiles, but it doesn't reach her eyes. She's still teetering on the edge when it comes to what she should do. She wants space, but I don't. I won't lose Sadie. I will fight to keep her—fight with everything I have.

"Yes, good luck," Ray says as she and Stanley come up behind Nick. Ray leans in for a hug, and I return it. That's a good sign. It's not until I turn to Stanley that I get a little nervous. How is this going to go? His face isn't giving me much. Finally, after what feels like hours, he stretches out his hand, and I met him halfway, shaking his hand. I'm the piece of shit these two prayed Sadie would never love, yet they are here, and I hope that works in my favor. I don't want to lose any of them—I won't lose any of them.

"Thanks, guys. Love you, baby." One last kiss and I make my way out. The low lights and building prelude are thundering in my chest. My heart kicks into overdrive. The thrill of performing brews inside me.

Taking a long sip of my water, I stay by the drum set and smirk up at JJ. The up-tempo electronic song ends, and the first notes to "Run, Baby, Run" start. Grabbing the mic, I begin our set.

"How the fuck are ya, Portland!" The crowd roars, and that's when the familiar high begins. This is the shit I live for.

Thirty-one

SADIE

"How the fuck are ya, Portland!" Ben yells into the mic, completely in his element. My stomach has been in knots all day, and I'm more torn than ever over what to do. I want to work it out with my husband—I don't want to lose Ben—but the choice isn't really mine to make.

The drugs, the fighting, the drinking, the way he only opens up on the surface—it's a deadly combination, and he has to be the one to stop. I can handle the drinking in moderation, but the drugs, fighting, and leaving me hanging—no, I can't sit back and watch my husband kill himself and beg for CliffNotes to his life.

Last night, I gave in to temptation, and now I'm stuck at a crossroad. Ben probably thinks he has reeled me back in, but little does he know he just complicated things by taking me home last night.

We shouldn't have spent the night making love; we should have spent it working out our issues and attempting to compromise.

"Will I ever get used to his crass language?" Mama chuckles in my ear.

I look over and smirk. "Sorry, Mama."

She shakes her head, waving me off. "We all have our vices, right?"

I nod, looking back to Ben. "We do." I believe Ben is my vice. He's the one person who has the power to shatter me into a thousand pieces while at the same time being the only one able to put me back together.

Nonetheless, here I am. One good thing about tonight: my parents showed up. When they asked to come, I wanted to tell them no. But I took a leap of faith, and I am glad I did. I need them here.

The band finishes a song, and the crowd quiets down slightly to hear what Ben says. "Oh man, it feels good to be home. I've missed you guys. Bet you've all missed me!"

"You're fucking hot, Ben Cooper!" some dark-haired beauty in the front row screams.

"Thank you, honey, I know it," he teases, and my palms start to sweat, the hair on my neck rising. I hate that he entertains them even if it's only part of the act. I'm as jealous as he is over me.

"Breathe through it, baby," Mama whispers. Looking over to my dad, I see his nostrils flare. He doesn't say anything, though, since he knows it's useless. This is part of the act, the rock star life, and I made the choice to be a part of it. I have no one to blame but myself.

"All right, this next song will be on our new album—this is the first time we are playing it live. Let's go, Portland!" He turns the second Eric starts the opening guitar solo. Grabbing a sip of his water, he takes a second to look over at me. He winks, and I shake my head. There is no denying that there is something magical when I watch him play.

He gets more passionate with each song, his onstage persona flourishing for the rest of the show. Mama and Papa are champs through everything, not letting Ben's comments faze them too much. I adore my parents for being so accepting of Ben and loving him even when it's hard to.

Ben has a way of doing that to people.

After my parents leave—it's getting late—Kate and I wait in the changing room while they do the meet and greet.

"They did really good. I take it you two talked?" Kate inquires. I shake my head.

"Making double entendres during sex doesn't count, does it?" I ask.

"Hardly. So it ended up being nothing but makeup sex?"

"Well, maybe even breakup sex. I don't know."

"Sadie, you two have to talk. Something has to give here."

"You don't think I'm aware, Kate? I'm the one in this marriage," I snap, instantly regretting it. At my tone, she throws her hands up in surrender. "I'm sorry, Kate, it's been a bad week."

Conceding, she nods. "I get it, babe, but make time to talk to him before they leave tomorrow. Okay?"

"I will."

"Fuck, yeah, shit was good. Baby, tell me how good I did!" Ben barrels in with a whiskey in his hand.

"You did really good." I can't believe he's already drinking; the show ended less than an hour ago.

"I think I made every person in that crowd wet." He runs his hand over his bare chest, and everyone laughs—everyone but me. I'm over the cocky Ben tonight. I want the serious one instead.

"Babe, the guys wanna go out tonight, you want to come?" Sitting next to me on the leather couch, he pulls me into his side.

"No, I think I'm going to head home for the night. It's almost eleven, and I need some sleep."

"Come on. Let's have some fun. We stayed in last night and all day today. Let's go out, baby," he begs, and I grow a little more irritated. He's going to try to blow off our problems—sweep them under the worn-out rug. Seriously?

"No, I want to go home. In fact, Kate, can you take me, please?" I stand.

Reluctantly, she follows suit with a deep sigh. "Yeah, I can do that. I'll meet you boys later." She kisses Eric's cheek, and Ben sits still, eyeing me up and down. His eyes form tight slits, and he looks pissed. The feeling's mutual. He doesn't even try to stop me as Kate and I leave.

Climbing into her car, I get a text almost immediately.

Ben: What the hell is your deal, Sadie?

Me: Nothing. I have things to do tomorrow, Ben. Have fun tonight doing whatever it is you do. I'll see you before you leave tomorrow.
Ben: So, what? I'm the dick because I want to go out?
Me: I never said that, Ben. You came up with that all on your own.
Ben: Bullshit, you really love to fucking pull the leash and make me feel like shit.
Me: The leash? What are you talking about?
Ben: You control everything I do, Sadie. I can't fight, I can't drink, I can't get high, I can't hang out with my bandmates after a kick-ass show. I fucking invited you out tonight, and you said no. But I'm the dick?
Me: You hang out with your bandmates every day. Sorry that I wanted to go home so we could work on this small thing called our marriage.

I wait for his response. I feel my blood flowing rapidly through my veins. He's being such an insensitive jerk right now, already falling back into old habits. How can he expect me to forgive him or trust him when he flips a switch like this?

Ben: You know I want to work on us. Don't make it seem like I don't. You act like you're a saint in all this.

His text just confirms everything I worry about day in and day out. I know he's on something; he's out of control tonight. The sober Ben doesn't fight with low blows. He doesn't say things that cut me so deep.

Me: Ben, have fun tonight. I need a minute.

After that, it's radio silence. Kate gets me home, and I drag myself into the apartment. Once inside, I slide down the door, emotions taking over as I cry into my hands. I can hear the echoes of my broken sobs carrying through the desolate apartment.

My phone chimes next to me, and I eagerly check it, hoping it will be an "I'm sorry" or "I'm coming home" message from Ben. I whimper when I see it's not. Opening Mike's text, I read it.

Mike: Hey, we still on for lunch tomorrow? I can pick you up?

I forgot I agreed to have lunch with Mike. I'm trying to maintain the friendship, and when I talked to him a few days ago, he agreed that when I got back from the tour, we would go grab something to eat.

Me: Sure, sounds good.

My response is bland. I don't have any energy left in my body tonight to even try to be excited. Throwing my phone on the couch, I decide I need a bath and some solitude to think everything over.

Turning on the faucet, I let the water run and pour in some bubble bath. As I step in, the bubbles drown me, covering the surface of the water. My thighs are to my chest, and my cheeks rest against my knees in complete defeat. I can't believe that at nineteen, this is my life. I'm in a bath crying after having yet another fight with my husband, and I'm seriously considering a divorce.

Six months ago, my life was so simple. I was focused on taking care of everyone else. Now, life is destructive and frightening. It's devastating and reckless—yet it's beautiful at times. After every low that Ben and I face, he fixes it; he brings me comfort and love. I don't know how he does it or why I continue to let it happen, but I can't stop it. Even now, I am convinced he's the only person I want, the only thing that will make me happy—even if he's the one thing that makes me the unhappiest.

Turning the water off, I hear movement in the apartment on the other side of the locked bathroom door.

"Ben?" I call out.

"It's me," he responds, his voice devoid of anything. I didn't think he was going to come home, but the fact that he did gives me a flicker of hope. Hurrying out of the bath, I wrap myself in my big plush towel and leave the bathroom. When I walk into our bedroom, he's sitting on the edge of the bed, his face wearing a scowl. He has my phone in his hands.

"Ben, why do you have my phone?" I ask, walking closer with steady steps. He doesn't answer; instead, he stares at the screen. As I get closer, I see him scrolling through my messages, and instantly my blood boils.

"Ben!" I reach out to grab it, appalled by the invasion of my privacy. He yanks his hand up by the side of his head and stands up.

"You're going out with Mike?" I stand on my tiptoes to try to grab the phone, but he pulls it further away. I see red in his black eyes, a dead giveaway that he is high. Did he do a hit of cocaine after I left?

"Ben, hand me my phone. That's my private business."

"Bullshit. Are you fucking him, Sadie?"

"Oh my god, Ben, you're insane, you—"

"Are you letting him fuck you, Sadie! Are you letting him touch you!" he screams, and all of a sudden I'm afraid to fight over my stupid phone. I back up slowly. I don't cower; that's not who I am. However, I am trained to de-escalate situations, and right now, that's best.

"Huh? Answer me! Why the fuck are you going to lunch with him! You been fucking around on me? Huh, baby!" he yells again, throwing my phone against the wall on the other side of the room. It shatters, and I scream, terrified.

"Ben, stop." I try soothing him. The fact he could think this when I've been on tour with him for months is irrational. How could I cheat on him when I was with him? Drugs will manipulate your mind, that's how.

"No, you want to let someone touch what's mine? You fucked him, didn't you, Sadie!" He cages me in. I grip my towel tighter, truly afraid of him. I have never been afraid of him.

"No, I didn't. Ben, we're friends, it's not like that," I whisper as he towers over me, his arms on either side of my head. "I had a life before you, friends, family, and it's all a part of me. I can't give everything up; that's not fair."

It's like Ben doesn't hear me, his mind trapped in a deadly rage.

"Was he good, did you like him fucking you? Did he touch you better than me? Did his cock feel good inside you?" he seethes, his eyes so far gone they have lost their warmth. His words sicken me, and my stomach rumbles, bile trying to make its acidic way up my throat.

"Ben, don't say that! Stop it!" I begin to cry, my body shaking uncontrollably.

"No, I want you to tell me if he was good. You want him again? Or do you want me to fuck you better and show you no one can ever fucking touch you like I can? I'll kill him if he touched you, Sadie," he bites out, and I drop down, sliding against the wall, covering my ears and crying harder. He steps back, and I feel his dark eyes boring into me.

"Ben, please stop, you need help. Look at you. Please—please stop." Taking a risk, I peer up at him.

"I'm not the reason you fucked around on me!" he screams, and I see it: the fear in him. His brows draw together with sadness. The expression fades faster than it came, but I saw it. Ben's afraid; he knows he's no longer capable of controlling the spinning wheel that his life has become. I swallow my tears and try a different approach; my only mission is to calm him down. I wanted him to be himself, to let his demons out and let me in. *You got what you asked for, Sadie. You think you can handle it?*

"Ben, baby, I don't want anyone but you. No one has ever touched me. I promise. Only you." I stand to my full height, and he breathes in and out deeply, his fists tight at his sides. I see his brows slowly loosening again, and his jaw goes a little more lax.

"Ben, please, trust in me, baby. I would never hurt you. I love you." I'm now face to face and toe to toe with him with no space between us.

I bring my hands up, shaking on the inside, unsure how he's going to react to me. My heart is breaking for my husband; he doesn't want to have all these crutches. Finally, I see the real him. Seeing my husband not knowing how to heal is devastating.

"Come back to me, Ben. I know you're in there, baby. Come back." I search his eyes and rub my hands against his face, hoping my touch will bring the real Ben forward. I do this for what feels like hours before he crumbles.

"Sadie? Fuck, what do I do? What do I do, baby?" He breaks, his jaw no longer tight, his eyes coming back to the honey brown I'm used to and his hands releasing their tight fists. He drops his head to my shoulder, his hands squeezing my hips as he lets out a gut-wrenching wail. "I'm so sorry. God, I'm so sorry, baby. I'm just like him. I'm like my father. Help me, Sadie. Please." I lift his face from my shoulder and navigate his focus back to me.

"Shh, you're not him, Ben, shh. I promise we'll get you better. Trust in me." I kiss his chest repeatedly above his heart. I stand on my tiptoes and kiss the underside of his jaw.

"How can you trust me? I've lied, I've hidden things from you, I fucking said terrible things!" His fists leave my hips, and he punches his chest hard. The echo of flesh being pounded chills me. I grab his hand, stopping him.

"Don't do that! Stop it!" I start to cry along with him. I stop his fist from another blow to his chest and kiss him there instead.

"No, I fucked up, and I need to be punished for that. Let me make it up to you, Sadie." I start to respond, but he falls to his knees. Dropping his lips to my feet, he kisses the top of them then continues a path up my shins, then my thighs, until the towel stops him.

"Let me make it up to you," he says again. He opens the flap of the towel and pulls so it leaves my body.

"Ben, take a deep breath. We got this. We can get through this." Ben has never broken down like this before. He has always talked about his past stoically. Never has he been so emotional in front of me. I knew there was something painful deep down, but I had no idea how bad it was until now. Nick warned me, and I naively thought that I had seen the worst. Not even close.

"Let me worship you, Sadie. I'm at your feet. Don't you see that? You're my saving grace." Without another word, his lips close around my core, his tongue licking up my slit. I grip his hair and throw my head back.

"Ben!" I cry.

"You're mine. I have to have you forever. I will quit any drug, any addiction but you. Don't give up on me," he says against my skin, inhaling my scent and kissing my thigh. He rubs his face all over my thighs and my center, marking himself with my scent. My broken, broken man. My beautiful lover.

I believe him. I actually believe him for the first time, but with this sacrifice from him, I will have to sacrifice too. I need to give up something—a life that once mattered more than anything to me.

"I'll leave with you. I want to go with you." I will forgo my planned future for the unknown with Ben.

"What?" He rises, pulling me against him. He bends, becoming level with my face, his hands gripping my sides under my breasts.

"I don't want a life without you, Ben. You need me. I made a vow to love you in sickness and in health. I won't let you be alone anymore." Though I speak these words proudly, inside I'm anything but strong. My heart is crumbling to ashes as I give up all that I have left in order to save Ben. Walking away from my dreams is like mourning a death, but Ben means more to me, and my greatest dream in this life is to see him healthy and happy.

"But you've worked so hard to get here. I can't let you give that up for me."

"Yes, you can, because you're giving up things for me. I love what I do, but I love you more."

"Sadie..." He trails off, his head hanging low as he sways back and forth in disbelief.

"That's what I get for loving you."

"Why didn't you come sooner?" He kisses me, sealing us together. I claw at him because I feel we're not close enough. I will never regret my choice to work on my marriage first and to protect and help my husband. He has never had a home where there wasn't pain. The only love he knew was overshadowed by brutality. But not anymore; now he has a home, and I have to keep that home safe.

I climb into his arms, my legs wrapping around his waist. His hands grip my ass, and he turns, laying us on the bed. I grab at him, helping him remove his clothes in an instant. Once he's naked, I eagerly grab for his cock. Stroking it in my hands, I see the thick veins grow more prominent as his full nine inches awakens.

"I want you," I moan, sliding closer and lining him up with my entrance.

"How do you want it?" he groans as the rounded head opens me up.

"Use me. Use me like I am your drug. Take everything from me so you can feel complete." I want to be his only addiction. I need to know—I want to know—what it feels like to be his object of obsession, someone he would do anything for.

Without a word, he shows me. Slamming into me, he lifts my legs above his head, resting them on his shoulders. I'm nearly ripped in half by his violent thrusts. He growls at me, and I scream out his name repeatedly.

Turning his head, he bites down hard on the side of my calf, and I bear down on him. "Ben!"

"You're my wife, my hero. I can't believe you keep fucking choosing me," he cries, and I keep looking at our connection, the root of his cock hitting against my clit with each thrust.

"Ben." I cup his face. I need him to understand what I am about to say. "I will choose you every time. Religiously. You have someone who isn't leaving. Please." I shake his face softly, his thrusts now slowing down. A tear falls and hits my chest, and he nods.

"I know. Goddamn it. I love you." Leaning in, he picks up speed and licks up my tears. This is so raw. I almost want to stop it because my heart feels like it might explode in my chest. My love for him is overwhelming. Ben mirrors my desperation as he tries to hold off his orgasm to make this last.

"Don't hold back, take a hit, take another blow, baby," I cry out as he grabs my breast in his hand and squeezes with bruising force. He begins to pound into me like he is enunciating each thrust.

"Kiss me, give me your taste." He leans down, and I give him my mouth. Licking his lips, he lets me in. Our tongues tango, fighting one another for more than we can possibly give with a kiss. I scream into his mouth when he pinches my nipple then slaps my hip. "You're such a good fucking girl." He bites my lip, causing blood to leak from it.

"Oh, don't stop, Ben!" His body slides against mine, and I wonder how I ever lived before him making love to me.

"I won't, I'm never gonna stop. You're mine, Sadie Cooper." With his ownership, I come, unraveling beneath him. "No way, baby, don't you settle down, I'm not done. Give me one more, angel." I come hard, my juices flooding us as they squirt from me. "I can't, it hurts!" He keeps at me, my spasms still going and my body shivering in response. The muscles in my stomach have begun to tighten then release repeatedly, and I lose all sense of consciousness.

"No, it doesn't. Let your man show you. I can make you do this over and over tonight, baby. Come again, feel me inside you." He slows down, letting my high slowly fall. When my spasms slow down, my eyes flutter open to see him staring down at me. "Good girl. Relax."

Pushing one of my legs down, he opens me up and stares down at our connection. He groans, the sound as good as his lovemaking feels. Pushing my knee into the bed, he keeps my other one high and against his side.

"Shit, look at that. Mmm, Sadie. Your heart may be pure, but your body was sculpted by the devil, my little temptress. This tiny, tight pussy can bring me to my knees." I choke on my own moans.

"I have to stop, baby, it hurts," I cry out, the new sensation building faster. It's one I've never felt before.

"That's good, baby, oh fuck, chase it, come on my cock again, take it, angel." He groans, and I do as he says: I ride that wave, chasing it or, better yet, running from it. The only problem is I'm not quick enough. I come apart, orgasming in a rush. Leaving my knee nailed into the bed at my side, I try to close my legs, but it's no use. My back bows off the bed while tears invade my eyes and heat coils in my spine, causing my toes to curl.

"Ben! Fuck! Ben!" I scream, losing my moral code.

"Too tight, fuck, so tight. I'm coming, baby, get ready." Finally, my vision refocuses, and I can watch him and enjoy his pleasure with him. His eyes are zeroed in on his cock sliding in and out repeatedly; it almost looks violent. He's large, and I'm still not fully used to him; my core pulls him back in greedily as he slides out.

"Ben, look at me," I call out to him, running my hands up his sides. He finally breaks his trance and gives me his attention. "Promise me something," I say.

"Anything, Sadie—fuck, I'll do anything."

"Promise me you will fight like hell every day for us."

"If you promise to never leave me."

"Never, baby. I can't. I need you too much," I cry, the severity of how badly I need him consuming me—the depths of danger I'm willing to enter in order to keep him. As he empties himself in me, I feel something, a stronger connection than I have ever felt with my husband. He is the man I loved first and the one I plan to love last—if I can save us.

Thirty-two

BEN

Sadie didn't deserve seeing the darkest version of me last night. The rage I showed was so out of line, even I want to beat the shit out of myself. What's worse, I don't know how to take her decision to come on tour with me. Making her give up her internship, which promises her a full-time job and a gold star on her nursing school application, may be the thing I feel most guilty over.

She works tirelessly and puts so much into us, but I'm selfish. For her to focus only on me—that is something I hate to admit I want more than my next fucking breath. I can't overcome my past and my addictions without her by my side—I can't.

Outside, on our balcony, I take a drag of my cigarette while she packs her bags for the next three-month leg of our tour. I'll admit, even with the guilt and the hard shit we're going to face the next few months, I find comfort in knowing I'll have her by my side. But will it ever be enough? Will it ever stick? The treatment? The healing? The will to be better?

Putting the bud out in my ashtray, I step back in and head toward the bedroom. I hear the faint sounds of Sadie sniffling, and I halt outside our bedroom.

"Yes, I know that I won't be able to get the internship back." My heart beats out of my chest. Fuck, I knew this would hurt her. "I understand,

Dr. Bailer. Thank you so much for this opportunity. Yes, thank you. Okay, bye." She hangs up, and I peek my head around the door. I watch as she drops her head into her hands and sobs. I think about going in there and comforting her, but the second my feet set into motion, the phone in her hand rings. Releasing a deep breath, she answers.

"Hey, Mama." I hear the faint sound of her mother's concerned voice on the other end of the line.

"I know, Mama, but I have to do this. He needs me, and I need him." She pauses. "No, please, this is what I have to do. I can't sacrifice us. No—stop, Mama. I can't talk about it. My mind is made up, and it's done with. I'm leaving with him."

I want to know what her mother is saying, but from what I hear, I can guess. Well, I almost made it to their good side.

"I can find another internship when he's sober. He can't walk away from the band; the industry is hard to get into. Can you and Papa respect that—for me?" I don't blame them—shit, I don't fucking respect myself for letting her do this. I can't believe I even got bad enough for her to need to do it.

"Papa, marriage is supposed to last forever. What we have means more than anything. You and Mama have to let me do this."

Her parents must really think I'm the scum of the earth, and honestly, I think so too. I don't deserve Sadie. My touch is dangerous, my love is poisonous, and Sadie could do so much better than me, but how do I even begin to try letting her go? The thought of losing her makes me murderous. I wouldn't be able to walk this earth if another man had her after I've touched her. I can't survive without her.

"Yes, Papa, and that's why you need to let me do this. I want to have a happy life with him, and if I walk away now and don't fight, I may regret it more than anything else in my life."

Sadie may be doing this to save me, but I'm doing this to keep her. The selfless loves the selfish.

"I will call you and FaceTime you on the road. I'll be back once a month with Ben to visit. I love you guys." They share goodbyes, and the second she ends the call, she cries again. She's giving up her aspirations, her family, her friends, and so much of herself to come with me—how can she even stand the sight of me?

I don't walk in when she's crying, deciding to make it easier on her. Approaching her when she's like this will only make her put her feelings aside and tend to mine. She will feel guilty and explain away her tears, thinking I need it. I don't need her to do anything else for me; she's already done way too much. Eventually, she stops crying before disappearing into our bathroom.

"Baby?"

Clearing her throat, she responds, "I'm in the bathroom. I'll be right out." I start putting more of my things in an extra suitcase. I hear the sink turn on and off, and she comes out a second later. The sight of her takes my breath away. Her hair is in a braid hanging down one shoulder, her big blue eyes are striking, and her face is a little red from crying. I stare at her while she packs and avoids my gaze.

"The bus will be here in an hour."

"Perfect. Do you want me to pack more of your hats or shoes?" she asks, moving to the closet.

"I got it, don't worry. Thank you, angel." See, there she goes. Her entire world has imploded, and she is offering to pack for me? Sadie can't be real.

"Sounds good. I need to run to the pharmacy really quick. I need to pick up some things. Will you be good while I'm gone?" Zipping her bag, she still doesn't make eye contact with me.

"Yes, of course." Rounding the bed, I bring her into my arms, and I don't feel any resistance. Instead she clings to me, letting me know that I'm her only hope, and I better not let her down. Fuck me, I better not let her down.

Thirty-three

SADIE

Ben has been extremely hard to be around these past few weeks. He has been weaning himself off the harder drugs, causing his attitude and irritability to be at an all-time high. He's been snapping at the boys and Nick—even me. Sometimes me more than anyone since I'm the one by his side day and night. We have made no progress on him letting me go to therapy with him, but he says soon. Every time, the answer is *soon*. When will soon come?

He's been taking the anxiety pills that his doctor prescribed and doing an hour of therapy three times a week. But there is something missing. Something isn't clicking for him, and it's not from lack of trying. He works so hard. Subconsciously, he has a wall deep inside that he can't see over, but he hasn't figured out yet what that is.

Today, he's been eerily quiet. The first time he said anything more than *good morning* was five minutes ago when they started sound check. They're playing Salt Lake City, and I'm worried Ben isn't going to be able to put on a full show. In fact, if I were a gambler, I would put money on him storming offstage. If this rehearsal is any indication, they might as well cancel tonight's show.

"That sounds like fucking shit, Eric. Tune the D string, fuck, man."

I swallow, keeping quiet in my chair. Nick sits next to me with his lips tight as well.

"Sorry, B," Eric apologizes, walking lightly on Ben's eggshells.

"Is this my fault, Nick?" I question, my voice low as Ben warms up his vocal cords.

"Sadie, he needs this. We all need him to get better. You should be proud."

"Hardly. I see it already."

"See what?"

Bringing my knees to my chest in the tiny seat, I answer. "The quiet resentment. He thinks that I'm doing this because I think what he's doing is wrong, but I'm doing this because I love him, and I don't want something bad to happen to him. I don't want to lose him, Nick," I admit, watching Ben as he messes with his earpiece.

"We know that, Sade, we do. That's why we all let him do what he wants to us. We know he'll be better one day, and it'll be worth putting up with all this." He smiles, and I give a forced one in return. I sure do hope that's the case.

※ ※ ※

"Nick! Where the fuck are my black jeans? I can't find shit!" Ben yells from the back of the bus. Standing in a rush, I urge Nick to let me go instead. I briskly move past the bunks and into the back.

"Which ones, baby?"

"Fuck! I don't know!"

"Let me look." I instantly start looking through the clean clothes I washed for him at our last stop. "Here are your pants." The jeans are at the bottom of the stack I folded a few hours ago. I lay them out on the bed next to his Chucks. When he doesn't move, I turn around and see him watching me.

"What?" I question.

"I need it." His voice is low, his chest not as red as it was when I first came back here.

"Okay. What can I do to help you, baby? You're doing so good, let's not give up," I soothe, crawling on my knees to his side of the bed. I kiss from his happy trail all the way up to his heart. His breathing is ragged and uneven, his fists clenching repeatedly at his sides. "Ben, you have to relax. You need to calm down; you can't be like this onstage. What can I do to help? We can cancel the show. You say the word, and I will cancel it." I start to rub his shoulders. I can see how hard this is on him. If it's hard on me, I can't imagine what being inside his head all day every day is like.

"I don't know. I feel violent, Sadie. Like I could punch a wall straight through."

"Do you want us to get you some gloves and a standing punching bag? We can do that," I coo, hearing Nick enter the room.

"Hey, man, we got to hurry up. We go on in ten."

I close my eyes and gulp.

"Fuck off, man! I'm talking to my girl right now. Why don't you give me a fucking minute!" His hands grip my hips, and I look over to Nick.

"Nick, it's okay. We'll be out there. Let me have a minute with him." Nick shakes his head, pausing for a brief second before leaving us again.

"Why can't they understand me, Sadie!" Ben yells, lifting his hands to his head and running them through his hair.

"Shh, baby. Why don't you let me take care of you? Hmmm?" I come off my knees to sit on the bed. Placing both my feet on the floor, my legs on each side of his, I kiss the dip of his *V*, my hands working on his belt buckle and zipper. I want him to relax; I can't imagine what he's going through. I've done quite a bit of research on his IED, and the empath in me can't help but want to take it all away. If I could take all his trauma on my shoulders, even only for a day so he could have a brief moment of reprieve, I would. Without question.

I wish I could break through to him and not struggle with the guilt eating at me daily. I feel terrible because I feel alone. I've spent all this time trying to help him, and I've lost a bit of myself in the process, but he's worse off. It pains me to know that I'm selfishly thinking about myself at a moment like this.

I wish I had the words to help the sleepless nights and the nightmares. I wish that my arms could give him the comfort he needs when he shakes in his sleep.

I wish I wasn't always drowning in his troubled waters, all so I can keep his head above them.

Thirty-four

BEN

Slowly weaning off drugs and alcohol over the past two months has damn near killed me. My skin is crawling, my eyes are constantly dilated, and I'm always looking for something to keep me engaged. My hands haven't stopped shaking, and my performances seem to be lacking a piece of me.

Sadie hasn't once tried to control my sobriety. She listens, she tends to me, she holds me, and she lets me use her, but it's not enough. It's never fucking enough. I've had to distance myself from the band offstage, spending my nights and days locked up in the back room. The only way it's fucking manageable is because Sadie's here, glued to my side as my own personal therapist. Yes, I changed my meds and have been meeting with Dr. Danivah three times a week, but how am I supposed to get better when I am balancing the band and my sobriety?

Sadie nurses me after my nightmares—the flashbacks that the drugs used to help silence. She sees me go from zero to sixty when someone steps into my space.

When it gets really bad and I think I might shatter into nothing, she makes love to me, feeding the one addiction that I'm damn lucky to have. I'll admit, my funny antics and romantic charm have taken a backseat lately, but she wrote me a love letter and gave it to me before my last show. That letter showed what we need. A night of me attempting to sweep her off her feet. Since she's out running errands with Nick, I reread the letter for the fourth time.

Ben,

    I know this hasn't been easy. I actually think this is the hardest thing we've faced, both personally and together. But I wanted to tell you how proud I am of you. I know you sometimes don't see me there on the side of the stage watching you, but I am. You shine up there with your astounding talent. You have so much talent in the tips of your fingers . . . it's beautiful. I'm blessed to be by your side on this journey, and I can't wait to see what's next for your music career.

    But mostly, I'm proud of your dedication and hard work getting sober, not only for yourself but for us. The therapy, the meetings, the late nights and aches and pains that you have had to endure to stay clean, I appreciate it all. You are the strongest man I know, and I cherish that beyond compare. I wrote you this letter so you could hopefully find comfort in it or encouragement whenever you are feeling confused, afraid, or like giving up.

    Read this and know that you have a home with me, Ben, and I love you. I'll never hurt you, and I will never let anyone else hurt you again. I will be a shield to protect you if it means that you will slowly mend and heal again. Your mother is proud, and I am proud . . . so you should be too.

I love you.
SJC

Still faithful to me during the battle of heaven and hell, it seems. But every word in that letter reminds me of the greatness I still have in my life, and that is Sadie. I still have her, and it makes every day worth fighting for.

    I take a shower and wake myself up, getting ready for a day off with Sadie. No show tonight means I get to spend the entire night thanking her for the gift of her love and her overwhelming patience for me during my journey.

Thirty-five

SADIE

Nick calls a rideshare and takes me to the store while Ben rests so I can pick up a few things—including a test. I think I may be pregnant, and I've never been more terrified of anything. The pill has a very small chance of failing, but with my body, we knew there was a chance. This wasn't in our plans, and with where we currently are, I don't know if we have the strength to bring a child into our marriage.

"You going to take it when we get back or do you want to take it here?" Nick asks next to me at the checkout.

I shake my head. "I never really thought about taking my first pregnancy test in a convenience store bathroom, so I'll pass." Squeezing my shoulder reassuringly, he smiles. I quickly pay, then we head back.

"I think I want to get us a nice hotel room and maybe take it there and then tell him if I am or not. You know, in private." My knee bounces briskly up and down next to Nick. My hands are shaking, and my insides are all discombobulated with nerves. I can't believe I might be pregnant.

"That's a good idea," Nick concedes. My last period was two months ago, and besides being so late, I've been tired and nauseous all week.

"Do you think he'll be okay with this? The tour will be over soon, and then he'll be back home to record."

"It's with you. I think he'll love anything you give him." He chuckles, and I blush. I love the fact that Ben loves me as much as he does.

Through this journey, I have seen Ben eat away at himself, letting guilt consume him. He feels bad for making me choose. But really, he didn't. I won't credit anyone for this choice but myself. He has been loving, even on the lowest days, and he has apologized relentlessly. I forgave him a long time ago. We all have to set boundaries and know when to walk away, but that time isn't here yet. There is still hope, and I love him for not giving up on us. We've both made the greatest sacrifices.

"What about you, kid? You sure you're ready?" I ponder that for a minute. Life has thrown me a curveball. Ben and I haven't talked much about having kids, but I knew it was going to be in my future eventually, even if this is sooner than I thought.

"It's scary. Definitely unexpected. But it's a piece of Ben and me, and knowing we're possibly going to be a family is . . . kind of like faith." Nick looks at me, confused. "I get that that sounds weird. But faith sometimes doesn't make sense. Out of nowhere, it has pulled me through some of the hardest times in my life. Ben and I could use some good news, a little reward for all the work we've put into our marriage. This possible baby could be a blessing, a reminder that we are meant to be together and can fight anything that comes our way."

"His battles, you mean?"

"They aren't his battles to fight alone. I won't give up on him just because the life I signed up for isn't the life I expected. I want Ben, and that means I'll have to fight his battles as if they were my own."

As we pull up to the bus, Nick looks over to me, dumbfounded. "You know, you are one of the strongest people I've ever met. You honestly have no idea how special and incredible you are. Ben is the luckiest man alive to have found someone so accepting and loyal."

"I'm not that great. Love isn't a choice."

"It can be."

"Is that why you're not married, Nick?" I tease, pushing his shoulder and breaking up the tension. We climb out of the car and head inside.

"Not for me. Been there, done that. Now let's get going."

Nick has been married before? Ben never said anything about it.

"Lead the way."

I'm curious to know Nick's story.

"Angel," Ben says the second we step onto the bus. I look up and smile at the version of Ben in front of me. He's freshly shaved and dressed like he's ready to go out.

"Hey! You look very handsome." I put my bag on the counter and walk into his waiting arms. This is the first time outside of him playing shows or promoting the band that he has gotten out of bed or left the back room. I can smell his body wash, and his warm body heat can be felt under his clothes.

"You look stunning. Did you get everything you need?"

"I did." My cheek lies against his chest, and my eyes meet Nick's as he gives me a knowing nod. This has to be a good sign—coming back to him in a good mood, freshly showered and energized.

The universe is listening. We are healing. Ben is healing.

"Good. I was thinking we could go sightseeing. I hear there's a fair in town."

"Ferris wheels! Yay!" I laugh like a little kid, all giddy and turning to mush on the inside.

"You like Ferris wheels?" I nod rapidly and lean up, planting a quick kiss against his warm lips before pulling back.

"I'll explain when you get me on one!" I yell excitedly, heading for the door. I'm ready to get off this bus and spend a worry-free afternoon with Ben. Whatever is happening feels good, and I chase out all the doubts to live in this moment.

"All right, guess we're going. See you later, boys."

***

"Snuggle in close, baby." We get comfortable on the Ferris wheel, stomachs full of hot dogs, cotton candy, and enough soda to have a sugar high for a month. I place the teddy bear he won me in the empty space next to me and snuggle in close.

The cart starts to rise, and I close my eyes, taking in a deep breath, feeling alive for the first time in weeks. I use all my senses and feel Ben all around me. I've missed him, missed the unexpected touches, the laughter, the passionate whispers. I love when he's fully here with me like he was when we first met.

"Why Ferris wheels?" he asks, planting a kiss on my temple.

"Papa asked Mama to marry him at the top of a Ferris wheel."

"Nice. I knew Stanley had game."

"Hardly. He was a romantic." I shrug, opening my eyes when the wind catches my hair and the ride stops. Looking around at the scenery from the top of the Ferris wheel truly brings me peace. Ben's brown eyes watch me intensely.

"About that. Sorry I've been slacking in the romance department." The Northern California sun is setting, and you can see the ocean in the distance, glistening with yellows and vibrant oranges.

"You've been preoccupied," I admit, kissing his neck.

"Thank you for helping me. I can't imagine it's been easy on you."

"It hasn't, but it's been worth it."

"Is it?" he questions. This gets my full attention.

"What do you mean?"

"Do you still love me as much as you did the day we got married?" I cradle his cheeks; the setting sun casts a halo around his handsome face. He looks like an angel.

"I love you more every day. For better or worse, remember?" I take my other hand and tangle our fingers together. Bringing his lips to mine, I give his ring a gentle kiss. I never want him to doubt my love for him. Ever. "You're my better half."

"You're mine." He smiles, and we kiss again, this time not separating. We go around a few more times until the sun is gone and the night air has grown colder.

"What do you say we get out of here? I got us a hotel room. I hear the beds are comfortable, and the hot tub is screaming our names." He is one step ahead of me. I was planning to show up at the nearest place and see what rooms they had. Clearly, we both need a night away.

"Sounds like a plan, baby." He winks, and we climb off the Ferris wheel and catch a cab, stopping at the bus just long enough to grab some overnight items before hitting the hotel. He planned this so well: this place is truly stunning, like something out of one of my romance novels.

Once inside the room, Ben excuses himself to have a smoke, and I take a minute to take my test. With all the time we have spent today laughing and talking, now feels like the perfect time. I wait the three minutes, thinking about a beautiful little baby who looks like Ben: big brown eyes, a raspy little voice, and pouty baby lips. All this time, Ben and I have never really talked about children. We agreed that we want to be sure I don't get pregnant right now, but that was it. Yes, we are young, but we were young when we got married. From day one, we were anything but traditional.

I can see a better life where Ben is content and sober with a little girl perched on his knee, learning to play the piano. I think of all the ways Ben would be a great father, and call me naive, but maybe this is the cure. My phone timer goes off, and I take the world's longest, deepest breath.

Here we go.

Lifting the test, I stare at the word flashing across the tiny screen.

Pregnant. Pregnant. Pregnant.

I read it over and over again; my eyes are glistening, and my smile deepens. We're pregnant. I'm going be a mother—Ben is going be a daddy—the best one there ever was. This is our blessing after a hard start to our marriage. All we fought for is here and now; it feels surreal, but our love's purpose is fulfilled. This has to be a good sign. The universe, God, anything that brings in blessings after storms is working for us.

"Baby, let's take a bath!" Ben calls from the other side of the bathroom door.

"Yes! Okay, one second." I hide the test, unable to wipe the smile from my face. Forget trying to calm the butterflies dancing wildly in my stomach. Closing my toiletry bag right as he opens the door, I spin and smile at him. His tall, lean, yet muscular form takes up nearly the entire doorway.

He's already undressed down to his boxer briefs, and I'm overwhelmed at the sight. Four minutes ago he was just my husband, and I thought that made my love for him strong, but now he's the father to our child, and that love seems to reach depths I didn't know existed.

"What's that big smile for, angel? You're fucking glowing." Wrapping his tattooed arm around me, he swoops me up in that breathtaking way he always does, but today it feels more special.

"It was a beautiful day with you. How about that bath?"

* * *

"I really loved your letter. You have a way with words, angel."

"I have to keep up with my lyrical husband." I'm snuggled between Ben's legs in the hot tub, his arms wrapped around my shoulders and his hands dangling lazily near my chest. I play with his long, thick fingers covered with callouses from all the instruments he plays.

"You do all right for yourself." We laugh in unison.

"How do you feel?" I ask the question of the day. I wonder if he feels the same way I do. Like there is a light at the end of this tunnel, and we are so close to the other side.

"About?"

"Your sobriety. Is it getting easier?" He waits to answer, his body relaxed behind me. I hope we're safe to talk about it. The last thing I want to do is burst this bubble of peace we made today.

"Yes and no. Some days, it's almost unbearable."

"Is the therapy helping?" Ben and I know that he's committed to this tour. Even though Dr. Danivah suggested we cancel the rest of the tour to see more effective results and for the overall benefit to his mental health, Ben insisted on continuing. In exchange, he has dedicated more time to therapy on the road, and when this tour is over, he has agreed to take a year off for proper treatment. Relapsing is more likely with this type of untraditional therapy, and Ben's circumstances are more complex than he and I first realized.

"It's working for the moment, but if I'm going stay clean, I need to get proper treatment and go to groups. The year off will be hard, but it's going to be what helps this stick." He says exactly what I'm thinking. In my opinion, his self-awareness and ability to admit what he once denied may be the biggest improvement he's made.

"You want that?" I'm hesitant to ask, that fear of his resentment sneaking back in. He can want this now, but will he want it forever? Did we do this the right way, or are we setting ourselves up for a bigger downfall?

"I want you, Sadie, and I can't keep bringing you down with me." I drop my eyes to the still water.

"Are you going to resent me one day?" The last thing I want in this life or any life hereafter is to have Ben look at me as a regret.

"You saved my life. Getting clean is something I needed to do."

"I'm not a savior, Ben. I'm selfish, and I want you here forever. The thought of you overdosing or fighting and getting…" I can't even mumble the word. I fall silent; he knows the dangers without me saying it out loud.

"I realize that. Don't worry, angel. I'm getting there. It's okay."

The water is hot, but my body feels chilled, and the shiver in my spine is all I notice.

"I want you to come to my next therapy session with me. The one I have scheduled when we get back. My first in person after this leg."

"What?" I turn, facing him, the water sloshing around us.

"I want you there." His eyes zero in on me. This is the one thing I've been holding onto. The last bit of space between us. He has never let me into that part of his life, and now he wants to. He wants me there.

"Are you sure you're ready for that?"

"I've never been more scared to let someone in that deep, but you aren't just someone, Sadie." I'm left breathless. I'm not just someone. I'm *the* one. He let me in. I broke down that wall. We have this. The battlefield fog is clearing, and we are finding our way back to safety.

"All I wanted was for you to feel like you'd gotten back something that you lost when your mother died. A home. I hope that when all is said and done, you will see what I see in you every day. You are not what he did. You are you, and your soul is so beautiful. You have power in you." My voice cracks, captivated by his strength and by the battles he has fought to simply let someone love him. To let *me* love him.

"Fuck, I love you."

"And I love you." With our love surrounding us like a bubble, I know it's the right time to share our news.

"I have to tell you something." I hold his face in my hands and straddle his waist. His cock grows under me, and reaching between us, I begin to stroke the smooth, pronounced shaft with my small palm.

"Oh shit." He drops his head back and groans, his throat bobbing.

"You know how much I love you?" He lifts his head with difficulty as I sit up on my knees and line him up with my entrance.

"More than I deserve." He grabs my hips and takes control, guiding me down on his cock. I moan from the invasion; it spreads me open, and the connection of skin on skin with our news on the tip of my eager tongue has me confessing.

"Ben, I'm pregnant," I cry as he slams me down again. Opening my eyes once I'm settled with no further movement, I see him staring at me wide-eyed.

"What?"

I smile, nodding. "I'm pregnant."

"No. No, you're not. Fuck." Lifting me off him, he puts space between us and stands, grabbing a towel and leaving the bathroom faster than I have time to process what's happening. When my brain starts working again and I regain my bearings, I realize he didn't take that the way I thought he would. I look around, panicked. I read this all wrong.

My body goes cold and numb. I told my husband I'm pregnant, and he physically pushed me away. I hear him cursing outside the bathroom, and that sets me into motion. Climbing out of the tub, I do a terrible job of toweling off and tie my robe sloppily.

Rounding the corner into the bedroom, I see he's now fully dressed and pacing a hole into the carpet.

"Ben, what was that?" I ask, stepping up to him.

"You're pregnant? Tell me this is a joke."

I step back, my body freezing up. A small gasp escapes from my lips. I'm more than hurt by that comment—I'm devastated. How could he call our child an attempt at a joke?

"You're such an asshole. How could you say that at a moment like this?"

"How could you get pregnant!" he yells, stopping his pacing and turning on me.

"Excuse me, but you were there too. I didn't do this alone or on purpose, if that is the next thing you plan to accuse me of!" I can't believe he's reacting like this.

"You are in charge of taking your pill. This is your fault!" I almost slap him after that degrading statement.

"I can't believe you. I don't even know who you are right now, Ben."

"You know who I am. I don't want a fucking child. Have you not been here these past few months, Sadie?" he yells, the veins in his neck swelling.

"Stop talking about our child like that! Stop talking to me like that!" I get in his face, ready to give him a taste of what he is dishing out. "You said one day, and yes, the timing isn't ideal, but we knew the risk. Any birth control can fail!"

"I said maybe." His voice lowers. "I said *maybe* one day when we talked about it."

Did he say maybe? Thinking back to that night, I can't remember. We were both in post-sexual bliss when we had that talk. I must have missed it. If he said maybe, I would have said something. But I didn't.

"Why didn't you tell me that *maybe* was actually a fucking no then, Ben!"

"Well, *maybe* sure as hell isn't a yes either. For me it isn't, at least!" It's as if I'm arguing with a stranger. The stark difference between a lover and an enemy is glaring. Ben is really doing this right now. His chest is heaving, and his hot breath comes out heavily against my face.

"I don't want a child."

"Well, I'm not going to give up my child." Is he asking me what I think he is? He wouldn't ask me to have an abortion, would he? God, who is he? I think I'm going to be sick.

"I guess we're at odds then," he hisses, leaving a cold draft in his wake as he grabs his jacket and storms out.

I fall to my knees and scream into my hands, the tears pouring out of me. My heart is trying to escape out of my chest by squeezing its way through my throat. I feel bile rising, and I run to the bathroom, losing everything—physically and emotionally. I vomit so violently, my ribs start to hurt.

When nothing is left, I stand and look in the mirror. I shake my head and continue to cry, my heart no longer whole, my mind no longer sane. I've lost a part of me, and Ben took it.

I see the test in my bag, and like my heart snapped, so do I. I take the test and throw it across the bathroom, watching it shatter and bounce off the wall. Looking back in the mirror, I see the broken woman I have become. I see everything I abandoned to be what he needed. The cross that adorns my neck every waking hour mocks me. I grab it and rip it clear off in one tug.

Just like he left me, I abandon myself and my faith. Nothing can take back what was said and done tonight. Nothing.

Thirty-six

BEN

How the fuck could she get pregnant? Why did this happen to me? Punishment? It must be punishment for what happened to my mother. Sadie and I talked about a family one day, but I made it clear I wasn't sure, especially with my life right now. The band, our success, our age, and my current state of trauma—I have to heal, and a child doesn't deserve that. Sadie and I both have to work on us before we even attempt starting a family. We were there, straddling a line of making progress, and now we've moved ten steps back.

I left her behind with a broken heart and lonely eyes, but I needed to get away. Things were going to get way worse. I don't think I have it in me to do anything but go completely black. Taking the stairs down, I call Nick and tell him to meet me at the hotel. I pace outside, waiting for him to get here. When Nick pulls up in a cab, he's on me immediately.

"Ben, what's going on? Where's Sadie?" I shake my head, and I give him my hotel key.

"I fucked up, and I need to get the fuck away. Don't leave her alone, and don't let her leave. Room four." Giving him the key, I ignore him as he yells after me. Climbing into the car, I tell the driver to take me to a local bar.

What the fuck have I done?

* * *

The bar is crawling with locals, a lot of them women and businessmen. I don't see anyone here that I would usually pick as an opponent. That's until the group of men in the corner catch my attention. I watch the girl next to the biggest asshole cower as he yells at her. The other men with him laugh at the way he belittles her.

Here we go.

Standing, I push my way through the crowd and approach the table.

"You're an idiot. You had one too many drinks tonight. So much for your diet," the man yells.

"The fuck is your problem?" I grab his collar and pull him from the booth. The table is right by the exit to the back alley, and I drag him in that direction. His buddies are right behind us. They know the drill: don't fight in the bar, wait until we're in the alley.

"Who the fuck are you! Get your fucking hands off me, dick!" the man yells as I throw him on the ground. Only thing is, I don't want to hit him. I want him to hit me—to bruise me and punish me for the bullshit I just put my wife through.

I want him to hit me for my child. Fuck—I have a child. How could I have been so careless as to create a son or daughter and make them live their life watching their father rage and regret?

His buddies are on me before I even speak, knocking me down from behind and kicking me all over. My sides, my legs, my arms, even a boot to my fucking face. I laugh through it, the sound sinister while I take the beating I deserve.

"Is that all you fuckers got?" I yell and take more, their faces blurring as blood from my cut brow seeps into my eye.

"Hey, break it up!" We hear yelling, and like roaches in the night, they all scurry off in different directions, leaving me bruised and battered, like I hoped for.

That one's for you, Sadie baby.

Through my blurred vision, I see one of the bar's bouncers come to stand over me. He helps me up, and I stumble back a bit.

"Hey, man, let me get you an ambulance." I wave him off and step back, gripping my side where my ribs are bruised and possibly broken.

"Don't. I'm fucking fine." I push past him and limp away.

"Let me at least call the cops," he yells after me.

"Don't call anyone. I said I'm fucking fine," I snarl over my shoulder, and he yells profanities after me, calling me a dick. I nod my head, laughing, because I agree. I'm so much fucking more.

It takes me a minute to order a car, but I do. By the time I get back to the bus, Nick is still gone, and the guys are all passed out. I decided to give Sadie space, knowing she's safe with Nick. Even after having my ass kicked, I have enough energy to mentally stew over all the ways that I deserve to be tossed to the curb by Sadie. I feel like scum. The smallest man who ever lived.

I take my anxiety pill and pass out, not sure who I am, where Sadie and I stand, or where the fuck to go from here. One thing I do know is I will not look pretty tomorrow. Physically, I'm going to feel this night for days—but mentally, I will never forget or forgive myself. Never.

***

"Get the fuck up." My eyes open, and the morning light blinds me. Nick kicks the side of the bed, and I sit up, forgetting for a brief second that my body got fucked up in a bar fight. I wince, my eyes adjusting to the light. "Take these, get your ass dressed, and meet me at sound check. We need to talk."

He's pissed, and I 100 percent back him up on that. I hate myself too.

"Where's Sadie?" I begin to worry, knowing that she left last time.

"She's at the hotel. And for whatever reason, she won't leave. Even though she fucking should."

"What do you mean she won't leave?" I stand and start changing. I hiss when I look at the bruises all over my stomach and legs. I don't even want to know what my face looks like.

"I tried to tell her to leave you and go home. To get the fuck away, but no, she said she won't leave." Is this a dream? There is no way in hell she should still be here. I lace up my shoes.

"You hate me—you should."

"I don't fucking hate you, but damn it, I don't fucking get you. I don't. She deserves way fucking more, and I hope she sees that." With that, he leaves. I agree with him. Sadie not only deserves better, she deserves to have her memory stolen from her so she forgets me and the damage I've caused.

Picking up my phone, I text her.

Me: I don't know what to say. I fucked up.

Stepping into the small bathroom, I see the crusted blood around my bruised eye. My lip is busted, and I look like the hell I put Sadie through. Holy fuck. I splash my face and growl through the pain.

I towel off then check my phone, seeing a text.

My muse: We only have two weeks left, and then we're home. The baby and I will leave then. You don't have to say sorry for something you clearly didn't want.

Me: You don't have to stay, I wouldn't blame you if you left.

I don't know why I'm saying this. The last thing I want is for her to leave, but what I did is unforgivable. The things I said can't be taken back. I love Sadie more than I care about my heart and my needs. I will set her free if that means she'll be happy.

My muse: I promised I would stay to keep you on track and get sober. I may not want to be around you right now, but I care about your health and safety. But the minute this tour ends, you are on your own back in Portland. Have a good show.

I can't believe that we're here, that I went as far as I did last night. My words are moot at this point. I've fucked up and suckered her back in with failed promises too many times. The words are past jaded. They are nonexistent. They are void and have lost all power.

But what do I do? Do I want to stay? Do I really think I could be a good father with the history behind me?

I want Sadie, but wanting and being good enough are two different things, and in our entire time together I've been nothing but a letdown who is undeserving of her. Even if I choose to stay and really commit to being a better man, I can't promise it. Shit, I can't even breathe a word of it to her ... I have to show her. Why couldn't I think this through last night? Why didn't I take a breather and tell her I needed a minute to process things? It's always the aftermath that leaves me broken and wishing I tried harder.

* * *

"Whoever fucked you up last night could have done a better job," Nick says as I step into the back entrance of the venue.

"They would have if security from the bar didn't show up." We walk back to the changing room, and one of the roadies hands me my earpiece. I remove my hoodie and set it up. Each movement is brutally painful. Tonight's show is going to kick my ass.

"I can't believe I'm asking you this, but how do you feel about everything?"

"Shit. Fucking shit, Nick. But what's new?"

"Why are you so damn afraid of a family with Sadie?"

"How can I not be? Look at my past—at my dad."

"Oh, that shit is tired. Stop using him as a crutch."

Eric comes in and sees my face, interrupting our conversation. "Damn, you look fucking busted. Rough night?"

"You could say that." He pats my back then pours himself a shot. It's only eleven fucking a.m.

"It's not a crutch, it's who I am, and if I care about Sadie and our child, I should stay away."

"Child?" JJ and Jason walk in at that moment, and all eyes land on me.

"Sadie is pregnant," I tell them, grabbing my hat and putting it on. I let them all congratulate me, taking all the praise that I don't deserve.

"Too bad he fucked it up," Nick says, and their cheers cease. They stand back and look between Nick and me, confused.

"What do you mean?" JJ asks, pulling up a chair.

"Yeah," Eric and Jason add.

"I told her I didn't want our child. I pushed her away then left her."

"Oh fuck, man, seriously? Shit. That's rough. I don't know what to say."

I nod, agreeing with Jason.

"So, did she go home then?" Eric questions.

"No." I shake my head in shame. "She didn't. She said she wants to stay to make sure I stay clean. She said when we get home, though, we're over." My emotions begin overtaking me. I don't want to lose Sadie. The pulsing in my head intensifies, and my blood seems to thicken in my veins.

"You're going to let your girl and your child go like that?" JJ asks, standing next to Nick.

"What other choice do I have? I can't take back what I said, and I still don't know if I can be a father."

"Well, you are, whether you want to be or not. You're a dad now. It's your choice if you want to try to be the best father you can or if you want to repeat history and join the long fucking line of Cooper deadbeats," Nick hisses, his face turning red and his eyes stone cold. If I didn't agree with him, his words would hurt me—tell me something I don't know. "Make a fucking choice, Ben, but make sure you do it quick because you have no idea what the hell you've done to her. Don't drag it out or make it worse." Nick nudges my shoulder aggressively as he walks out. I keep my head low and look around the room, feeling guiltier than before.

The guys don't say anything after that, and we make it through sound check in silence. I take the rest of the time before the show to pace the venue and talk myself out of going to Sadie a hundred times.

I pull myself together enough to get through the show. When the meet and greet ends, I take a cab and drive around town for hours, mulling over every part of my pathetic life.

Where do I go from here? What do I do next?

Thirty-seven

SADIE

When Nick first came to the hotel after Ben left me there, he told me Ben had taken off on him. Instantly, my mind went to the worst-case scenario. A relapse? A fight? When I saw him the next day at his show, he looked like he'd walked in front of a bus.

When we see each other now, it's beyond awkward. We pass by each other with barely a breeze to let us know that we are in the same room.

We haven't talked all week since I sent him my last message. I plan to keep it that way. We'll only speak if we have to. He sleeps in a bunk, and I stay in the back bedroom of the bus. All this past week he's disappeared after shows, sneaking in at all hours of the night. What he is doing, I don't know. Most nights, I fear that maybe he is with someone else. I can't help it. What is he doing that is keeping him away?

I tell my parents about the baby. My father once again shuts down. He tells me this isn't the best time, and we can't keep putting bandages over bullet holes unless we want to become a disaster. Unfortunately, we already are, but I leave that detail out. To my parents, Ben and I are getting better every day, our marriage is a work in progress, and Ben's excited to be a father.

This is the hardest, most painful lie I have ever told, not because I'm saying it to my parents but because I'm trying to believe it too. Regardless of what I wish, in just one more week we will be done. I want to choke on those words and the realization that this is where we are. The papers will be filed, and I will be divorced at age nineteen. In one more week, I will lose my best friend, my husband, the one man whom I will never be able to replace. Divorced, heartbroken, and pregnant. What a tragedy, right? God, I am truly pathetic. When did I become this girl? The one who accepted excuse after excuse and fell down the rabbit hole? The one who lost her identity to fit into his perfect mold? This isn't what I thought I was missing. In fact, it's exactly what I wanted to avoid in my life. I fell in love, and I broke. I am no martyr. I have no one to blame but myself. I could blame Ben, but there was no loaded gun to my head. I made this choice, like I always have. Sacrifice myself to keep others happy, safe, and loved.

I'm tired. I'm over being on a bus with four rock stars and zero female interaction. This bed in the back of the bus is giving me a severe case of cabin fever. I miss Kate, I miss my parents, I miss nursing—and pathetically, I miss Ben.

Grabbing a shirt from Ben's suitcase, one I can drown in comfortably, I pull off the sundress I wore to go out today. Removing my bra, I throw it in the hamper. Before I get the shirt on, Ben walks in, causing me to jump and cover my chest with my hands.

"You scared me."

He eyes my body up and down, and for a split second I forget I'm pregnant. His eyes fixate on my stomach, the tiniest bloat where our baby is growing; it's enough to take notice of, but only if you look close enough. I suddenly think about doctors' appointments—I'll be doing those alone.

"Sorry."

I grab the shirt and slide it on quickly, hiding the evidence of our child. Evidence of the one person I love more than anything—but to him, the innocent child who ended us. How could our baby be the cause of our marriage ending? Shouldn't we have built a bond so strong that it brought us closer together?

I never thought a child would be anything but a blessing until I became pregnant with Ben's.

"It's okay. We're gonna head to dinner, do you want to come?"

"No, I'm ready for bed, and I'm not feeling well. Thanks, though." Climbing into bed, I bury myself in the heap of blankets, the cool sheets feeling nice against my overheated skin.

"I can bring you back something; you're both probably hungry." That's the first time he has referred to the baby.

"No, I'll order some pizza or something. Have fun with the guys." I feel the tears forming in my already swollen, tired eyes, and I badly wish I could make us better, but he has made it very clear that our child is not something he wants. As a mother, I choose our child above anyone or anything, but it still kills me to be losing him.

"Call me if you need me."

"Mm-hmm."

With those vague words, he leaves.

My eyes are beginning to drift closed, heavy from all my crying, when my phone goes off. I debate answering it for a long while when I see *Mama* on the screen. Then I widen my tired eyes and put on an effortless-looking smile.

"Hey!" Papa's face comes into view alongside my mother's. The sight of them is overwhelming.

"Baby, how are you?" my mother asks.

"I'm okay—super tired, and I feel so bloated." I chuckle, rubbing my belly.

"You don't look bloated. You're glowing, baby girl," Papa chimes in. Regardless of his reservations, he still shows up. My father is a great example of what a real man and father should be like. I wonder what Ben would be like if his father loved him this way. Ben deserved better.

"You have to say that because I'm hormonal and I could either snap or sob." We all laugh, and I hear the doorbell ring in the background. Dad leaves to go grab it.

"Who's there? You guys have plans tonight?" I ask.

Mama smirks. "We have someone who wants to see you." With that, the loud and familiar sounds of Kate fill the echoing kitchen.

"Sadie Jay!" I begin to cry the instant I see her face. I haven't talked to her in over two weeks, not since she left for Paris with her parents. She has no idea I'm even pregnant.

"Oh no, don't cry, you're going to make me cry!" I drop my head and wipe away the tears. No one knows that I'm filing for divorce when I get home.

"Sadie, why are you so upset?" my mother asks, and I shake my head. I sniffle and sob, a mess on the other end of the video call.

"I miss you guys. I can't wait to see you next week. I'm just a little homesick." The lie rolls off my tongue like a truth. I never used to be able to lie, it never sat well with me, and now I can do it without so much as a blink.

"Oh, Sade, don't worry! Only seven days and we'll be together, and I promise we'll have a girls' night, with a sleepover and *Cosmo* magazines." We both chuckle—I even let out a snort. I wipe the tears and decide I better tell Kate about the baby.

"Hey, Kate?" She stops laughing and looks into the camera.

"What?"

"I have something to show you." I'm only wearing Ben's shirt and my tiny white thong, so to keep my father from getting an eyeful, I pull the blanket up to my hips.

"What?" She tilts her head.

Lifting my shirt with one hand and tucking it under my breasts, I extend my arm up and out so she can see my growing little bump—it's nothing extreme, more like water weight.

"Is there a reason I am staring at your stomach?" She laughs.

I smile and giggle. "I'm not food bloated, Kate. I'm baby bloated." The phone drops from her hands and lands face up. I can see her hands at her mouth and my mama rushing to pick up the phone, giggling under her breath.

I laugh as my mom checks over her phone then holds it in front of Kate.

"You're pregnant? Bun in the oven? Pregnant with a baby?" She screams behind her hands, jumping up and down excitedly. I feel butterflies, and it makes me forget for a split second that Ben isn't happy—that he said he never wanted a child. Everyone but him has reacted so beautifully—everyone who doesn't matter as much as he does.

"Yes. I'm mostly bloated; I'm not that far along." I run my hand up and down the center of my warm stomach.

"Oh my god! Sadie! You're pregnant! Oh! If it's a girl you have to name her Kate!" We all laugh, and I roll my eyes, secretly loving every second of this.

"Okay," I reply sarcastically.

"No, seriously. It's your best friend duty to do so! I would name mine after you!"

"We never discussed this." I shake my head, laughing, the feeling welcome after a week of nothing but gray skies.

"Sadie! I'll convince you! We don't have to talk about it, it's the order of things."

Shaking my head, I respond, "Okay, good luck with that."

"Whatever, you just watch. But have you and Ben talked names yet?" My stomach drops, my light mood drifting away.

"Uh, we have, but nothing has stuck." I lie again, two times in less than five minutes.

"You'll find it, baby. Papa and I didn't know what we wanted to name you until we held you in our arms. Then, out of nowhere, he said Sadie, and I looked down at you and saw a Sadie. We hadn't discussed that name at all—your dad had actually just heard it that day. So it'll happen."

"I guess." I think briefly about the moment I will hold our child, and that's all I see—me and our child. The bedside will be empty because Ben won't be there; our child may never know their father.

"Speaking of Ben, where is that loser? I haven't seen him in weeks!" Kate asks.

"He went to dinner with the band. I'm not feeling too hot, so I stayed back. I think everyone has left." The door is closed, and I don't hear anything coming from the front.

"Make sure the bus door is locked. I hate you being alone in a strange place," Papa chimes in.

"Ben wouldn't leave me here without locking it. Don't worry. But hey, I need to get going. I'll talk to you guys later?" I need some alone time right now; I've had enough roller-coaster emotions for one day.

"Okay, baby. Get some rest, we love you!"

"Yeah, get some rest, preggo, and sleep on that name!" Kate gets the final word in, and I wave them all off and end the call.

Standing from the bed, I go to search the little fridge for some soup or something for my hungry baby. When I walk out, I see light from the TV and someone's feet up on the couch in the living area.

"Hello?" I call.

"Hey, it's me," Nick says. I double-check the shirt is covering all of me before I step out.

"Oh hey. How come you didn't go to dinner?" I ask, stepping in front of the fridge.

"Ben wanted me to stay and make sure you were good and didn't need anything." This stuns me.

"He did?" I didn't think Ben cared once I told him I was pregnant.

"He did. Anyway, you hungry? I can take us to get some food. We can get an Uber and drive around till we find something?" He sits up, and I debate it for a second.

"I would like that. Let me throw on some pants."

"Cool." I walk into the back and find my black ripped skinnies. I pull off Ben's shirt to throw on a bralette, then throw Ben's shirt back on. Slipping on my flats, I make it back out in less than two minutes.

"All right, ready!" I announce. Nick nods, throwing on his jacket.

We leave the bus and head toward the front of the venue we're parked at.

"They'll meet us up here." The night is chilly, but I didn't grab a jacket, so I have to deal with the crisp air.

"You want my jacket? You look cold," Nick offers as the Uber pulls up. I shake my head as he opens my door for me and helps me slide in.

We sit in a comfortable silence, and my mind has time to wander as we watch the tall buildings and small businesses pass us by.

"Does he ever talk about the baby?" I don't let my eyes drift over. Nick doesn't answer for a few drawn-out seconds.

"He does. He asks us about how you're feeling. He's been pretty secluded, keeping to himself."

"So we think," I mumble, finally peering over at him.

"What do you mean?"

"It's nothing," I lie.

"Sadie, you think he's stepping out on you?"

I nod and frown. "Maybe he is. Ben's mad, he's hurt, he feels like I betrayed him by getting pregnant. He knows the marriage is over." Using *the* instead of *our* shows how much distance has been wedged between us. I'm separating myself from who we were.

"Listen, yes, he disappears at night or in the middle of the day sometimes, but I don't think he would cheat on you, Sadie. You're too good of a woman, and regardless of how he feels about the baby, he does still love you."

The mixture of the silence in the car and the bustle of the outside world sounds deafening, like the world is closing in on me.

"I never knew that love could feel so much like pain—like hate. I never knew that it had the power to destroy you."

"That's all love is, Sadie. I hate to admit it, but love isn't always picking who makes you happy but more who you want to stand beside. It's about deciding who you want to survive the pain with—who you want to stand with as you burn to the ground."

"We already burned. Now what?" What he said is true, but now we don't stand together at all—we couldn't survive the fallout. How do I start to heal? When will I worry about me and not about Ben being happy? I should hate him, look at him with so much disdain I can taste it, but I don't. Instead, I only worry about what his life will be like without me.

The feeling that comes with thinking *without me* is excruciating.

"You walk away, Sade. You are the best thing that ever happened to Ben, know that, but you have to walk away now that you've played all your cards. Learn to accept what is and save yourself. You did your part; he has to do the rest." Nick has always supported me; we bonded very early in Ben and my whirlwind relationship, so I trust him. But even he knows there's nothing left to fight for; I will say goodbye to not only Ben but this entire life.

"That's what I plan to do. I'm going to file for divorce. We can't do this anymore." He doesn't beg; instead, he lets my tears fall and pulls me into his side, running his hand up and down my arm.

Goodbye never felt so devastating.

"Tacos? Does baby like tacos?" He breaks the silence, and I snort, wiping away my tears and the snot that has escaped. How charming is that?

"Who doesn't like tacos?"

"Good. Hey, man, can you let us out right here?" The driver pulls up outside a taco joint. The smell catches my and the baby's attention instantly. Oh, that smells so damn good.

Nick orders our food, and while he gets us drinks, I study his side profile, noticing the slight wrinkles around his eyes and forehead as well as the sharp details of his chin. He's handsome and rugged. You can tell he has seen so much in life, and it's made him wise.

***

"Nick, were you really married?" I ask, taking a sip of the ice-cold Coke, remembering what he said last time we talked about it. He sits across from me at the round table. Looking around, he nods.

"I was married once. Almost twice. But then I realized the first marriage was a shit show, and I didn't want a repeat."

I snort, watching him sip his drink. "I have to admit, I wouldn't have pegged you for the noncommitment type. You're always so kind, and I see the way that you love the boys, especially Ben."

"Don't forget *you*, kid." He winks, earning a grin from me.

"Me too. So why didn't it work? What messed you up so bad?"

"Oh, that's a story. Hold on," he says as they call our order, and he grabs it. "All right, two steak tacos with extra sour cream for our hungry mama." He places my tacos down, and I salivate—I'm starving. Clapping my hands together, I moan and start to dig in.

"You *are* hungry. Damn."

"Don't avoid. You know all my dirty laundry, time to spill." I push him before taking a big bite of my taco. I must look like this is my first meal in days, sitting here with my legs crossed in front of me, wearing my big loose tee and my mouth full of food. When baby lets me eat, I eat. No slowing me down.

"I met Suzy."

I snort, halting his story. "What?" he asks, taking a bite of his shrimp taco.

"Suzy? Really, that's the best you can come up with? What was her real name?"

Shaking his head, he smiles around his food, bringing his napkin to his lips to shield his mouthful of taco. "I'm serious." He takes a sip of his drink to wash it down. "I married Suzy when we were both seventeen." Assessing him, I almost call him on it again, but he's completely serious.

"Seventeen? Wow, I thought Ben and I were young. So it was young love?"

"Yup. I was an arrogant, cocky son of a bitch, and she was high-maintenance and everything I now try to avoid—she always knew how to push me."

"Is that why you divorced? Couldn't get along?" He shakes his head, looking out to the street beside us, his eyes becoming distant. I struck something there.

"No. Shortly into our marriage, we realized we had no money. I barely made enough to put soup and bread on our table. She wanted the finer things, and when I couldn't provide, she would make me feel like shit, so I started using."

"Heavy using?" He nods, finally looking at me.

"Yup. The real shit. I was on coke, heroin, ecstasy, anything I could get either free or dirt cheap." Putting his taco down, he stretches his arm across the table. I gulp just thinking about Nick on anything. I haven't seen him touch a thing—not a cigarette, not drugs, not alcohol—so I can't imagine him being into anything hard like that.

"See these lines?" He points to the three solid black lines tattooed on the inner side of his elbow where his arm bends. I nod. "Each line is a five-year sober mark. I am now sixteen years sober. I got them here to cover up the marks from all the fucking needles I used."

I swallow thickly, my heart hurting for him. I see those years before he was sober flash in his eyes.

"Hey, you don't have to tell me. I don't need to know," I reassure him, comforting him by rubbing my hand up and down his arm.

"No, it's all good. This is who I am."

I let him go on without another word, taking small bites and little sips.

"Well, one day I started to owe people money for my addiction, and I had to start selling stuff. I sold her ring—her nice jewelry. One day, I came home on a trip, and it all changed. My eyes were blurry, and everything was loud. I was gone. Rightfully so, she started getting after me about my drugs and my stealing, calling me a worthless piece of shit, and one thing led to another, and I hurt her. Broke her arm and bruised her up bad." His eyes go a little misty, wandering anywhere but at me, and my heart cracks in two for him. "I didn't even know I was doing it. I didn't really know where I was when I started hitting her, too far gone at that point. When I woke up in jail the next day with a restraining order, charges against me, and a foggy memory, I knew I'd fucked up."

"Nick... I'm so sorry. I shouldn't have asked." I shake my head and reach for his hand, wiping away my tears.

"You deserve to know. Sadie, listen..." He pauses, leaning in and giving me his green eyes. "I get why you stayed with Ben. One day, I fucked it up so bad that I went too far. I hurt the love of my life. Ben has never hurt you like that, but the wounds he has caused, those are as deep. You deserve better, and if he isn't willing to get better for himself, for you, or for the baby, then you need to let go."

"They really do hurt," I say. Nick is right. Ben would never hit me, but that doesn't mean that he will always want me or love me, no matter the obstacles. Ben can't love me or our child the way we need if he can't even love himself.

"I love him like a son. I took him in after he left the foster system, and I have tried to sober him up every day since, seeing myself in him, but it didn't work. I had to get better, but I never could until I was willing to do it by myself and for myself. Losing you will always be his biggest regret. Don't let him be yours. You did all you could, Sadie." I nod, knowing the truth. Knowing I can't help Ben or make him stay with me. I can't force him to accept our child—and I don't want to.

Ben Cooper is the man I fell for way too fast and lost even faster.

"You were wrong earlier," I say as I stare at Nick, seeing him in this new light. It makes more sense to me now why he loves Ben and why he's the silent father figure. He was once broken, and slowly, with time and self-love, he glued himself back together.

"How so?"

"You said this is who you are, but it isn't. That's who you were. You're a survivor. I hope Ben will be one day too." His face softens, and he accepts my words.

"Me too, kid. Me too."

I mull over everything he said, envisioning Nick as a broken young adult and seeing Ben as the broken man he is, and I hurt for them both. Even though Nick is sober and clean now, it doesn't mean he's free of scars on the inside. He's still as wounded in there now as he was then. In time, I believe Ben will also be a better man, damaged underneath but overcoming each day.

Thirty-eight

BEN

"You have been quiet the past couple sessions, Ben. You want to start with why that may be?" Dr. Davinah asks. The entire bus is empty. Sadie is out with Nick, and the guys went to walk around the city and sightsee.

"No." I shrug, looking around the bus. I'm stationed at the kitchenette with the doc on a video call. I am highly aware that no one is here, and the silence is deafening.

"That isn't going to help us much. I will allow space for you to stay silent if that's what you think is best, but is it?" he presses. I hate that professionals can see right through us. Read our minds, our body language, and have the innate ability to know we are anything but fine.

"No," I answer again.

"Why don't we talk about what I have been asking you for some time now. Do you feel right now is a safe space?" he asks. My neck begins to tighten, my spine tingling in the worst way.

"What is it going to do? I hate him," I spit out, gritting my teeth through my snarl.

"Yes, you do. That's why I think that in order to process more of your trauma, Ben, we have to open the possibility of closure with him." Darren. My donor.

"What will it do? How is that going to bring me any closure?"

"Who is to say it wouldn't? What feelings are you having right now?" He gestures to his body, encouraging me to look inward. We do this often.

"Anger. My blood feels hot. My neck is tight. My nails are digging into my skin. I suddenly feel like I want to throw up."

"Okay, why?"

I scoff. "Because we are talking about the man who killed my mother. The guy who beat me black and blue. My body. My spirit. My mind. He took everything. Am I supposed to feel warm and fuzzy inside, Doc?" I snarl again.

"No. In fact, your emotions now are very normal, but they come from a deep place of never finding a way to let go. You want to tell him these things. You need to shut the door to your past life so you can open the one that leads to the here and now." I shake my head, running my hands through my hair.

My knee starts bouncing rapidly in sync with the speed of my heart.

"I burned that door. Took a fucking torch to it. I never want to open it again," I tell him, my eyes staring him down on the other side of the screen. Some days, I look at him with dread and beg for him to end this suffering. Other days, days like this, I look at him like I want to see him crumble under my gaze.

"All you did was singe yourself when you burned it instead of closing it." He shrugs, unfazed by my agitation. "Part of healing is really a simple concept that has been complicated over the years. In order to heal from trauma, you have to be uncomfortable for a short time. And I mean unbearably uncomfortable. Because you have to face it, relive it, recall the moments that you buried. But once you face them and sit in that uncomfortable space, you see it's a temporary pain for a future of freedom."

I look down, focusing on my hands clasped tightly in my lap. Tears fall slowly, leaking from my once-dry eyes.

"I have lived years with that torture—why hasn't it healed like you said, then? If I've been living in that uncomfortable place since I was young, how come I am still fucking suffering?" I groan, my soul crushing under the weight of my own existence.

"Because the discomfort that you are living in is a lie. It's a blanket that you placed over your head like children do when they are scared of the dark. The monster can't get you, but after enough time covered in that blanket, it becomes suffocating. You need to pull the blanket down, look around, and face the fact that part of growing is realizing that demons can be faced, that they go away." I think about his words. Is it true? I mask a lot of pain—hell, that's why I am getting sober. That's why I am sitting here. So why isn't that enough? Fuck, maybe he is right.

"I used to dream, when my mom was still alive, about what our lives would be like if he were happy. If he didn't hit us." I pause, wiping under my nose and sniffling. The hardest part about therapy? The raw, vulnerable emotions that you never want anyone to see. "My mother would smile more. She would laugh. I even imagined what my father's real laugh would sound like. I only ever heard his sinister one. But the one I made up in my head? It was so peaceful. It was like safety." I sniffle again. "I could feel him holding me." I wrap my arms around myself, keeping my head low. "Rocking me to sleep." I start to rock myself in my own embrace. "He loved us in those dreams, and Mom was happy."

"And you?" Dr. Davinah asks as I keep rocking myself.

"I was fucking whole. There wasn't anything I was afraid of. I wasn't broken and damaged. I was sheltered from the pain and darkness in the world. But then I woke up. Then I fucking woke up." I wail, the sound so loud I can hear it. It vibrates off the wall and shudders in my chest. This sob rips through me like a tornado. "He took everything. He still takes everything." My shoulders bounce up and down, and I don't hold back anymore. I don't care what I look like or how much I wanted to hide this part of me. These pieces of my pain. I bare it all, and I let it go. Years of suffering and torture and torment all come crashing down.

"Let it have space, Ben." He encourages me to fall apart. I have fallen apart in silence for so long that I can't do it alone anymore. I suffered and made everyone suffer with me. Just like *he* did. But for the first time, I don't blame myself. I accept that he made me this way. That what he did made me a lost, lonely, and frightened child who turned into a broken man. But I don't want him to have that anymore. I want to let go. I need to let go. My heart can't take it anymore. And in this most vulnerable moment, in my weakest hour, I have never felt prouder of myself as a man.

The only way out of this is to go through it. The past can't be rewritten, but I can put ink in my pen to draw my future. My future with her. With Sadie. With our child.

"What about Sadie. How do I fix that? It's too late. Saying goodbye to Darren and getting that closure won't bring her back." I push through the tears; this is one of those times I look at him and hope he can end the suffering.

"You can't lean on her anymore. You need to get to a place where you can lean on yourself. Understand that you are not your trauma. You're not your father. You are your own person with your own wants, regardless of what you thought you wanted because of him. Maybe then you can show her that you can lean on one another. It's a give and take, Ben, in any relationship." He jots something down before looking back up and continuing. "Now, I'm your therapist, and I'm always in favor of your growth and healing. You don't see it, but you have healed many things. You've come a long way, and you will continue to improve, and I don't want to see you discredit yourself. Yes, we have work to do, and there is a lot of self-reflection that will take place, but you have done very well, Ben. Maybe you should extend yourself some grace too." Grace. My mother's name. I'm not a believer in signs—you wouldn't catch me looking at a dragonfly and thinking it's anything more than an insect—but right now, I feel warmth surrounding me, and it feels so much like the warmth I used to find in my mother's arms.

Grant me grace, Mother. Grant me grace, Sadie, I think to myself.

"Okay, I'll do it. I will go see him." I look up at the good doctor again, this time with my head high and my shoulders squared. There isn't a life I want to live without Sadie or our child. There isn't a world I want to live in where they aren't there. I see that now. I crave it, and I will fucking crawl on my bloody hands and knees if it means that my past can be the past and they will be my future.

"All right, let's plan it. When?"

We talk about it for the rest of my session and decide that I'll see him my last day of this tour. We'll be playing the city where he's in prison. How poetic. The end of a tour and the end of generational curses.

And for Sadie? Well, with only seven days left, I have to prove to her that I'm ready, not just say it. I need to give life to my words for the first time and make her fall in love with me again. I made her love me in three days the first time; let's hope I can do it in seven after all the damage I caused.

***

After therapy, I go for a walk, clearing my head and decompressing. For the first time, it feels like I'm not gasping for breath but actually filling my lungs. A heaviness has left me, and I can physically feel it. I think about the next couple of days and all I need to do. Dr. Davinah gave me a list of things to mentally prepare myself for before visiting my father. We even went over some of the questions I think I may ask, but at the end of the day, I really don't know what I'll say when I'm face to face with him. When I head back to the bus after dinner with the guys, it's dark out.

Opening the bus door, I step in and find Nick sitting up at the end of the couch with his head rolled back, asleep. Sadie's laid out beside him with her feet in his lap; the tiny blanket covering her body looks like it's doing nothing to keep her warm, but her pouty lips are puckered and she's breathing deeply, fast asleep. I grip my chest at the sight.

I get down on my haunches and flip my hat backward so I can get closer to Sadie. My leather jacket tightens around my back as I touch her delicate face.

"Angel, you gotta wake up." I run my thumb across her cheek, and she stirs. Blue eyes flutter open and adjust to my face. For a moment, she shares a smile, happy to see me, but it passes like a bolt of lightning.

"Hey, sorry, we fell asleep watching a movie," she whispers, sitting up, careful to not wake Nick.

"You're good, let's get you to bed." Helping her up, I walk behind her, my hands on her hips. She tiredly says good night to the boys as we pass them, swaying back and forth in a haze. She hasn't pushed my hands away, and I absorb this touch. It's been too long since I've touched my wife. Once in the back room, I close our door to give us some privacy.

I help her strip out of her jeans. "What did you guys have to eat?" She yawns, shimmying her hips to help me remove her skinny jeans. I groan inwardly when I lower to my haunches to grab her pants. Her beautiful skin is so smooth, and her pussy smells sweet, so potent I can smell it from inches away.

"Tacos. That seems to be the baby's favorite." She giggles lightheartedly, relaxed and deep in a food coma.

"The baby gets that from me. You know that's my favorite." I smile up at her, taking advantage of the moment. Sadie doesn't let me in anymore. This is rare, and I've craved it so much.

"Don't do that." Suddenly she is fully alert, and she steps away from me.

"Do what, Sadie?" I stand, looking down at her petite frame.

"Talk about the baby and your similarities like the past few weeks have been bliss. You didn't want this, remember?" she bites out, and it stings, but she's right.

"I deserve that," I admit.

"Ben, you deserve for me to walk out right now. You pushed us away like we were trash."

"I did. I've done a lot of shit, Sadie. I have pushed and pushed all while pulling you in and taking everything from you."

She snorts, looking at me incredulously. "You did. The worst part about all of this, Ben, wasn't your IED or your drug use or the alcohol. I understood that you needed help, and I was willing to lie down like a fucking doormat! But you pushed me away and kept me at arm's length, taking the parts of me you knew you could use, and you abused that. You pushed me and my child."

"Our child," I interject.

"It's my child! You made it clear that this is my child and you don't want them. You made it clear that you don't want this!" she screams, tears ricocheting down her cheeks and onto her chest. My heart breaks. I want to pull her in, but pulling her in is what I always do. I bring her in when she is ready to leave, and I touch her and ruin her more. *I have to prove it*, I remind myself.

"I fucked up. I see it. I feel it. But am I allowed to redeem myself?" I ask, dropping to my knees.

"Ben . . ." She cries harder. "A million times. I gave you so many chances! You've done enough to destroy me. Don't make it worse."

"Destroy you?" I choke, swallowing my emotions.

"Yes. You destroyed who I was. You broke me so far past healing, and all I ask is that you have mercy on my heart and let me go," she cries, sitting on her side of the bed.

"Please don't say I destroyed you. I didn't, angel, come on," I beg, hoping she will take back those words. I move closer to her, gripping her arms in my hands. I shake her slightly as she cries.

"You did, Ben. I can't even look at you anymore because all I see is the end of who I was."

"No! No, baby. Come on, we can work through this, okay? Don't fucking say that, please." I grip her hips and drop my head in her lap, broken because I had a plan. I spent all day going over it in my head, convinced I had a chance to save us. Seven days will never fix this; they can't even scratch the fucking surface.

"Give me seven days, please. Seven days of you and me. Nothing else. Give me seven more days with you to fix us," I beg, kissing her legs and moving my shirt so I can kiss her little belly. "If not for me, do it for our child."

"You don't want us, Ben." She tries to push my lips away from her, but I don't let her. I kiss harder, sucking and crying over the skin of her belly—leaving my marks of ownership over her and our child. They are mine, my life.

"Ben! Please!" She cries harder, pushing me away.

"No, please, Sadie, please, please, please." I lay us back as she bangs on my chest, screaming and fighting under me. "Please," I plead, kissing her chest, her neck, her cheek, her lips. I remove her shirt, bra, and panties as she cries, and she slowly starts to fold into me. We need each other.

We have officially shattered, and there is nothing more we can do but heal.

I remove my jacket and shirt—I want her skin on mine, for her to feel that this is home. We are each other's home.

"Ben . . ." she cries.

"Take it out on me, Sadie. I deserve it. Take it all out on me. Hurt me so I can heal us, angel." I pull her naked chest to mine, and I cradle her as she cries. I need this moment, her skin on mine, our heartbeats thundering against each other as I attempt to undo the worst of the damage. She wraps her arms around me and punches my back—hard—screaming against my chest.

I whisper in her ear, "Shh, baby, please." There's a knock on the door, and Nick's voice comes through the thin wood.

"Ben, what's going on in there?"

"Leave us alone, Nick! I got this!" I yell. I turn to Sadie and soften my voice. "Breathe, baby, relax. I'm sorry." Finally, her punches get weaker and fewer in between her sobs. I hear Nick outside the door, and I swear I'll lose it if he comes in here.

Sadie cries over and over while I beg for this last week, her eyes going dull and her body becoming stone under my touch.

"One week, baby. Just one. I promise I'll fix what I've done to you, then you can leave me, and I will never bother you again." That's a lie, because I'll never let her leave. She shakes her head repeatedly, telling me the damage is done. I rub her back until her body gives out and she shuts down. I have to convince her to stay—I have to.

Thirty-nine

SADIE

I have no idea how last night transpired—it happened so fast. One second, I was asleep after a night out with Nick, and the next Ben and I were fighting and screaming as he begged me to give him more time while I begged him to set me free.

I wake up to his arms around me. I stay still, not wanting to wake him, afraid if I do we will do it all over again. His arms feel nice around me for the first time in what feels like an eternity. I won't deny that I miss the Ben I once knew. I miss him when I reach across the sheets and find cold emptiness, when I no longer see his eyes when I first open mine, when I can't feel his touch as we're lost in one another.

"Good morning," he whispers, and my eyes close tight.

Crap.

"Morning." I shift a little, and he tightens his grip.

"You hate me, and that's okay, but I promise I will make this right. I will fix us." I shiver, and the tears find their way out. I'm already crying three minutes into the start of my day. He has no idea the depths of pain he has caused me, what he has truly done to my soul. They say heartbreak feels like death, and right now I'm six feet under.

"You say that now, but you've never been able to keep your promises. Ever. And I don't know if I have it in me to ever trust you again," I admit. His arms tighten around me, and my body grows colder.

"I don't blame you for that, and all I can do is show you. No more empty promises, only actions and results."

"Why? What do you want?" I finally ask, wiping at my tears.

"I want my family. I want to change the future and leave history where it belongs: in the past. I will be the best husband and try to be an even better father. You wait, angel." He releases me, and I let him leave me alone to cry, not watching him retreat from me.

I catch myself almost believing him but urgently shut it down when I remember how seriously damaged I am. I have to make a choice, and it will not be easy. Do I stay and fight or give up and try to pick up the pieces? I have always chosen the former, and look where it got me.

How can I trust him when I don't know if I can trust myself to make the right choice anymore?

I get up and start to get ready for the day, one foot at a time.

* * *

I made it. I fulfilled my promise, even when I had to do it by walking on broken glass and the shattered pieces of me. I stayed. And now I will say goodbye. Ben has spent the past seven days being soft. He has been reserved with his words and actions; it was like peace followed him around. He came back to the bus after every meet and greet. Sober. He would pull out his notebook and lie next to me in bed writing songs while I read. He made sure I was always fed, that I was never alone and had everything I needed. Oftentimes, he would join me and the guys in the front of the bus, telling jokes and making everyone laugh. It was like looking at the Ben I spent those first few days with right after we met. But I still have a wall up. A wall so high that I know he can see it. I expected him to ignore it and bulldoze over it, and I was surprised he didn't. In fact, he respected every verbal and invisible boundary I set. Honestly, I don't know how to take it.

I am wearing a pair of ripped skinnies and a loose-fitting Roes tee on the last day of the tour. My hair is in a high ponytail, and my makeup is light. Ben spent most of the morning in the back of the bus having a meditation session with his therapist while the guys and I went to breakfast. My appetite has snuck back up on me, and little baby is loving every second of it.

We make it back to the bus around one, giving us a few hours before sound check. Wandering into the back with a take-out box for Ben, I find him sitting up in bed, playing his guitar. I didn't have to bring him food, but for some reason, some small part of me wanted to make sure he at least ate before taking his medication and performing.

"Hey, how was breakfast?" He starts the conversation first.

"It was good. I brought back some food so you can eat before sound check."

"Smells like biscuits and gravy."

I nod. "Nick found me a restaurant with all my favorites."

"I'm starved. Besides, I need to hurry up and eat. I need to be at the prison in about an hour."

"The what?" I set the box down next to him and look at him, confused.

"I'm going to see Darren." Am I dreaming? I look around and debate pinching myself. What did he say? His father. He is going to see his father?

"Ben, why in the hell would you do that? Not only in general but also before a show?" My eyes are wide as I watch him. He is calmly eating his breakfast. It's like he just casually told me the sky is blue and grass is green. What the heck is happening right now?

"I know I never talk about my sessions, but I want to tell you about the last one. If you're okay with that?" He looks up from the food. His eyes are soft. He looks so handsome. Everything about him is mine, and I want to reach out and touch him, but I resist.

"If you really want to. You don't owe me anything anymore." I sit on the edge of the bed and remind him that we both know today is the end. Today we part ways.

"Dr. Davinah has been asking me about seeing Darren. He thinks this is the last part of me that needs to be addressed if I am going to properly start healing." This is a lot to process; what do I even say? He never talks about this with me, so I don't have any idea how to approach it.

"Okay, do you feel that way too?"

He takes a bite and nods. "I don't know if it will work, but at this point, I will do anything to make this right. To get you back."

Is that why he is doing this? For me? I shake my head. "No, Ben. This can't be for me. This has to be for you. You understand that I wanted to help you for you. Not for me. Right?"

"I understand, and I want to heal for me too. Trust me. But I made a vow. And I want this for me, for you, and for them." He looks at my stomach. Instinctively, I place my hand there and start to rub.

"Okay." I entertain this. "What if it goes in the opposite direction? Did your therapist and you talk about a plan of action to make sure you're okay?" I ask.

"We did, but that's not for you to worry about. Let's focus on us." How is he so damn calm? Mentioning his father in the past was like lighting a fire and throwing it at his gasoline-covered body. Now it's casual. Who is this man, and where the hell is Ben?

"You seem . . . normal with all this. Like you're not worried." His whole demeanor is throwing me off.

"I'm terrified, Sadie. But Dr. Davinah says I can't start to fully heal until I face the source of my problems. That would be Darren."

I nod. "I hope this is the right thing for you. Regardless of where we stand, I want what's best for you. And it is terrifying, but you are capable of so much. You have already come so far."

Ben is on the other side of sobriety. That isn't an easy thing to do. He is still going to therapy, and even though he couldn't let me in and work on us, he has come a long way, and I am proud of him. He deserves peace, no matter how much it hurts to know that our child and I are not part of that peace. Ben said that night that he wants us, and I believe that he wants to believe it, but I have lost the ability to know what he really wants and to tell if what he says is true.

"I have, and that's why I know I am capable of showing you that I want you and our child. My words are shit at this point, and the only way I can prove myself to you is by my actions." I close my eyes and rest my hand above my heart. Ben seems so sure, and I really want to believe him. I do. But there is this huge void in the center of my chest where he ripped out my heart each time he promised me something then turned around and broke his promise.

"Okay. Let's go see Darren." I stand, not ready to talk about this anymore.

"Wait, you want to go?" He joins me, closing the box on his half-eaten breakfast.

"Yes. I promised to stay by your side until the end of this tour. This is part of it, and I'm not a complete monster, Ben. As much as I want to deny it, I do love you and care about you. Darren hurt you; he took away your mother. I won't let you do this alone." With that, I head to the front of the bus. If I stood there any longer and looked at the longing on his face and that glimmer of hope in his eyes, I would have crumbled. I'm growing stronger, but I am not invincible.

***

The table we're seated at in the room full of other families and inmates is a concrete block cube. It's uncomfortable but fits the mood perfectly—desolate. Ben's leg is bouncing up and down, and there is a slight shimmer of sweat beading around his hairline.

Regardless of whether we're at odds, I comfort him. "Hey, relax. You got this far, you're strong enough to do this." Leaning in, I whisper in his ear, "You have me." He turns, his leg ceasing moving and his eyes shimmering. I don't want to offer him hope for us, but I know this can't be easy, and I still care about him getting better. This is a huge—if not the biggest—part of his recovery.

"I really love you, Sadie." My mouth opens to tell him he needs to focus on what he's here for, not on me, but someone else speaks before I can.

"Son?" We both look at the man standing opposite the table with a chain between his feet and his hands in cuffs. He looks like Ben; his hair is gray but thick like Ben's, and his facial structure is similar, but his eyes aren't as kind. They are the same color, but Ben's have a softer feel to them because Ben is still good, like his mother.

"You look so grown-up, And who is this beautiful young lady? She looks like your mother."

"Stop!" Ben snaps, and I grab his hand, squeezing it between mine below the edge of the table. He takes a breath and starts again. "Stop. Do not talk about my mother like you aren't in this place for murdering her." I keep my eyes on Ben for a moment. He is trying to calm himself, breathing deeply through his nostrils and releasing the air through his mouth. That's new. Is that something his therapist taught him?

"Ben, I did a terrible, unspeakable thing, but I've changed, and your mother would have forgiven me." My eyes fly up and zero in on him. Out of everything he could say, he chose that? He really must not know his son at all, and that's devastating.

"Forgiven you? How in the world do you think that you can sit here and assume she would forgive you? We hated you. You broke us," Ben spits.

"Because your mother taught me forgiveness." Wow, he really is brave.

"You have no idea what you're talking about—what you have done to me."

"I do, son—"

"Ben, My name is Ben." His dad nods, briefly silent. He looks offended, and I almost call him on it. He lost the privilege of calling Ben his son the moment he laid a hand on him. He has no right to act hurt. The only ones who got hurt in this family are Ben and his mother.

"Ben, I know what I've done to you, and I am sorry. My father did the same thing to me, and look where it got me." He gestures to the surrounding walls.

"You blame him for what you did, but you made a choice."

"I did, and how does that make you any different? I'm sure you blame me for all the fucked-up things you've done in your life. I made a choice, and it was mine alone, but you need to know that whatever I did to you, I'm sorry."

Ben scoffs, shaking his head. I keep my hands tight on his. I want to scream at the man across from me and tell him how vile he is, but this isn't my battle—it's Ben's. If I could say anything to his father, I would spew out words of hate because he hurt my husband, my best friend, so badly that even after all these years, there is still a broken child trying to heal inside of the man.

"You can't even say what you did. You say 'whatever I did to you,' like it was no big deal. You hurt me every day. You hurt my beautiful mother and took her away from me when I needed her. I didn't even get to say goodbye to her!" Ben slams his hands down, and the guards straighten up and look over at us. I hold my hand up, and they stand their ground.

"Relax, baby. You got this," I whisper, and Ben looks at me.

"Who is she?" Darren gestures to me.

"She's my wife."

"What's your name?"

With no enthusiasm, I respond, "Sadie."

"Sadie, you're very beautiful. I hate that I'm meeting you this way, but welcome to our family."

"She is not your family, she's mine, and I'm not your family either. I came here today to close this chapter and forget you altogether."

"Ben—"

"No, you listen to me. I do not forgive you. I never will. But I can forget you, and that's what I plan to do."

"I'm sorry. Why can't you take my apology and let this go?" I don't know much about the man who hurt my husband, but this man right here, he isn't sorry. He hasn't changed. He is only saying this to gain something—maybe a way into Ben's life to ask for money and new lawyers? I bet that isn't too far off.

"You will never be sorry. I needed to see it in your face. To look in your eyes and not see myself in you. To know that I am different. I want you to know that you are dead to me, and my mother deserved better than you. She never deserved what you put her through. I hope that while you rot away in this place, you know I will walk this earth being a better man in spite of you. I hope you go the rest of your life knowing that you are a fucking monster." With that, Ben gets up and leaves. The guards open the door, and I watch him go.

I go to stand without a word when Darren stops me.

"He's better than I ever was. He may not know it, but I will never forgive myself for hurting them and losing him and his mother because of it. Take care of him for me."

"Darren, this wasn't for you. You taught him everything he shouldn't be, and he is a better man. He doesn't need you or your approval. And I hope he is right. I hope you spend the rest of your days knowing he is better than you are. That he is not the wonderful man he is because of you but in spite of you." I shake my head and leave. With his father's words heavy on my heart, I catch up with Ben and walk silently behind his tense form.

What I saw back there helped me understand Ben and his struggles. There is a deeper heartbreak there than Ben has ever let on, always shielding it with hate instead.

I will never forget that moment or the words his father left him with. Suddenly, it's apparent to me that I'm a part of Ben's old wounds but also a part of his newly healed scars.

***

"Ben?" We have been driving for a few minutes; I wanted to allow some space for him to breathe, but I can't stay silent after what we went through back there with Darren.

"Yes."

"What was it like in that home? Please tell me." Ben has mentioned very briefly how bad it was, and sometimes how great it was, but there is so much more there.

"My mother was a saint, my father was a coward, and I was always in the cross fire."

"Please," I plead. That isn't what I meant. He is slowly rebuilding that wall, the one he uses to keep himself safe. I need to see him knock it back down. Pulling up to a red light, he looks out the driver's window, one hand on the wheel and the other rubbing the stubble on his chin. I hear a sniffle. Oh, Ben. God, I want to reach for him, but now isn't the time.

"That house was like a dream and a nightmare all at once. The best memories I have, the only things I have left of my mother, took place there. But the same place holds memories that I so badly want to rip out of my head." He takes the back of his hand and runs it across his cheeks, wiping at the tears. The light goes green, and that's when I get a better look at his profile. His cheeks are red, the tears are brimming again, and he lets them fall. Ben being comfortable enough to cry and be vulnerable is admirable. There is nothing more mature than a human who can bare their soul.

"All I want is to take time to sit with those memories of her. To have that. But I can't because they all lead back to that fucking house. That fucking coward. And me being selfish and not coming home." Once again, I have to resist the urge to remind him that he wasn't selfish and that it was not his fault. We both know that. His logic and his trauma are battling right now.

"Memories can be heaven-sent. But they are often more like a curse," I say softly.

"You're right. That's why I try to run from them. But clearly running makes it worse."

"Do you remember her voice?" I ask, and he nods.

"She used to sing all the time—hymns, oldies on the radio—and she was always humming." He smiles. I love that smile. My stomach turns in terrible knots. I will never forget his smile. Maybe our child will have the same one. Maybe one day he will decide to be in the child's life, and they will make him smile like that. I would be lucky to see it. No matter the ending of us, I will always miss everything that makes me love him.

Ben starts to hum a tune, a haunting but beautiful melody. I can't place it, but within seconds, the humming is broken up by sobs. Maybe he is remembering her voice. Her smell. Her smile.

"Ben. I am sorry for everything. I know you miss her, and you want to remember the moments you spent together, but if it hurts too much right now, try to hold onto these things: her smell, her voice, and the looks she gave. Memories don't have to be just places. You can let their being, be the memory." I reach over and place my hand on his leg. He nods but doesn't say anything else.

Ben and I may be over, but he doesn't deserve to suffer. No one deserves to suffer. Ben is good. All he needs is someone to help him navigate life. I wish that person could have been me, but it wasn't, and regardless of my pain, I want him to find happiness. There has to be happiness after me.

Forty

BEN

Sadie offers me the comfort that I crave, and she does it so beautifully and in a way that only she can. The conversation solidifies that I cannot go on without her: she is what I want. She and our child.

We barely make it back in time for sound check, then I have the show. This time, she attends. It is our last show, after all, but that's not why she comes. She's coming to support me after what she saw. I wonder what it was like seeing that through her eyes. Maybe she will tell me. Maybe this will be the start of something for us to rebuild our foundation on? Who knows . . . tomorrow we were supposed to fly home, but she doesn't know I canceled that flight. Our future is hanging in the balance, and the time before we fly out is all I have to get her back. Every second counts.

I put all the anger, the pain, and the release of seeing Darren after all these years into my show tonight. Every song wears a new emotion from relief to pain to heartbreak. I will think back to this day often. I'll remember sitting across from him and saying goodbye for good, letting him know that I have set myself free. I will look back on it when the hard days come. Because trauma can heal, but the scars will always be there, and sometimes I am going to feel it, but all that matters now is how I face it. Do I hide under the blanket or look the monster in the eye and live in temporary discomfort for long-term peace?

"This is the last night of the Run, Baby, Run tour, and I have to say it's been a fucking ride!" I say that in both the best and worst ways. I started to get sober. I bared my heart to Sadie. I saw the man whom I once called Dad. I pushed Sadie away. But I also had the best moments. The biggest one is finding out I am going to be a father. At first, I ran from it, but now I dream of it. I want this with her. They wrote headlines about me and Sadie and my sobriety, but they have no idea what really happened. This tour has been a peak in my career, all while my personal life fell to shambles. This time in my life has been a paradox. A bittersweet time. And now there is the after. What is it going to be?

The crowd cheers, and I take a second to look over at Sadie. Her eyes are on me, and she gives me a sweet smile. Nick and the stage crew move my piano out to the stage for the last song of our set list. Part one of my grand gesture begins now.

"So, as many of you know, this year I married the most beautiful woman I have ever met, and somehow she said yes and stuck around." I sit at the piano, and the crowd roars, cheering for my love. I look over at Sadie, and she is biting at her lip, tears ready to fall. I refuse to let those tears be wasted.

"Well, I found out a few weeks ago that we're pregnant, and I have to say I'm on fucking cloud nine right now. Let's cheers to that!" The crowd whoops and hollers in congratulations. I bring my eyes back to Sadie and see her holding a hand over her mouth while Nick stands with his arm around her.

"So I want to end this show with a cover of one of her favorite songs by her favorite artist. This one is for you, baby. I hope our melodies that night stay in your mind forever." With that, I begin the first notes to "Lust for Life" by Lana Del Ray and the Weeknd. The crowd knows the words, and they sing along with me, but my eyes stay on Sadie.

Each word I sing is directly to her; the thousands of people disappear, and I hope Sadie feels every single word.

My words have left her scarred, my actions have caused her love to waver until she wants to leave me, but she has stayed because she loves me. Even when she lost hope, she still stayed to help me.

When the piano solo starts, I look her right in the eyes, unashamed in front of a crowd of our fans and my bandmates. I mouth *I love you* before I sing the final chorus, and when she mouths it back, I feel her in my heart. She is letting me in like I need her to tonight, because this night is all I have left to make her fall in love with me again.

I play the last few notes at the end of the song, and I see a flashback of every moment I've had with Sadie. I see her in the front row at the show where we met, I see her on that kitchen counter letting me touch her like she's never been touched. I see the lake, the whipped cream fight, the day I first said goodbye to her. I see the moment I asked her to marry me and the second she said yes in front of that courthouse. I see our first time together, and I see how I broke her. I see the pain I selfishly caused.

But tonight I'm going to make new memories, better memories, with her and our child. The greatest memory we ever created.

After the show, I meet my fans. I do my best to speed it up so we can make it to the fair before it closes. When we finish, I head to the hotel room Nick booked for us while he keeps her distracted. I shower and change, cleaning myself up with a shave and styling my hair how she likes it. I put on my black jeans, plaid button-up shirt, and leather jacket.

Grabbing my wallet and phone, I head back to the bus, where they're all waiting for me. Sadie's in the back bedroom writing in her journal when I come in. She's still dressed from the concert, and she looks beautiful in her red dress that hits a few inches above her knees with a scoop neck and a low-cut back that shows off her creamy skin. She wore that on our wedding night. Another memory to smile over. Her hair is down and wavy, and her blue eyes stand out against the red of her lips and dress. She looks like a fucking angel.

"Hey, you mind if I drag you out tonight?" She pauses from writing, taking a deep breath before peering up at me.

"Ben, it's eleven at night. Besides, I don't think we should do that." She means we shouldn't be alone. She is worried there may be a chance it isn't over.

"Sadie, I know these past two weeks have been confusing, but please, give me tonight. Just one more night with you." She looks out the tiny bus window and contemplates what to do while I stand waiting anxiously and sweating under my shirt.

"Fine, okay."

"Perfect. Grab your jacket, it's gonna be chilly." I step out for a second to let her get her shoes and jacket. Finding Nick in the front of the bus, I pull him aside.

"Don't fuck this up. It's your last chance, buddy," he reminds me.

"I won't let her go without a damn good fight."

"Good. You better not." He punches my arm, and I smile, anxious as all hell, like this is the first fucking time I'm meeting Sadie. In a way, it is. I'm sober and getting the help I need. I'm letting go of my past, and that's a man she's never met.

"Ready?" she asks, joining us.

"I sure am, angel."

Forty-one

SADIE

The last show was incredible, but it also symbolized the end. Ben sang our song, and it was the hardest start to our goodbye. We love each other, and we always will, but love isn't enough. In the short time I've been with Ben, I've matured in some ways. I once believed love was the answer. But being married, especially to Ben, has taught me that love is just the beginning.

"A fair. You brought me to a fair?" I question, shocked this is what he wants to do on our last night together—one I wasn't going to give him but decided to because truthfully, I want it too. It's selfish, it's playing with fire, but if it's goodbye for us, I want it to be a damn good one.

"You'll see. Trust me?" he says, shutting the cab door after helping me out.

"I think I always have. That's why we're here." I'm not referring to our location but rather our marriage. I trusted each and every word he said, every promise that he could never keep.

"Don't do that. Please." He puts my hand in his and gives me his Ben eyes, those deep brown eyes with honey dripping from them.

"Don't lead me down another road that I can't travel on," I warn him with a heavy sigh.

"I won't. Come on." Taking my hand, he makes a beeline toward the Ferris wheel.

Approaching the Ferris wheel, I smile discreetly. The small gesture feels meaningful.

As we climb on, he tells the ride operator to let us go around until he signals us to get off. I find the request odd, and I begin to wonder what he could be up to.

We ride around a few times without saying a word, watching the moon over the water. The sounds of other games and rides go off in the background, but he says nothing. I feel him watching me, waiting for me to speak first, but I really have no idea what to say. This is the last night we will be together like this. What can I possibly say?

"Today was hard." That's the best I can come up with.

"How?"

"You confused me even more, Ben. You say you love me and want this baby, but all I can see when you say that is you pushing me away that night." The image comes back in a rush, and I shake my head to try to get rid of it. I can't think back to that. I can't.

"I'm so fucking sorry, angel. I will regret that forever," Ben tells me, wrapping his arm around me and turning my body into him. I want to reject the embrace, but I don't. Call me a glutton for pain.

"You live with too many regrets and too much guilt. Aren't you tired of always adding more to your list? Aren't your shoulders heavy?" I ask, searching his face.

"The only regret I have left is how I've pushed you away and caused you pain."

"Then why are you trying so hard to get me back when you know that?" I ask with a huff.

"Because I love you. I could try to give you more words to define that love, but there aren't any that can justify it. I love you, Sadie, and I want to fight to get us through this. I want to look back years from now and know that the two young kids who fell in love when they had no clue what kind of shit they would go through made it out. That we made it through."

He searches my face, and I shake my head in disbelief, my eyes swimming with tears. Is there such thing as overcrying? Or running out of tears? I think we have both cried more in this marriage than smiled.

"How can you expect us to get through all we have been through. How can I forget what you did the past few months? Ben, how can you expect me to do that so fast?" I'm yelling as we pass the ride operator, but he pretends he doesn't hear us. I wouldn't care if he did. I'm completely wrecked.

"Because I'm getting clean. I'm working hard every day to become a better man, and when we get home, I will continue on my road to recovery because I have you and our baby."

"You took my people-pleasing and abused it, Ben." I sneer at him, because that trait was something I said I wanted to run from, but after everything, I gave in the most with him.

Quickly, he grabs my face in his hands. "Because I was wrong. You are right. I saw what I wanted, and that was you, and I did so many things to ruin it. But this is different. Things have changed, and I think deep down you know that."

"I want to believe it," I whisper, trying to break from his grip, but he keeps it tight, giving me no way out.

"You're my grace. You were sent here to fucking save me, Sadie. You have my soul in the palm of your hands, in your heart, on your wedding finger, inside our child. I won't lose the only two people in my life that I've loved more than my mother."

I choke, letting out a soft sob. How come he's never said that to me before? Where were those words the whole time I needed them? My soul softens a little more, and that little wick of burned-out hope is slowly sizzling back to a burning flame.

God, I've needed him to make this right for so long. I don't say anything, but I urge him with my eyes to go on, to keep telling me what I need to hear, because he's holding onto my heart, and I don't want him to let it slip away again.

"You and our child are everything to me. Please know that I will not lose sight of that again. I need you to bring me back to where I feel most at home. In your arms, in your heart, baby, right here." He lets his hand travel to my heart, the warm touch making it beat again. I swear I can feel it thundering as he revives it with his hand.

"Ben," I cry, pulling him in and locking my hands around the nape of his neck. We kiss for the first time in weeks. The taste of him mingles with the salt of my tears, and he takes over, grabbing my hips and placing me in his lap. The bucket we're in rocks a little, and he breaks our kiss with his own tearful laugh.

"When the boat goes a rockin'. . ." he teases, bringing his lips to mine again. We do this for an entire circuit before we find ourselves in the air at the very top. Pulling away, I rest my forehead against his, placing my hand on his heart. His hand drops to my stomach. I swear I feel an energy where two souls that are drawn to one another—made for one another—finally find one another.

I've fallen in love with Ben all over again. Like the first time, all it took was a moment in his world to know that he is my everything, to know that his life is my life and my life is his.

"Sadie?"

"Hmm?"

"Marry me?" I chuckle and peer up at him.

"We're already married, Ben."

"We are, but I want to marry you again. This time with your parents there, the way it should have been. With the version of me that you deserve."

"Ben, I love every version of you. I only wanted you to stop hurting me. To stop hurting yourself." I need him to understand that I don't blame him for the path he traveled to get here. He isn't a bad person, and he shouldn't try to be someone he isn't. The real Ben was there the whole time, but there was a giant wall blocking him from accepting and truly giving the love that he wants and deserves.

"I never doubted that. But this time, I love this version of me. This is the version I want you to marry." He places me back beside him and very carefully drops to one knee in the bucket.

"I'm asking you to marry me like your dad did with your mom."

My heart dances, and a beam of light radiates from the center of me.

"Ben. I'll marry the same you, just in a different light." With that, I pull him back up by his shirt, and we kiss, my heart beating wildly for this man, every doubt I ever had vanishing.

"I can't believe you're trusting me and giving me another chance," he says, pulling away. Looking into the eyes of my other half, the better side of my soul, I get lost inside him.

I pause for a moment and sculpt his face in my hands, gazing lovingly into his honey-brown eyes before I speak the realest words I will ever speak in my life. "That's what I get for loving you, Ben Cooper."

And right here, Ben Cooper shows me what I have been searching for for so long. Someone to love. A person to test me in ways that make me a stronger person. I lived to please others and protect others, and though I did that with Ben, in the end, I broke through. I learned to see my strength and find what I want in life. That is him. That is us. It was wild and toxic and all-encompassing, but it was real. All of it was real.

Epilogue

BEN

Sadie Cooper not only saved me from a long life of regret and loneliness, she gave me a permanent melody—our child—to remember everything we had to sacrifice to have our fast, reckless, and all-consuming love. She is a mirror that reflects all the parts of me that I searched for for so long.

Epilogue

SADIE

"Married twice before I'm even twenty. That is definitely the wildest thing I think I have ever done." I play with the lace of my wedding dress. We are in the back of the limo on our way to the reception.

The feeling is similar to two kids falling in love. Maybe that was the thrill when we first met: finding that love that everyone tells you you're too young for. The kind that you will fight the world for.

"No, I think it was the time we got married after a month." I smile, kissing his cheek. He looks dapper, as handsome as ever in his Frank Sinatra–style suit with his hair slicked back. I decided on a tight-fitting mermaid-style dress. The lining is nude, and the white lace overlay hugs me, showing off my five-months-pregnant belly.

Ben's hands haven't left me all day, even holding me tight to his side during the ceremony with his hand glued to my bump.

"You know, I was thinking about what we could name her." I place my hand over his and watch his profile. He is staring down at our joined hands over the bump.

"Oh?" We found out we're having a little girl last month, and we haven't been able to think of a name, but as we said our vows, the perfect name came to me.

"You know how you are always telling me that she is the greatest song you ever wrote?"

"Yes," he says.

"And your mama's name was Grace, and her favorite song was 'Amazing Grace'?"

"Yes?" He laughs, nodding his head, waiting for me to spit it out.

I giggle and shoot the driver a wink, and he lifts the divider between the back of the limo and the front.

"Call me cheesy, but I think Melody should be her first name because she is our greatest melody, and Grace should be her middle name for your mama. Melody Grace Cooper."

His jaw relaxes and tightens repeatedly, an attempt to hold back tears, I'm sure. Finally, he relaxes and smiles, his brows drawing in softly. He doesn't have to say what he's thinking because I can feel it; so can our little girl as she kicks in my belly.

"Oh, Sadie, you're going to fucking destroy me," he growls, leaning in and ravishing my mouth. His hand leaves my stomach and travels up to my breast. I moan into his sensual kiss.

His hand reaches up to the speaker button that connects to the front. Pushing it, he speaks. "Take us to the hotel. I need a minute." The driver responds, but we ignore it, going back to kissing, not caring if we miss the first half of the reception. It feels more urgent to be alone with one another than to be in a room full of people.

The driver gets us to the hotel and parks, and we run inside. It's just like us to act like this. We're young, crazy, reckless, and in love, and even when we're old and gray, I'll still feel this way.

"Help me remove this dress before I rip it off of you," he growls the second we enter the room. His words send a shiver of arousal through my entire body. Lifting my hair up, I turn my back to him and show him my zipper. With steady hands, he unzips me in one quick swoop, and my dress loosens. I drop my hands, and it slides off my shoulders, over my bump, and down my legs, leaving me in nothing but my sheer white thong and my lacy white bra.

I turn to face him, and he looks me over, spending time on each part of my body like it's a work of art, because to Ben it is.

"You dirty little girl, putting those nipples on display for me."

"Yes." He tweaks my peaks over the fabric, and I whisper a moan.

"Say it, say you're mine."

"I'm yours, Ben, oh!"

"Yes, you are, pretty baby. Now how about you let me have that delicious cunt so I can get my cock nice and wet to fuck that ass." His words stun me. An excited thrill races up my spine. We've never gone that far before.

I put on a show for him, loving everything about this moment—renewed love, a bright future, and heated passion all making the perfect moment on the most perfect day.

"Why don't you take me like this? I know you like it, baby." I climb on the bed on all fours, thrusting my ass up and out like he likes it. My engorged clit is touching the fabric of my thong.

"Fucking dirty girl, you want it bad today."

"So bad." We had a really busy week, and I purposely held off on sex so we would both be begging for it today. That didn't stop me from teasing him over the past week, though, so we're both ready and practically salivating for it.

Without another word, he rips my panties from me, and the harsh burn on my skin feels more pleasurable than painful. With a slap on my ass, he thrusts into me, sheathing me fully on his hard cock. I feel every inch, skin on skin, every thick vein gliding against my tight center. I scream out, my body thrusting forward, and he growls, making no attempt at moving until I've adjusted.

"So fucking tight. I love being inside you."

"I love it too. You own me, you know that." He groans out a yes, gripping my breast. I lay my hand over his.

My veins are alive with smoldering heat, and my stomach is coiled and heavy. I'm ready to come, and my legs and arms are a quivering mess as I try to keep myself up.

He's slow but deliberate with his movements, sliding out slow then pounding so deep.

"I want you on top. Come here, baby." He drags out a few more thrusts, both of us feeling that pull that we don't want to stop. Finally he moves us, him lying on the bed and me over his hips.

Grabbing his base, he lines me up with his cock and helps me down. I practically yelp at the new angle, my core overly sensitive from our last position. Roaming his hands over my thighs, he tilts his head, keeping his lip between his teeth while he looks me over from my breasts to my face, then to where we are connected.

The look he gives me sets me ablaze, and I become unhinged, going wild. I begin to buck, rising and falling fast. He leans up for a brief second and unhooks my bra with little effort, and I remove it without stopping.

"You are so goddamn beautiful. Ride me harder, angel, let me see your body."

"Oh!" His words spur me on, and I do exactly as he asks, using all the strength I have in my legs to help me move.

"Fuck, come on my dick, baby—come on. Let go and get me wet." Throwing my head back, I scream and let go, feeling my orgasm rippling through me like a riptide.

Pulling my eyes back to him, I watch as my juices pour out onto that triangular patch of smooth skin.

"Just like that, fuck, oh fuck!" I feel him expand, and I tighten down on him, squeezing him like a glove as he loses himself, exploding rope after rope of hot come.

"Yes, Ben, come for me!" I scream, chasing a second orgasm, my chest shuddering as my body shakes with ecstasy, and we both twitch.

We come down, still connected with him inside me, but now we're sitting up chest to chest with our foreheads touching. His hands roam my back lazily, leaving a trail of goose bumps behind. My hands tangle in his hair at the back of his neck.

"Say them to me again, say your vows," I whisper into the tiny space between us.

Smiling up at me, he doesn't miss a beat.

"I will always be the man that you deserve. I'll never run from you and always trust in you. I will take solace and shelter in the home of love that you built for me when I needed it most. I will forever worship you like my own saint, and when the time comes, I will worship our daughter and remember how hard we worked to get here. I will spend forever loving you as you have loved me, Sadie Jay Cooper."

With a lone tear on my cheek, I listen as those words echo in the quiet of the room. I hold them close to my heart and remember them like a beautiful poem told by the greatest poet of all time.

"I love you, Ben Cooper."

Acknowledgments

To my readers. I love you. For almost a decade we have had the highest highs and lowest lows together. You have supported me in chasing this dream. I'm here for you, because of you, and I'll never be able to thank you enough. Enjoy Ben and Sadie. Here's their new story. The manuscript isn't mine anymore. It's yours.

My husband and sons. I love you, my boys. You three give me so much purpose. Making you proud is all I strive to do. To show you that your dreams are important and you should chase them until they are your reality. Toddy, thank you for being the best husband. The one who cries with me when he sees me with my readers and hitting Publish. Thank you for loving me every day.

Lashelle, Leila, Heather, Sav, Ness, and Taylor. Your friendships have saved me time and time again. Forever and always. Friendships are so very important to me, and you have held my fragile heart in your hand and healed wounds you didn't cause. Thank you.

Anna, Deanna, and the Frayed Pages team. Thank you for believing in me. For opening the door with open arms. Ben and Sadie's story has always been the book I dreamed of being in stores, and one day on the big screen. You all read it and saw the importance behind their tragic yet beautiful story. You gave them space to grow and flourish. Thank you from the bottom of my heart. You are dreamers like me, and together we have created magic.

Xoxo,
CC Monroe

About the Author

CC Monroe was born in the sunshine state of California. She now lives in Utah with her real-life book husband and beautiful sons, spending her days working and her nights locked away writing the stories her readers can't get enough of: angst-filled, plot-driven, insanely sexy stories—just the way we like them. CC has one-liners, can be witty on the spot, and curses like a sailor. Her best friend is coffee with a side of sarcasm.

MORE FROM
FRAYED PAGES x WATTPAD BOOKS

Unleashing Chaos
by Crystal J. Johnson
& Felicity Vaughn

Meant for Me
by Tay Marley

The Starlight Series
by Pia Mia

ANNA TODD'S BRIGHTEST STARS TRILOGY

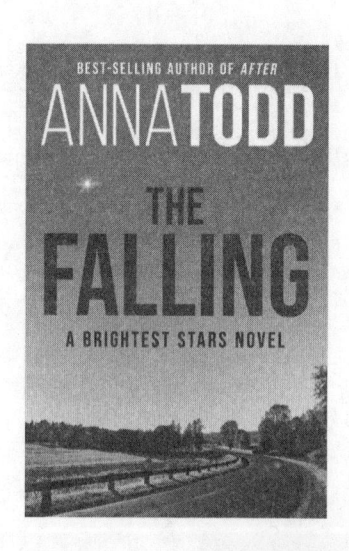